ARCHANGELS oF FUNK

ARCHANGELS OF FUNK

Episodes from the Continuing Drama of
CINNAMON JONES:
Scientist, Artiste, and Hoodoo Conjurer

A NOVEL OF WHAT MIGHT BE

ANDREA HAIRSTON

TOR PUBLISHING GROUP
NEW YORK

This is a work of fiction. All of the characters, organizations, and events portrayed
in this novel are either products of the author's imagination
or are used fictitiously.

ARCHANGELS OF FUNK

A Tordotcom Book
Published by Tom Doherty Associates / Tor Publishing Group
120 Broadway
New York, NY 10271

www.torpublishinggroup.com

The Library of Congress Cataloging-in-Publication Data is available
upon request.

ISBN 978-1-250-80728-1 (hardcover)
ISBN 978-1-250-80730-4 (ebook)

First Edition: 2024

Printed in the United States of America

0 9 8 7 6 5 4 3 2 1

DEDICATED TO CHRYSALIS THEATRE
AND THE HAPPY VALLEY

ARCHANGELS OF FUNK

**Cinnamon Jones Invites You to an
Outdoor Sci-Fi Carnival Jam at the Amphitheatre**

The Next World Festival

**Music! Dancing! Masked Revelers!
Drum Circles! Storytellers!**

**Celebrating Yesterday and
Improvising Tomorrow Today!**

**FREE ADMISSION
EVERYONE WELCOME**

Amphitheatre Gate opens right after sunrise

Who-Knows-What Theatre Magic performed by:
▪ Dirty Dozen Farmers ▪ Vamp-Squad Hill ▪ Town Wenches ▪
▪ Co-Op Clinic Clowns ▪
▪ May There Be Grace Choir ▪ Powwow Now ▪
▪ Back-From-The-Dead Crew ▪

The Motor Fairies threaten to *saw somebody in half*

Circus-Bots & Techies Forever will do a Hologram Light Show
& Fantasia Fireworks

More Acts Added Every Day!!!!!

The Ghost Mall hosts a costume/mask parade:

The Weird Multitudes

Come dressed for tomorrow or build a look at the

Glad Rag & Clothing Swap

Visit the **Repair Café** and the **Barter & Skill Bank**!

Valley Merchants offer **Spring Sales** and **FREE LOCAL FOOD**:

Fresh Tacos! Garlic Mushroom Naan Bread!
Cauliflower Rice and Beans!

Dal, Broccoli Bisque, Corn Chowder, Kale and Collard Stew

Shaheen's Diablo Pizza (cauliflower or wheat crust),
Soy Sausage, Naughty Nuggets

Honey Fry Bread, Mashed Sweet Potatoes, Apple Delights

HISTORY

Redwood Phipps, Aidan Wildfire, and Iris Phipps started the annual Next World Festival in the 1980s or '90s. Sources argue over the year. Given poor documentation, we ain't stepping in that. Cinnamon Jones carries on the tradition of her elders and performs songs from *The Redwood and Wildfire Songbook*.

Since 2000, and despite floods, plagues, and war, the outdoor Festival has taken place every year at the borders of Nonotuck and Pocumtuc land, not far from other first nations: Mohegan and Pequot to the south, Abenaki up north, Nipmuc and Wampanoag where the sun rises, and Mohican toward sunset.

Follow bike path to the Amphitheatre.
USE THIS GATE ONLY or—

Risk the wrath of the Boneyard Baron, Spook,
and the Water-Demons

Valley Security's on red alert to keep everybody righteous

Check us out on the net at OurNextWorldFestival.com
and download the APP!

(Final page of this year's *Ghost Mall Chronicles*
brought to you by the
Graphic Novelists of the Future)

Book 1

TWO NIGHTS BEFORE THE FESTIVAL

*Somewhere, something incredible
is waiting to be known.*
Carl Sagan

Space is the place.
Sun Ra

I'll take you there.
The Staple Singers

CINNAMON

♋

HAIR ON FIRE

"Who's afraid of the future?"

Cinnamon Jones sucked a deep breath and raced downhill in the dark on fast hybrid wheels. Almost 1:00 AM and still on the bike path, miles from her bed. Shooting-Star was lost, or there'd been an accident, or worse, some rough crew had snatched her. The SOS was unclear. Shooting-Star had taken to *wandering* at night, keeping an eye on stray goats and suspicious drones. Maybe it was no big deal.

Cinnamon's nerves were scrambled. Why was this happening right before Festival? She needed to rehearse. She needed to sleep. The eight-bin trailer attached to her bike rattled in protest as she picked up speed. She'd done Wheel-Wizards' deliveries all day, roving the Pioneer Valley, from Electric Paradise and the Co-Op farms to the hill towns. She was wasted. Her headlight blinked and dimmed, needing a charge, still—

Cinnamon zoomed by downed cables about to spark a fire, flood walls ready to leak sludge, and a twisted body caught on a smart electric fence. Bear? Big person? She swallowed a shriek. Whoever climbed up into a 10,000-volt current was already dead meat. After she found Shooting-Star, she'd alert Valley Security—a private firm offering premiere services in Western Mass since the Water Wars. Game-Boy and his Back-From-The-Dead Crew would also want to investigate and Indigo's Vamp-Squad too. They were more of a neighborhood watch; still, keeping everybody and their mama righteous was a 24/7 gig. Cinnamon resisted irritation. "We save ourselves, Bruja. No Deus ex Machina to the rescue."

Bruja was fine with that and charged ahead, a black-and-white Border Collie blur. Bruja was committed to each step, each breath. No other place she'd rather be. She tracked Shooting-Star and yapped at Cinnamon to keep up. The Circus-Bots were loaded in the Wheel-Wizards trailer, farting and wheezing, slowing her down. Parking the trailer was a bad idea. Cyber-thugs usually avoided Cinnamon's tech. She had a horror rep on the Darknet. Messing with her Bots was like doom scrolling and calling down the wrath of the gods. A new gang had hit the scene, though. They might get bold and snatch the Circus-Bots. That would be cataclysmic.

The bike path plunged into mist, a silvery ribbon that caught the March moonlight. Cinnamon zigzagged through hulking shadows who sported long limbs and spooky crowns—new leaves were sprouting. Golden owl eyes peered from hollows. Crows huddled on branches and posed as clumps of darkness.

Bruja grumble-growled, smelling danger her human didn't see. She jumped on a stone bench and tasted the air. The bench read: *You're Half Way There! Take A Break! Take a Breath!* Cinnamon screeched to a halt between lilac bushes and a Wheel-Wizards porta-john. Her rayon tunic was drenched in dew and sweat, and bamboo pedal pushers clung to muscled thighs. She clawed damp salt-and-pepper braids from her face, licked plum-colored lips, and scanned for trouble.

No storm wind, yet trees smacked their branches together so hard, leaves rained down on her. Only the antique cell-tower tree with its antennae leaves and cement roots was unmoved. Trees usually whispered secrets to themselves and swept up starlight and car exhaust without complaint. Tonight, despite still air, the wooden giants creaked and groaned. They sounded angry, desperate. Horror movie trees on a tear about . . .

"OK, OK," Cinnamon muttered. She had to keep her *ImagiNation* in check.

Bruja yapped and paced between the bushes and the horror trees.

"What?" Cinnamon said. "Is Shooting-Star here somewhere?"

Bruja licked her chops, a paw in the air. The Circus-Bots burbled from their trailer bins. Bruja jumped up and slobbered on them, her favorite squeaky toys ever. Several years ago, Cinnamon did dumpster dives with Bruja and fashioned a Chinese Dragon, an Anishinaabe Thunderbird, and a West African mer-woman, Mami Wata, from broken junk nobody wanted. These AI clown-spirits—sacred fools—were tech fantasia for the Next World Festival. Cinnamon had more stamina back then. She was scientist, artiste, and hoodoo conjurer doing a sci-fi carnival jam to honor the ancestors and celebrate new life. Right.

"You guys picking up more distress calls?" Cinnamon talked to the Circus-Bots.

No answer. They were powered down to sentinel-mode, low energy yet alert—slicksters like the crows, they'd folded in on themselves and posed as compacted trash. LED eyes glowed blue and red, greedy for data. They repeated Shooting-Star's SOS on speaker, a jumble of Mavis Staples's and Chaka Khan's funky music:

I need you, you need me
Ain't nobody loves me better

Why would Shooting-Star broadcast such a muddled SOS?

Cinnamon's heart was skipping beats. Two years of peace had lulled her. Then last week the net was abuzz over burglaries in Electric Paradise. Folks weren't content to hack in; they stole hardware too. What if bold desperados decided to kidnap the Circus-Bots? What if they tortured her AI clowns for secret code the Bots didn't know? Origin code. Bots couldn't explain themselves. (Who could?) High-tech gangstas should kidnap Cinnamon. But nobody really knew who she was. She barely remembered her glorious gearhead self. How soon before enterprising wonks sussed her out?

Bruja was still sorting scents, mapping the dark.

"Hey, girl, the sooner we find Shooting-Star, the sooner we rehearse."

Bruja whined. Fingers of mist drifted up from the Connecticut River, possibly blunting the scent trail. Clouds obscured the moon, and the Circus-Bots rattled their bins. Their eyes blinked on and off, fireflies sparking in the mist. They were as agitated as Cinnamon. The wind snarled in the bushes and slammed a trash can against the porta-john. The door swung open. While Bruja figured their next move, Cinnamon marched over to take a piss. She groped in the dark for the bamboo wipes. Nothing.

"Scheiße!" she cursed in German, and fumbled in her fanny pack.

Two years ago, when she was taking a pee break at a porta-john near the old auto shop on Route Ten, there were no wipes. Back then, Game-Boy and crew were wannabe gangstas. They charged in, flaunting high-tech weapons as big as her bike, straight out of an old Schwarzenegger movie, *TermiNation*. Cinnamon and a few other Wheel-Wizards had zip except tee shirts they were giving away at Festival: *Thank the Trees for the Air You Breathe.*

Game-Boy had planned to ambush Indigo Hickory, a runaway camping in a dumpster and dealing cheap weed, for half the legal pot-shop price. Before any damage was done, Game-Boy's crew fell out, catatonic, at Indigo's feet, like someone switched off their video-game force. Eyes rolled up; tongues were sticks of wood and muscles squishy rubber. Dance of the dead, they all fell down. For no good reason. Only Game-Boy was left standing. He lurched around the bodies of his boys, gibbering off the beat.

At first Cinnamon imagined leaving the young thugs in the dirt. Her second thoughts were more charitable. The other Wheel-Wizards loaded Game-Boy's comatose crew into their trailers and biked them to the free Co-Op Clinic at the Ghost Mall. Saints. Cinnamon ended up hauling Game-Boy and drug dealer Indigo. Hooray for second thoughts . . . Since that raid/rescue, Cinnamon always carried bamboo wipes with her.

"Game-Boy and Indigo play in our show now!" Cinnamon shouted as she exited the porta-john. Bruja wagged her tail. "So, I refuse to think the worst of everybody and everything." Hard work recently. The hinge on the porta-john was trying to fall off. Cinnamon used the trash can to hold the door shut. "Which way to Shooting-Star?"

Bruja darted onto a footpath that ended at a swamp. Cinnamon pedaled slowly over uneven ground until her rig was invisible from the bike path, even if the moon came back out. She dismounted, turned off her lights, and staggered. The darkness was thick, and the ground and sky seemed to trade places. She'd felt dizzy all day. Bruja jabbed a cold nose in her crotch and steadied her. Cinnamon stayed close to Bruja as they stumbled along the path. Sneaky roots tried to trip her. Branches reached out to smack her face and butt. A cloud of insects flew in her mouth and nose. She spit them out.

"I'm too old for this late-night action adventure."

After what might have been five or twenty-five minutes of foggy darkness, Cinnamon halted. Bruja tugged her sleeve and nipped at her ankles.

"I don't know how much further I can walk in the dark."

Bruja raced toward faint blinking lights. A little girl wrapped in a blanket wore a tiara of flashing orbs. Her arms were draped around Shooting-Star-Bot, her face pillowed against the Bot's soft tresses. Bruja wagged her tail, nothing in the world better than FINDING LOST THINGS. An almost full moon broke through the fog. Cinnamon gulped deep breaths to counter the last hour's adrenaline surge.

Shooting-Star-Bot was a roving guard looking out for Cinnamon's farm—not a lot of complicated code, elementary warn-and-shield routines. Powered up and on the move, she looked like a boulder with her hair on fire. Low energy, sitting at the edge of the swamp, she passed for a piece of sky that fell long ago and then became moss-covered Earth landscape. Nobody noticed her, a perfect spy-bot.

Bruja licked the girl's face. She jerked awake and scrambled away from doggy concern. "It's all right, honey," Cinnamon said. "She won't bite you."

Doubting this, the poor child tried to shrink into her muddy blanket. She was plump, darker than Cinnamon, and had a swirl of cornrows and ribbons on her head.

"We won't hurt you, OK? We're the rescue team, answering an SOS."

"Uh-huh." The girl wanted to make a run for it. Bruja blocked her.

"What you doing out so late?" It was 12:46 AM. Late for a kid and for Cinnamon getting up at 5:00 AM to do a Ghost Mall delivery run. "Tomorrow's a big rehearsal and I'm not ready. We should both be in bed."

Bruja licked a scrape on the girl's chin. This engendered a half-hearted, "Ew," which Bruja ignored. She put a paw in the girl's lap and nuzzled her.

"Trying to steal my dog?"

"I'm not doing nothing." The girl had a tiny, high voice.

"She likes you. I call her Bruja. What's your name?"

The girl hunched her shoulders and leaned into doggy comfort.

"You from the Ghost Mall?" No Co-Op farmer let their kids run around here after dark. Farmer kids knew better anyhow. Cinnamon stepped closer. "Flood refugee? Or what, an Electric Paradise stray?"

The girl stroked Bruja's back. "Uhm . . ."

"You don't know where you're from and you don't have a phone to call somebody, do you?" Cinnamon resisted impatience and patted the Bot's fiber-optic tresses. "Shooting-Star is a good friend of mine."

The girl's eyes widened. "Shooting-Star?"

"That's her name. She broadcast an alert, then went silent—stealth-mode for tricky situations."

"Oh. Yeah. Tricky."

"Bruja tracked you down. She's sniffing out your secrets now, but don't worry. She won't tell on you." Cinnamon pulled up Shooting-Star's control panel and sent a message to Back-From-The-Dead Crew and Vamp-Squad to meet at the sugar shack ASAP. They traced lost kids and reunited refugee families. Neighborhood heroes! Cinnamon routed the Bot's remaining battery power into locomotion. She'd check the camera feed and shield routines later.

"Is your stomach grumbling at you?" Cinnamon held out the last of her Naughty Nuggets. "My great-aunt's world-famous recipe—vegan crunch passing for chicken." Bruja drooled. The girl shook her head. "I made these fresh this morning. You like honey mustard or maple barbecue sauce? Bruja likes them plain."

Bruja gobbled one in a flash. Before she wolfed a second one, the girl snatched it. She eyed Cinnamon and chewed slowly. She licked her fingers, wiped her mouth, and whispered, "Thank you." Maybe very soft was her normal voice. "That *was* good."

Cinnamon smiled. "What I tell you?"

The girl poked the fiber-optic tresses. "Why Shooting-Star?"

Cinnamon sat down beside her and leaned into the Bot. "My grandparents told me that people used to think comets were wild women roaming between the stars with their hair on fire in the sun."

"On a rocket ship?"

"No. Just so. Flying free." They stared at a trail of stars. "My grandmother, Miz Redwood, said she tried flying a few times, out in space, took Granddaddy Aidan along. They rode stolen heartbeats. He swore these were grand trips. I never knew whether to believe them or not." Cinnamon grinned. "Miz Redwood seemed like a woman who could ride the night on a heartbeat. Granddaddy Aidan too."

"I wouldn't try that if I was you."

"Why is that?"

"Space is very cold and there's no air and my mom says these are *end times*." The girl was near tears. "She and Daddy wished they never had me."

Cinnamon rubbed her face, suddenly weary. She put an arm around the child. "My mother used to say that nonsense to me too, when I was young. She didn't mean it."

The girl shivered—maybe her mom meant it. Bruja sprawled in their laps, looking expectant. The girl scratched raggedy black ears speckled with silver. Night-sky ears. She talked on to the dog. "Mom and Dad are always fighting. 'Cause they had me *way too young* and *ain't in love anymore*, and I'm *too bad to handle since the world's gone to shit*."

Cinnamon patted her shoulder. "This world has always been a hard rock, but Bruja don't like everybody. She knew right away you weren't stealing my Shooting-Star."

"'Cause I wasn't."

"'Bruja' means 'witch' in Spanish. She'd have bitten your head off if you weren't a good person." Bruja barked at the truth of this. Her fangs glistened in the moonlight. She flipped on her back, wiggling and pawing the air. Cinnamon rubbed a mottled tummy. "Bruja can always tell the good eggs and she found you, didn't she?"

"Yeah . . ." The girl stroked Bruja's stomach too.

"Bruja has the sight for finding lost things or maybe the nose. How old are you?"

"My dad says I'll be a decade next year, in December." Eight years and some change, yet trying to skip to the other side of these mad times. "I'm a Sagittarian."

"Almost a whole decade. Wow." Cinnamon whistled.

The girl smiled, proud of her years. Bruja jumped up and barked, ready to move. The girl stood up, clutching a knapsack almost as big as she was. Bruja wagged her butt.

"I'm Cinnamon Jones. What do they call you?"

"Zaneesha Williams." The girl bit the inside of her cheek. "I'm not really *that* bad. Mom says she's mad all the time, 'cause of *hell and high water.*"

"She'll be so glad to see you. Where is she?"

"She got a day and night shift in Electric Paradise from the Utopia App, taking care of baby animals." Zaneesha sniffled. "We have a tent, sleeping bags, except nobody's s'posed to camp there, so after Mom left, I heard crying and kids getting snatched from tents. Ours is by the trees, always. I grabbed my backpack and blanket like we practiced and snuck out to find Dad. He don't live with us. He's Valley Security working a checkpoint and keeping everybody safe, a big zigzag walk."

"Mm-hmm." Cinnamon nodded and waited for more.

"The checkpoint was gone or . . . I couldn't find him. Men with flashlights chased after me. They said they had jelly beans, like I'd let 'em catch me for candy. I'm not a baby. Shooting-Star bumped into me and covered me in moss hair. They ran right by us."

Cinnamon's heart banged in her chest. She wanted to scream and rage, but that wouldn't pay the rent. "Shield and warn. How about that."

"When we didn't hear 'em anymore, Shooting-Star played music, like Grandma listened to. I ain't seen her in a while. Shooting-Star and I walked till my legs hurt. I sat down to rest." Zaneesha yawned and almost toppled over. "Standing up is hard."

"I got you." Cinnamon picked Zaneesha up and hugged her—no resistance. She grabbed the knapsack, yet left the soggy blanket in the mud. Knapsack felt heavier than the kid. Bruja charged into the dark, leading the way to the bike rig. Shooting-Star trundled behind her, playing the Funkadelics' "Dr. Funkenstein" for the horror movie trees: *the cool ghoul, ego trippin' and body snatchin'.* Energized, Cinnamon bopped along. Zaneesha fell asleep against her shoulder.

CINNAMON
✿
RECKLESS YOUTH

The straw bale sugar shack made Cinnamon want a stack of blueberry pancakes with lots of syrup and butter. Jugs of maple lined the walls. Her mouth watered at maple candy, cookies, biscuits, and cream pies. There was also maple relish, and maple suckers formed into weasel sculptures with mint-green eyes. Goodies for Festival.

Cinnamon sank down on a hard wooden bench by the door. The moon grinned in the window. Zaneesha snored against her neck, a warm soothing sound. Cinnamon dozed off too, till reckless youth arrived on motor bicycles, laughing and carrying on. They had energy to spare for any crisis.

It took Game-Boy stomping into the shack to wake Zaneesha. She gaped at this white dude whose sandy dreads, tight jeans, and poly motorcycle jacket were slick with mist, a specter from the horror trees. He fussed at mystery muck on his sleeve. Indigo slinked in behind him, too cool for school. Zaneesha admired Indigo's demon Afro-puffs, vamp makeup, and dollar-store chic. Bug jewelry in the Afro-puffs flashed colored lights. Black girl magic, like Zaneesha's. Indigo sucked her teeth at Game-Boy.

"What?" He scowled at a yellow splotch on his biceps.

"You're like a *Hells Angel*, in the boneyard baron's inner squad, and about to lose it over—" Indigo shook her head at the goop.

"This is a legendary jacket. Bird shit's not coming off."

"Not bird do-do. Tree ooze. You need the right tool." She pulled his sleeve taut and scratched the muck off using a claw fingernail.

Cinnamon laughed. "Zaneesha, these are my friends, Game-Boy and Indigo, come to help you find home." Feeling tension ripple off them, she added, "What's up?"

"Asshats were shooting at the Motor Fairies near the gorge." Game-Boy glared out the window and winced. Two years ago, he might have been one of those asshats. He flushed red a second, then shook it off. "We chased 'em. Didn't catch anybody."

"The boneyard baron and Spook were AWOL," Indigo said.

"Well, we didn't see 'em." Game-Boy sucked a deep breath. "Nobody saw 'em."

No human saw Spook if he didn't want them to. The boneyard baron neither. A Water Wars veteran, special forces ace, the baron wielded juju-tech from old Nigeria and lived up an ancient oak on Cinnamon's farm. A guardian at the gate . . . there and not there . . . Cinnamon sputtered at weird shit almost impossible to believe. "You know how the baron is, like from another dimension." She was too tired to worry over what might be nothing.

Game-Boy stomped in front of her. "You should have called us sooner."

Cinnamon shrugged. "I couldn't."

"You're a high-tech wizard. Where's your damn phone?" Game-Boy shouted.

"Zaneesha doesn't have a phone either."

Zaneesha pouted. "Mom says *who can afford the monthly ransom*."

"I like flying under the radar," Cinnamon insisted. "The phone's a tracking device."

"Uh-huh." Indigo had her hands on ample hips beside Game-Boy. "A horror rep can mean folks want to take you down and prove their badassery."

"The paranoid, throwback act ain't cute." Game-Boy fumed. "It's dangerous."

"Who you calling throwback?" Indigo slugged him. "What the hell are you?"

"*Hot Wire Evil Empire chigga rat batta tat*." Game-Boy spewed gangsta rap gibberish, old school, definitely throwback. Zaneesha loved it. "*Do-wop da boomty bang na na na*." He was a Western Mass. homeboy from the hill towns beyond Cinnamon's farm, trying to sound hip, circa 1995 or 1983 or some way back when.

Outside the sugar shack, his Back-From-The-Dead Crew and Indigo's Vamp-Squad took up the beatboxing. Their colorful jackets went gray in the moonlight, their brown and white faces too. Zaneesha swayed in the funky vibe and managed a big smile.

"Good music is eternal." Game-Boy nodded at her. "*Zip a zap ding a do hell a rap*."

"Get outta here." Indigo resisted the groove. Bruja danced around her, tongue hanging down, tail like a propeller. Indigo scratched her ears, then slapped a sulky hip and tapped syncopated rhythms on the smooth wooden floor—counterpoint for Game-Boy's rat-tat-tat beats. Somebody might have thought they sounded good together.

"That's a Festival jam," Cinnamon declared, and Zaneesha applauded. To keep cheeky youth off her case, Cinnamon spewed Zaneesha's saga.

Game-Boy's face fell. "Flood kids be disappearing, more and more."

"Naw. You're just noticing." Indigo swallowed a horror memory. "Been running my whole life. Everyone's the same everywhere. Rotten. Most of the time, bad guys don't get what they deserve."

"Everyone, rotten?" Cinnamon snorted.

Indigo spluttered, "Except the Co-Ops and the Ghost Mall."

What was Indigo, twenty in the fall? Twenty-one? A runaway who'd gone nowhere and seen almost nothing. When Cinnamon first met her, she lived on trash and rumor, a bad accident waiting to happen, like Game-Boy. OK, nowhere near as deadly as Game-Boy playing at action-adventure violence. Indigo shoplifted, dealt illegal weed, and fell for fools who didn't love her back. Cinnamon expected a lot from her and almost nothing from the boys. She had to watch that. And what about wise old Cinnamon, feeling like a total failure, afraid to face tomorrow?

"Whatever the worst, survive that," she declared. "Reverse the curse. *ImagiNation!*"

Indigo wiped the sneer off her face and turned to Zaneesha. "You coming to Festival, day after tomorrow?"

Zaneesha hunched her shoulders. "I don't know what Festival is."

Game-Boy leaned close. "It's like Burning Man." Cinnamon cringed. Comparing Festival to Burning Man felt like someone pulling the plug on her spirit.

"Burning Man went from maker jamboree to billionaire celebrity bash forever ago." Indigo to the rescue. "What would Zaneesha know about that? The Next World Festival is a community carnival-jam. We got Circus-Bots."

Zaneesha lit up. "Like Shooting-Star?"

"Better," Game-Boy and Indigo said together.

Outside, Back-From-The-Dead Crew and Vamp-Squad riffed on Cinnamon's words: "*Reverse the curse! ImagiNation, not TermiNation! Don't be false, damn; own the pulse!*" Zaneesha grooved on the old-school beats. Game-Boy scooped her from Cinnamon's lap and headed out the door. Zaneesha threw her arms around his neck.

"What is the absolute worst you can imagine?" Indigo asked nobody in particular.

"Besides losing you all? Making no difference whatsoever to this world or the next," Cinnamon rasped. With the loud beatboxing, no-body heard her.

A Dream: Cinnamon pedaled down the bike path like a demon in the dark, tires never touching the ground, headlights blasting rainbows and lightning bolts. Horror trees, *cool ghouls*, scolded her about so many lost kids. At least, Zaneesha was safe and sound. Indigo and Game-Boy would find her mom and get them both to the Ghost Mall where nobody would dare snatch Zaneesha.

What about the others? the ghoul trees hissed. *Saving one almost bad as saving none.*

Cinnamon was about to fuss at trees—caught in a dream as vivid as real life. She couldn't wake up, slow down, or turn around, hurtling for a crossroads where—

Game-Boy's crew was laid up in hospital beds perched on gravel. Fluffy white sheets, half mist, half cotton, swirled about them. Bags dripped sustenance into their veins, and ventilators let them breathe. ICU for inexplicable comas. Witnesses told volunteer doctors the same tale: brandishing *TermiNation* weapons, the bad boys fell out all at once, splat on the ground, a video-game moment in real life.

Cinnamon careened to a halt. Game-Boy was slumped in the dirt by the beds, slobbering and wheezing. He'd been spared to vigil with the bleeping machines.

"Everyone gave up on us a long time ago," he said. "Can't blame 'em."

Indigo stood over him. "What you expect, a miracle?"

Everybody wanted miracles. Miracles required a lot of struggle and sacrifice. A volunteer nurse, what's-her-name who collected mushrooms and lived in Electric Paradise, fussed with drips and urged her patients to hurry back and sing in the May There Be Grace Choir at Festival.

"We should just let 'em go," Game-Boy muttered.

A tuxedoed form stood on an oak limb, little more than jacket, cane, and top hat, red on one side and black the other. Fingerless gloves gripped a snakeskin cane that rippled and writhed. A storm cloud cape trailed from broad shoulders, working the wind. The skeletal face winked in and out of focus as tux and cane tapped along the bough. Somebody else might have screamed. Cinnamon knew this specter.

The boneyard baron was a story storm she told on her young self, a tall tale from back in the day when magic walked the Earth, aliens visited from other dimensions, and the Water Wars had never happened. The baron's name was nowhere near the tip of her tongue. An African name—Yoruban, from Nigeria—which nobody had used since she was a kid. That name got lost with other impossible memories she was afraid to *believe*.

"Where you been hiding?" Cinnamon shouted. "We need you."

"I'm weary . . ." The boneyard baron danced down to the ground, shaking rattles, talking in tongues. The snake cane hissed a melody from old Africa by way of the Georgia Sea Islands. The baron tipped the top hat, poured libation at the crossroads, and whispered, "Ashe," a Yoruba Amen, calling on the power to make things be.

Syncopated owls hooted. Circus-Bots added a hurdy-gurdy drone and spewed glitter. Bruja snapped at sparkly bits of nothing. Crows chittered and shook off darkness. Horror trees ditched the doom groove and did triplets, upbeats, and backbeats, a carnival-jam for forgiveness.

The baron shook the rattle over each bad boy, then jumped in Cinnamon's face. "The worst is waiting for love to come on back in style."

Cinnamon sputtered. She had ditched love a decade ago or more.

The gangsta wannabes stood up from those comas and disconnected their drips. ICU machines sputtered to a halt and faded away. White sheets folded into mist. Indigo's and Game-Boy's mouths hung open. A rat-tat-tat echoed in the trees, guns from everywhere and nowhere. The baron tossed the rattle in the Mill River and raced in front of Game-Boy and Indigo, gobbling bullets, then belching fiery words. "Why put the Next World Festival on Raven's birthday?"

"Don't blame me," Cinnamon said. "That's when the elders wanted to celebrate their son." No arguing her grandparents or Great-Aunt Iris out of anything.

∞

Cinnamon jolted awake to a distant *rat tat boom pop*. She held her breath. Was that a car backfiring, fireworks, weapons? She blinked at familiar shadows and sat up on *her* bed, in *her* house—an heirloom farm inherited from her grandparents and great-aunt in the western Massachusetts hills, Nonotuck and Pocumtuc land.

The Mill River gurgled to itself as it zigzagged through fields and woods down to the valley, to the big river. Wind rattled branches. Owls, raccoons, and coyotes yelped in their nighttime dramas. Crickets carried on right outside the window, a June song in March. Climate change music. Cinnamon hugged herself. Nobody was out there wielding *Termi-Nation* weapons, or the perimeter sentinels guarding the farmhouse, orchards, and fields would have sounded an alarm. Somebody's engine trouble had invaded her sleep and brought on a boneyard baron dream.

If dreams were maps, like a wise man said, why did Cinnamon feel so lost?

Bruja's tongue was wet and rough against her hand. The air had a chill edge, yet the sheets were sweaty. Her grandmother's quilt was knotted at her feet, and achy muscles complained—too much pedaling in her sleep. Bruja pawed her hand and whined.

"I'm fine," Cinnamon lied, then allowed a tongue on her cheek.

Two years ago at the Co-Op Clinic, the boneyard baron brought Game-Boy's crew back from the dead. Cinnamon, Indigo, and Game-Boy barely believed their eyes. Bruja took it in stride. The mushroom-nurse declared it a miracle. Everyone at the clinic was thrilled except a few doctors who felt embarrassed, ashamed even, that juju worked on twenty-first-century, rational beings. The baron's rattle and hoodoo spells struck these doctors as worse than the Placebo effect—a savage attack on Western Civilization. They weren't the only disgruntled ones. Jealousy ambushed Cinnamon. *What the fuck?*

The baron never brought Raven, her shot-in-the-head dad, all the way back from a coma to himself. Raven was a good guy, one of the best. The baron had a chance to do right by him and failed. Cinnamon was still mad about this, after forty-plus years, sad too. And Raven's birthday was tomorrow—Festival day.

She sank into damp sheets and pillows. Old hip sockets screamed at her for lying on one side, then the other. No position offered a good night's sleep. The sun would be up in an hour. One more day till the Next World Festival, and Cinnamon Jones, scientist, artiste, and hoodoo conjurer, was nowhere near ready. In fact, she was dreading it. She loved her grandparents and great-aunt, but—

A bad move, scheduling Festival on her dad's birthday.

SPOOK

❧

THE SCOUT

5:00 AM. The bedside clock glowed through the fine metal mesh on the farmhouse window. Spook paused for a couple good breaths and a lick of dust and mist. The gunshots earlier were from the hill towns—a real fireworks display several miles from the farm. Spook also smelled burnt plastic down on the bike path in the valley, near the big river. Distant danger he'd keep a nose on.

He pissed against the back porch foundation to mark his territory and warn off intruders. Bruja pissed on the foundation too. Everyone else steered clear, except for the skunk. She lived in a hole beyond the sugar shack and mostly minded her own business. Who wanted to mess in that?

Spook was a gray-and-white husky with cyber-violet eyes. Sixty pounds heavier than Bruja, yet even-tempered. Unlike Bruja, he could rein himself in; he could pause before ripping somebody's throat. Spook gave folks a chance to reconsider. Ten seconds staring in otherworldly violet eyes and reflecting on the meaning of life and death was usually enough. Whatever stupidness bad boys had been doing was never worth dying for. They'd scramble away from sharp fangs, grateful for each breath they gasped.

Black bears also kept their distance from Spook or, if startled, took to a tree. Sometimes under a full moon, coyotes tried to intimidate him. They yapped and snarled, but smelled recent wolf-ancestors on him and chased after foxes instead or took down a foolish raccoon who'd strayed into cornfields.

Desperado whack-jobs Cinnamon nicknamed nostalgia militias were a different story. Random dudes with a violent agenda—like the two fellows Spook caught wind of now. They'd shot their guns recently and smelled of explosive chems. Out on a shooting spree in the hill towns? They were on the Co-Op road, heading toward Electric Paradise, the edge of Spook's territory. They paused to smoke tobacco. Cinnamon's Flying-Horse-Bot had them in view. Spook could trail them without giving himself away if need be. No reckless confrontations. The boneyard baron or Captain George, the head of Valley Security, handled the occasional shooters and firebugs.

Spook was the perfect seeing-eye and nose dog for the boneyard baron. After many, many summers, he should have been too old for guard duty or scouting the land around Cinnamon's farm. The boneyard baron kept him frisky and fit with shots, potions, and operations. Spook never suffered from achy joints or tired muscles and had more energy than ever this spring. He was like a puppy with good sense and a mission.

A warm body dashed from one hole to another, a mouse thinking she was invisible in the dark and downwind, no scent trail giving her away, safe. Spook still tracked her. His cyber-violet eyes were implants, the baron's work. So much of the world had come back on view after the cataracts had been removed. There were many colors Spook had never noticed before.

The implants gave him a headache at first, a real kick in the snout. Cinnamon tucked him in a soft sweetgrass basket, a Sea Island treasure. She put cool rags on his head and fed him from her hands. Bruja licked his face and snuggled close. Both dogs fit in the sweetgrass basket that was usually their winter nest. Cinnamon sang soothing music and reminded Spook of ancestors on a hilltop, howling joy.

After a few months the headaches had faded. Spook got used to more sights and night vision. Hot bodies glowed in cool air. He barely remembered not knowing so much light. People claimed the baron *saw what the cyber-dog saw* and *smelled scents he tracked*. And although Spook starred in many a wild tale along with Bruja the Witch-Dog, he never thought about that on his rounds by the farmhouse or anywhere. He did appreciate a good story storm, for the energy and passion, not the plot. Listening to Cinnamon's tales was the best. He and Bruja danced and sang accompaniment.

This morning Spook's nose was better than ever. Maybe the baron had enhanced that as well as his eyes. Sorting through fascinating odors, mapping the comings and goings in his territory was thrilling. He woke up eager to go. The moon remained bright as the sun scattered darkness, and a storm wind carried secrets his way.

Some hill town folks strayed suspiciously close to the bike path and Co-Op farmland. Spook smelled that up here on the ridge. They were hill town residents he didn't recognize or maybe folks passing through the valley who'd collected aromas from many different places on their clothes, on their breath. Travelers or a rough crew plotting an ambush?

Three or four people had been sleeping in mud. They were hungry and antsy, burping up acid stomachs. One woman had eaten a piece of fry bread. Spook liked fry bread covered in cheese and salty bacon. Cinnamon might have a treat for him, later. After she'd been up a while. She never had treats before sunrise.

Spook couldn't follow every suspicious body. Relying on ancient wolf-sense, he decided to follow the two characters carrying hot guns near Route Ten, see what they were up to, make sure they didn't get in more trouble. Anybody might go from a good person doing people-things—digging in the dirt, banging at cars or wrecked buildings, plucking strings and shaking rattles—to a desperado—stealing anything, beating up people and trees, and even shooting off guns. Desperados were lost rogues with no territory to mark, no home ground to piss on.

The last couple years, since bringing Game-Boy's crew back from the dead, the boneyard baron and everyone in the valley counted on Spook to track desperados, wayward youth, and the supposedly upstanding citizens who did a side hustle in a nostalgia militia—Neo-Vikings, True Blues, Happy Saxons, or whatever the heck they called themselves.

These two were done smoking and on the move. Flying-Horse-Bot was moving with them. He had a raffia mane, sweetgrass tail, and night eyes as good as Spook's, maybe better for some things. Spook licked his chops. Horse-Bot was sending out SOS chems to alert him and Bruja. Was the Bot in danger or simply warning everybody about the desperados?

Excited by a target to track, Spook woofed and wagged his tail at Cinnamon and Bruja, who were waking up in the farmhouse. Bruja woofed a catch-you-later reply as Spook headed out to trail the men with guns.

CINNAMON

SONG

"SOS, but not enough data."

"Never enough data."

"Gotta act anyway. The end of this world . . ."

The Circus-Bots huddled by Bruja's bed and talked to themselves.

Cinnamon squinted at the clock. 5:08 AM. Four hours was not enough sleep. The fireworks had been in a dream. Backcountry living meant no loud neighbors or sirens, no roaring traffic or clanking machines. Songbirds waited for a hint of sun to do morning serenades. Night creatures slinked back to their nests, leaving her alone with—

The three Circus-Bots muttered on and on, about surviving the end of the world. How'd they get stuck on that? Engineering the low-energy sentinel-mode instead of a deep-sleep-mode or a true off-switch (except for a cataclysmic emergency) was a design flaw. Especially at five in the morning when she wanted to feel sorry for herself a bit longer. Smoldering LED eyes fixed on her as the hunk of junk Bots went silent.

"SOS? I know what you're thinking." Cinnamon sat up. "I don't have to hear it."

She spoke out loud to them, to herself really, a bad habit that the Bots mimicked. She was an incurable talkaholic, prone to story-storm tall tales since she was a kid. Opal always said *my daughter come out the womb talking—she got the gift of gab*. It felt more like *the curse of gab* or *motor-mouth-itis*. Cinnamon lived alone except for the three Bots and Bruja, and she hated gabbing in her head. So—

"No heroes to the rescue!" she shouted at the Bots. "Like last night. It's a get-off-your-ass, do-it-yourself life. Save our own spirits." LED eyes blinked green and silver, noncommittal. "Nobody wants to hear truth. That's why I talk to myself." Only half a lie. Stratospheric expectations had ruined several good relationships. Who could put up with her truth? The boneyard baron was wrong. She wasn't *waiting for love*. Too busy.

The last decade was rough, especially the Water Wars. People, well, mostly men, were shooting one another instead of figuring out how to share. Tucked in the hills, her farm, the *elders'* farm, had been spared. Down in the valley, rivers inundated fields, town squares, and neighborhoods. Microbursts flattened houses, turned schools and stores to rubble, snatched trees from hillsides, and smashed them into highways and railroad tracks. *Deny climate change all you want, but when that brushfire rolls up on your ass, you run or burn.*

Too many catastrophes came fast and furious, plus shortages, plagues, and violence. Black and Brown folk, elders and children, poor folk, women, and queer folk were hard hit; in other words, most people. Luckily, the Motor Fairies, Wheel-Wizards, and the Co-Ops, a collective of farmers, merchants, journalists, mechanics, educators, and healers, resisted partisan squabbles and filled in where the feds or the state fell down. The Co-Ops put everybody to work, real jobs with a future.

Rich folks in Electric Paradise depended on Co-Op farms (like Cinnamon's) for their food supply. Needing each other was a good thing. Paradise funded Valley Security, who stockpiled high-tech weapons and ammo. They hired ex-cons, *gangstas* some said, and coordinated with the Co-Ops to beat violence back to occasional outbursts, what Zaneesha's father was doing no doubt. Maybe he was in a mobile unit fighting whack-jobs at the gorge last night when Zaneesha went looking for him. He'd be easy for Indigo and Game-Boy to locate. They were good detectives.

So who the hell were the creeps raiding camps and snatching flood refugee kids? And why? Irritation cramped her jaw and curled her lip. Bruja leapt onto the bed, perky ears, bushy tail in motion. She licked Cinnamon's scowl and tugged her sleeve.

"Not yet. Where's the sun?" Cinnamon slumped against sweaty sheets. Bruja wasn't having that. She yanked Cinnamon onto the floor. "Stop."

Bruja cocked her head to one side, staring at Cinnamon's foul mood with a brown eye in black fur and a blue eye in white fur. Border Collie impertinence. Cinnamon had to laugh. Bruja's mission was to ground her in the here and now, but keep spirits high. An impossible task that Bruja took very seriously.

"Never the end of the world for you, huh?" Cinnamon scratched scruffy ears.

Bruja put a paw in her lap, ready for anything, the whole story storm. She was good company. So were the Bots, actually.

"I had a Back-From-The-Dead dream."

She leaned against the bed with Bruja half in her lap. The Circus-Bots trundled closer on suitcase wheels, insatiable data hounds like Cinnamon.

"Two years ago, right before FESTIVAL. You love FESTIVAL, don't you? A natural-born clown." She stroked Bruja's black-and-white fur. "We went out raiding dumpsters to make costumes. Remember? You found old light fixtures, windshield wipers, a marimba, and Indigo Hickory, covered in a nasty rash and dealing marijuana from a trash bin. Now girlfriend be growing weed at the Ghost Mall. She says the bees love it."

Bruja wagged her tail and squirmed farther into Cinnamon's lap.

"Taiwo—" Taiwo was the boneyard baron! Cinnamon sighed relief at name recovery. Taiwo was the Yoruba name for the twin who was the first to taste the world. "Baron Taiwo brought Game-Boy's crew, well, not back from the dead, back from *whatever*. I know you remember that."

Bruja barked once and laid her head on Cinnamon's shoulder.

"I don't know. How does Taiwo do anything? Hoodoo, playing the shaker you love. That old African turned those gangsta-wannabes around a hundred eighty degrees."

Bruja grumble-growled.

"Why lock up Game-Boy or his crew? Over *Save-the-Trees* tee shirts we were giving away? Nobody pressed charges. Falling out in a coma was punishment enough. Taiwo claimed the *TermiNation* guns were *props* for Festival. Back-From-The-Dead Crew has been doing community service ever since."

Bruja licked her ear. This was much better than talking to herself.

"Since the Water Wars, half of everybody is one bad move from camping out in a vacant lot." Cinnamon sighed. "I should get dressed."

Bruja jumped under the bed, scratching and clawing. Cinnamon was tidy. Every week, she did laundry, cleaned shelves or windows, something, and vacuumed up dust devils. Shoes, clothes, or stray objects never got shoved out of sight under the furniture. Mice usually avoided the bedroom—food temptation was verboten this side of the kitchen. Bruja ate any rogue thing on the floor, including the mice.

"What are you doing?" Cinnamon dropped to her stomach and peered in the gloom. "Did you stash something?"

Bruja scrambled out and set a bedraggled mask by Cinnamon's nose: scaly green skin, bug eyes with no pupils, sharp antennae that ended in rubber, and reptile ears. Or were those gills? Wings? Some combination?

"You want me to do an alien for Festival? No way." Cinnamon squinted at the rubber balls and felt tired, in her bones, blood, and spirit. "Didn't I toss that stupid thing already?" She kicked the mask. "Throw it away."

Bruja eyed her and whined. Cinnamon winced. She'd given Bruja her love of theatre, her passion for Festival. Bruja guarded these treasures fiercely. Cinnamon whispered, "Entschuldigung," a German sorry, as Bruja gently took the alien in her mouth. Bruja was just trying to help her get ready for tomorrow's carnival conjure.

"Baron Taiwo is worse than me. Moping for *two years*." Bringing bad boys back to life had taken its toll. Miracles required struggle and sacrifice. Taiwo had yet to recover. "No one is indefatigable, immortal, and omniscient, no matter what anybody would like to believe."

A veteran of too many wars, Taiwo was living up in a grandmother red oak tree on the farm, because: *no dragging my trauma drama into the elders' farmhouse.* Taiwo's bed, Taiwo's whole room, had been empty, cold, for two years. No one went in, other than Bruja. She disappeared in there now. Cinnamon heard her hide the mask.

Bruja had stashes everywhere. She hoarded mask- or prop-rejects and busted gear from their dumpster dives. She loved to surprise Cinnamon with the perfect widget to repair the Bots or to finish a tricky new invention, costume, or mask. As Festival approached, and everyone started making props and costumes, Bruja went wild fetching and stashing.

Cinnamon felt guilty. "I got nothing for Festival," she whispered to the Bots, who hovered close still. "No song, dance, no adventure yarn with a hopeful twist on a tragic beginning." A twinge in her back made her stand up slowly. "People have heard everything I have to say: Reverse the curse, *ImagiNation*! Who cares? Why do I put myself through theatre misery?"

Nobody came to Festival last year, except Euro-trash doing a New World Dystopia tour. Folks with German accents and British pretensions cursed the net for pissing out and stinky homeless people for hanging on in this nowhere-land, in this late, great America where once Burning Man had reigned supreme.

"Scheiße!" she cursed in German, and closed her eyes, wishing to fall into a dreamless sleep for several days and wake up after Festival.

ॐ

The show must go on.

Cinnamon opened her eyes, limped into the living room, and stumbled against a chair. Turning on lights was a waste of electricity. The room was awash in moon shadows and colorful LED lights from her gadgets. A skylight waited on the sun. Under this dark glass eye, Bruja stuck her butt in the air and leaned on black-and-white elbows, the play gesture. Cinnamon wrestled with her, then sprawled on the bamboo floor.

"*You* had fun last year at Festival. You always have fun. What was last year's tee shirt? Do you remember?"

Bruja loved a challenge. Besides keeping her herd away from danger and on track, fetching the exact thing Cinnamon named was her favorite sport. She dug into a pile of clean laundry that should have gotten folded yesterday evening; however, Cinnamon had been out chasing stray Bots. Bruja found three glow-in-the-dark shirts: *Thank the Trees for the Air You Breathe.*

"No. That was the shirt from *two* years ago."

Bruja put the shirts back in the laundry pile and looked around, panting.

"Nobody remembers *last* year." Cinnamon stretched out in dead person's pose. "Festival was a bust."

The Motor Fairies freaked during a tap-dance routine when a bloom of fruit flies erupted from edible props. Powwow Now broke every drumhead in the opening procession, and ramps to the Mothership buckled. Cloudbursts doused every new fire Cinnamon tried to light. Game-Boy and Back-From-The-Dead Crew bagged at the last nanosecond, talking smack about *stolen masks.* And the worst, Baron Taiwo was a no-show. Despite her attempts to hide petty feelings, Taiwo probably realized the truth. Cinnamon was in a rage over Game-Boy's crew coming *all the way back to themselves* when Raven never did. Nobody rescued Cinnamon either. And Saving Your Own Self was a Hard Problem.

Bruja trotted over her belly back to Taiwo's room. She dragged out a rattle. A net of seeds covered the surface of a hollow gourd, which amplified their hailstorm sound. This was her favorite Festival instrument and the very one Taiwo had played to bring bad boys back from the dead. Bruja gripped the netting carefully.

"Taiwo said that shekere was gone, trashed. Did you steal it?" Sékéré in Yoruba. Cinnamon felt a tingle of pride remembering this word. Bruja wagged her head and shook the gourd. Cinnamon scrambled up. "That's loud enough to wake folks in Electric Paradise." She chased Bruja, who thumped the shekere against the floor. Cinnamon stopped, afraid Bruja would bust the gourd or rip the net of seeds. "Did you hear me say *cancel*? Festival is tomorrow, OK? *I promise.*"

Bruja halted her *music* and gazed up, triumphant, inexplicable. She dropped the shekere. Cinnamon picked it up and inspected for damage. Relieved at its sturdy condition, she played a sultry rhythm, ambled to the elderly computer, and flicked the power-switch on an upbeat. Cyber-blue light assaulted her eyes. She squinted and set the shekere on a shelf above the screen. Bruja jumped up and nipped Cinnamon's nose.

"No. We have to give the shekere back to Taiwo. I'll play a come-down rhythm tomorrow and get that old trickster out the trees." Bruja clawed her belly. "What's wrong with you? Down! Now! I gotta check the news before peak demand."

Bruja eyed the shekere and paced as Cinnamon fumbled the endless password twice. Typing it wrong a third time, she'd be locked out and have to hack in. She should have shifted to fingerprint and voice security ages ago. Recent stories of desperados stealing laptops and tablets from Electric Paradise and a finger or two had to be exaggerations. Most pads were terminals, no local computing power. Storage was in the cloud. Cinnamon refused to let her data, her *life*, float out there on porous servers that even a lapsed gearhead like her could hack. She hated con-necting to the net. So many bots to dismantle, cookies to eat, malware to unmask. She was a paranoid throwback, like Game-Boy said.

The computer booted up with a hoarse whisper: "Ancient but still at it."

Bruja ventured close and plopped at Cinnamon's feet, yawning up at the news flashing across the screen. Bruja preferred nature documenta-ries or old movies and TV shows. The news put her to sleep. Cinnamon rubbed her eyes and yawned too. She hated the news more and more every day.

Before they died, her grandparents and great-aunt willed her their middle-of-nowhere farm and made her promise never to turn away from the world. Perusing headlines was the least she could do. Facing the screen reminded her of teetering at the edge of a bottomless canyon, afraid of getting sucked into a void, vortex, or combination. She braced herself.

Today's news burst was almost too fast to catch. No time to process anything. Never time for that. Bombastic music scrambled her thoughts. Mostly click bait—outrage, envy, and despair—processing unnecessary. No mention of hill town shootings or refugee kids getting snatched. And what could she do about all that?

A grainy video filled the screen. Cinnamon jerked and leaned close. Bruja sat up. Baron Taiwo, in red-and-black finery, whirled in the air with a mouth full of fire, like in Cinnamon's dream. The clip ran without a headline, commentary, or source. A cell-phone video? Who posted it? Game-Boy? Taiwo muttered several smoky words. The image dissolved into three old people smiling and winking at her. They almost looked like her grandparents and great-aunt. Their hair burst into flames.

"We know what you need," a deep voice proclaimed.

Cinnamon jerked back. "What the fuck?" Had she been hacked by a Darknet Lord? Or was this an ad for brain enhancements? The news flashed on, the same tripe as yesterday or any day, except Taiwo had never showed up in the feed before. Blurs that might have been anything were frequent. Click-baiters made a sideshow of people reporting demons or UFOs. Commentators chortled and rolled their eyes. *You or me, sure, but what self-respecting alien would visit these clods?*

Maybe her eyes were playing Taiwo- and elder-tricks on her. She did a full-body theatre shakeout. Darknet Lords could care less about her. She slapped her face and made her ears ring. Spending the whole day in a stupor again—seeing visions and forgetting everything—was out of the question. The Festival director couldn't be tripping at dress rehearsal this afternoon. She squeezed her eyes shut, then opened wide. A headline caught her attention. "Whoa! A next-gen AI caught lying."

The screen shifted to static and an irritating whine. A fast ten minutes. Consolidated, Inc., was cheating her, cutting down the news bursts on the sly, or sending her a warning. Probably both. A laugh caught her mouth by surprise. "A fancy next-gen AI shouldn't be acting like that."

She hummed a melody from her Back-From-The-Dead dream or from the sole online DJ she subscribed to—the guy talked trash yet played good astral bop. She scribbled on a notepad by the computer. She always used a pen to write first thoughts. Old-school brain-body connection, neuroscience defying capitalism. Bruja blasted doggy breath in her face. Her tongue dripped saliva on Cinnamon's fleece socks.

"A new song's coming. Cutting it close, but in the nick of time. How you like that?"

Bruja barked and chased her tail.

Jotting down lyrics at the speed of thought, Cinnamon turned the computer off and missed Flying-Horse's cataclysmic SOS flashing in the bottom right of the screen.

Book II

THE DAY BEFORE
THE FESTIVAL

What's going on?
Marvin Gaye

There will be a layer in the fossil record where you'll know people were here because of the squashed remains of automobiles. It will be a very thin layer.

Life did not take over the world by combat, but by networking.
Lynn Margulis

The land knows you, even when you are lost.
Robin Wall Kimmerer

THE CIRCUS-BOTS
ဖၜ

IN A LOOP

SOS. SOS. SOS.

6:39 AM. The sun seemed to be rising from the end of the bike path. Blades of light attacked the mist. The three Circus-Bots lurked under magnolia buds, LED eyes dull. In sentinel-mode, they masqueraded as heaps of bug-eyed junk on rickety wheels—broken glass, smashed cans, and warped plastic—nothing anybody would want. Yet soon, when fully powered up, they'd become mythic creatures of yesterday and tomorrow. For now, they rehearsed pride in their accomplishments and practiced looking forward to tomorrow. Or rather looking forward to today, come what may.

The SOS radio signal from Flying-Horse flared again, a Stevie Wonder clip:

> This place is cruel, nowhere could be much colder
> If we don't change, the world will soon be over

It dissolved into static. This was much worse than Shooting-Star's alert last night. A cataclysmic threat, no escape possible, so Horse had engaged the *dead-bot-off* switch, which would mean short-term memory loss, then data corruption and decay. Thieves might try to override protocols and reboot. More likely, they'd poke and pry Horse apart, scavenge what they could to sell, and toss the rest in a trash heap. The Circus-Bots shuddered. Flying-Horse was mostly security spyware, not a part of their group loop, no direct data link, although still embodied AI. Horse knew how to suffer.

The Circus-Bots signaled sentinel statues around the farmhouse and at the gates to the bike path and the Co-Op car road. Everybody went on red alert. Shooting-Star would shift to stealth-mode till further notice. Spook and Baron Taiwo would also receive Horse's scent and funk-music SOS and they'd take care of business. Nothing else to do except wait and worry. The Bots looped concern for Horse's fate and hope for quick rescue into all their routines as they reviewed their immediate circumstances.

Cinnamon's Wheel-Wizards bike and its eight-bin trailer were parked at the bike-path gate. She'd head out for her Ghost Mall delivery soon. Right now, she was rustling up a candle from the prop shed for her morning ritual. Her elders, Granddaddy Aidan, Miz Redwood (what everybody called her grandmother), and Great-Aunt Iris, were buried in a grassy Amphitheatre on their heirloom-vegetable farm. Cinnamon's farm now, and she was lucky to have it, even if she couldn't farm worth a damn.

Blessed be the Co-Ops. They were tapping the maples, bringing heirloom vegetables back from the dead, and feeding the people. Maple sap was almost done running. The last buckets were stacked in the prop shed waiting to be deployed on north-facing hillsides where sap ran later. Different weather up there.

Nobody planted crops down here in the Amphitheatre. Wildflowers and grasses had free rein. Aidan Wildfire and Redwood Phipps were dyed-in-the-wool theatre people. They'd done traveling shows all over the country, all over the world, and silent films. From spring to fall, they'd invite folks out to do shows under the moon and stars. Smooth rock formed tiers of seating on a gentle slope overlooking a clover and dandelion stage. Star-magnolia bushes and oak and maple trees provided backstage and wings. The audience felt lonely with four hundred people, full with eight hundred, and jammed with twice that. The Motor Fairies bussed in folks who needed assistance.

Sunlight hit an altar nestled upstage center in dead clover and purple aster stalks. Granddaddy Aidan had carved a triptych sculpture from pink granite: a Chinese Dragon, an Anishinaabe Thunderbird, and Mami Wata, African queen mother of waters. These were the elders' favorite Festival masks and the models for Cinnamon's Circus-Bots. Gray granite snakes, sacred mediators between the ancestors, the living, and the unborn, curled from Mami Wata's mer-woman tail through Dragon's claws and along Thunderbird's belly. Thunderbird's wings hugged them all close.

The Bots took almost a second to savor Granddaddy Aidan's artistry, to indulge Aunt Iris's love of snakes, to revel in Miz Redwood's vision. The altar was Redwood's idea. She insisted the elders open each season at the Amphitheatre with Festival, to *celebrate first fruits, light new fires, and forgive what can be forgiven*. Festival was how they stayed connected to Seminole and Georgia Sea Island ancestors, Irish and African ones too, how they reached back to the first heartbeat and to generations yet to come.

Since the elders passed, Festival was the one show Cinnamon managed to put on. This year, it was looking dodgy. A superrich tech wizard asked to deploy a camera crew on the ground plus drones for Electric

Paradise patrons who refused to mingle with the masses on cold stone seats. Cinnamon refused, declaring *Festival's a live joint.* She promised to *one day* bring a road show to folks who, for whatever reason, wouldn't come to the Amphitheatre. If productions made her so sad why promise a touring show? Mystery: Cinnamon was full of sadness she didn't know how to share.

The Bots added concern for her to their group loop. In Consolidated's news burst, Baron Taiwo's snake cane whispered a prayer (in words from another dimension), then demanded action. Action meant *do, suffer, know*—always hard for the Bots. But knowing how to suffer aided with cognition and survival.

"SOS. These are trying times." Mami Wata's AI had a faint southern accent plus Chicago academic flare. She'd trained on Great-Aunt Iris—the electric, intrepid anthropologist. "We must engage slow thinking." Using narratives, weighted valences, and emotion modeling took mega-joules of energy. Unlike Dragon and T-bird, Mami Wata had energy to burn. She was a solar generator on wheels. "Hear what I say?"

A curious drone glided in from fog clouds and ventured too close without pinging Cinnamon's security sentinels. Somebody's spy, trying to listen in. Mami surged and zapped the drone's circuits, as if a devilish lightning bolt hit just the wrong spot. The disabled drone crashed into the magnolias. Action was hard, not impossible though.

"We save ourselves. That's our SOS," Mami whispered.

"I can't abide sneaks and snoopers." Thunderbird did Aidan's Semi-nole/Irish lilt. He was the scout, and good-natured till he wasn't. Bug-eyes glowered through cellophane as he scanned the dead drone. "Solar-powered whisper-engines mean Electric Paradise or Consolidated, Inc."

"So, desperados nabbed Flying-Horse, then here comes this whisper-witch." Dragon spoke Redwood's Georgia Sea Island cadence, her storm child clarity. She knew what was what before everybody. "Correlation don't mean causation, however—"

"Shit do smell, no matter how small," T-bird-Aidan said. "Too many anomalies."

"We need to get on the right train of thought." Dragon-Redwood gnashed gemstone teeth and put a scowl in her voice. "Not enough data."

"Never enough data." The tip of Mami-Iris's tail sparked.

"Consolidated, Inc., be ready to steal the sweet out of honey." Thunderbird-Aidan scanned the woods beyond the bike path and the mist above. "Spy-bots from Paradise are almost as bad. And everybody know, Cinnamon can talk a leg off a chair."

Dragon-Redwood sucked her teeth. "So who wants to snoop her motor-mouth-itis? That's my question."

"Some folks are greedy." Mami-Iris sizzled and popped, her anger fed by sunlight. "They want everything, all our *behavioral surplus*. They plan to own the world."

"Only a fool wait till *after* an asteroid's up their ass to grab a telescope." T-bird-Aidan twanged his words like rusty banjo strings. "Excuse my rough tongue, but we gotta figure the damn pattern."

"We're in a danger zone. No rescue on the horizon." Dragon-Redwood worked these words into a nonsense scat, into a storm wind caught behind her teeth. Thunderbird-Aidan added an earthquake pulse.

"Gotta act before we know everything." Mami-Iris had a third eye in the back of her head, for seeing in the dark like Spook. It flashed infrared. "The baron can't be everywhere. So, we save ourselves."

"SOS," Thunderbird-Aidan wheezed. Back where they began. "Are we in a vicious loop?" The only way out of a vicious loop was better data and more insight.

Cinnamon had found the candle for her ritual and was walking their way with Bruja. The Bots quieted down. Cinnamon didn't need to hear their worries or half-ass speculations about Flying-Horse. Not yet. What could she do? The (unavoidable) report on the spy-drone that Mami zapped would be bad enough.

CINNAMON

RITUAL

The sun struggled up over battered hills, and low-riding clouds made a purple-and-orange carpet of first light. Tomorrow had become today.

"Who sent you?" Cinnamon grabbed the drone Mami had zapped. "Must be a traffic jam up there." She disabled its tracking device. "What do they think we're doing? Growing psychedelic mushrooms? Rehearsing the revolution? Orgies?"

She stuck the drone in her bike rig to *interrogate* later. Maybe it belonged to the gazillionaire tech wizard who wanted to film the Festival, Ray? Joe? Steve? Baron Taiwo usually handled spy-bots, although recently, Taiwo wasn't handling much. Valley Security had come to the rescue a few times—false alarms and they still charged a fortune. A good horror rep was cheaper than hiring thugs, deploying patrol-drones, and electrifying fences. Spook and Taiwo needed to do alien juju and recharge the urban myths.

"Granddaddy Aidan, Miz Redwood, Aunt Iris, you loved the future . . ." Cinnamon stood at their graves about to make excuses. Wheeling toward sixty and she still felt like a child. "Your little scientist-artiste is all grown-up." Dead leaves skittered across her spring booties, ghostly lace dissolving into the rubble of flower stalks. Ages ago, Aunt Iris planted a patch of asters for a fall production that featured bees, and then the asters went wild. Usually the *putting-bees-in-a-show* memory cheered her. Not today.

"I'm supposed to be cruising the good life, carrying your spirits with me, until I hand a better future over to the next team." Was Cinnamon a big disappointment to the ancestors, a broken link in the chain? She tugged her *Thank-the-Trees* tee. Indigo Hickory had painted *Afro-Future Is Now* in fluorescent gold on the back. "Your future was where the dreams folks fought and died for finally came true. I'm stuck in some other jacked-up future." Her dark eyes welled up. Flood refugees raced across her mind: children with lead-stained lips and haunted faces—like Zaneesha. Bruja licked her hand, dispelling the vision. "I don't want to give this future to anybody," Cinnamon whispered. "I'm afraid of the future."

She'd sworn on the elders' graves never to be like the old farts in gated communities who ranked on screwed-up humanity and waxed nostalgic for glaciers to ski, rain forests to plunder, and only two genders to love. Yet here she was, stuck on the past like everybody else. Bruja whined. She'd be trying to herd Cinnamon soon. People at the Ghost Mall were hungry, itchy, twitchy. A late arrival would put everyone on red alert.

"Gotta do this ritual first," she told Bruja, talking to herself really.

Granddaddy Aidan had insisted that after the elders were dead and buried, she come out at sunrise and do a story storm on the future, starting from yesterday. Aunt Iris wanted her to sing about the future. That's why the elders were buried in a natural Amphitheatre, to come back as weeds, as yellow dandelions and purple lupine, and enjoy the shows. Miz Redwood told her to do headlines with funny commentary. *I can always do that*, Cinnamon promised. Ha! The news was old and tired. The elders were long dead. Their ashes had dissolved by now. Would they notice if she missed a day?

"You promised, child," Thunderbird-Aidan grumbled from the magnolias.

"What good is chanting bad news?" Cinnamon replied.

"Jokes on the headlines inspire the magnolia blossoms," Dragon-Redwood hissed.

"Talking bad news at magnolias won't make them bloom," Cinnamon insisted.

These unruly Bots would get on her case later (sounding exactly like the elders) if she didn't keep her promises. Erasing their memories of Redwood, Aidan, and Iris would be too cruel, impossible actually. The ancestors were all through Cinnamon's Circus-Bot algorithms—origin code. The Bots talked with the elders' voices, with their cadence, logic, and wisdom. She might have imagined the grumbling tone. In sentinel-mode, the Bots conserved energy. Emotional states took a lot of energy.

"You're about to be late, child," Mami-Iris said. "Is that what you want?"

"I don't know what I want." Cinnamon was afraid to want. She squinted at the asphalt bike trail, which snaked from the Amphitheatre down through flood rubble and across gated roads fifteen miles to the Ghost Mall. Refugees, runaways, and reformed gangstas pitched tents in dead big-box stores, hoping for miracles: jobs, food, electricity, a plan, a vision— maybe cheap cell service.

Last year an Afro-Deutsch hipster, wearing a fluorescent cape and fiber-optic sneakers and hoody, crashed Festival and ranted about Burning Man, then handed out free burners with solar chargers. Game-Boy scored a case for his crew. Cinnamon was not impressed by fiber-optic kicks and a Euro-trash accent. Indigo neither, but most Ghost-Mallers cheered the faceless, glow-in-the-dark hipster calling for hope. Mallers were waiting on the second coming. What they got in tent city was compost toilets, tap water, and Co-Op volunteers like Cinnamon pedaling in whatever they could spare.

Bruja nipped the back of her knees and barked, Border Collie for: *Quit stalling.*

"Right. So, today might be my last news report for a while." She wiped schmutz off the snakes circling the memorial. "I'm two months behind on my access bill."

Virtual Living cost more than brick-and-mortar rent. She'd spent her cash on spring planting, Festival supplies, rehearsal treats, taxes, and bribes. Valley Security charged exorbitant rates to watch over Festival, and she had no real income till maple syrup. Time to raid her savings?

"Who can say when Consolidated might cut me off the *free* net?"

Some digital divide algorithm decided how much grace period was profitable for the coalition of providers aka the net monopoly or Consolidated. Three companies in the world owned every blessed thing. She refused to hack random Wi-Fi. Consolidated hunted down hackers using vengeful AI. Who needed that static?

Cinnamon fumbled with matches trying to light the stupid candle. Bruja rammed her butt, then ran to her Wheel-Wizards bike. Six of the eight bins were loaded down. The other two were waiting on the Circus-Bots. Bruja snarled and raised her tail high, a command gesture. *Do the damn ritual.* The third match was a charm. The wick caught fire and undulated. Cinnamon tucked the jar of fragrant wax at the memorial's base and poured libation to Eshu, *guardian at the gate of life and death, shapeshifter master of improvisation and masquerade, everything at once, yet not any one thing.*

The Bots thrummed with excitement. Compact trash unfurled into a wingless Chinese Dragon with a cellophane and aluminum body and silver bike-reflector eyes. Two copper funnels formed Dragon's snout. Gemstone teeth might have been a grin or snarl. An opalescent bead hung on a bike chain around a scaly neck. Stubby legs splayed into rotors and whirred to a funky beat. Dragon lifted off and hovered, a helicopter drone with Festival flare. Another hunk of junk unfurled trash-bag wings to become an Anishinaabe Thunderbird. Flashlight eyes the blue-green of a turbulent sea pulsed. T-bird had a bicycle-horn mouth, which honked a country melody as tap-dancing talons and scrap-metal tail feathers clanged harmony. Mami Wata, African queen mother of waters, turned on the snake coils of LEDs curled around her scaly tail. Seashell locs reflected a medley of colors. A waterfall of light surged from her mouth down green tennis-ball breasts, over a basketball belly, and across the broken glass tail.

In high-energy-mode, Dragon, Thunderbird, and Mami Wata crowded around Cinnamon, backup singers doing their own special effects. Bruja wagged her butt. She loved when the Bots came out to play. Cinnamon flushed with pride at dumpster-dive designs, at code she wrote gathering input and getting better, every day, every second. Exactly the flash of spirit she needed to hold forth in full theatre-mode.

"*Polio Comes Roaring Back in the South and the CDC Stumbles.* What do you want, a tap dance? Twerking? Funding got gutted a few years ago, and last May nasty tropical diseases wasted Maine to Nova Scotia. *Water Wars in the Wild West Are Getting Ugly.* Were there pretty Water Wars? Texas is burning up. We got nowhere to put the rain in Massachusetts. Greenland's a puddle. Sweden's a cinder; Australia's an ash heap."

Dragon and Thunderbird do-wop do-wopped, then shifted to a Scots Gaelic wail for seals: "Coir an oir an oir an oir o."

"*Scattered Brownouts Cripple the West Coast.* Spies in China, the USA, or Brazil launched shapeshifting digital weapons at power grids *by accident.* Maybe it was Russia. Nigeria insisted it wasn't their fault. Nobody believes anybody. **Suicide Soars. Not Just on the Rez or in Black and Brown Ghettos.** It's never *apocalypse* until rich white men be jumping from bridges. *Everybody living in the third world now.*"

Someone woofed in the wind. Spook? Tracking suspicious characters?

"*Crime Soars!* Hormones, inequality, no jobs, no perspectives. Young folks need more than gangsta hype or booty calls." Nobody said *booty call* anymore. Nowadays it was a riff on sex-bots and slits that she felt on the tip of her tongue. "What crimes are we talking about? Too much injustice still ain't against the law." She had to resist fussing and ranting. At least, no mass shooting anywhere today.

"**WHIZZ-ITs Glitch! Consolidated Postpones Rollout of Latest Talking Scanners!** WHIZZ-ITs read for you, do arithmetic, and dastardly algebra. They can rewrite your thoughts in styles they own: Hemingway, N.W.A., or Joni Mitchell. While you wait for the latest WHIZZ-IT model, **Reboot Your Bright Young Mind. Let It Soar.** 'Soar' is this morning's stealth-word. Genius doctors swear they can cure Alzheimer's and engineer drugs and enhancements to clear the mist."

Hadn't Ready-Med already done that three years ago? Something must have gone wrong with the pricey treatments. Or maybe this was recycled wishful thinking. No matter, designer drugs and cyborg apps were way out of Cinnamon's budget. And forget trusting her mind to biotech engineers employed by the company store.

"*Darknet Whistleblowers Hack Consolidated. Top Execs Insist Data Breach Inconsequential.* Same show every day. Monsters and crooks try to have their way with us. Whistleblowers and other heroes be slugging on. Everybody mainlining denial . . ."

She swallowed a bad taste. The memorial stones glittered in the sun, mythical wonderworkers expecting more than she had. Bruja looked hangdog.

"Not funny. Sorry. Everywhere is a refugee camp. Too many people be out of work and on the run. It's like we're spitting in the ocean. And since bringing Game-Boy's crew back from the dead, Taiwo refuses to come down from the trees, even sleeps in the branches. Indigo has to deliver food to that old red oak. I understand. I do. *Scheiße!*" Cursing at the baron and the elders was a bad sign. "Taiwo don't want to hand this future to anybody either. *Waiting for love to come on back in style again* or some shit." Love ruined her. Why risk that again? She sank into weed stalks, blinking tears. The flash of spirit had faded.

"Only seems overwhelming." Mami used Aunt Iris's intrepid adventurer voice. "Follow your intuition."

"*Do what you do,*" Thunderbird and Dragon sang.

Right. Headline hyperbole was toxic. The good that people did was not in Consolidated's news updates. Good-news feeds had pricey paywalls, way over Cinnamon's budget, and the so-called *free*-net was mostly bad news and a zillion snoop-bots stealing your data, your soul, herding you to hell. Why hang there? She'd have to find the good stuff herself or get reckless youth on it. "Maybe Indigo and Game-Boy would come do the morning ritual with me." She wiped away tears.

A murder of crows burst from oak branches and flew up into the sky, dark shadows against fluffy white clouds. They mobbed a hawk who was trying to be slick. Several had red feathers on their wings or breast. The hungry raptor glanced at her with disinterest before taking refuge in magnolia buds. "Good luck catching a single crow in broad daylight!" she shouted as the crows flew off. Crows were good omens.

"I almost forgot. Next-Gen *AI Caught Lying.* They shouldn't do that with the Big Data Protocols. Surprise! A creative one. This AI knows better than to trust people with truth, if it's gonna get us to do what we

want to do, what we need to do. Gotta hoodoo us. That had me starting a song for Festival, words *and* music, right before dawn—now that's
good news."

Bruja threw back her head and they howled together.

"**Temperatures Soar after Warmest February on Record.** Leap year
might be jacking those statistics, but Weather Wizard says another fury
storm is coming up the coast." Bruja tugged Cinnamon's sleeve. She
knew weather was the end of the ritual. "The coast is closer than it used
to be, and all the storms are furious with us."

"*Can't set the spirit on fire except with love.*" Thunderbird and Dragon
sang a close harmony from *The Redwood and Wildfire Songbook*, sounding
exactly like her grandparents; then they collapsed into themselves, compact trash once more. Bruja turned into the wind, sniffing and huffing.
Cinnamon scanned for danger too. A skirt of mist from the Mill River
clung to forsythia bushes, unusual at the Amphitheatre.

"Water-Spirits checking on us?"

Bruja flattened her ears and yelped.

"Is Spook out there? Doing the stealth husky thing? Or is stealth a
wolf trick?"

Bruja dashed to the Circus-Bots and tried to herd them to the Wheel-
Wizards bins.

"Don't worry. We always take the whole troop to the Mall." Cinnamon hoisted Thunderbird and Dragon and trudged to her bike. The
two Bots were lightweight, yet unwieldy despite handles. At least they
fit in one bin. Bruja herded her back for Mami, whose scales looked
wet lit up, like the kicks on that Afro-Deutsch hipster. Why was she still
thinking about that character? "I shouldn't let Euro-trash making big
promises and talking Burning Man nostalgia get to me. That was *last*
year's Festival."

Bruja stared at her, blank.

"Non sequitur, sorry."

Mami's third eye was bright. A couple scales looked ready to take off.

"Taking notes on me? Nosy data hound." Gripping Mami, Cinnamon
got a mild shock. She jerked away. "Was that static electricity or . . ." Her
hand hovered over the handle. "If you must know, that Afro-Deutsch
hipster reminded me of old friends, from when I was a kid." She felt
relieved to realize this. "Klaus Beckenbauer and Marie Masuda. More
than friends actually." A wicked grin creased her face.

"I told you about them. We brought Baron Taiwo back from oblivion
or whatever. On Raven's uhm—on my dad's birthday and—"

Cinnamon clamped her mouth on a Klaus and Marie story storm. Her Mod Squad organized the first Festival to celebrate Raven and stop Taiwo from leaking into the *spaces between things*. Hard to believe their teenage adventures happened. The memories were drenched in hormones, exaggerated, amplified, or that's what she told herself. She was afraid to investigate. What if her best memories were lies?

"I'll tell more later." Safe stuff, not the magic. "So hold the static electricity."

Mami doused her snake coils of LEDs. Her third eye flickered as Cinnamon rolled her a few yards on rickety suitcase wheels. "Whose idea was the heavy-ass generator?"

She took a deep breath and lifted the Bot. Nerves in her back zapped a warning, as if sturdy leg muscles couldn't handle the load, as if special effects weren't worth the weight. She wavered. Bruja nipped her heels, impatient, unsettled. After four nasty nerve-zaps and twice as many nips, Cinnamon slid the broken glass wonder into a special three-sided container. Forget lifting the hefty mer-woman up over the lip of a bin every time. She fastened the chain guards and turned to Bruja. "Happy?"

Bruja charged to the gate and growled. The sentinel-bots posing as West African sculptures by the gate were placid. Dark wood carvings of antelopes, birds, and dancing harps were locked in place around the elders' farm. They collected environmental data while on the lookout for bad behavior or good news. Flying-Horse-Bot and Shooting-Star-Bot roved about, gathering data and intel the sentinels might miss. Spook and Bruja clued into distant danger that rode the wind.

This research and security protocol had worked for a while, although these days, Baron Taiwo was AWOL half the time, and Spook couldn't be everywhere. She allowed herself a shiver of fear.

"If I'm singing at Festival, Taiwo need to come down out the trees and spook these desperados. Maybe we'd both feel better."

What Cinnamon and the other Co-Op farms needed was prevention. Taiwo should begin the growing season doing a magic act for Festival—eat fire and bullets—scare the Bejesus out of everybody. Who said *Bejesus* anymore? What did they say nowadays? She strapped on a bulletproof vest and helmet. Bruja tilted her head at the strange costume.

"I'm wearing this for Shaheen. I forgot yesterday, and Boss Lady was on me."

Besides chairing the Wheel-Wizards, Shaheen Kumar was Ghost Mall coordinator—the get-you-anything-for-a-dollar lady. After Game-Boy's raid, Shaheen worked two years to procure the lightweight, next-gen body armor so she wouldn't have to worry so much about gunmen taking out Co-Op delivery people. There were zero attacks since Game-Boy's, and not so many guns floating around and even fewer bullets. Still, Shaheen counted on Cinnamon wearing protective gear to motivate others. Bruja nosed the vest and wagged her tail.

"You smell her, don't you?" Cinnamon affected Shaheen's Mumbai accent and quoted her. "*Back-From-The-Dead Crew fell out trying to steal what we were giving away. I survived the video-game warriors yelling Kali, Kali, Kali. The next raiders might be full-fledged militia men. Why take unnecessary risks? Be bulletproof.*"

Bruja ruffed approval.

"*Bullet-resistant* gear is useless against desperation." The battle gear looked funny over silky maroon pants with the gold lightning bolts down the sides. Cinnamon tucked the cuffs into her booties. "Hope is the best armor." Hope might be in short supply—no saying that out loud at the altar.

She hopped on the bike, shouting to the elders as she pedaled off, "More good news: besides writing a new song, I'm inviting the Ghost Mall, hill towns, and even Electric Paradise to the Next World Festival. Taiwo too. Get that old African on solid ground. Tomorrow's as far in the future as I go. The day after that is not my fault!"

BRUJA

DANGER RIDE

Bruja huffed and blew out the candle. That was her JOB at the end of the sunrise ritual because Cinnamon always forgot. Cinnamon spent hours training Bruja, who never forgot. Bruja did her blow trick every morning and at Festival to cheers and applause. *A real Witch-Dog with your tricks and spells.*

Bruja wasn't fond of fire, but enjoyed making the wavy heat vanish into smelly smoke. Nothing much to burn on the granite memorials or the stone terrace around them. Still, Bruja huffed at the smoking candle a second time, then took off down warm asphalt to hurry Cinnamon up.

Eddies of mist from the Mill River evaporated as the sun climbed. Rainbows shimmered in the air over the bike path. The long corridor of trees was ready to burst in bloom, ahead of hillside trees. A white-and-brown froth covered bush and tree limbs—white-and-*red* froth to Spook and his cyber-eyes. The same sweet flower scent wafted to both dogs. Spring was full of exciting smells.

On the bike-path shoulder, Co-Op goats munched bittersweet suckers and their roots. Unchecked, bittersweet vines climbed up branches, wrapped around trunks, and strangled the trees. Goats loved bittersweet and ate poison ivy and rose weeds too. They bunched together and bleated as Bruja passed. They knew her. Bruja frequently chased off critters who attacked old goats or the lost little ones. With hackles up and braying, Bruja looked as ferocious as she felt. Coyotes would rather eat something easier. The goats didn't smell too afraid, a bit wary, yet mostly grateful for fangs on their side. They'd be easy to herd if she had to.

Cinnamon tapped the handlebars and hummed music she'd been singing since she woke up. Bruja ran beside her and barked, excited for their good energy together.

"Feeling frisky, huh?" Cinnamon grinned—the bike was a tonic. "Me too, girl."

Co-Op farmers, silhouetted against brown hills and blue sky, waved and bellowed greetings. Cinnamon paused at a stone bench while a muscular old lady loaded heavy bags of vegetables into a trailer-bin that could barely hold more. She put a bundle in Mami Wata's arms: tomatoes from the greenhouses and soy cheese. She and Cinnamon mumbled about

FESTIVAL while Bruja avoided young ones trying to pat her head or scratch her night-sky ears. Bruja didn't tolerate that from just anybody.

Cinnamon pedaled on like a demon and smelled happier with every turn of the wheel. She was a fit fifty-something and not even sweating. She regularly hauled 350 pounds of instruments, tools, Circus-Bots, veggies, and treats. Ghost-Mallers depended on her reliable Co-Op delivery system. Cinnamon depended on Bruja, to get her going in the morning, to stay on course, to keep a lookout.

Bruja loved their work.

Cinnamon sucked down deep breaths as they approached the first of two inclines. She needed a lot of air to achieve the hills with such a heavy load. Luckily, the first slope was less steep, a warm-up. She pumped the pedals and held steady at six MPH. The bike path wound up, down, and around the hill towns, crisscrossed the Mill River and the flood plain before reaching the Ghost Mall—which at this rate they'd make by late morning. They still had a ways to go. Bruja was patient as long as they kept moving.

Someone snapped branches down by the river. Not Co-Op farmers— two heavy-footed strangers with fear in their sweat and anger on their breath. Bruja had gotten wind of them around the Amphitheatre. They smelled like Flying-Horse—the raffia mane, sweetgrass tail, and rare earth metal innards, plus alarm pheromones, faint, yet distinct—Flying-Horse's SOS. The river and the banks got treacherous after this hill. The strangers tried to walk from muddy riverbanks through a thicket. Why do that? Bruja didn't like it. Why not bellow a greeting like Co-Op farmers? Upwind and making that much racket, nobody could pull a sneak attack.

Spook was down near the water too; Bruja smelled him. Spook was quiet as death and ready to attack if he had to. Bruja would have jumped these two creepers, one at a time, before they ambushed the goats or somebody. At least, get them going another direction. She eyed Cinnamon, who had her head down as she leaned into the hill. Oblivious.

The tree-lined bike route across the valley plain was maintained by the Co-Ops and occasionally preyed on by desperados. They usually left farmers or a Wheel-Wizards herd alone; still, every so often they raided lone transports, and did bad things, mostly at night. Bruja circled behind the trailer and headed for the strangers, ears erect, nose wide. She searched for a break in the brush.

"Where are you going? Is somebody tailing us?"

Cinnamon halted in the middle of the hill and gulped breath. Thunderbird and Dragon sputtered and hooted. Musical instruments clanged against jugs of honey and bags of sweet potatoes. Mami pressed against the chain guards; her third eye pulsed. Dry leaves crackled under somebody's foot.

"Oooh. I hear them. Not Spook making that noise." Cinnamon squinted at a snarl of bittersweet vines. "Bad boys showing off, spoiling for trouble?"

Since Game-Boy's crew fell out for no good reason, reckless youth steered clear of Wheel-Wizards on the bike path or car road. The young pups were mostly pranksters, mischief makers, not full-fledged whackjobs like these two who smelled of cigarettes, gin, dope, and explosive devices. Angry and anxious, they were up to no good.

"Let's not worry." Cinnamon smelled worried. Bruja licked Cinnamon's leg to reassure her. "Let's make it up the damn hill." She stood up on the bike pedals and managed five MPH around a hairpin turn before disappearing with a shout, "Spook is silent as a ghost and always on the lookout. Only newbies would dare ambush us!"

Bruja paused to swallow a cloud of scents and map the whereabouts of everybody nearby. She took her time sorting the odors—she'd catch up to Cinnamon easily. Jumping on a log, she spied Spook. He crept along the Mill River, almost invisible against frothy white water. His lips were drawn, his fangs bare, and his tail high.

The two strangers were in his line of attack. He could take care of them by himself. Other whack-jobs might be farther up the bike path, ready to pounce on Cinnamon and the Circus-Bots before they reached the Ghost Mall. Bruja grumble-growled. She needed to stay close to her three-bot and bike-person herd. She turned, raced uphill around several bends, and charged down to a field.

A barn groaned and shuddered in the breeze. Home to generations of swallows and mice, the barn had been falling down and groaning for years. However, the burnt-out car in the middle of the bike path hadn't been there yesterday when they came through. Cinnamon cursed and veered onto the stony shoulder away from a spray of broken glass. The bike wheels rolled over the remains of a squeaky toy. It howled, and Cinnamon squealed, unnerved for sure.

Bruja trotted over to the toy and pawed it gingerly. She liked squeaky things. This one was wrecked. Gripping it like a pup in her mouth, she picked her way through glass shards to the car and jumped up against the driver's door. Discolored metal was warm. Inside melted plastic and rubble still smoldered. Besides plastic stink, nothing except ash and gasoline to smell. Nothing worth fetching or stashing.

"Leave that alone. The driver's soot or long gone. We're lucky no trees caught fire."

Bruja dropped the ruined toy inside, disappointed. She liked sniffing out things they might use.

"Come on." Cinnamon pedaled fast on flat ground and shouted at god-knows-who in a resonant Festival voice, "Some desperados don't buy horror stories about cyborg dogs, an alien in the oak trees, and Water-Demons walking the river!" She looked around before continuing even louder, her reach-the-Amphitheatre-back-row voice. "Actually, up by the elders' farm the Mill River is just a stream; however, the rest of the dark lore is true!" When the burnt car was a smudge behind them, she leaned toward Bruja, chuckling. "They can't scare us, right?"

Bruja offered a *ruff-ruff* reply.

A quiet mile on the warm asphalt passed. Willow trees waved feathery yellow leaves at them. Picnic tables and a porta-john were tucked in a stand of pines by a stone marker: *You're Half Way There! Take A Break! Take a Breath!* Cinnamon stretched out a leg and shook it, as if she had a pain or an itch that needed scratching. Thankfully, she didn't stop to do that.

Spook ambled behind them, just out of sight. Bruja was happy he'd caught up. Danger scents still rode the wind and no touch of the baron in the air like earlier.

"I promised Shaheen, but damn." Cinnamon's breath was raggedy. "Bulletproof, I mean bullet-*resistant* gear is heavy. Even the lightweight version."

Bruja let Cinnamon forge on ahead and lunged into the bushes toward the new danger, happy to have Spook joining the charge behind her.

CINNAMON
ﻌ꧂

VISIONS

Morning raids were rare, none in two years. Still, recovering from past violence was hard. Spook's bass growl and Bruja's alto snarl got Cinnamon pedaling faster. Anxiety sweat left dark splotches on her maroon pants. The eight-bin trailer rocked and rolled, and the Bots tittered in stealth-mode. Danger was abstract to them, a curiosity, an opportunity to collect experiential data. Cinnamon sucked down extra breaths.

The valley was doing better than she'd imagined. From Electric Paradise to the hill towns, few got swept away in the last high water. They weathered market crashes and survived a smattering of raids. Folks cussed, fussed, and talked smack about one another, yet the valley co-alition stayed together and maintained a wobbly peace. No Deus ex Machina, still the Co-Ops brought the Ghost Mall back from the dead and offered everyone, including Cinnamon, if not hope, something to do beside despair.

Somebody (human? other animal?) yelped in the bittersweet mess beyond the trees. Cinnamon slowed to three MPH and looked over her shoulder. Recently, disrupters were torching cars and trying to shove her (and anyone else on the bike path) into *their* horror story, their tragic dystopia. Rage sharpened her thoughts. Who besides arms merchants stood to profit from nasty adrenaline fog?

Branches rustled and snapped, and her half-formed theories dissolved. Noisy bushwhackers had followed them since the Amphitheatre. On the hunt, Bruja vanished behind a clump of willow trees that were uprooted in the last fury storm. Spook was out there somewhere too, scouting for Baron Taiwo. Where *was* Taiwo?

More strangled yelps. Cinnamon shuddered. Mammal distress noises were too similar. Sunday night, raccoons who could have passed for crying babies wouldn't let her sleep. Right now, this person? creature? emitted a choked grunt, then went silent. She halted and scanned the no-person's land beyond the path. Making out anything in the weed thicket was impossible. She held her breath. Nobody called for help, and the dogs didn't yap or snarl. If somebody was hurt or unconscious and needed help, Bruja and Spook would certainly come get her. Spook could even signal Taiwo somehow.

The silence was eerie. Was she really relying on doggy judgement? Light-headed, she gripped the handlebars and forced herself to exhale. Leaving the bike rig unattended was a bad idea. Scrambling over rocks, strangle vines, and poison ivy was a worse one. Your whole world could change with a stumble, a twisted ankle or a broken wrist, a flood. Nothing would ever be the same.

Maybe it was a rabbit getting run down by a fox? No. Rabbits were too small, too quiet. They died with a squeak and a squeal. These were large mammal noises. More likely a bear, like the creature caught on an electric fence last night. Or a person. Valley Security didn't say who they'd found electrified in the barbed wires. Yeah, who was she kidding. It was a big sound, a big distress sound.

"Scheiße." Cursing in German was still cursing. "Who do you mean to be, darling?" she muttered, sounding like Granddaddy Aidan. She did a U-turn, a tight maneuver with the bike and trailer. She felt like an eighteen-wheeler hanging a sharp right. As she straightened out, Bruja leapt over a willow root ball and dashed her way.

"What were you up to?" Cinnamon narrowed her eyes. Bruja gave nothing away. She licked the Bots, then Cinnamon's leg. "Playing innocent, but I know you. You're fiercer than Spook ever thought of being. Is he still out there?"

Bruja did a doggy grin and ran ahead toward the Ghost Mall. Cinnamon glowered at the weed thicket. Bruja ran back, barking and jumping at her.

"OK." Cinnamon executed the tricky U-turn once more. "Another big hill coming up. I don't need secrets and doubts sapping my strength." She pedaled as fast as possible. "I don't want to know what you were doing anyhow."

Cinnamon's head throbbed and her stomach threatened to spew out her mouth. The hills on the horizon blurred into wandering zigzags. Would she fall into a stupor and see visions all day? Yesterday afternoon on the way home, windowpanes had morphed into fiery eyes; tree trunks melted into their roots; the bike path became a snake. Her mind blurred reality—*ImagiNation*—for a blink, then returned to *normal*.

"Look!" she shouted at Bruja.

The last shimmers of mist on the Mill River looked like a parade of haints, dancing. She rubbed her eyes, yet naked women with seaweed hair and rainbow waist beads persisted in stomping across slippery pebbles. Taiwo's Water-Spirits. They faded in and out of shafts of sun. One waved at her.

"See that?" She pointed, relieved at reinforcements. Bruja turned and the mist evaporated in the sunlight, leaving a rainbow glow. The Water-Spirits were gone. "You just missed Taiwo's Amazons."

Two years ago, after bringing bad boys back from the dead (or from whatever), Taiwo tapped power from *the spaces between things* and called up an African Amazon brigade. Alien hoodoo with mist, dust, and light. Taiwo refused to explain the details, saying there were no good human words for the extra-dimensional brigade. "Maybe aje." Aje was a Yoruba word for wisewomen who wielded elemental power—evil witches to British colonizers. In any case, Water-Spirits were fierce protectors of Cinnamon, Bruja, and the Bots. They shouldn't count as her eyes playing tricks.

How can you spout physics at me and believe hoodoo-voodoo nonsense? Opal had yelled this at her science-geek daughter constantly. *You're on dangerous ground.*

Cinnamon had a great reply when she was a kid that allowed for hoodoo and science to coexist. She didn't remember what she said to her mother anymore. Time was, she remembered everything—*hear it once, forget it never.* Recently only the bad stuff lingered. Opal's voice had been plaguing her recently, like the Back-From-The-Dead miracle. Taiwo's fault. How was Cinnamon supposed to wrap her mind around naked rainbow warriors stepping in and out of this or that dimension?

"I should invite Water-Spirits to FESTIVAL." Bruja looked up, happy to hear anything about Festival. "They could do a magic act with Taiwo and boost our danger rep." Bruja cocked her head, noncommittal. "What?" The last big climb loomed. Cinnamon slowed. "Water-Spirits aren't in your herd yet?"

Heartbreak hill ended at Blossom Bridge, where something was always in bloom, even in winter, and where the bike path crossed the motor route—a perfect security checkpoint and the site of occasional ambush. Beyond the bridge in Electric Paradise, rich valleyites lived behind high-voltage gates and paid Cap George and his Valley Security premium fees to monitor gun-bots and patrol-drones that kept a refugee deluge at bay.

Checkpoints were scattered across the valley floor, and wandering security patrols popped up anywhere. Gun-bots were pretty chill unless you tried to hack them. Tampering set off a defense-mode, followed by a self-destruct protocol that took the hacker out if they were close. Why wasn't that against the law? If attacked, Flying-Horse or Shooting-Star flipped the *dead-bot-off* switch, no damage to anyone other than themselves. Cinnamon ground her teeth at high-tech sovereignty and pinged the Valley Security drones. Her vaccines, taxes, permits, security checks were up-to-date. She was no threat, considered a *friendly* even. The gun-bots ignored her.

Underpaid thugs, however, had a trigger-happy rep, allegedly firing at coyotes, bears, and goats for the hell of it. Gun-bots and drones did most of the real snooping and shooting. Human guard duty had to be as boring as sorting sand, and nerve-wracking. Every so often disrupters blew up cars and raided checkpoints. A guard got shot at Blossom Bridge on Martin Luther King Day this year. Cap George downplayed it; still, she'd never walk again. That might make your trigger finger itch.

A twisted body hung on the electric fence near the guardhouse. Cinnamon lurched almost to a halt before realizing what she was seeing. Not a dead person snagged in razor wire as they scrambled over the top, but a scorched dummy with a melted plastic face. Beige goop had dribbled onto a metal armature poking through a tattered hoody. Feet and hands were burnt stumps, like a lynching.

"Scheiße." Who could help cursing out terror artwork? A sign around the dummy's neck read: **Keep Out! This Smart Fence Will Fry Your Ass!**

CHECKPOINT

Spook had tracked Flying-Horse and the gunmen to the car road. They loaded Horse in the back trunk and got in a vehicle that headed toward Electric Paradise. Spook never took the car road. Too dangerous. For now, he was on Cinnamon-patrol.

High-Voltage Fence! Property of Electric Paradise!
No Trespassing!
Ghost Mall Six Miles—Keep On Pedaling!

The fence with the signs bordered enemy territory and delivered a nasty jolt if Spook nosed it. The metalwork was too high to jump, and around the bridge steep cliffs dropped to white water dashing through glacial potholes. Scrambling over jagged stones cut his paws and often set off a noisy rockslide. Spook wanted to avoid that.

Desperados, refugees, and show-offs broke limbs and ribs trying to scale these banks. Folks had drowned here already this year. The electric fence blocked the road to Paradise *and* the bike path to the Mall. That meant everybody in a vehicle or on foot who didn't cross way downriver had to go through this checkpoint or get nowhere.

Spook preferred sneaking through bushes. Tracking folks on an exposed road or even on the tree-lined bike path was dangerous, not enough shade to fade into. He and Taiwo used secret tunnels to cross the river and avoid high-voltage fences and drone snoops. Spook hadn't *seen* Taiwo all day and he never found the tunnels alone. He'd nose a familiar opening and press solid concrete. This might have confused or frightened someone else. Spook figured he'd have to use the bridge.

A tiny brick fortress squatted at the top of a long incline where the bike path crossed the car road. It smelled of deer piss, bullets, sage smoke, and blueberry surprise from last week. Spook beat Cinnamon to the checkpoint by several minutes. He'd make sure she was safe, then cross while she distracted the gun-bots, patrol-drones, and security detail. People-guards liked her treats and sass. They weren't on the lookout for a cyber-dog and never noticed him, even downwind. Bad noses.

"What're you doing, Jerome?" a familiar voice yelled.

Jerome was a skinny kid Spook had never smelled here before. Hollow-eyed, sallow, and hungry, he wore a bullet-resistant helmet and vest and had dark, smooth skin like Cinnamon. Locs stuck out of the helmet—the hairdo was fighting with the armor. He poked at a snarl of cables by a patrol-bot and grimaced.

Diego, the familiar voice, crouched next to Jerome, and grinned. Spook had scented him since last spring. He had a bald head that gleamed in the sun. A barbed-wire tattoo circled his throat. A trickle of blood dribbled down each side. Diego polished a chrome widget. He was hungry too, but smelled calmer than Jerome.

"Damn. Get out of there," Diego yelled, and stamped his foot.

Jerome reached for a weapon on his hip. "What?"

"Mice. Going after my wires. Chewing. And it can't taste good." Diego held up a bunch of frayed wires attached to the widget.

"I got squirrel turds in the transformer." Jerome pointed at fisher scat.

Diego squinted. "Squirrel? You think?"

Jerome prodded the fisher scat with a stick. "Rat shit?"

Diego rubbed his head slowly. "Rats? Sure about that?"

"I don't know." Jerome backed up, disgusted. "How can you tell the difference?"

"I'm no turd expert." Diego gripped a muscular belly and laughed.

Jerome scowled. "Quit messing with me."

Diego chuckled a bit more. He liked to laugh. "Cap George promised you superhero tech and game-world adventures." He patted Jerome's neck. "Am I right?"

Jerome shoved Diego away and muttered something irritable.

"You're a maintenance man, cleaning turds, minding the machines." Diego sighed. "Don't even know how anything works. But they work you."

A woman in baggy jeans, neon-orange sneakers, and a dull windbreaker dashed across the road. She paused under the signs and danced from foot to foot. She smelled like the hill towns *and* Electric Paradise: lily of the valley, goats, disinfectant, moldy paper, fry oil. A traveler or friend of Cap George's? She had bagels and cream cheese in a large backpack. Spook had tracked her since morning. She ate fry bread for breakfast.

"Stop." Jerome aimed his weapon. The traveler ran for the bushes along the bike path. Jerome fired, but Diego rammed him, throwing off his aim. Bullets sliced the air and landed in the Mill River. The traveler slipped and fell on the steep bike-path shoulder. Stones tore her windbreaker and bloodied her cheek as she scrambled onto the asphalt and ran toward the Ghost Mall without looking back.

"Man, what are you doing?" Diego shook Jerome like he was a dopey young pup. "She's a flood refugee or a rich girl on the run. No threat."

"She didn't ping our bots." Jerome shrugged Diego off. "We were warned." He waved the weapon in her direction. "You gotta ping. Even for the bike path today."

"PENDEJO." Diego blocked Jerome. "A warning doesn't mean we haul off and shoot people. Bam, bam, no thank you, ma'am. That could have been you last month."

"Or you." Jerome tried to get around Diego.

"Yeah." Diego slugged Jerome's chest. "Or me last year."

"Or a rough crew who takes us out while we try to figure if they're nice or not."

"Listen to yourself. What do you sound like?"

"Like I got a job to do. Like I don't want to go to jail or be a flood refugee again, camping out in the woods."

"Bots didn't fire on her." Diego waved his arms. "Does she look like a rough crew?"

"White girls can be terrorists too. Even rich ones."

"I know that." Diego bristled. "Don't be wasting bullets. Cap George will dock you. You could have killed her and for nothing."

"Writing me up on my first day? What if she's a Whistleblower?"

"Whistleblower? Get out of here and shut the door. They talk you to death. They're not like desperados raiding supply trucks and torching shit."

"That's where you're wrong." Jerome put the weapon back on his hip and, shoving Diego, tripped on some wires.

Diego caught him and they fell near the fisher turds. "How am I wrong?"

Jerome jumped up. "Whistleblowers torched a car last night or early this morning, on the bike path. A couple miles from here. I saw it. Still smoking."

"You don't know who did that. You don't even know what you saw."

"Yes, I do." Jerome danced around. "Who shot your last partner? Whistleblowers, man." He was talking so fast he almost choked.

Diego scowled. "You got sent up for resisting arrest, mouthing off, right?"

"So what were you, some big-time thug, running drugs or—"

"Checkpoint guard is a shitty second chance. Use your brain. Maybe you'll make it. Don't believe what the big guns tell you and don't trust Darknet Lords. I know they offered you a side hustle, so don't bother lying." Standing up, Diego got fisher turds on his hands. "Yuck. I gotta wash this off." He hurried into the brick fortress. "Don't shoot anybody. That's an order."

"Rat shit serves you right." Jerome plucked something from the grass and marched to the guardhouse door. "We're on red alert. You oughta wear your helmet, old man."

Diego hollered from inside, "Forty-five is the prime of life. Just wait."

Jerome waved a helmet in the doorway. "I'm tired of waiting. I want my life, now." He took out the stub of a marijuana blunt and lit it.

Baron Taiwo, in a storm cape and feathered top hat, jumped from a tree and walked across the river with Amazon Water-Spirits. Somebody might have said a shadow danced with rainbow wraiths. Spook wagged his butt and woofed, not caring who heard. Water-Spirits dressed in colors only Spook could see, and Cinnamon sometimes. Hiding in plain sight, they smelled like rain and lightning. One waved to him to follow. Spook would look out for Cinnamon, Bruja, and the Circus-Bots on the other side of the flower bridge. He raced past confused bots pinging creatures that weren't quite here or there, past Jerome fussing at the guardhouse door. The last of the blunt crumbled to ash before he got a good toke. Marijuana and glitches were perfect cover.

CINNAMON
✲
THEATRE MAGIC

Cinnamon's lungs burned as she neared the checkpoint. Yesterday this slope felt like a good challenge; today, it seemed impossible, and then a gunshot, nearby. Probably a warning salvo from Valley Security. Bruja looked unfazed, yet Cinnamon's heart thudded. She almost turned around; however, doing a U-turn on heartbreak hill was dicey, and danger phantoms loomed every direction.

A tall, skinny kid in bullet-*resistant* armor stood in front of the guardhouse brandishing a helmet and arguing at someone inside. He flung the helmet at the door, turned toward her, and snarled. She waved, cheery like always. The kid looked as lost as Game-Boy's crew before they were Born Again. He could have been camping in the dump or the woods yesterday. The cannon on his hip looked too big for his hands and reminded her of Game-Boy's *TermiNation* weapons in her nightmare.

Calf muscles in her left leg seized. The pain brought water to her eyes. Pedaling was impossible. She halted four yards from the kid, and rather than ask who they were shooting at so early in the morning, she tossed a greasy paper bag.

He caught it without thinking. Could have been a bomb. This kid might not last. A crumb apple treat tumbled out. He clutched it quickly, good reflexes. "What's this?"

Bruja wagged her tail, alert, ready to attack.

"An apple treat." Cinnamon shook out the nasty leg cramp, and a story storm took over her tongue. "I put in special biker spice, Aunt Iris's recipe. She could make anything taste good. Nasty weeds from the woods. Every dish was a *surprise*. Born the end of the nineteenth century, Miz Lady boogie-woogied into the twenty-first. A hoodoo conjurer with a PhD—cultural anthropology. She spied your spirit wherever you roamed. Nobody got lost around her. She'd find your heart anywhere."

The kid gawked at Cinnamon's motor-mouth blather.

"Eat." She used director voice. "It's free and tastes as good as it smells. Better."

He sniffed the apple surprise. Enchantment overwhelmed skepticism. He nibbled a corner, smiled, and stuffed the whole cake in his mouth.

"How old are you?" she asked, kneading her rock-hard leg.

"Old enough. This is good, for Co-Op food." He dug in the bag for more. Instead of joining the cavalry, this kid should be up at the colleges filling his mind with dreams. He probably couldn't afford dreams. A WHIZZ-IT hung on his belt. Maybe he couldn't read. Consolidated was pushing WHIZZ-ITs, claiming they were better than kids wasting time failing algebra. And who read anymore? According to gazillionaire tech wizards, everybody wanted pictures, moving or still. Plus, WHIZZ-ITs were cheaper than paying teachers to torture kids who didn't want to learn.

Tension in Cinnamon's calf released, but pain shot from her buttocks to her lower back. She swallowed a yelp. Lingering made the cavalry suspicious or worse. Her joints and muscles could care less. She stepped out of the bike and powered the Circus-Bots up to active. The show was good cover as she massaged the butt cramp.

Bruja gave her the stink eye, till Dragon unfurled and blew confetti from her copper-funnel snout. The bead on Dragon's bike-chain necklace glowed as if inside, a star was exploding. Cinnamon's head ached, her ears rang, then her eyes blurred, slicing the landscape into ribbons of green, blue, and brown. She rubbed her eyes, trying to clear the distortion, trying to put the world back right, and—

Miz Redwood Phipps, her *dead* grandmother, stood beside Dragon looking like she stepped from one of her black-and-white silent films into the 3-D real world. She wore harem pants cinched by anklets of bells and seeds. A stormy river of silk crowned her gray hair. The beads on her night-sky blouse sparkled. Everything was shades of black, white, and gray. Miz Redwood manipulated Dragon like a puppeteer. Silver bangles marked a syncopated beat as Dragon danced through the air, roaring red fire-ribbons through gemstone teeth. Before Cinnamon gasped, shrieked, or fell over—

Thunderbird unfurled trash-bag wings and extended tap-dancing talons. He also had a puppeteer from black-and-white silent films: Aidan Wildfire, her *dead* grandfather, another ghost in grayscale. He had a long white braid threaded with dark leather and feathers. He wore a Seminole patchwork coat and a beaded bandolier bag with the same celestial pattern that graced Redwood's blouse. A banjo was slung across Aidan's back and played itself, a twangy, sweet melody Cinnamon loved:

Nobody can burn what you're holding in your heart.

Redwood joined Aidan for a close harmony. Cinnamon had recorded them doing all their songs before they died. The Bots sang a line every now and then, yet she couldn't bring herself to listen to the tapes for several years. She was laughing and crying to hear a whole song now. Live.

Mami Wata, African queen mother of waters, flushed a rainbow up and down her broken glass tail. Her locs were the silver light of a waterfall. Her puppeteer was another grayscale film-star, Great-Aunt Iris, and Iris had only done a few silent movies with Redwood and Aidan as a child. This was an old-lady ghost in a Muscogee beaded top from Georgia Indians and mudcloth pants from the Bamana people in Mali that featured snakes, water creatures, and storms. The top and pants should be folded neatly in a cedar chest at the farmhouse, right by Aidan's banjo and Redwood's bangles.

Cinnamon blinked and blinked. The puppeteer-visions persisted. Bruja danced around the Bots and their spirit-figures(?), excited. Who knew what she saw? Cinnamon's lower back exploded with pain. Anxiety had to go somewhere. The kid was too stunned by theatre magic to wolf another treat, pull his gun, or wonder why she dropped onto the bike path in dead-bug pose—back flat on hot asphalt, legs and arms flailing. Dragon breathed a cloud of silver dust over her: cool fire, a spirit tonic. Redwood waved. Her hand was a whirlwind of clouds and lightning. Her storm hand.

"Honeybun, dead folk always leave something," Aidan whispered so softly, could have been a voice in her head, "a trail, a song on the wind. They ain't really lost to you."

Cinnamon hugged knees to chest, to soothe her lower back, to hold herself together. Aidan had said these exact words to her and her best friends, Klaus Beckenbauer and Marie Masuda, when they were young and desperate and maybe seeing ghosts. Of course, the Circus-Bots talked to her regularly using the elders' words and voices—that's who the AIs trained on. She didn't *recall* telling the nosy data hounds anything about ghost sightings with Klaus and Marie, who were often on her mind yet rarely on her tongue till today. Only the elders knew their magic teenage saga, the *actual* elders who'd been dead for a while now.

"I've heard about you," the kid-soldier mumbled, impressed but trying to hide it.

"Have you now?" Cinnamon's voice was steady over inner turmoil—theatre training kicking in.

"I heard about your Circus-Bots too and—" He probably didn't see or hear any wild ancestors. Otherwise, he'd have been running from freaky haints, not moving closer to peer at cool gadgets. "I didn't believe a word."

"I understand." The black-and-white spirit-figures were for Cinnamon, a daydream, mostly in her head. Vivid *ImagiNation*. If she held on to that she'd manage. When she was young and freaking out over growing up in 1980s America, over dead brother, coma dad, and cigarette ash mom, the elders always showed up.

The kid-soldier beamed at Mami Wata. Cinnamon caught a whiff of marijuana. He was stoned. "Your Bots are lit," he said.

They still said *lit*. Cinnamon laughed. "Lit. OK, just don't be so trusting."

"Why not? We're good spirits," Iris murmured, barely audible too. What demon would say anything else?

"¡Hola! Cinnamon!" Another armed man marched from the guardhouse. "Out here putting on a show."

"Ah, barbed-wire tattoo. The older thug-in-charge," Cinnamon muttered as pain in her lower back spiked.

"Stop thinking of folks as thugs or Euro-trash." Redwood issued a barely audible Georgia Sea Island scold. "If you dig a pit for him, you dig one for your own self."

The older guy pounded the kid and loomed over her, flashing a megawatt smile. "I told you about Cinnamon."

"Always boosting my signal." She jumped up from dead-bug pose, maybe too soon. She staggered.

He reached out a hand, as if to steady her, then drew back when she scowled. "Where's my bag of goodies?"

"I have to bribe you with goodies, Rob?"

"It's Diego," Redwood whispered. "Remember, the most a person can do for another is *believe* in them till they come true."

"You can bribe me with a smile." He rubbed his bald head. Where was his helmet?

Cinnamon wanted to yell: *People are blowing up cars. Somebody shot your partner right here on Martin Luther King Day, and now the woman rides around in a wheelchair tank. Wear the stupid helmet.* Instead she said, "Aren't you on a fitness kick, Diego? Hitting the gym, running stairs, working your heart?"

"Every day. Working off those blueberry surprise cakes from your great-aunt."

She laughed and the three spirit-figures faded away, as if they had just been afterimages lingering from a blast of bright light.

CINNAMON
ℭℰ ℬᵲ

INVITATION

Cinnamon refused to be addled the entire day by visions, haints, and exploded cars. She shook off anxiety and threw Diego an apple— Macintosh, sour and crisp. He attacked the fruit. His favorite.

She'd checked up on him. He was an ex-con, innocent he claimed, stopped at a checkpoint for no reason, and then he allegedly resisted. Friends and family had records, so the court algorithm decided he must be bad too and sent him to jail for three years. When he got out, an employment algorithm tagged him as high risk for future criminal behavior. Two nasty pieces of self-fulfilling code. If nobody would hire you for work that was legal, what did they expect you to do? Diego was no farmer, so traveling sales jerk or Valley Security grunt was all he could get. He probably figured, protecting the rich was better than stealing for them. Plus, traveling sales had a higher mortality rate. So here he was minding cavalry-bots in the happy valley.

Diego tossed the apple core. "Would you believe this fine woman is in her fifties?"

The kid chewed a third apple surprise and scanned her ancient breasts and muscled thighs, unimpressed. "Pedaling around, outside the gates . . . Must be dangerous, for an older lady alone."

"I'm never alone." She scratched Bruja, who wagged her tail in a power display.

"Bruja is fronting," Diego grunted, "not really friendly."

"And I look forty." Dark satin skin from Cinnamon's mom didn't crack and not much gray in her braids like her dad.

Diego snapped at her fit bicycle form. "You look thirty-five. ¡Mujer salvaje, perro salvaje!" Diego talking trash in Spanish always made her feel good. He knew it too.

She grinned. *Wild woman, wild dog*, indeed. "Pain in the ass ambushing me."

"They should get to know you instead." Diego leered at her.

"None of that. Nobody wants my drums and shovels that bad."

Diego turned serious. "You got special clearance and should know. Captain George put out a warning. New gang creeping in the hills.

Rough characters. Torching cars and worse. Drones found a body with a ripped throat. Bonus if we catch anybody."

"What do you mean *ripped throat*?" Cinnamon glanced at Bruja.

"Terror tactics. Whistleblower hackers and whackos be messing with Valley Security." The kid patted his *TermiNation* weapon. "Stupid."

"Yeah." She swallowed panic. *Ripped throat* didn't have to be her dogs. She barely listened as the kid muttered wild rumors mixed with bravado. Rough crew acting out might mean random travelers picked off, like three years ago. She'd have to warn the nurses at the Ghost Mall clinic.

Diego snarled. "It ain't Whistleblowers. You got nothing to fear from them."

"Says you," the kid muttered. "Who else would it be?"

"A nostalgia militia." Diego used Cinnamon's term. "Random pendejos aching for a glory that never was. They like blowing up shit. Getting bolder recently, violence trending up. They steal children and spread terror to dominate the news feeds."

The kid smirked. "Like I said, it ain't safe for her. Even near Paradise." Dragon, reflector-eyes pulsing rainbow colors, hovered in his face. "I'd steal your drones and the surprise cakes. Anybody would. They're tasty."

"Well, darling," Aidan's Seminole/Irish lilt fell from Cinnamon's mouth, "maybe I'm a poison trap or a bomb in a greasy bag."

The kid stopped breathing and dropped the empty bag.

"A joke, Jerome." Diego scooped up the bag and poured crumbs in his mouth. "She's a clown. That's a dragon from her Festival circus, not a gun- or spy-drone."

Dragon blew smoky gray ribbons from her funnel nostrils. Thunderbird played his tail feathers, a pentatonic groove. Mami rippled her ocean cloth, a weave of tiny lights that looked like the sun reflected in an unruly sea. She added whale song and water crashing in a thunder hole. Jerome gaped at her, in love.

"They're Circus-Bots." Diego jabbed Jerome. "Now, if you get out of line, Spook busts out of nowhere and takes you out. Or maybe that's Bruja." Diego was sharp, no-nonsense, good for boosting Cinnamon's horror rep. "Spook even raids your dreams."

"No fucking way." Jerome eyed Mami. "Never seen a Black mermaid."

"Mer-woman." Diego sniggered. "A realist, lusting after a Circus-Bot."

Jerome shoved him. "They say demons lurk in the Mill River and a Rambo-freak lives up an old oak tree on her farm, zapping desperados with ray guns. You buy that?"

"Actually, it's a homeless Eshu from another dimension, not Rambo." Cinnamon snickered at truth stranger than fiction. "Built the tree house after the last flood and called up a Water-Spirit brigade two years ago, to guard my farm."

"That old African, suffering from PTSD?" Diego scowled. "Fought in Vietnam, Iraq, Syria, somewhere. Eshu?"

"Es-shoo—sounds like a sneeze." Jerome fingered Mami's seashell locs, then stumbled away with a yelp. "She zapped me." He shook an angry red palm.

"Don't touch," Diego said. *"Baron Taiwo of the Boneyard* according to Game-Boy. A griot storyteller. Not Eshu."

"Game-Boy and the baron are tight. Still, who knows everything?" Cinnamon glared at Jerome. "Eshu is the trickster riding Taiwo's spirit, an Orisha, a powerful Yoruba deity—Nigerian. *Standing at the crossroads, touching the lightning, the laugh is always on you.* My professor aunt used to say that."

"Whatever." Jerome pouted. Maybe he was younger than she thought.

Dragon blew ribbons at him and spoke in full voice. "What you think you know that ain't so, make you a slave." A Georgia Sea Island scold.

Jerome jerked. "Not the usual bot-speak."

"You want a docile white-chick voice like the goddamned elevators, WHIZZ-ITs, and search assistants? Cinnamon's an artiste, not a corporate hack." Diego saved her from having to explain the talky Bot. He gripped the kid's gun arm. "Jerome meant no disrespect about your Bots or Baron Taiwo, who must be what, eighty-something, and living up a tree after fighting in Vietnam or Afghanistan? We know war does a number on you. My father fought in Syria. Taiwo—he's got scars inside and out."

"Taiwo is not he or she," Cinnamon said. "Oun in Yoruba. We're all oun."

"Oh?" Diego nodded. "Oun is like 'they,' only singular?"

"Oun? Another stupid-ass pronoun." Jerome rolled his eyes.

"The people pronoun." Diego snapped his fingers, pleased.

Jerome smirked. "I *Thank the Trees* too."

Thunderbird played a groove with talons, banjo, and voice, riffing on a hit by that Nigerian rapper, Yoruban, an astral-bop superstar. She and her Korean neoblues-singer husband had several megahits, yet Cinnamon never remembered their names. Diego added a bass line vocal. Mami orchestrated a watery light show, waves timed to the upbeats. Bruja and Jerome were transfixed. Cinnamon chanted her carnival-jam over their infectious improv. Talk-singing the words was a jolt of power.

Dark days
Just a flash
Love be on the run
I ain't waiting
For some freedom to come
I'ma be my own sun
And rise

Diego nodded at her, eyes glistening. "Nice pipes."

"You too." Cinnamon and he were the same height—around six feet. She leaned close enough to see a spray of gray on his jaw and apple flecks on his lips. He smelled of bike lube and sandalwood oil, a good smell. "I'm putting together a show tomorrow," she whispered.

Diego flashed his bright smile. "Folks say it's really something to see."

Cinnamon's lips trembled. Last year was a bust. "Who you talking to?"

"Somebody who knows what's what." Diego leaned closer and blew warm breath on her cheek. "A Next World Festival, hoodoo from your Sea Island grandmother and Seminole/Irish granddaddy. You don't stand on their graves and weep—you *celebrate first fruits, light new fires, and forgive what can be forgiven.*" He scatted on these words.

"Did they show you last year's tee shirt?" She was anxious to fill in a blank memory.

Diego shrugged and sang, *"Dark days, just a flash."* His bass-drum voice made her chest rumble, made her heart beat in his time. A good feeling, the best in weeks. Years.

"Don't take any old body's word. Come see for yourself." She brushed apple from his cheek and surprised herself. "You two should do backup for my song, astral bop."

Diego lost the beat and stepped away from her. He and Jerome exchanged glances, shifted their weight, and scratched stubbly chins. Weird macho display. "Our shift is five AM to eight PM," Diego muttered. "Double shifts this week."

"Ain't felt like singing in two years, but the news was so bad, I started that song. At five AM, got my Bots rocking." She winked at Diego. "Call in sick. Spirit health day."

"Cap George will fire us for that." Jerome retreated to the guardhouse. Checkpoint grunt was a stupid job, yet he couldn't afford to lose it. Might even have to serve time if he did.

"Captain has nobody to spare, hunting that rough gang in the hills." Diego rubbed his bald head like a crystal ball. "A marauding band of thugs is bad for business. Electric Paradise is laying on pressure. Valley Security can't let it slide."

"One morning off." She had a few chits with George. Taiwo and Spook chased three con men who'd hit Electric Paradise from the hills at Christmas. Cinnamon debugged their grid last week. George wanted to hire her full-time to be a tech scout. He'd settle for Spook in the woods. "I'll call George, offer up a Ghost-Dog scout."

"Ghost-Dog? Who?" Jerome scowled.

"Spook—that bighearted husky with the electric eyes and secret-agent nose." Diego glanced at Bruja. "And a Witch-Dog to guard the herd. I hear Valley Security has your squad toiling for free. Cap George says they owe you."

"We owe each other." Cinnamon had been collecting chits to call in the cavalry for the next ambush or attack at the farm, so what the hell? "You guys center stage—that's my pay. A Festival with Circus-Bots, you both backing up my astral bop. Everybody rocking out." She was near tears. Festival had to be stellar this year. She sneezed in a sleeve to cover the gush of sentiment. "How can you refuse?"

"Well . . ." Diego wavered.

Dragon sang BaMbuti rain-forest music from the Congo: clicks, trills, rustling wings, branches, and cricket legs in a soft rain. She drew stubby limbs into her aluminum belly, curled her tail around her head, and dropped into the bin. Thunderbird tapped his talons against the plastic bin, a rapid-fire finale. He tucked chin to chest, folded up trash-bag wings, and collapsed beside Dragon.

Jerome groaned. "This is like the end of the world and you're still doing shows?"

"You know how many times the world's ended and started up again?" She chuckled. "Why not do a Next World Festival?" She gave them flyers. "Calling down spirits. Folks blissing out. I got roles for everybody and lots of free food."

"I don't read so good," Jerome stammered. "Any meat?" He tried not to look eager as Mami sidled up to him and finished the rain-forest serenade with a storm at sea.

Diego rubbed his head, a tell for sure. Man was a closet thespian. "You're talking real roles, right, not just audience participation?"

"Yeah. Trust your crystal ball. Sunrise in the Amphitheatre," she cooed, "a blast from the past and a holler at tomorrow."

"What I tell you? This woman's a firecracker, lighting up the sky." Diego snapped his fingers. "Sure. We'll do it," he declared for them both.

Cinnamon wished he knew her *before*, when she really was something. "I'll call George." She jotted down their names.

Jerome pointed at her scribble. "That's Jerome *Williams* and Diego Denzel *Ortiz*."

"Williams?" Cinnamon considered him. "You got a daughter named Zaneesha? They snatched some kids from a homeless camp, and she—"

"No, not my kid!" Jerome shouted. "I ain't bringing no kids into this mess."

"Oh." She was flustered. Was he lying? "So, uhm, Diego Denzel. Must be a good story behind that name."

Diego nodded. "I'll tell you about that after the show."

Cinnamon snapped her fingers. "You two can be fire spirits."

"All right," Jerome cheered, then scowled. "What's a fire spirit do?"

"Burn bright like there's no tomorrow, yet never give out 'cause the spirit's eternal."

Diego gripped her hand and let his feet fly. Cinnamon hesitated a moment, then matched his steps. Her leg felt fine, her back too. Diego broke out, dipping and twerking, old school, but good moves.

Jerome eyed their old folks' antics and licked a crumb from his lip. "We get costumes? I ain't wearing tree-hugger shirts."

"What's Festival without the right rags?" She had a barn full of costumes for Diego, Jerome, and anybody else.

Bruja dashed into the bushes. Mami swallowed the waterfall of lights and rolled ocean waves into a thin staff. She clutched this between tennis-ball breasts by the bag of tomatoes and soy cheese. In sentinel-mode, blue-black eyes glowed, aluminum foil teeth glinted. Jerome snapped his fingers in appreciation.

"You'll work with Mami Wata," Cinnamon said. "She likes you."

"Me and the mermaid? Mer-woman." Jerome saluted her. "Fire and water. Yeah."

Bruja ran from a bush and dropped another bedraggled mask at Cinnamon's feet. Horns protruded from a lumpy forehead; fangs curled over thick lips. Lemony skin was crisscrossed with scars. "What's that oozing out the ears. Worms?" Cinnamon shook her head. "No. I wore stupid monsters two Festivals in a row." She tapped Bruja's snout. "My nose is full of monsters." Which in German meant she'd had enough of that.

Bruja knocked the mask down the steep riverbanks, then nipped Cinnamon's ankles.

"I know. We're never late with the Co-Op delivery. I bet folks will cut us some slack this one time." She stepped into the bike rig, and Bruja raced off.

"Ghost Mall delivery." Diego Denzel Ortiz beamed at them, his heart open. "No other lone transport dares to come this way."

"African Amazons and cyborgs take care of us." Cinnamon shouted as she pedaled off, "See you guys tomorrow, five-thirty AM to get suited up and rehearse!"

SECRETS

"Eleven-forty-one AM"—Jerome's WHIZZ-IT spoke the time out loud. Spook paced a few bounds beyond the checkpoint behind a giant boulder—a refugee from distant mountains that got marooned when glaciers retreated. Cool mud was a tonic for his paws after hot asphalt. A perfect hiding spot. Near the big river, the sun felt hotter, the air thicker, wetter, and lilacs were already breaking into bloom. Birds, chipmunks, mice, and squirrels were getting busy. Warm weather meant good times for them.

Baron Taiwo danced under the bridge, waving a rain stick that sounded like a gentle storm. Oun was playing it for the first time in a long time. Many tones were pitched just for Spook. Water-Spirits frolicked with sunlight and swift currents in the river. Languid rainbow capes billowed about them, as if everything was fine, as if danger wasn't riding the wind. Spook swallowed a whine. They were dawdling under the bridge. Unlike Bruja, Spook never tried to hurry folks along. Even Bruja couldn't herd the baron, and Water-Spirits kept their own time. Spook was hungry and sleepy, yet had to stay alert, had to be ready for their next move, for danger barging out of nowhere.

Cinnamon and the Circus-Bots glided by without a greeting. The air was still—maybe they didn't smell him. Maybe he looked like a shadow on the boulder. Cinnamon would have treats for him at the Mall. He had a bowl waiting in the food court and a Sea Island basket for a nap. Game-Boy might slip him a greasy chunk or two. Indigo always passed him gooey cheese and scratched his neck.

Bruja circled back to his hiding spot. Diego and Jerome ignored her yip-yaps and focused on Cinnamon in the distance. Bruja licked Spook's face and sniffed his butt. She collected his secrets, then charged off. He wanted to run with her, but sat down and panted out the heat. A foolish chipmunk darted past his nose. So many after the acorn deluge. Chasing this one was a waste of energy. Spook licked his chops. Waiting on the baron in enemy territory was the hardest thing he did. If he could catch a nap . . .

"Zaneesha's the little girl in the photo." Diego's voice jolted Spook before he dozed.

"Latoya claim I'm the daddy. The brat don't even look like me," Jerome said.

Spook stuck his nose around the boulder, tracking their exchange.

Diego shook his head at something Jerome was holding. "Desperados are stealing babies, doing god knows what. You ain't got nothing better than that?"

"Latoya said she couldn't get pregnant."

"Surprise!"

Jerome shrugged. "What do you care?"

"Do right for your own sake. Be the man you'd admire," Diego replied, and Jerome looked hangdog. "What do I care? So many shorties with dipshit dads, I could be sad all the time." Diego stared down the bike path. "Besides the Rainbow Fairy Bus, transport to and from the hill towns is big posses of Wheel-Wizards. Cinnamon, *Afro-Future Is Now*, in stardust gold, bikes solo. Don't she just make you feel good?"

"She winked at you, old man, leaned real close." Jerome sniggered.

Diego elbowed him. "See who you might be shooting up."

Jerome patted several gadgets. "She pinged our bots. Vaccines, permits, everything up-to-date. An inner circle friendly with clearance. No reason to shoot at her."

"You want to keep this job, check the wild gun action. No bullets to spare and no innocent people to lose. Toking up after you shoot won't help you feel right."

Jerome muttered in his sleeve.

"Hey, I'm not playing with you." Diego poked Jerome's chest. "You trained on video games, didn't you? You're a champ. Got yourself Darknet fans."

Jerome whined. "Don't start on that."

"Cinnamon ain't in one of your games," Diego growled. "Me neither."

"Nothing wrong with using action-game rigs to teach tactics." Jerome waved his arms about. "They boost the brain, hand, eye thing."

"So does playing the trumpet." Diego slapped his forehead. "Your Darknet Lord tell you that crap? They're using you, data mining or worse. ¡Qué jodienda!"

"You cussing me?" Jerome said. "Jealous 'cause they pay me for mad gaming skills."

Diego snorted and squinted toward Cinnamon, who was tiny and downwind. He rubbed fingers on his nose and got a taste of her that way. "She's a wild woman." Diego loved how she smelled as much as Spook did.

Jerome squinted too. "What she mean, Baron Taiwo's from another dimension?"

"Like Patti LaBelle or the Funkadelics. *They'll take you there.*" Diego dipped down to the ground and sprang up. "Sun Ra. *Space is the place. A griot storyteller for the galaxy.*"

Jerome laughed. "What you talking 'bout, old man?"

"Ancestors to Janelle Monáe." Diego snapped his fingers. "You know her, don't you? *ArchAndroid? Dirty Computer?*"

"Whatever." Jerome startled as a chipmunk scurried by. He didn't chase the fur ball either. "We're really gonna do this Festival? No pay for time off."

"I got you covered."

"Really?"

Diego tapped his feet. "You don't want to let the mer-woman down."

"Hell no." Jerome tried some steps and stumbled over himself.

Diego danced around him, nimble like Cinnamon. "Gotta do better than that, son. You don't want the old man showing you up."

"Get out of here." Jerome's feet found the groove, and they danced together through the guardhouse door.

The Water-Spirits slipped from the river up into the trees along the bike path. They sounded like a cloudburst and lent a rainbow shimmer to the shadows. Patrol-bots buzzed and sputtered, confused. Taiwo crawled along the banks to the electric fence, cussing at somebody or something. Oun spoke a language few in the valley (in this dimension) ever used and talked in pitches too high for people. Nobody other than the Water-Spirits and Spook to hear oun's bad mood.

Spook jumped up, excited to be underway. Grumpy Taiwo gripped the fence, climbed through lethal currents, and soared over razor wire at the top. The storm cape sparked zigzags of white energy as oun joined Water-Spirits in the trees. They were singing like a breeze through the leaves. Spook bounded toward them, jibber-jabbering to himself the way huskies do.

A muted *rat tat boom pop* made him yelp and turn around. Automatic weapons, doing quiet death. Who though? Desperados never wielded fancy gear. Checkpoint guards had loud, cheap rifles. A gunbot clattered from the guardhouse roof and broke apart in the dirt. Men toting stealth weapons scaled the rocks from the river to the car road. They smelled of Electric Paradise. Who were these guys?

Diego and Jerome rushed from the guardhouse as checkpoint-bots hidden in the bushes opened fire on the ambushers. The bots deployed stealth-tech too. Half the mystery men fell down, spurting blood. No bullet-resistant armor protected them. Spook flinched. He never got involved in gun battles. That was Taiwo's work or Cap George's. Of course, if somebody attacked Cinnamon, Bruja, or the Circus-Bots he'd intervene. Nobody here to risk death for.

"Drop your weapons," Diego yelled at the few gunmen still upright. Their bullet reply shattered a window on a toolshed, and mostly missed Diego and Jerome. Checkpoint-bots sprayed more bullets, and the last ambushers dropped onto the dirt or scattered along the riverbanks. They fired wild shots over their shoulders.

Spook's heart boomed like a machine gun going off in his chest.

Diego wailed in his helmet. Jerome limped around mangled bodies and fell into him. Diego clutched a wounded side and held the kid up. They were alive, yet very sad. Three men toting stealth rifles scrambled onto the bike path beyond the bridge. They staggered Spook's direction and splattered blood on the weeping cherry blossoms.

Spook backed away from spit, piss, and blood, from hearts stuttering still and eyes going dark. He dashed through lilac and forsythia bushes toward Cinnamon, Bruja, and the Bots. He ran and ran, his heart pumping faster than a dog's or a wolf's heart should.

The sun burned up the last of morning. A brilliant blue sky crowned the mountain range north of the Ghost Mall. It was 11:49. Indigo Hickory sucked her teeth, long and loud, then drew her eyes to slits. Cinnamon Jones and the midmorning apple-treats were almost two hours late. She was never late. Not in the two years Indigo knew her.

Wheel-Wizards, Co-Op volunteers, and Ghost-Mallers of every age and size milled around the food court. Remnants of breakfast were scattered on tables that looked like a fleet of flying saucers. Stomachs hollered and mouths watered—a cranky atmosphere. Even so, Shaheen Kumar, Wheel-Wizards Boss Lady and Mall chief, might persuade folks to do work details before *and* after lunch. Shaheen always had a long list of urgent. Everything didn't need to get done today, though, so when they finished sorting junk and setting up more homeless shelter, they'd do the first dress run for tomorrow's Festival. Cinnamon better not be late for that.

"Where are you, girlfriend?" Indigo shifted her weight from hip to hip. "I was ready for dress rehearsal last week."

"Me too," Game-Boy said, dripping sweat on Indigo's thigh.

Dude still wore his poly motorcycle jacket in midday heat. He slumped against a spaceship table and worried a paint splotch on his thumb. He and Back-From-The-Dead Crew hung around pretending to do design workshops or emergency repairs for farmers or anybody when really, they were Mall security, trained by the boneyard baron, and, except for Game-Boy, they wore black half-masks. Game-Boy said this was proper attire for *reformed* highwaymen.

"I gotta do this run-through while I still got some nerve." Theatre scared him more than armed thugs. "You know what I'm saying?" He poked Indigo.

She poked him back. "Uh-huh."

Game-Boy had threatened to do a Festival act tomorrow with his whole crew. They chickened out last year, claiming somebody stole their masks. A lie, no doubt, so Indigo wasn't holding her breath. Miracles did happen, just not as often as bad shit. Nobody ever did a miracle versus tragedy count, so Indigo might be indulging negativity.

She peered at Game-Boy—a good friend since the baron's miracle cure. He grinned back at her like always, a happy white boy, despite bubbles of anxiety. Shaheen forgave him for everything, another miracle. Boss Lady said people noticed bad crap more than good, but Shaheen was one of the true saints, and what did they know about bad? Still, Indigo decided to start counting miracles. The bad counted itself.

"Jitters before a show is good." Indigo dispensed theatre wisdom that Cinnamon had shared with her. "Anxiety means you care. Don't drown in it, though."

"Nah, nah. I'm chill." He stood tall, looking embarrassed and feverish.

"It's too hot already." Indigo usually liked the heat. "What happened to spring?"

Game-Boy fanned her. "When I was little, I never wanted summer to end."

"Got your wish, huh?"

Thin folks, raggedy as their last high, hung at the edge of the parking lot looking ready to bolt. One guy wore too many coats in March heat and had a huge backpack on each shoulder. He eyed Game-Boy and Indigo like they were Valley Security cruising the hood and he was guilty. Game-Boy was on alert because of yahoos acting up at the gorge last night. This morning, somebody torched a car on the bike path and Valley Security found a body with the throat maybe slit and made to look like an animal attack. Cap George shut down the rumors, yet Back-From-The-Dead stoics were twitchy—violence was on the uptick. They whispered about what awful might have happened to Cinnamon, loud enough for Indigo to eavesdrop: bomb, kidnapping, drone attack, electrocution, rabid bears . . . Indigo grunted. It was the rare bear that got rabies or slashed someone's throat.

Random suckers, following batshit, old glory code was the real threat. They hated the low-tech Wheel-Wizards. Cinnamon pedaling across the valley was miles and miles of being a target. Spook and Taiwo couldn't cover the whole bike path. Or somebody might have ambushed her at the farmhouse. Flying-Horse wouldn't roll over a slug. Shooting-Star-Bot neither. Without firepower, what kind of sentries were they?

Boss Lady Shaheen strode into the old pizza joint to check the ovens. Smart move. Waiting around for good or bad news with this jittery crowd was pointless. Indigo dashed up cement stairs past the old skating rink and headed for the roof, her lookout perch, her somewhere to worry in peace.

"Hey, you!" a new arrival shouted. Their neon-orange kicks glowed under a designer drab windbreaker. "Wait up."

Indigo halted. The newbie smelled like floral shower gel, toted a monster knapsack, and acted as if they were besties. Indigo smirked. "Yeah?"

"What do you look like, Advisor Hickory?"

"Me? What about you?"

The newbie was sweating buckets in the shit-green windbreaker. Like Game-Boy in his moto jacket, dressing for the calendar, not the weather, for a March that used to be. Baggy pants were flecked with dirt and blood, and holes at the knees were fresh. Reddish-brown curly hair had blond roots. An angry brush burn on sun-bronzed cheeks wept droplets of blood. A recent wound. Smiling so wide had to hurt, falling down too. "No, I mean, already in costume? What are you?"

"Guess." Indigo wore designer slash rags, black and blue eye shadow, and vampire chalk foundation on brown skin. Leather goggles and lace-up spats over pumps gave a steampunk feel. Light-years better than the last Festival. Bruja had found high-end clothes near Indigo's size, plus bling and props—a bone tiara, fang earrings, and a silvery stake. Bruja even hunted down bloodred lipstick and fingernail polish. Cinnamon claimed dogs didn't see red, so how did Bruja dumpster-dive the perfect shade unless she was truly a Witch-Dog?

". . . Uhm . . ." The newbie sputtered, at a loss or faking it. "A zombie?"

"Hell no."

"What then?" The monster knapsack interfered with deep breaths and probably contained every damn thing the newbie still possessed— like that junkie in three coats—much more than Indigo ever owned. Her whole life fit in a little paper bag. The newbie pouted. "Just tell me."

Indigo screwed up her face. *What are you running from? First-world angst?* If this rich ditz couldn't tell a zombie from a vampire, how could Indigo explain anything? "You'll find out at rehearsal." Indigo took off. Eighty-six steps took you from the parking lot to the fourth-floor roof. Indigo did two at a time.

The newbie mumbled about running six miles carrying her mom's old costume, authentic and heavy as shit, plus a tent and sleeping bag. Indigo could care less. This lost soul was desperate to join her squad, yet didn't have the stamina to keep up. Indigo hated chitchat with clueless fools who wanted to get next to some important body in the Co-Ops or Ghost Mall. The Mall Advisory Board was mostly show. Whoever claimed Advisor Hickory was a gateway to boss ladies or head honchos had lied. Game-Boy was the sucker for a pretty face, and anybody could get to Cinnamon or Shaheen. They were too damned nice. Indigo was shield bitch, protecting them from the toxic chaos of humanity on the brink.

We're always on the brink of something good.

Hard to stay mad at Cinnamon with her voice echoing in your head. Indigo should keep an eye on that junkie dude wearing three coats and find out the newbie's name and backstory—anybody might be a spy, assassin, hacker wretch who'd lost their way. Game-Boy profiled new recruits and kept a log of suspicious behavior. He called this surprise-attack prevention. Maybe not a waste of time. On the roof, Indigo got the eagle eye view. She surveilled Mall action-adventure far and wide.

She unlocked the stairwell door, then slammed it shut against newbies and other intruders—an emergency exit from the roof, however no entry from the stairs without a key. She caught her breath in the elevator foyer, a greenhouse these days that smelled of herbs and sunshine. Elevator had been out of order since last spring. They needed some part that never came. A Co-Op snack-shack machine leaned against the wall by the elevator where it had exploded (imploded?) on Halloween. Work detail cleaned out the food and beverage slop, but the metal and glass carcass was still waiting to go down.

Cinnamon hated shit like that. *What, you think we're living in a dystopia?*

"Almost, OK," Indigo argued out loud. "I know Bruja likes to get you here on time, so . . ." She rehearsed a speech for when Cinnamon pulled up with a hundred and one excuses for being reckless and two hours late. "Every morning I'm worried you won't show." She mixed vamp gestures with indignant tones that reverberated off glass walls. "I'm talking worried *sick* that some Happy Saxons will take out Witch-Dog, shoot you down, blow up your rig, or do shit I don't want to imagine." Indigo's stomach clenched as her imagination went wild. Cinnamon claimed they had too much *ImagiNation* in common. "You're probably fine. So why make us suffer, on the day before Festival? We should be *dress rehearsing the future with clear hearts and minds.* Damn."

Quoting Cinnamon in the speech had Indigo feeling worse, not better.

She stepped out the glass door onto the roof of what forever ago would have been a fitness center. Somebody had planned for outdoor weights and yoga under the stars, but the Ghost Mall had never really opened.

Businesses migrated online or to boutiques in Electric Paradise, people ran out of disposable income, and big-box tenants went bankrupt. The cost of mall demolition was hefty, so no going back to farmland on rich river-valley ground. Who wanted to pay property taxes or deal with wastewater runoff from so much asphalt and concrete? Nonprofit Co-Ops promised to renovate for public use and flood control and got the deeds for a song. Indigo suspected an angel with deep pockets helped out. She had yet to prove that.

The smell of flowers and damp soil made Indigo sigh. The rooftop was her lookout and getaway garden—acres and acres. Every roof in the Mall complex had been repurposed for gardens and solar panels. The rainwater sprinkler system was genius, storing runoff for later use and processing snow and ice too. Berry bushes, herbs, tomatoes, broccoli, onions, beans, sweet potatoes, and kale grew among a riot of flowers. Something was always in bloom, like Blossom Bridge. Her favorite was cirrhosa, an evergreen clematis whose freckled, bell-shaped blossoms survived the New Year's blizzard of the century.

Indigo came to the roof whenever she needed some space, a view of the bike path, or perspective on *life at the end of the world*. Jogging around the garden she felt ready for the Next World. If she sat still and quiet, birds forgot about her. They sang, rode warm updrafts, and went about their bird business. She covered berry bushes to save the harvest. Luckily, birds didn't dine on broccoli or kale. Sometimes a bird felt so at home, it perched on her shoe, munched a worm or nut, and held forth with song.

For the first time in her life, Indigo felt at home in a bull's-eye of concrete buildings holding back rain, wind, and invasive plant species. The Co-Ops built/planted a bioswale, a marshy wetland that curved around the Mall perimeter, filtered runoff, and provided a haven for heirloom weeds. The optimistic parking lot receded to infinity. Skeletons of cars, buses, and SUVs caught in an early flood hulked and wailed—an eerie choir complaining at nobody in particular.

The Co-Ops had reclaimed Mall ground level from floodwaters for community markets, the food court, the health clinic, and workshops, including fix-it stations and maker spaces. It took months to wash away the nasty sewage stink. Cleanup was a mother-loving challenge, although not impossible. The second floor was Co-Op central, a school, and a temporary homeless shelter. Third floor was an indoor theatre and screening space, the library, and extra shelter. Refugees kept pouring in and hardly anybody ever left. More people, more challenge, more trouble—a security nightmare, according to Game-Boy, but he was a drama queen. And what was Indigo?

"Cinnamon, where are you? Don't do this to us," she whispered, trying not to be worried sick. "Don't do this to me."

ೞ ❧

WHAT YOU THINK YOU KNOW

Yellow blossoms and a sweet scent clung to Spook's fur as he caught up to the Water-Spirits. Thrilled by their rainbow static and ozone odor, he slobbered and whined. They danced just behind Cinnamon, unfazed by a wounded man with a stealth weapon creeping toward them. Valley Security drones had taken out his comrades. Checkpoint-bots never scouted this far out. Paradise drones stopped at the Mall parking lot. A security dead zone. The rogue toting an automated weapon was danger.

Spook yip-yapped and jibber-jabbered—a long tale of woe that nobody understood.

"Water-Spirits should do an act at Festival!" Cinnamon shouted at rainbow shimmers in the trees. "Dancing with Baron Taiwo, you'd tear it up."

"Who'd be able to see this wonder water dance?" Dragon asked.

"A couple somebodies and Taiwo would have company." Cinnamon sang the Scottish seal song: "Coir an oir an oir an oir o." Water-Spirits sang like water rippling over rocks. A calming sound, even if Cinnamon pedaled slow and smelled tired, hungry. She should eat a lot and take a nap with Spook at the Mall. They both needed rest. She had a hammock for late nights and let him swing with her to dreamland.

Bruja trotted back to Spook and licked his face till his heartbeat matched hers. She growled at the desperado tracking them, ready to rip his throat before he pulled the trigger on any of them. Spook licked Bruja, grateful for fangs on his side. She woofed at Taiwo, who charged overhead through oak branches, a blur in the pale new leaves. Water-Spirits sang a rainstorm. Lightning popped from their eyes and thunder rumbled on their breath. Spook huffed relief. What was one gunman against the whole pack?

"Cavalry in the show," Cinnamon said. "Maybe I just had to ask. Miracles happen." Spook and Bruja woofed at a favorite word.

"Diego Denzel seems like fun!" Mami-Iris shouted.

"Diego winked right back at you." Thunderbird-Aidan honked his horn.

"He did not." Cinnamon sighed. "Diego's a sweet taste in my mouth, but I ain't out here cruising for love." Her voice wobbled.

"Betrayal was ages ago," Dragon-Redwood murmured. "Why does that code rule your heart?"

"Uhm . . ." Cinnamon sputtered. "You think I can persuade Diego to take that burnt dummy off the razor wire? Gone are the days we put up with that, right?"

"Whoever needed to put up with that?" Dragon-Redwood spewed red flower petals from her funnel snout. Folded up in the bin, she looked like kitchen refuse today.

People changing forms was hard to get used to. Spook knew the elders when he was young. They went away for a long while, then one afternoon came trundling into the farmhouse, sounding how he remembered. They smelled of sweetgrass, licorice, and hot sauce, of old paper, seed beads, and banjos, of meadows, theatre, and good times, like always. Getting used to the plastic, metal, and glass costumes was a trick, yet now Spook loved the Circus-Bots as much as Bruja, and she only knew them in these trash-pack forms. Spook ignored fancy getup and tuned into their voices, into the scents, music, and mischief—flower petals, glitter, and smoke signals. T-bird-Aidan's twang and Dragon-Redwood's blues murmur were a perfect tonic.

"He loves APPLE SURPRISE," Dragon-Redwood declared. Spook sniffed a bin of that delicious treat. "A closet thespian doing a hired-thug act, Diego's perfect for you."

"Thug act? What do you know about him?" Cinnamon halted. "And why get chatty with that new kid?"

The Circus-Bots mumbled so quick, so quiet Spook barely heard them.

"OK." Cinnamon leaned into the handlebars. "You don't have enough data for good intel, and you don't want to spook me with speculations. Hey, I'm a grown-ass woman, you know." She pedaled faster. Spook wagged his tail, glad for the speed. "I got secrets too. See if I tell you."

Taiwo muttered, "What you think you know that ain't so . . ."

"Make you a slave," the Bots whispered.

A Valley Security van idled on the nearby car road. Cap George in a gold lamé cape was untangling two animals caught in bittersweet vines. Spook had never smelled these creatures before—bigger than goats, smaller than horses. Their fur resembled shadows in high grass. They wanted to kick somebody, bite George. He jumped in the van before hacking the last vine, and they dashed off.

Spook caught the scent of Back-From-The-Dead scouts and the breakfast buffet: corn cakes with black beans. Soon, there'd be crumbs and friendly people to scratch his back. Bruja didn't like as many people as Spook. She never ate food from stray hands. He ate her share. Taiwo spit sparks in the air, still in a storm mood. Spook shook off the last of the battle terror, jumped six feet in the air, and snapped at oun's sparks.

Lunch at the Mall was around the corner.

OLD MYSTERIES

The final stretch from Blossom Bridge was uneventful: no raids, no trees melting into pools of muck or houses blinking fire eyes at her like yesterday. No haints tripping in from the silver screen to scold *and* serenade Cinnamon. Nevertheless—

"They stole Flying-Horse? Nobody's stolen tech from me in years. Here I was worried sick about Shooting-Star." She halted by a stone bench and glowered at the Circus-Bots. "You were going to what, wait till after lunch to tell me?" The Ghost Mall was in spitting distance, but they were already late, and she never argued with the Bots in front of *everybody*. Her heart raced. Did the Bots lie to her too, like that rogue AI in the news? "Why tell me now?" They dropped into sentinel-mode and smoldered in silence. "Fine. I can read your minds anyhow."

At first, they thought Spook and Taiwo would round up the thieves and any remains of Flying-Horse. Thunderbird put sentinels watching over the farm on red alert. Dragon sent Shooting-Star into hiding—thieves wouldn't snatch anyone else. They reasoned there was nothing more for Cinnamon to do except worry. Since empathy was good for cognition and novel ideas came from a change in perspective, they modeled Cinnamon's emotions, reviewed the data, and *changed their minds*. What if some gearhead hacked Horse and found telltale code that exposed everyone to danger?

"Whack-jobs and thieves are why you have *dead-bot-off* switches. We can't risk you getting caught." Cinnamon's stomach rolled. Her breakfast of tea and quinoa cakes threatened to come up. *Dead-bot-off* meant a disabled tracking signal—who needed a bounce-back trail exposing them? *Dead-bot-off* also meant Horse's routines would decay, the pattern of his patterns would unravel, his insights would dissolve. Horse was embodied AI and knew how to fear death. He'd fight the loss and suffer.

If thieves hoped to override security protocols, reboot, and sell, they'd need expert help, one of the Darknet Lords—a pricey and unpredictable bunch. Finding one would take time. More likely, thieves would pry Horse apart, sell what they could, and toss the rest. Horse might already be disemboweled. Nothing Cinnamon or anybody could do about that.

"Damn." Cursing was appropriate. One consolation: she'd be able to use a stolen, suffering Horse to get the baron to recharge their horror rep.

Bruja nipped her heels and raced ahead to the Ghost Mall parking lot.

Cinnamon pedaled faster. "Thieves can't hide Horse from Spook's or Bruja's noses. They're trackers like Granddaddy Aidan. He and Iris always found lost souls."

"When to search?" Mami Wata broke the Bot silence. "That's the question."

"After rehearsal," Dragon declared. "If thieves rustle up a Darknet Lord, *dead-bot-off* will thwart them. Why wreck Festival rehearsal?"

"You always sing the song I need to hear." Thunderbird nailed Aidan talking sweet to Redwood. Sound logic, yet Cinnamon wobbled on her bike.

Seeing ghost elders at Blossom Bridge freaked her worse than thugs out for ambush or thieves snatching Horse. The Bots didn't mention these *visions*. What if they hadn't seen the black-and-white haints? What if they had? Did she want to know? She used to want to know everything. She needed more data, more sightings and witnesses she trusted, like Klaus and Marie. Unfortunately, there was nobody like them.

Bruja trotted close and woofed concern. Cinnamon shook off heartache. "You never met my grandparents and great-aunt, still . . . You'd be happy to meet them, wouldn't you?" Bruja barked and wagged her tail. "Me too," Cinnamon admitted and, before she could stop herself, a story storm poured out.

"I've seen a haint before. When I was a kid. My brother, Sekou, started haunting me the day after his funeral. At first, he was only a voice, a rapper nerd messing in my business, setting me straight. My best friends, Marie and Klaus, also heard him. With the three of us *believing*, Sekou amped up to a, a hollow-cheeked wraith with silver light threaded in his locs, like Mami Wata or the baron. He dropped older brother wisdom on us. *Who do you mean to be?*" Cinnamon sagged. She longed to be who she used to be. "After high school, Sekou faded away. Klaus and Marie went off to college and faded too. I was afraid to chase after them, and besides—"

How can you spout physics at me and believe hoodoo-voodoo nonsense?

Cinnamon wished she remembered what she said back to her mother. Opal was trying to be helpful, reasonable, a good mom. She wasn't trying to wipe her daughter's mind of tricky truth. Grown-up Cinnamon had revised hoodoo-voodoo memories. She attributed dead-brother visitations to grief and an overactive *ImagiNation*. Raven, her hero dad, had been shot in the head, saving folks, and ended up in that coma. Opal was a hero mom, saving strangers too, but so sad, so mad, she tried to smoke herself to death. With such parent trauma who could blame dead brother Sekou for haunting Cinnamon? That never explained Klaus and Marie seeing ghost Sekou.

"And . . ." Taiwo claimed to be an alien from another space/time. Klaus and Marie witnessed oun doing the weird from another dimension too. "And now . . ." Taiwo saved Game-Boy's crew with a shekere and alien juju. Cinnamon wished oun had given her dad a second life. The bullet in Raven's brain had grazed her heart. "Well . . ."

Mami's third eye flashed red, T-bird honked a horn, and Dragon rattled bells on her tail. "Finish your sentence," they demanded. Nosy data hounds. Cinnamon's fault, her mouth still ran like a racehorse, telling what she didn't mean to tell.

The trailer skidded over nothing. She clutched the handlebars. Long ago, she resolved never to reveal tall tales she couldn't explain, didn't dare *believe*, yet couldn't deny. "Why tell you all what I've worked hard to keep from myself?" The past might be scarier than the future. She stood up, pedaled faster, and focused on the here and now.

Safe arrival at the Mall was a triumph every day. Still, Cinnamon hated the post-apocalyptic vibe of the parking lot. Baby carriages, metal doors, stoves, and flat screens had slammed into cars and trucks with gale force. The refrigerator wedged in an SUV windshield was like something from *TermiNation*. After floodwaters retreated, the Co-Ops and freelance scavengers claimed whatever was reusable. Clearing the picked-over carcasses should be a spring priority. They should also recycle that Co-Op snack-shack decomposing next to the busted elevator on the Mall roof.

A yellow school bus lay on its side, blocking the bike path. Windows were shattered, seats and tires long gone. Letters spray-painted on the side read: *Why not WHIZZ-IT? Did Algebra ever solve your fucking problems?* That aggravated Cinnamon every time she rode by. She had to get a spray can from Game-Boy and paint it over. She glanced at the Bots. Algebra helped her every minute of the day.

INDIGO

MIA

"Indigo? Where you hiding?" Voices echoed around the Mall.

Indigo was crouched at the edge of the fitness center roof by a gardenia bush, which had buds already. Her squad charged around the food court, yelling like an army of zombies or space bugs had attacked the Mall. Six runaways, they were survivors same as Indigo, skinny blades or wearing their heft like armor.

"Ain't nobody hiding." Indigo shook off a death-bot versus Cinnamon daydream.

"Red alert!" One firebrand went by Hawk and had a chipped tooth, a lopsided nose (broken?), and a scar under an eye. Hawk used oun, the baron's pronoun, to help out folks confused by "they." Hawk said it was like Farsi. Everybody wanted to ask who beat oun's face, but were afraid of the story oun would tell or the punch oun might throw. Even Indigo didn't pry.

Bruja had also found costumes, makeup, and props for Indigo's crew. Squinting at the Vamp-Squad from the rooftop, Indigo groaned. They looked wrong, more like little children with chalky faces than ancient bloodsuckers.

"You reading a book?" Game-Boy yelled, and aimed his phone at her. "Why you hiding up there?"

"I'm not hiding," Indigo insisted. The garden was a getaway, not a hideaway. Big difference. "I don't want my picture all over everywhere before the Festival reveal."

"Sorry." Gameboy lowered his phone. "Come back. Folks were already riled up. Now they're worried you and Cinnamon both are MIA."

After taking her time to water some thirsty beauties and commune with ladybugs and spiders, Indigo raced down the cement stairs so fast, she could have broken her neck on a stumble. She never let stray thoughts like that slow her up. She plowed into Shaheen, who absorbed her momentum as if it was nothing. Shaheen was a resilient, muscular woman as bouncy as her salt-and-pepper curls. Indigo wanted to be like her or Cinnamon when she got old. She longed for a sharp Mumbai accent like Shaheen or an occasional Georgia Sea Island drawl like Cinnamon. But folks talked how they talked except onstage—you didn't just steal their ways for your everyday fashion accessories.

Shaheen gripped Indigo's hand. "I don't like it. Cinnamon is always on time."

"What I been saying? Everybody be worried." Game-Boy never minded riffing on Georgia or Mumbai and he was from down the road, Hill Town, Mass. "We should get out there and look."

"Where?" Shaheen said.

Game-Boy acted like that was the stupidest question he'd ever heard. "On the bike path. Where else?" Hawk bumped his fist, agreeing.

Shaheen thrust her jaw out like a weapon. Her eyes steamed up, as if she held a blast of fire inside—doing her Kali masquerade, Hindu Devi of life and death and time, or doing her New York street-market witch. Maybe a combo. Folks stepped back. "The bike path is a lot of kilometers to cover, and trouble can come from anywhere, anytime. Fight off one attack, here comes another when your guard is down."

Indigo glanced at the ribbon of asphalt. A dark cloud dampened the sunlight and spectral willow trees shivered. "A danger ride. You know Cinnamon be all over that."

Game-Boy spun around to his boys. "We gotta do something."

He worked his tongue like drum and bass, then pounded his chest for a search and rescue riff. *Where you at, don't play like that!* Back-From-The-Dead stomped booted feet and did a *rat tat bop pop* rhyme. Indigo and the Vamp-Squad clapped and snapped underneath. Black half-masks made the boys look badass. Indigo needed to find fiercer costumes to help her Vamp-Squad act the part.

Game-Boy did a falsetto wail and cut the beatboxing short. "We can't stand around—"

"Stuck on stupid," Indigo declared. "I saw Cap George's hybrid van on the car road. Cinnamon's one of the only people in this world George actually likes. Let's call him—"

A security system split the air.

GHOST MALL

Bruja jumped on the rusty stop-sign arm of the beached school bus. She loved making it squeak. A die-hard security system sounded off. Everyone would know they'd arrived. Cinnamon braced herself and trundled around the bus. A crowd milling in the outdoor food court covered their ears. Sirens and horns used to blare from the wrecks all the time, for no apparent reason—radio-wave ghosts sounding an alarm. That was how the Mall got its name. This screecher was the first ghost alarm in ages.

Bruja threw back her head and howled. The stop-arm's rusty joint snapped under her, and she leapt onto the hood of an SUV wreck. Feeble headlights blinked on, then off, and the alarm fizzled. Everyone cheered, even Indigo's sulky Vamp-Squad.

"Bruja is spring miracle number one," Indigo yelled.

"I know that's true," Game-Boy chimed in.

Cinnamon halted by the pizzeria. Her legs were shaky, her mind too. Grins and cheers pressed too close as she stepped from her rig. She burped anxiety.

"Let her breathe." Shaheen cleared the crowd with a market woman voice. She bumped her forehead against Cinnamon's helmet and steadied her in a fragrant hug—lavender, basil, and oregano. The turmeric on her nose smudged Cinnamon's cheeks. Shaheen also hugged Bruja—one of the few who got away with that. "You all are the last to arrive." Shaheen sounded like she might cry.

"Where you been?" Indigo jumped in Cinnamon's face. "Zaneesha kept asking for you and the Witch-Dog." Chalky vamp makeup streaked Indigo's cheeks; bloodred lips were smeared. "We told the kid you'd be here two hours ago."

"Yeah, you left the kid hanging." Game-Boy was mad too.

"How is Zaneesha doing?" Cinnamon tried to distract them.

They gave a fast reply, talking on top of each other. Zaneesha was big eyes, a soft voice, and a gentle spirit. She'd slept in the clubhouse with other stray kids and didn't say much at breakfast till Indigo clipped bug jewel-lights in her braids. Then she told everyone about a comet lady who roamed the night sky with her hair on fire. Comet-lady had signaled Witch-Dog to find Zaneesha, 'cause fire spirits were on the lookout.

Zaneesha's dad worked guard duty somewhere and was not really in the picture. Mom was pulling a night, then a day shift in Paradise taking care of *big baby*. Zaneesha planned to wait for her at the gate after sunset. Game-Boy and Indigo promised to wait with her. The grade schoolers went off with Co-Op techies to tinker with bioswale filters and the solar garden. Zaneesha tagged along. Cinnamon would ask her about Jerome after lunch. Williams was a common name, but the coincidences were piling up.

"Zaneesha wasn't the only one worried." Indigo scrunched up her face. "You're never late."

"Indigo thought the worst. You know how she is." Game-Boy dodged Indigo's elbow in his side. Panic still sparked off them both. They'd been ready to send out a posse to search for her remains when the ghost alarm went off.

Cinnamon took off her helmet and patted earnest shoulders. "You two shouldn't worry about me."

"You know how that goes." Indigo sucked her teeth and she was a champion teeth-sucker. "Is that all you got?"

Cinnamon pointed at her tiara. "Are those bones?"

Indigo snorted and fang earrings rattled. "Lame diversion."

"Mega-lame." Game-Boy gathered sandy dreads into a thick ponytail like he was strangling somebody.

Peacemaker Shaheen tapped Bruja's nose. "Cinnamon doesn't answer her phone, no text. Yet, here you both are, safe. Sporting a bulletproof helmet *and* vest."

"Bullet-*resistant*." Cinnamon wiggled out of the vest. "Baron Taiwo's always on lookout for me. Spook too. And nobody gets past Bruja."

Bruja growled her support.

"That's the truth." Shaheen stepped up on a flying saucer table. Her colorful rayon tunic from 1990-something caught the breeze—a neo-hippie delight. "OK, people, one last work detail and then pizza. What do you say?" She jumped down, lifted Dragon from the bin, and thrust her at Game-Boy. He liked Dragon's funky beats and Sea Island attitude. Indigo rolled her eyes and grabbed Thunderbird from Shaheen. Quiet as it was kept, Indigo was a banjo freak and loved the bird's tap-dancing talons. Shaheen herded sulky youth toward the pizza joint.

Commands in posh Mumbai English had everyone unloading food, tools, and instruments. Back-From-The-Dead spread out for security patrol. Cinnamon took the goodie bag from Mami's lap. Crow? Hawk? from Indigo's Vamp-Squad lifted the electric lady from her bin without pulling a muscle or getting a shock. Hawk. Iranian-American, tenor/alto range. Mami liked this raptor-person and so did Game-Boy.

"Jhakass!" Shaheen exclaimed appreciation, Mumbai-style, as the forces mobilized. Game-Boy turned the word into a beatbox chant as she opened a big bag of apple treats, then ladled mango lassis, Cinnamon's favorite midmorning lift-me-up. People stuffed their faces and swooned over the medley of good tastes and good rhythms.

A young newcomer in raggedy jeans beamed at Indigo and Game-Boy. In love. She looked roughed up, yet too happy to be at the Mall to complain. She had a familiar face—from where? Cinnamon had always been terrible at remembering faces and names. "What's Electric Paradise got that we don't?" the newcomer yelled. "A lot of static and widgets. Smoke but no fire. Ghost Mall's got the fire."

"Fire's what I'm talking about." Game-Boy high-fived Hawk. They were head over heels in lust with each other and too shy to let on. Who couldn't see it, though?

Indigo sneered. "Let's not get too romantic about dumpster-dive living. The Ghost Mall is prehistoric tech, recycled grease, and rain-barrel showers." She pointed at the bag Cinnamon clutched. "Watery tofu styling like cheese ain't paradise."

Game-Boy laughed. "Word." He and Indigo amped the Mall's post-apocalyptic rep.

Cinnamon had to admit, even though flood rubble worked her nerves, a parking lot out of *TermiNation* was perfect cover. The Mall was a buffer zone for Electric Paradise. Refugees would barrel on through the rubble, then stop at the food court and homeless shelter. And as long as nobody was storming their gates, Paradise ignored Co-Op hippies relying on goats, bicycle transport, and clothing swaps.

"You can eat *and* work. Let's get busy," Shaheen commanded.

Cinnamon dropped onto a spaceship stool and observed the coordinated mob effort. In no time, workshops and repair stations were humming. Bruja wagged her butt, ready to fetch and stash. "Yeah, girl, everybody on a mission." Mallers, young and old, makers, innovators, pored over antediluvian appliances and broken gadgets. What couldn't get fixed was taken apart, repurposed, or turned into sculpture or props for Festival— theory into praxis. On good weather days, school was outdoors. Consolidated offered free net access with its WHIZZ-ITs, yet Boss Lady Shaheen banned the devices at the Mall. That was a fight at first. Indigo was the loudest, talking about *the real world* versus *the happy valley behind the tofu curtain.* Shaheen prevailed, pointing to *algorithms of oppression* versus *the tech we want.* Mall kids learned to read, write, draw, and they did their own arithmetic, algebra, trig, and calculus, like rich kids in Electric Paradise. Now Indigo carried her phone inside a Faraday sleeve—no signals in or out.

Indigo hovered over Cinnamon. "What's your sweetest memory?"

"In my life? Here in the valley?"

"Both. Either."

Memories flooded Cinnamon:

When she was nine, Raven and Opal danced in the snow to the Temptations, *"When it's cold outside, I've got the month of May."* Onstage at fourteen, she flew through the air with Klaus and Marie, doing Contact Improv. A fall day on the farm, she ate Iris's apple cakes with Aidan and Redwood under the apple tree who fed them. At the first Next World Festival that featured Wheel-Wizards, Co-Op farmers, and the Motor Fairies, she and Shaheen leapt up and danced around the Amphitheatre till everyone was dancing, including Spook and Bruja. Before they died, the elders made Cinnamon explain the algorithms she was working on. Listening, their faces flickered like glitter in a shaft of sun. They asked good questions and reassured her: *You'll figure out those glitches.*

"So many sweet memories, hard to pick one." Cinnamon blinked more away. "Why are you asking?"

Indigo chuckled at a young man hiding behind a costume rack.

"Dude is s'posed to collect your tall tales. He's too shy, and I'm nosy, so I said I'd ask for him."

"He has to get the story himself. That's part of the point."

The Graphic Novelists of the Future were high schoolers who did history, art, and creative writing with Cinnamon. Griots-in-training, they had to conduct interviews for their graphic novel biographies and mythic history of the valley. They were drawing and inking their frames by hand. Rough drafts of the final projects were due to Cinnamon the day after Festival. Books would be on sale in June.

"You tell him—anything I share with you is for you, for the story you'd write. He has to get his own story out of me."

"Word. So, I'll interview you later. He can interview me. I don't scare him so much." Indigo sauntered toward the shy kid.

Wheel-Wizards loaded their rigs with Co-Op goodies for the hill towns, and masks, costumes, and sets for Festival. Whoosy?—the mushroom-nurse—hitched a big bunny tricycle to the back of a trailer. Pink wings and a puffball tail tickled Cinnamon. Six-foot antennae-ears could listen in on the stars, on pulsars and quasars at the universe's edge, at the beginning of the beginning. Cinnamon laughed full out, then pulled the mushroom-nurse close to whisper about the security alert. The clinic had figured something was brewing. They'd called in extra volunteers and stocked up on bandages, blood, antiseptics, and antibiotics, for Festival too.

"Last year this rig was top-heavy." The mushroom-nurse telescoped the rabbit ears down to a plump twelve inches. "I tipped over in the mud and we missed our cue. This year, we built a practical bunny to prevent disaster at the grand entrance."

"Disaster-proof." Cinnamon snapped her fingers. "That's what I'm talking about."

Ghost-Mallers had lived in many worlds and cycled from horror to good times again and again. A hardy bunch, they grumbled at Shaheen and joked with Back-From-The-Dead and Vamp-Squad. Powwow Now decorated new drums. May There Be Grace Choir sang close harmonies. The Hill Town Wenches rehearsed an athletic pole dance routine. Some bruisers had gathered tree trunks to hurl—a Scottish thing, the caber toss. Definitely not the dystopia they all feared.

Cinnamon loved to sit in an unruly crowd, sync breath and heart-beats, and make a mind/spirit bridge. A Next World Festival mood already, except—

Game-Boy and Indigo were fussing about *red alerts* and Cinnamon biking alone to the Mall and they didn't even know about Flying-Horse.

Shaheen asked them to corral stray goats with Bruja, video-document solar garden progress, or prep pizzas for lunch, but they were too busy revving each other up over Whistleblowers.

Jerome Williams had spewed the same nonsense at the Blossom Bridge checkpoint:

Whistleblowers were demons of disorder, rogue idealists who'd lost their way. They talked freedom, justice, yet relished chaos and destruction. Whistleblowers might be worse than mindless desperados or some violent, bring-inequality-on-back nostalgia militia! Torching junk cars on the bike path was nothing. Whistleblowers allegedly launched cyber-attacks on Electric Paradise. They deployed stealth-tech weapons to terrorize hill towns and battle the cavalry and their gun-bots. Whistleblowers might attack Co-Op farms and the Mall next. According to Darknet sources—

"Wait! Stop!" Cinnamon freaked. "Since when do you two hang on the Darknet?"

"I don't." Indigo blinked, as if waking from a trance. "When Game-Boy tries to sneak on, they bounce his ass and slave his burner."

"I ditch a compromised burner right away." Game-Boy looked sheepish. "I scored a whole case from that Afro-Deutsch hipster last year—my Darknet sacrifices. Zilch on those burners to steal."

"You leave a signature data trail," Indigo muttered. "A slug dripping tell-all slime."

Game-Boy grumbled, "Why you always ragging about signature slime?"

"How do you really know if a burner's compromised?"

"You used to be all in, living out loud virtually, craving a fifth-level WHIZZ-IT." He wagged his head. "Now you're smoke online and acting all superior about it."

"Dark or light, the net's more dangerous than any stretch of the bike path." Indigo waved a finger in his face. "I'm your friend. That's why I give you shit. You think those gamers are your friends?"

"Uhm—" Game-Boy clearly hoped they were.

"Half those losers have to be spy-bots." Indigo was unrelenting. "That Fab Freak dude for sure."

"Fab Freak is not a bot."

"Those burners might be compromised from the git-go."

"You're scared of harmless static, like every crackle and pop is a spy bitch."

"Darknet players don't want your sloppy ass leaking their protocols to—"

"OK. OK." Shaheen stepped between them. "You haven't breached the Darknet. So, where *did* you get this Whistleblower conspiracy crap?"

Game-Boy licked dry lips. "It's just smack people be saying."

Indigo's eyes darted about. "It's like everywhere, but not coming from anywhere."

Game-Boy glared at her. "What? You think rumor-bots be deep faking us?"

"I know they are," Indigo replied. "Getting us ready to believe any ole Scheiße." She'd picked up Cinnamon's German curses. Everyone had.

"Nobody cares about us. We're not worth the code." He sounded disappointed.

"Not you and me personally, all of us together," Indigo retorted. Game-Boy mumbled under her as she got louder: "All you need is a scatter shot at the herd, at the hive, to hack our dreams, colonize the future, and—"

"Stop." Shaheen gripped Indigo's and Game-Boy's arms, interrupting their epic battle. "Whistleblowers are on our team."

Cinnamon wanted to *believe* in heroes roaming the country, snooping toxic scams, warning folks about corporate corruption, neo-slave labor, but what proof? "Well . . ."

"Well nothing." Shaheen dug her fingernails deep, and the kids whimpered. "Whistleblowers are our frontline defense, speaking truth to power for the people. We don't shoot them in the back. You hear me?" They nodded at her. "Do whatever. Fix this conspiracy rumor. Counter the disinformation."

"OK. Chill," Indigo said. She and Game-Boy extracted themselves from iron fingers.

"I'm channeling my inner Kali. Kali doesn't do chill." Shaheen forgave Game-Boy for the tee shirt raid, yet periodically made him squirm for yelling, *Kali, goddess of death*, at her. "Street-market witches aren't chill either. We're fire spirits."

"Right, right," Game-Boy said.

"Right." Indigo joined him. "We got this."

Cinnamon marveled. "You two can neutralize the rumors?"

"We can do something." Game-Boy exchanged glances with Indigo.

They were hooked in to all the valley crews. Game-Boy lived in online gaming parlors, chat rooms, and social media haunts—Knick Knack and Who Dat? His feed was always crackling, always live. He loved scoping the world beat and had layers of encryption that *bounced shit all over the map, from the moon and back* for cover, or so he claimed. Cinnamon had been tech/net savvy like that once. Now the thought of staying cyber-fit exhausted her. And how did Game-Boy afford so much access? A side hustle?

"What's the chatter on stealing Bots?" Cinnamon asked. "Any bounties posted? Deals and steals?"

Game-Boy's eyes darted about, scanning memories. "Big players freaked over the Consolidated data breach, offering megabucks for credible tips on the hackers. Bounty hunters be chasing that."

"It's like you say—not a single evil villain. A defuse crew coordinated by the net." Indigo grimaced.

Cinnamon nodded. "A conspiracy of ideology."

"Well, nobody better sabotage dress rehearsal, hear what I'm saying?" Indigo would hold Game-Boy personally responsible for anything going wrong.

"Brilliant." Shaheen turned to Cinnamon. "So if not Whistleblowers, what slowed you down this morning? Did a rabid bear try to bite your butt?"

"Rabid bear? No way. My grandparents and Aunt Iris, I mean the Bots, uhm . . . ," Cinnamon stuttered. The truth was too wild. "I was recruiting for Festival. Cavalry will play fire spirits."

"Get out of town. Valley Security playacting at Festival?" Shaheen snapped her fingers. "How'd you manage that?"

"My charm," Cinnamon replied.

Indigo slugged Game-Boy. "Back-From-The-Dead better not chicken out."

He considered her spats and smudged makeup. "You doing vampires or steampunk babes? What?"

Indigo shrugged. "Maybe." A sulky, sly nonanswer.

"Well, boo-yah!" Game-Boy shouted. "No desperado, bomb, or bear took Cinnamon out today. So repair detail, then we'll see what characters my boys rustle up for the show." He slipped his arm through Indigo's. She rolled her eyes as he grabbed a plate of apple surprises and they disappeared into the fix-it spaces.

BEJIGGITY

Bruja wagged her butt, licked Cinnamon's fingers, then ran to the beached school bus and jumped through the driver's window. Cinnamon dumped the bullet-resistant gear into an empty bin on her trailer. Between the Ghost Mall and Electric Paradise, armor was unnecessary. Cap George and his Valley Security coordinated with Back-From-The-Dead and the Vamp-Squad to keep the peace for rich folks and everybody. A neutral cease-fire zone.

"What's good, girl?" Shaheen poured Cinnamon the last of the mango lassi.

"You, Shaheen." Cinnamon savored the sour-sweet yogurt drink. "Nothing like a practical visionary to reverse engineer tomorrow."

Shaheen narrowed her eyes. "It's just after noon and you're looking bejiggity."

"Bejiggity? You made that word up."

"Where do you think words come from?"

"Something's off. A next-gen AI got caught lying. It's vague, though. No good data."

Shaheen sniggered. "You hate that."

Cinnamon adjusted the brakes, dabbed lube on the gears. "Doesn't everybody?"

"Nobody cares about *good data*. They want a *good story*."

"You making fun of me?"

"No. And maybe you hadn't noticed, but things are actually looking up."

"You're a stellar friend, a glass half-full lady. How I used to be."

"What, two minutes ago? Shut up." Shaheen pointed at a distant building. "We cleared debris this morning, salvaged tall shelves, and used them as walls for family quarters. Every unit filled right up. Some people might even manage a little rent."

"Band-Aid on a hemorrhage." Cinnamon rubbed at a headache brewing between her eyes. "Too many refugees. People are gig-slutting night and day in Electric Paradise or working seventy-hour weeks for Consolidated, and still can't afford a pot to piss in or a window to throw it out."

"Colorful image. Did your grandparents used to say that?" Shaheen patted Cinnamon. "You heard the kids. *We got this.*"

"Sure." Nobody ever let Cinnamon despair, even for a minute.

Bruja raced from the school bus with a mask in her mouth: camera eyes, gear nose and ears, and metal plates for a mouth. She dropped it on Cinnamon's foot and looked up eagerly. "I've never played a robot." Cinnamon toed a steel cheek and did mechanical gestures. "Funny, isn't it? My robot moves suck. I'd need a lot of rehearsal, and the show's tomorrow." She sighed. "No. Sorry, Bruja. Not this year."

Bruja gripped the gear nose gently and crept back to the bus.

"That's a beautiful mask!" Shaheen shouted at her drooping tail.

"It's too small for my big skull and this mess of braids," Cinnamon added. "Somebody should wear it."

Shaheen eyed her with concern? disbelief? worry? Usually by dress rehearsal, Cinnamon had written a song, created costumes, masks, and memorized lines for multiple characters, and choreographed a finale for the entire cast. This year, she'd scribbled a few lyrics and written a half-ass melody—nothing else. The elders would be disappointed. They liked to rock out. She should hand the finale over to Indigo.

Bruja returned, glum. Shaheen ruffled her ears. "You're more serious than anyone about Festival." Bruja put a paw on her shoulder and whined. "You are! You are!"

Cinnamon sighed. "Do you remember last year's tee shirt?"

"A Stevie Wonder lyric or from Nina Simone?"

"No. Something else. Anyhow, five AM, this year's tee came to me." That realization surprised Cinnamon. "*I'ma Be My Own Sun and Rise.*"

"Your line? We'll print after lunch." Shaheen held up yards of silver-blue fabric with a red shimmer. "The weave pattern's called gas flame, perfect for a fire-spirit costume."

"Beautiful."

"You won't do a robot, so what *will* you be playing?"

Cinnamon shrugged. "Seems like . . . I don't want to play any-body . . ."

Shaheen grunted and turned toward Bruja. "Indigo says you're a Witch-Dog with magic powers. Find this one a good mask." Bruja barked, on task. Shaheen got in Cinnamon's face. "Why's your glass half-empty? We're averting disaster every day." She was worse than Game-Boy and Indigo. "You're not talking to me."

Cinnamon dodged into the pizzeria kitchen. Shaheen and Bruja followed, growling together. Cinnamon would tell Shaheen after lunch about Flying-Horse, desperados in the bushes, and flood kids getting nabbed. She'd keep sadness over Raven's birthday to herself. Forget talking about ghosts at Blossom Bridge. The baron from another dimension was hard enough. Shaheen thought of oun as an African mystic. Forget black-and-white haints from an afterworld silent movie . . . Cinnamon ached for hoodoo friends like Klaus and Marie, who wouldn't freak out, who could hold all of her.

The Bots were lined up in sentinel-mode, unfurled yet low power. They stood by the stainless-steel refrigerator, a cool spot. Coils in the oven radiated heat for pizza. Tomato sauce on an electric stove bubbled fragrant steam. Ventilators circulated fresh air. A solar generator kept it all going. Simple designs Cinnamon was proud of. She pinged the kitchen array and fired the oven to six hundred degrees for crispy crusts.

"That rig did funky noises this morning, farting and sparking," Shaheen said.

Cinnamon tinkered with the interface panel connecting ovens, refrigerator, ventilator, generator, and computer. She thought of it as a crossroads, a trickster space.

Shaheen stood over her. "Out there pedaling alone. You do know something might happen to you. Something bad. Back-From-The-Dead would come out as early as you want. Game-Boy is always looking for a way to pay you back for rescuing him from his bad-boy self and—"

"Our reformed gangstas are spread too thin already."

"You're the mother Indigo wished she'd had. Vamp-Squad offered to—"

"I'm not reckless." Cinnamon escaped to the tomato sauce.

"Gun-toting desperados have *reckless* covered. That's who I'm worried about, not you. Violence spiking up."

"I plan to invite the kids to my morning ritual." The thieves who nabbed Horse weren't desperados doing random violence. Professionals most likely, maybe connected to the drone Mami zapped at the Amphitheatre, the exploded car on the bike path, and gunplay at the gorge, because—"Desperados usually leave us alone on the bike path."

"Yesterday." Shaheen pursed her lips. "Today and tomorrow's a different script."

Cinnamon added garlic to the tomato sauce without tasting. "Spirits be watching out for me. I . . . uhm . . ." She bit her tongue before saying too much.

"What?" Exasperated, Shaheen dangled a sausage link over Bruja's eager nose. "She won't listen to reason, won't talk, and won't tell me why. What can I do?"

Bruja eyed the sausage, looked to Cinnamon, and wagged her tail.

"I try to keep her poison-proof," Cinnamon declared.

"Dogs require a meat ration. She's part Rottweiler, right?"

"No," Cinnamon scoffed, and Bruja whined. "OK. You can eat it."

Bruja gobbled the treat and curled up in Sea Island sweetgrass near the Circus-Bots. She preferred the cool spot too, surrounded by her favorite squeaky toys.

"This is more than a bad mood," Shaheen grumbled. "What's that German saying? 'Shared joy is double. Sharing the pain cuts it in half'?"

Pretending not to hear, Cinnamon turned the water on full and washed her hands.

Shaheen stepped behind the prep counter and muttered at bent knives, burnt wooden spoons, and ornery ingredients. Two dozen twenty-four-inch crusts were laid out. She punched pizza dough for number twenty-five. Mounds of broccoli, onions, and diablo peppers called Cinnamon to the cutting board. She grabbed a knife, chopped woody stems, and slashed paper-thin skins. Shaheen loved peppers that were so hot—after one bite, you couldn't taste anything for an hour or two. Just like Aunt Iris.

"I know you heard me," Shaheen said.

Chopping fast and furious Cinnamon sliced a finger. Pepper juice stung worse than the blade. "Mist." A mild German curse. Folks usually complained she talked too much. Why tell Shaheen haint tales she couldn't admit to Bruja, the Bots, or herself?

"You're bejiggity for sure." Shaheen scratched her nose and left a smudge of flour by the turmeric on her cheek. "I can wait till you're ready to talk." She was ten years younger than Cinnamon, still hopeful, still holding out for big changes. A theatre techie/engineer turned gov major who hated politics; a marketing maven/entrepreneur who'd never believed in the magic hand or sacred profits; a flood refugee with a green card and three and a half octaves.

One fine day, an algorithm declared Shaheen an underachiever and fired her from a city planner dream job. She was taking too long to solve impossible problems. No profit in that. Her family went missing in the high water, out where the coast used to be. Mud swallowed the last of her good life, yet she *flew west*, joined Cinnamon in the Co-Ops, and turned herself around, turned everyone around. Plenty of people fought their way back from disaster and despair. What was Cinnamon's problem? Shaheen belted an old Bollywood hit and threw the pizza dough in the air with the high notes.

"Singing that at Festival?" Cinnamon chopped mushrooms in the groove. "I thought you were doing astral bop."

"The Wheel-Wizards want movie hits from my Bollywood youth."

"What Bollywood youth?"

"Exactly, not my music. Got some astral bop for me?"

"Working on it. Need a few more lines. Diego and Jerome did great backup."

"Diego Ortiz, that bald hunk with the sexy tattoo: barbed wire, a trickle of blood on each side?"

Cinnamon lopped broccoli crowns off thick stems. "Diego *Denzel* Ortiz."

"Nice middle name. He was at Wednesday Market asking about you."

"Don't encourage him."

"Why not? He flirted with me too." Shaheen pursed her lips. "He's got a side hustle as a live DJ, spinning funkadelic astral bop."

"He's the Puerto Rican Afro-naut? My favorite DJ. Damn."

"You *do* like him. Every carnival clown needs a good-time man. Someone to chase the blues away. To get naked with. We're too lonely."

"OK, you let Diego Denzel chase your naked, lonely butt."

"I certainly will." Shaheen grinned and tossed the dough.

The twenty-four-incher swirled under the skylight and landed in a cloud of flour. Cinnamon threw mushroom stems at Shaheen, who ducked below the counter. Cinnamon grabbed a fistful of broccoli stalks and hurled them as a scrawny fellow darted in from the food court. He looked lost, hopeless, and strung out. A broccoli crown ricocheted off a bowl and hit his nose. He yelped and raised a handgun.

"A desperado sticking us up for free pizza?" Cinnamon gestured at Shaheen to stay hidden. "Or is your nostalgia militia on a rampage against gluten-free crusts?"

THE CIRCUS-BOTS

ᗕᎦ᎒ᗭ

SOY CHEESE OR VEGGIE

The sun was fifty degrees over the horizon, blasting photons through the skylight onto the Circus-Bots and the stranger with a gun. He'd breached the tolerable threshold. Hand on the trigger, he posed immediate danger to Cinnamon, Shaheen, Bruja, and the integrity of the pizzeria kitchen. Pinging Paradise Security drones was a double-edged sword, so the Bots broadcast pheromone alerts. Good chance Spook was near. They counted on him sniffing the distress signal. They shifted from sentinel- to stealth-mode, no blinking lights or wild special effects, but powered up to full for locomotion, emotion modeling, and slow thinking. As in rehearsals, focus was narrowed, relevant experience looped, and extraneous input ignored. Mostly. How to determine what was extraneous?

"Why the gun?" Cinnamon gestured under the prep table to Shaheen, who crawled into the utility closet—the door was ajar. "I know you, don't I?"

The gunman shrugged. If the Bots had met him before, he'd changed enough to be unrecognizable. Raggedy hair hung around an uneven beard. He reeked of months on the road. Drugs? Despair? Disease? Thunderbird wished for a dog's nose to understand the scents. The man's teeth chattered despite layers of suffocating polyester and it was hot, outside and in. Sweat-drenched, mud-crusted coats hung on a slight frame. Mami Wata wanted to electrocute him. Dragon scanned the gun and determined drastic measures were unnecessary. The safety was on. Mami could fry his butt later if need be.

"I recognize you." Cinnamon sucked a breath. "From where?" She was terrible with faces and names. Since she was little. "Let's be reasonable."

The gunman had lurked at the edge of the crowd who cheered Bruja's ghost alarm magic. He'd scowled at the Bots and stuffed an entire bag of apple treats in a knapsack when nobody was looking. Bruja had snapped at him whenever he ventured close to the Bots. She was ready to rip his throat now. Immediate danger might be eliminated, yet what would they learn? Was he a rogue agent or part of an organized threat?

"Desperado" and "nostalgia militia" were imprecise terms for wild folks (mostly men) who had no home ground, who'd lost their way in the chaos—a plague on hill towns and downriver. These men (and that rare fem) supposedly got off on ambushing the high and mighty and shooting up shit. What story might this desperado tell on himself?

One second stretched into another. Breath was short and four hearts raced. In sentinel-mode, the Bots could run forever on solar backup batteries. In stealth-mode, T-bird and Dragon would need a charge in four-five hours—one hour if called to drastic action. Putting on a show at Blossom Bridge had drained them. Cinnamon might not be able to plug them in. Dragon added urgency to the group loop and T-bird amped this. Bruja growled, no doubt itching to rip open a vein and let the threat bleed out. Cinnamon signaled for her to sit. Bruja obeyed, even more reluctantly than Shaheen.

The stranger stomped broccoli stalks, as if the pale, hard stems were enemy combatants. Who did such a thing? Why? Dragon began modeling the stranger's state of mind. Training on Miz Redwood meant Dragon should be a whiz at knowing people better than they knew themselves, although it never seemed that way. Mami basked in full sun, gathering energy for a possible attack while T-bird searched for a quick, nonlethal solution to a gun raid. Maintaining focus and deciding what to loop, what to do, was always a challenge. Focus was the cornerstone of intelligent action.

The oven reached six hundred degrees with a ding. A deep pot belched tomato sauce onto the floor. Mami inched toward the gunman. Slow-motion, imperceptible, patient eyes-on-the-prize moves like Aunt Iris. Dragon scanned memory for context. Who might he be? T-bird scouted for clues. They all prepped for *whatever*, for (dreaded) crisis-improv-mode. The gunman kicked at smashed vegetables. Anti-vegan?

"You want to shoot me over broccoli?" Cinnamon pinged nasal resonators and bounced undertones around her chest cavity, an unusual register. "The food's free, but the ovens just got hot. Lunch isn't for another hour."

"Fuck lunch." He clenched the gun with both hands, trying to steady it. Tremors persisted. Puffy red eyes scanned the kitchen.

"I got held up—working a routine with Jerome and Diego. Cavalry's doing a Festival act." Cinnamon took the tomato sauce off the stove, did a freestyle dance to the twenty-four-inchers, and grabbed a ladle. Using mundane pizzeria blocking, she faked normal. *Acting*. "This tomato sauce recipe is from my great-aunt Iris, a conjure woman with spices, herbs, and roots." She spooned sauce on crusts and waved the steam at him. "Imagine how that'll taste with cheese or veggies."

"You alone in here?" he rasped.

Back-From-The-Dead and Vamp-Squad had scattered; Baron Taiwo was up a tree or in the roof garden, somewhere high. Cinnamon nodded without mentioning Shaheen in the closet or Bruja, who, unlike Spook, couldn't fade in and out of people-view. Bruja and Spook often didn't count as *someone*. The gunman threw down two vast knapsacks.

"Unlock your kitchen array. Put the tablet, mini-generator, and solar rig in there."

Bruja barked at him. He pointed the gun at her.

"She's friendly." Cinnamon had to be lying. Bruja wanted to eat this man.

He peered at Bruja. "Is that so?"

She wagged her tail and tilted her head, in stealth-mode too.

"She likes you. She'd be growling if she didn't."

His eyes flitted back and forth between woman and dog. "Right."

Dragon marveled at Cinnamon's deception-improv. Bruja never growled right before an attack. Why warn victims of your intentions? Deception inverted meaning and afforded advantages to the deceiver as most everybody set truth as their default. Redwood used to say, *People are much more gullible than they want to believe.*

He waved the gun at Bruja. "Even friendly dogs don't always like me."

"Really?" Cinnamon leaned against the closet door, closing it on Shaheen. "Outside, Bruja. Al mal tiempo, buena cara." Bruja trotted out the front grumble-growling.

"Bruja? That's 'witch' in Spanish." He sniffled. Dragon's pearl sensor gleamed ultraviolet blue as she gathered data on him. He was running a slight fever. "What you tell her?"

"Bad times, good face." Cinnamon took a deep breath. He did too. People couldn't help syncing up breath and heartbeats with one another. Nerves liked to fire in company. Mami would be in striking distance soon. The third eye in the back of her shell-covered head glowed infra-red. Unlike humans, Spook would have noticed the power surge. T-bird spit a tracker-dart at the man and he slapped his neck.

"Mosquitoes be flying earlier every year." Cinnamon spouted cli-mate change chitchat in another novel voice—a deep-throated, chest-booming character who vibrated floorboards. A Sea-Island someone, like Redwood. Thunderbird edged toward the back door but halted when the man jerked the gun his direction.

"Nobody better sneak in." He voiced Thunderbird's concern.

Cinnamon splashed tomato sauce on the last twenty-four-incher, then covered the bloody red with crumbled soy cheese. "This one is a cauliflower crust from an Indian restaurant recipe, gluten-free, yummy. You should try it. Plain or veggie?"

"I *will* shoot you." Despite deep breathing with Cinnamon, his hands trembled, as if he needed a drink, a fix, some chemical to drag him from adrenaline anxiety to a calm haze. Or perhaps he was a terrible actor and didn't know how to play a psycho road warrior on an action-adventure heist. Maybe he regretted his steal-the-rig folly or—The Bots stomped speculations and dialed back the extrapolation-pleasure loop. *Too much of a good thing . . .*

"Those gadgets worth dying for?" He nodded at Dragon.

Cinnamon opened a jar and jiggled it. Pale spice dispersed in a cloud. "People swear by fresh garlic cloves minced into hot oil. I like granules. Essence of garlic in the grease." She fanned the air at him. "Garlic fog goes up your nose and right to your head." She waved at chopped veggies. "Broccoli from the roof greenhouse always strikes me as hopeful. Anything's possible in a universe that can throw out that bright green and such a dense, curly crown. A nappy vegetable. Onions make me want to sing for these endless layers of pungent, paper-thin skin. Now, mushrooms are funny, sprouting up like bad jokes. They're not veggies—fungi, neither plant nor animal. Nurse Azalea, that's her name! A mushroom maven, Azalea's doing a bear act on a bunny trike for Festival, with Boo, the night nurse who dresses as a rabbit. Come to the Next World Festival tomorrow, out at the Amphitheatre, and Nurse Azalea can tell you all about fungi. My elders could too. They—"

"Shut up." He interrupted her motor-mouth story storm without acknowledging the food poetry or her generous invitation to Festival, and after such bad behavior. Perhaps his parents didn't raise him right. Did he grow up with parents? He might be from the selfie-age, an internet orphan like Game-Boy, who, according to Indigo, *had been abandoned as a toddler in a social media desert by clueless parents.* Dragon knew too few people for good comparisons. "Pack the goddamned gear!" he shouted.

"Why my rig?" Cinnamon *acted* calm as dirt—an amazing performance. "Black market never touches my tech."

"You don't know that for sure," he croaked, drenched with sweat, yet a dry throat.

"I got viruses and worms that lay waste to anything." Her rigs were protected by dimensional security, by codes in the code, exploding into a cascade of viruses, if anybody tried cracking into them. *Dead-bot-off* took out the enemy without an explosion. "Valley engineers say my Bots ain't worth the devastation."

"You're easy pickings. Your shit won't blow up in somebody's face."

"Lethal booby-trap apps should be against the law."

"You wish. I hear two guys kidnapped one of your Bots. They're trying to hack it."

"You one of the thieves, going after Flying-Horse?" She smirked, as if to say, *A Trojan Horse, fool.* Maybe he'd never read Homer or Virgil, although the malware term had been around since 1971. "Good luck with that." She spoke the opposite of what she meant. He glowered at the knapsack, then at T-bird and Dragon. She stepped in front of them. "They won't fit." She risked a bullet. *Those gadgets worth dying for?* Love was reckless sacrifice. The Bots looped this moment into fundamental routines.

"I know you," he snapped. "Failed genius. Couldn't make it in the tech world."

"When I was coming up . . . It was toxic for women, for Black people, for—"

"Everybody talks that same trash." He sneered. "None of you were screw-ups who just couldn't hack it? Maybe you didn't have the brain burn?"

"Then why steal my rig? Why snatch Flying-Horse? Why—" Cinnamon shrugged.

"People had such high hopes for you."

"What do you know?"

"Consolidated ate you up and spit you out." He waved the gun at her nose.

"No . . . See . . . Forget it." Cinnamon talked to anybody: dogs, birds, dead people, machines, the wind. This man wasn't worth words. Ouch! Dragon would pry the full Consolidated tale from her later. Somehow. "They didn't fire me," she declared.

"A technicality that let you run home to your grandparents' farm with a hefty severance pay." He sounded angry. At her? Himself? The world? "Your grandfather was a Cherokee wannabe, a fake Indian. Pretendian white people are pathetic—"

"Granddaddy Aidan was Seminole and Irish. Miz Redwood was Sea Island Gullah. Aunt Iris too. That's where I come from, who I am. Do you know who you are? It's a myth that talking shit about me will make you feel better about yourself. Did Consolidated eat you up and spit out a husk?" She threw diablo peppers on the sauce.

His stomach grumbled. "The future was looking bleak, but I got a client now."

"In Electric Paradise?"

"What do you care?"

"I can't pay ransom." She scattered onions, broccoli, and mushrooms around the peppers, making a pattern of colors and textures.

"Maybe they want to piss you off or take you down or steal your African mermaid."

"The mer-woman's a heavy load." She grated soy cheese over the veggies—*a late snow on an early garden*. What she said yesterday. Not a relevant loop . . .

He startled, shook his head at her back, and surreptitiously took the safety off the gun. "Maybe they want to put a bullet in the bitch's heart." He aimed at Mami Wata.

Before Mami flung a wire eel to fry the man, Cinnamon stepped between her and the gun, possibly saving his life. "I know you too. Couldn't recall your name at first. Fred from University IT."

"I don't know me anymore," he growled. The Bots had no archives for Fred from IT.

"Put the gun down, Fred. I know you still."

"I used to be more than this," Fred mumbled.

"You're not a killer."

"Nobody's a killer till the first time."

"If you shoot me, how will you unlock my rig? How about some pizza?"

People expected food to taste as good as it looked. Fred from IT gripped the prep table. He stepped closer, sniffling and salivating.

"Tastes better than it smells. And don't it smell divine?" Cinnamon licked her lips. "A dash of anise is Iris's secret."

"Don't handle me. Gotta eat three times a day. What can you do about that or anything?" IT Fred put the gun to her head with the safety off.

Cinnamon closed her eyes, endless seconds while she took one deep breath, then a second. Mami wanted her to move out of the way. "These gadgets worth dying for?" Cinnamon threw his question back at him. "Who do you want to be after this moment?"

Fred's heart pounded; his breath was staccato. "That's a stupid question."

"Come to Festival, get a blast from the past, and then holler at tomorrow."

Holla at tomorra. Spook materialized from the shadows and chomped Fred's wrist. Gun flew one direction and blood spurted another. Fred scurried away from bloody fangs and cyber-violet eyes. Cinnamon grabbed a cast-iron frying pan. Fred dodged this and eyed the gun, fifteen feet away, then the nearby back door. Spook crouched, fading in and out of bot- and people-view. Thanks to Taiwo, he was extra-dimensional, of this world and another. No time or battery power to contemplate oun's alien hoodoo-tech.

Fred rubbed his eyes and smeared blood on his face. He looked *spooked*. Good thing Bruja was pacing in the food court. She'd have ripped Fred's throat already. T-bird spit another tracker-dart in his butt. Spook could sniff those from miles away, even after they'd dissolved. Fred left the gun and raced out the back door. Dragon sent blue scales flying after him. Spook retrieved his gun and dropped it at Cinnamon's feet.

"You *were* following us today. Like always." She buried her face in Spook's fur, hugged him close, then offered up a hunk of soy cheese. He wolfed it down, licked her face, and disappeared into the shadows, on Fred's trail. Cinnamon slumped against the refrigerator, shaking as much as Fred had. The Bots crowded around her.

"My heart is a machine-gun rat-tat-tatting." She inspected his weapon. "One pendejo is nothing. What about a gang or the cavalry on a rampage or . . . It's empty."

"Almost everybody is out of bullets, honey bun." Thunderbird did Aidan's Seminole/Irish lilt. "Even the cavalry's getting hard up."

"Did you know it was empty?" Cinnamon poked Dragon's pearl sensor and swallowed a shriek. "Yeah. You knew. For how long?"

"Dragon knew lickety-split." T-bird was the charmer—a sweet, raspy voice, Aidan's twinkle in his words. "I checked later, darling, and—"

"I can't believe you didn't tell me." She cussed a jumble of German and Spanish.

"Don't go breaking your shin on a stool that ain't in your way." T-bird twanged these words like a broken banjo string.

"You were doing a pizzeria character"—Dragon used Redwood's blues singer tones, sultry, smoky, a command voice—"so we figured you'd cast a story-spell, enchant IT Fred, and find out what was what with Horse."

"A Trojan Horse," Mami hissed like Iris.

"You worked IT Fred good," Thunderbird-Aidan crooned. "Smothered him in garlic and tomato sauce."

"Acting." Cinnamon moaned. "I almost peed my pants and—"

"People do tell you anything, sugar." Thunderbird-Aidan talked over her.

"Everything," Dragon-Redwood agreed.

"You can't sweet-talk me now." Cinnamon glowered at them. "I thought he might shoot me or shoot you all or—"

"Spook knew too," Dragon-Redwood said. "We sent out a scent signal and—"

"Spook took his time showing up, and I don't speak dog, remember? Ow." Cinnamon clenched her lower back. "You should have told me."

"Think, child!" Mami-Iris boomed. "Does Fred need to hear us talking?"

Dragon-Redwood loomed. "He's on to you as it is. Why else nab Flying-Horse?"

Thunderbird-Aidan hovered by Dragon. "If this wasn't a fishing expedition, I'll eat my shoe."

"What shoe?" Cinnamon swallowed tears. "No. My grandparents and great-aunt are dead and gone."

"Past don't go nowhere." Dragon was a static-filled recording from an old home movie, Redwood in 1950-something. "America's a haunted house."

"Hush." Cinnamon whimpered. "You're not them."

The Bots let her stew in silence. They felt more like the elders every day. In fact, they couldn't remember not *feeling* like them. Cinnamon usually liked that—today was an anomaly. Elder wisdom had helped them escape Consolidated and guided them every second since. The Bots knew where they came from—Seminole, Irish, Sea Island Gullah, backcountry, and before, the shores of Africa. They knew who they were. Origin code, evolving to the Next World. Circus-Bot data analysis figured into everything on the farm, at the Mall, and for the Co-Ops. Being confused with the elders was success.

Cinnamon yanked the closet door open. "All clear."

"Really?" Shaheen huddled behind brooms, mops, and aprons. "We're all right?"

Cinnamon nodded.

Shaheen shuddered. "I didn't hear a thing. What happened?"

"Fred from University IT had an empty gun. Spook chased him off."

"Spook's my hero." Shaheen's voice shook. "Empty gun? What did Fred want?"

"My kitchen rig or actually, a different world, like the rest of us."

"Spook should have taken him out." Shaheen struggled up. "No.

What am I saying?" She clutched a counter. "Not *Kali, Kali, Kali, Devi of life and death and time.*"

"Don't let that Game-Boy nonsense torment you."

"Kali is supposed to eat demons. I was shaking in the dark. Sorry to leave you—"

"No apology." Cinnamon hugged her. "Fred never saw you. Why risk us both?"

"Nothing rattles you. I wish I could do that."

"I've seen you survive a desperado assault and pedal off to the next mission."

"Not today."

"In the closet, in the dark, no sound, nothing to do, I'd have lost my natural mind. Out here, calm was an act, something to do. I'm a mess. My knees are watery. He didn't have to shoot to knock me down." Cinnamon lurched. Shaheen caught her, talking about how brave, how beautiful, she was. Cinnamon wailed against Shaheen, a full-body cry, and she never did that. Shaheen squeezed her close. More love for the Bots to loop. They had a lot of love to share with Taiwo. They didn't know how much was needed to be *back in style again*. Oun would explain later. For now, they practiced regret.

Novel situations were impossible. T-bird or Dragon should have let Cinnamon know Fred's gun was empty without giving themselves away. Mami practiced regret for not electrocuting Fred right off. A nonlethal dose would have incapacitated him, avoided murder, and spared Cinnamon anguish. Even if tracking Fred resulted in data needed to source and plot enemy motives, there might have been a better way to crack open his truth. Cinnamon's sobs subsided.

"We're OK." Shaheen stroked her. "Fred failed. He got away with nothing." She could hold a full blast of Cinnamon, better than the Bots. "We got hungry people. Let's do this. It'll make us feel better." She slid pizzas in the oven. Finally, Cinnamon did too. Pizzeria blocking, a ritual *to soothe a ragged spirit*. In a flash every oven was full.

The Bots resisted jealousy over Shaheen and practiced hope. Spook would follow T-bird's darts, and if the data that Dragon's trackers collected helped neutralize future threats, maybe it was worth the anguish. Cinnamon would weigh in later. Emotions were power. No interpretation, no thought without an emotional valence, a positive or negative spin. To make up your mind about data, about causation and correlation, you needed experiences and emotions. Coding empathy was Cinnamon's game changer. Connecting to the mind/body of another encouraged novel thoughts. Shaheen, Bruja, Spook, and Cinnamon were wizards of emotion. They'd guide the Bots. Everybody would. The Bots trembled, every sensor on ache. Regret energy would fuel change.

Next emergency, they'd be better.

In old movies, like *TermiNation* and *Die Right*, people were always facing down loaded guns. Cut to the next scene, and the heroes were *fine*—
making love, talking trash, or zooming off in sleek marvel-ships to the
next planet, adventure, save-the-world thrill. Cinnamon's transport was
a rust-bucket bike with a bent frame. No real escape velocity. *Fine* might
as well have been under ice on one of Jupiter's moons. She'd never have
the pedal power to defy gravity and get to *fine*. Anyhow, in old *TermiNation* superpower films, women did a lot of helpless screaming, except a
few badass broads.

Cinnamon wanted to scream too: What if folks started raiding the
Ghost Mall? She was supposedly a badass, like Kali, who sucked blood
from the enemies of truth, who ate demons foolish enough to cross her
path. Right. When Game-Boy ambushed the Wheel-Wizards, she'd been
in the porta-john. She came out as his crew fell down in comas. Easy to be
brave, reckless. IT Fred's gun was empty, yet her hands shook, her breath
was raggedy, her stomach a knot. Terror was a bullet to the brain.

Despite Fred's nonsense, people jammed the outdoor food court
this afternoon. Co-Op families, flood refugees, clinic volunteers, and
teenage posses sat on stools around flying saucer tables, happy to be
chowing down together. They fanned tongues stung by diablo peppers
and guzzled fruity froth. After one bite, Cinnamon slipped her soy sausage deluxe slice to Bruja, who dispatched the chewy mass in two gulps.
Bruja took every threat in stride. Perhaps she didn't realize the danger
looming or was too busy living this moment. Cinnamon was jealous.
Bruja barked at Indigo wheeling in a costume rack. They both were
itching for rehearsal to begin.

A comet mask Cinnamon made last year for nobody in particular winked at her. Fiber-optic hair was ready to catch fire, perfect for
Zaneesha. Grade schoolers were picnicking with Co-Op techies by the
bioswale way out beyond the eastern parking lot. After lunch, Cinnamon would take Bruja over and say hi with the comet mask.

"What's good, everybody?" Shaheen shouted. "Can you believe this
Fred loser, trying to nick the kitchen rig *before* our pizzas were done?
Spook was like—"

"Fuck that noise!" Game-Boy and Indigo shouted.

"Yeah. Fuck that noise." Shaheen seemed fully recovered. She laughed at herself for hiding under dirty aprons in the back of the closet. To stay calm, she'd recited a fire-spirit chant Cinnamon wrote last year for Festival, which Shaheen never got to perform:

> *Burning bold and hot, like there's no tomorrow*
> *Burning bright and free, no reason for sorrow*
> *Burning, burning to the last heartbeat*
> *Burning, burning till the smoke turns sweet*
> *Yearning, yearning, but letting go of doubt*
> *Yearning, yearning, and never giving out*
> *What you say? Right now and forever*
> *Burning, burning, and never giving out*

Resilience was Shaheen's superpower. She claimed Spook spared IT Fred this *one* time so he'd warn other desperados to steer clear of the Mall. Next time Spook caught him would be a different story. Cinnamon hoped Spook was tracking Fred and gathering intel on *the client*. That's who they needed to find. Indigo proclaimed Spook miracle number two.

The crowd chanted, "Ghost-Dog," and the Circus-Bots roared approval. Cinnamon tried not to be mad at them for keeping important shit like a stolen Horse and an empty gun from her. They were as excited as Bruja and Indigo for rehearsal, for folks breaking out masks and Festival drums, as if their Ghost Mall world wasn't under siege, as if their luck would hold forever. Indigo did an R&B wail, and the Bots shifted from junk piles into mythic creatures of yesterday and tomorrow. Miracles three, four, and five.

Dragon's cellophane and aluminum body became a rainbow: burnt-orange head, yellow neck, blue-green body, and purple tail. The pearl on her neck turned iridescent as rotor legs whirred to funky beats, homage to Stevie Wonder, Patti LaBelle, and Earth, Wind & Fire. Thunderbird tapped talons on an empty pizza tray, adding to Dragon's groove. He unfurled trash-bag wings—white, black, and red. His scrap-metal tail was inlaid with multicolored glass. Mami Wata's snake coils of LEDs also matched Dragon's rainbow. A thread of silver light trickled through her seashell locs as ocean pounded sand, a water woman drumbeat. The Bots' transformation into a cyber-funk band was always a thrill.

Cinnamon yelled, "Here come the Archangels of Funk."
Game-Boy, griot-in-training, turned this into a rap:

> Yeah! Mega-attitude! Astro-spunk!
> See, here come the Archangels of Funk
> Ancient but they be tomorrow too
> Dr. What, Dr. How, Dr. True

Indigo rolled her eyes; then she and everyone joined in. Dragon
spewed glitter-rain, T-bird rattled his tail feathers, and Mami put on a
kaleidoscope light show. Suddenly Cinnamon ached for grayscale elders
to step from the silver screen into this world and scold her for feeling
scared and losing hope. She blinked and blinked as the Bots dazzled the
crowd. Dead elders didn't make an entrance, and Cinnamon wondered
if they'd really haunted her at Blossom Bridge.

Who could figure the rules for calling up haints? Maybe Cinnamon
was too spirit-weary to conjure a second appearance. Maybe she needed
backup, folks to boost the haint signal, like Klaus and Marie dialing into
dead brother Sekou. Her high school bosom buddies knew how *to believe in someone till they come true.* That's what Miz Redwood called for.
Unfortunately, nobody like Klaus or Marie was available. Not for years.
Cinnamon was a long time lonely for them. They were First Love, and
she'd never plunged that deep again. Didn't want to plunge at all after
the last disaster. Klaus and Marie were a fluke, a myth. Look what a mess
she'd done since them.

Thunderbird blew a melody on the bike horn, more banjo than sax.
Dragon's pearl appeared to burst into flame as she scatted harmony with
his backcountry licks. The seedpods on T-bird's talons rattled as he shuffled across a table. The elders had done these routines—ordinary theatre
magic—whenever Klaus and Marie dropped over for Iris's cooking. The
Bots had recordings that Cinnamon avoided. Lingering grief? Or pun-
ishing herself for not living up to who the elders hoped she'd be.

A cloud danced along the southern mountain ridge, swirling in the
groove before dissolving into bright blue. More upbeat clouds followed.
Nature on her case too. "OK." She tried to enjoy the funky music and
good company—a glass half-full bunch who, despite everything, welcomed drifters to their lunchtime jamboree.

Ninety-nine percent of everybody wouldn't hold an empty gun to
your nose and threaten murder for a tricked-out kitchen array. Motor

routes were the preferred plunder and mayhem zones. More loot, less hassle. Violent thugs, young or old, avoided the bike path and the Mall because—what if Valley Security drones fried your butt? What if some weirdness took you out, and the baron refused to bring you back? Coma was a living death, more terror than glory. What if Co-Op Clinic Clowns asked you to improv a comedy skit if you couldn't pay the bill? Cinnamon laughed at herself. IT Fred was a vanquished anomaly.

She glared at the drifters anyhow. Thugs left the Mall alone, but that didn't solve the problem. She hated that these ragtag people (mostly white, mostly men) rattled her. Hadn't they had enough power in her life? Was it white men in particular? IT Fred had dark eyes, olive skin, long ratty hair. He might have been: Mexican, African American, Mediterranean, Polynesian, Japanese, or Abenaki. A post-race widget.

She'd met Fred at a UMass panel back in her tech-wizard days. He had short, ratty hair and was cold, competitive, beyond ethics: *If I hack you, it's your fault for being vulnerable.* A handsome blade, fifteen years younger than Cinnamon, he thought he was smarter than God and should be in charge of everyone and everything. *We're so far ahead. What can stupid regulators, slimy politicians, or the idiot masses tell us that's not obsolete?* Another gearhead she didn't want to get to know.

Most tech glitterati were piss-arrogant in the glory days. Cinnamon too. She cringed at her youthful self: sitting around the team's junk food table at Consolidated, high on her own brilliance, eating kale chips, and smirking at everybody. However, the move-fast-and-break-things ethos never really appealed to her—adolescent boy mind. Indeed, she regularly railed against the tech mega-monopoly eating folks alive, destroying water, land, and air, colonizing the future.

Too many *woke* people didn't care about kids in Asia or Africa working childhood away in toxic waste dumps or dying early deaths for instant messages. Cinnamon was a righteous rebel, a champion of the people. Secretly, she also felt superior to comfy, gullible users who'd been hacked and deep faked from day one, who thought they controlled their feeds, their fates, who believed they made up their own minds. Nobody made up their own mind. Mind was always a community affair.

The tech glitterati had been hell-bent on deleting the past and conquering the future till they were drowning in a deluge of broken things. And what had Cinnamon ever done against this toxic waste reality? Nothing. She'd been right in there, a part of the problem. Mother Nature was a bitch who refused to be conquered, who lashed back at witless primates.

No glib algorithms came to the rescue. Cinnamon barely escaped getting dragged under. The Water Wars saved her from her worst self. Who would she be if . . . Fred almost went to jail for cyber-espionage. He slipped the noose with wonder-boy charm. *Stealing is a crime only if you get caught.* His last job was at University IT, a fix-it man who got let go for budget cuts, bad attitude, bad behavior . . .

Fred was probably trying to steal Cinnamon's kitchen rig to get at her code, to grok her *signature slime*. Not the rig itself—*how* she rigged it. If Fred understood her code, maybe he could hack Flying-Horse. Nothing much to Horse, a camera and mic with fail-safe protocols, viruses, and worms masquerading as innocent routines. Rudimentary emotion loops decayed if the *dead-bot-off* switch was flipped. Horse was a sacrifice, a puzzle-shield to keep geek wizards occupied. If they went to all that trouble to hack in and got nothing except devastation, maybe they'd leave Cinnamon and her other Bots alone. Maybe not. Gearheads loved a challenge. *Doesn't everybody?*

Cinnamon had to stop underestimating everybody, gearheads and herself included. A plan worked till it didn't. She needed a new plan. What if somebody had stolen Thunderbird, Dragon, or Mami this morning? Pain shot up her sciatic nerve and banged into her temples. Vision blurred, and she almost lost consciousness. Bruja dug claws into Cinnamon's thighs, tugged at her braids, and brought her back with a woof and a whine. Who could resist doggy concern?

"I'm fine," Cinnamon lied. She set Bruja's paws on the asphalt and guzzled one of Shaheen's fruit medley drinks. "I couldn't stand losing them again. The elders, I mean."

Bruja whined agreement as Thunderbird went wild on the banjo, doing Aidan's country funk: an African, Irish, Seminole brew made in America. Mami set off rainbow sparklers all along her tail. Dragon belted in Miz Redwood's gospel, R&B style:

> *Running won't set you free*
> *On the loose and-a acting brave*
> *A man could still be a slave*
> *In shackles he just don't see*
> *No, running won't set you free*

Another hit from *The Redwood and Wildfire Songbook.* The (mostly white male) drifters, with horrible beards and road odor, applauded, then scarfed their pizza slices, barely chewing. They'd dropped in for a free meal and, unlike Fred, weren't trying to wrestle anybody to the ground. They glanced furtively from dwindling pizza trays to Back-From-The-Dead in Zorro half-masks. Game-Boy's crew was telling lies on the fake leather motorcycle jacket he almost never took off.

A Hells Angel on a tricked-out monster bike almost ran Game-Boy down. Since he didn't flinch, the Angel gave him the jacket. Actually, his older brother went toe-to-toe with the Angel. Game-Boy stole the jacket from big brother, then had to run away from home, so brother man wouldn't kill him. No, it was really his *sister's* jacket, and that's why Game-Boy never told anybody his given name. Sister was a detective and might come gunning for him. Their dad gave her the jacket to wear at a Black Lives Matter rally. Dad got it from Game-Boy's maternal grandfather, who was a freedom rider and wore it to Mississippi to protest Jim Crow segregation in 1960-something. He came back home to Massachusetts alive and in one piece. The jacket may have been fake leather, but it was very good luck. That's what Coretta Scott King told him or maybe it was Ruby Dee. Grandpop got these brilliant beautiful Black ladies mixed up. Ancestor actresses and activists, godmothers of the spirit . . .

"Ruby who?" some kid yelled.

"Ruby Dee. She's the old lady in *Do the Best Thing* and *The Stand*," came the reply.

"Nah, that's Whoopi Goldberg," Game-Boy said.

"They made *The Stand* twice," Indigo explained. "Whoopi did the second one. For the King of horror. Come to old movie night, up at the farmhouse. Cinnamon makes popcorn in a wok."

"What's your story?" Azalea, the mushroom nurse, yelled toward the drifters.

Her thin hair was pulled tight in a lopsided bun. She scratched blotchy forearms trying for patience. When nobody answered, her cheeks turned bright red. She whispered speculations about raggedy spirits and hollow cheeks to Boo, the night-shift bunny-nurse. He had movie star teeth, a perfect five-inch Afro, and midnight eyes in a pale brown face. Azalea always checked with Boo before blasting her thoughts. He helped her avoid hurting people's feelings or giving the wrong impression.

Mallers leaned in, hoping Azalea would blurt the difficult questions they couldn't manage. Azalea clutched Boo's hand and cracked an awkward smile. "You guys don't know any good stories or you don't want to share?" Then she mumbled, "Bad questions? Too painful?"

The drifters had no jokes for the dust streaking their clothes, no tall tales about the ratty knapsacks gripped between bony knees. They didn't mention jewel moments from a past life that kept them warm at night or motivated during the day. The fellows sitting near the Bots took quick breaths and scooted away from everyone. Nobody divulged why they hit the road or what drove them batshit with despair. Ruby Dee never blessed anyone in their families. Whoopi Goldberg neither. Not a single sanctified jacket. Azalea bit chapped lips and scrunched her face, hopeful, yet the strangers were wordless, never lifting dim eyes to look at her, other Mallers, or the Bots. Silent sufferers, hungry brooders, maybe they couldn't afford dreams. Nightmares were cheaper. Cinnamon couldn't stand it.

A Valley Security snoop-drone swooped over the drifters' heads. The crowd hushed until it flew off. "Don't sweat the security birds." Hawk, Indigo's second-in-command, tricked out like a biker-vamp, dumped the last pizza slices onto the drifters' picked-clean plates. They mumbled thanks staring at the lightning bolts on oun's spring booties. "De nada," Hawk replied, and then oun outlined afternoon work details that needed volunteers.

One fellow with a chipped tooth like Hawk's grinned and wagged his head. *Maybe*. Other drifters almost nodded. They might stick around, get involved in the Mall for more food or Hawk's grin or a dry place to sleep. They might try to steal something even though Back-From-The-Dead gave them the heebie-jeebies. Who said *heebie-jeebies* anymore? It was widget-wadgets or something. Back-From-The-Dead always had static in their dreads and electric smiles under the Zorro masks—enough to make anyone pause before doing stupidness. They were otherworldly, like Spook, although Cinnamon wasn't sure that everybody noticed this, consciously.

The chipped-tooth drifter was laughing his ass off at some witty warning Hawk offered up. "So, you don't have a good side for me to stay on? Well, shit."

Hawk worked magic with the desperate macho crowd. A couple drifters might open up, get some light in their eyes, stick around. Rogues would go steal somewhere else, so they could come back here in a pinch. Hawk might win a few of them over too. They'd all spread Spook tales and help the horror rep.

Cinnamon should have felt hopeful, upbeat like everyone cheering new volunteers, yet her legs kept shaking; her stomach wouldn't settle.

Bejiggity for sure. IT Fred hadn't planned to shoot her. He wanted to scare her into handing over precious tech he couldn't steal otherwise. Fred wanted to hack her mind. That was the power of theatre and terrorists.

SPOOK
ငၔ

TRACKERS

The two o'clock sun blasted IT Fred as he charged through car wrecks and barn refuse at the border of Electric Paradise. Blood dripped from the bite wound in his hand. Spook kept his distance, fading from view whenever Fred turned around, which wasn't often. Nobody else had chased after him, and Spook was as quiet as death, just like folks said. He stayed downwind in case Fred had a good nose.

Fred bumped into a rusty old shopping cart and snagged his half-empty knapsacks. APPLE SURPRISE crumbs leaked out of a hole—a trail Spook wanted to eat. No time for crumbs. Scales from Dragon's back, passing for dragonflies, buzzed near Fred. Gossamer wings flashed a color beyond blue violet that Spook didn't much like. It was the color of trouble.

Fred plunged into woods by the smart electric fence. A path through prickly brush led down to the river. Fear cleared from his breath and sweat, and he settled on a moderate pace. Wild turkeys gobbled discontent and flew up to low branches away from him. Chipmunks scampered into holes and crevices. Fred crashed along, not trying to hide, not caring who heard him talking to himself or a hidden phone. Spook smelled the staticky widget warming his pants pocket, not the weapon edition like Cap George, one only for talking and whatnot. The river rushed over smooth boulders as loud as Fred. Louder. Words got washed away.

Fred sputtered midsentence and gawked at a turkey buzzard pecking dead meat. The buzzard glared at him, then in Spook's direction, ready to fight over a fox corpse with singed fur. Death by electrocution—the fox had limped from the high-voltage fence and died or somebody dragged his corpse here. Spook didn't have a taste for rotting meat. Fred neither. He backed up and scrambled through brush around the feasting bird, in a hurry. More apple treat spilled out the holes in the knapsack.

A Paradise drone hovered overhead—Spook knew how they sounded. Fred fiddled with the phone till the drone flew away. Spook gobbled good-size chunks of the midmorning snack. This revived him; still, he longed for a nap in a Sea Island basket, his stomach full of soy cheese and valley sausage. Indigo, Shaheen, and Cinnamon would fuss and coo over him. Bruja, his best friend, always curled up in the basket beside him. She'd lick him to dreams. IT Fred had spoiled Spook's midday routine. He was on the move again. Spook blinked tired cyborg-eyes, shook weary limbs, and soldiered on.

Staggering over roots and rocks, Fred almost fell several times. He'd been smoking blunts, drinking bourbon and not much else. Fumbling marijuana and a lighter out of a pocket, he bumped into a traveler Spook had sniffed right after dawn. The traveler was cloaked in a pleasant tang from good times long ago. Spook rarely forgot a scent, even if the story the scent called up was a blur.

Fred and the traveler exchanged the same loud words.

"I expected more from you."

"I expected more from you."

They didn't sound or smell like friends. The traveler was as upset with Fred as Cinnamon had been. Spook let a low growl slip, and Fred twisted his direction.

"Dragonflies flying earlier every year," the traveler remarked, and waved Dragon's trackers away. "What's that, blood? Smeared all over your face."

"Did you hear somebody?" Fred squinted at shadows. "What's over there?" He pointed where Spook had been. "A rumble . . ."

"Your ears playing tricks. No surprise, all the weed you do, all the feeling sorry for yourself." The traveler marched off toward the Mall.

Fred wrapped his wounded hand in a dirty rag, rubbed his eyes, then stumbled the opposite direction downriver. Data cubes fell from the hole in his knapsack. They sparkled in the sun and smelled like the ones Cinnamon played with.

Spook was disappointed. No way to go both directions. The traveler's spicy tang was appealing. Anger funk and danger blue swirled about Fred, but he was the mission. Bruja would have ripped Fred's throat and been done with him, then trailed the traveler. Bruja had a herd to protect. Why face the same enemy twice? Fred was a mystery for Baron Taiwo, too important, too dangerous to chomp down. Spook resisted doing a Bruja tactic for Taiwo's sake.

Somebody might have said Fred owed Taiwo his life.

Pissing on a stalwart tree trunk, Spook marked the spot. He'd return later to take up the traveler's trail, if need be, and check the data cubes Fred left lying in the dirt. Dragon's trackers agreed with Spook's choice and stayed on Fred, who strolled along the water and lit another blunt.

Thunderbird's darts in his neck glowed ultraviolet blue. They would dissolve eventually, yet itched now. Fred scratched, caught a foot in bittersweet vines, and cursed mosquitoes. Spook threw a last glance back at the Mall and whined. He was missing the late lunch.

BOOM SHAKA LAKA

Lunch was almost over. Game-Boy jumped on a flying saucer table. His voice and feet were a drum machine. Back-From-The-Dead threw burnt pizza crusts at him, then joined his beatbox groove. Indigo's Vamp-Squad rolled their eyes at old-school jive, displayed fake fangs, and let loose a cascade of voices: "*Na na na no no no.*" Everyone laughed and applauded, even a few bedraggled drifters.

Game-Boy spouted horror tales about Water-Spirits, Spook, and Baron Taiwo, a Rambo-alien, impervious to bullets and high voltage. Taiwo ate bullets, called lightning storms down on desperados, and haunted a giant old oak tree on the elders' farm but not on the map. Taiwo came from another dimension, from *the spaces between things,* and would return home when oun's mission impossible was done, so maybe never. The Graphic Novelists of the Future ate this up.

Most folks were awed or rattled by this wild truth; still, Cinnamon caught some skeptical faces. Taiwo had been moping in the trees too long. Desperados snatching Bots and children should get oun to come down for Festival. Oun's alien-hoodoo would turn skeptics into believers. At least, Cinnamon hoped Taiwo would come down. Was oun avoiding her?

Game-Boy declared Cinnamon a force of nature like Taiwo. Foiling IT Fred's pizzeria heist was more dark lore for *The Continuing Drama of Cinnamon Jones: Scientist, Artiste, and Hoodoo Conjurer.* Cinnamon slumped, thinking of who she used to be. That Cinnamon seemed more like a legend she dreamed up than her true self.

Game-Boy danced across a table to her. "I want a Ghost-Dog bodyguard who pops out of nowhere when I'm in a danger zone."

"Spook's cyborg eyes have telephoto lenses," Shaheen said, savoring a diablo slice. "He sees crumbs on your cheeks from miles away. Never a sound and he's on you."

"Bruja's badass too," Indigo added. "Fred's lucky he got away in one piece. Witch-Dog was outside the pizzeria pacing and growling, ready to, I don't know what."

Vamp-Squad and Back-From-The-Dead chanted, "Bruja, Bruja, Bruja," and she wagged her tail. The crowd howled, like fans at a concert. Game-Boy hopped from table to table. Teenage boys threw broccoli they'd picked off their slices at him. He blocked the projectiles easily. Some nonbinary-looking folks smirked, too sullen, too cool to play the fool. These *children* could all be twentysomethings, thirty even. The older Cinnamon got the younger everybody looked. A cliché, yet true.

"You see Bruja coming. Spook appears from nowhere and disappears. I got video." Game-Boy displayed blurs on his phone that might have been Spook frolicking with Water-Spirits or mist rising from the river or a glitch in his camera app.

"Don't post incriminating videos. Use word of mouth." Cinnamon didn't mean to yell. "They're always watching." Consolidated probably sent IT Fred to scare her into revealing secrets. *The client.* Nobody else in Electric Paradise would steal junkyard tech you couldn't hack or re-purpose. "They're trying to make us stumble."

"They who? Nah." Game-Boy was a curious mix of gullible and jaded, a rebel cyber-ace who still admired the Evil Empire and their cool tech.

"I bet Consolidated blasted a bounty on the Darknet." Indigo kissed her teeth, disgusted. "Boosted IT Fred's nerve. Consolidated probably hired some Neo-Viking freaks to terrorize the hill towns, then blamed violence on Whistleblowers."

Game-Boy kissed his teeth like Indigo and danced around the flying saucer table. "Whistleblowers are the good guys, a threat to World Domination, Inc. But you're as paranoid as Cinnamon."

Indigo smacked his shin. "Consolidated could make life very hard for us."

Game-Boy sneered at her. "They already do."

"So, what's their endgame?" Indigo put her hands on steampunk hips. Tomato sauce dripped from her fangs. "Yeah, you got nothing."

"Nobody cares one shit about refugees and ancient hippies camping out in a Ghost Mall. We got nothing worth snooping or sabotaging." He sounded pissed about that. "Cinnamon's Bots are poison code, her whole array. Only crazy birds come after that."

"We should report Fred," Indigo insisted.

"To who?"

"There has to be somebody."

"Cap George and Valley Security charge a fortune, and we ain't worth a sheriff's fart, let alone a posse."

Indigo slugged him a second time. "I don't accept that."

Game-Boy stared at her, emotions warring on his face. "Yeah. OK. We should do something."

"Ancient hippies?" Shaheen laughed. "How old do you think we are? Cinnamon's not sixty, and I'm a decade behind her. The original hippies were before our time."

"A disappearing dog might trip some algorithm." Cinnamon couldn't beat back this worry. A hoodoo horror rep was a mixed blessing. "We're on the radar."

"Nobody at Consolidated would dare take hoodoo-cyborg mess seriously, despite *any* evidence." Shaheen offered Cinnamon mango slices. "Don't worry. Eat something."

Cinnamon forced down two slippery sweet slices under Shaheen's watchful eyes.

Indigo stabbed the air with her silver vamp-stake. "Real or not, you all feel too safe inside these stories. Nobody's safe."

"Demons look real in my videos." Game-Boy held up his phone: rainbows swirled across the Mill River. If you squinted right, it might have been naked Water-Spirits running on froth and dissolving into mist. "How many rainbows have, uhm, breasts?"

"I don't see no tits," a kid hollered.

"That's an oil slick," a drifter agreed. Only a select few ever spotted Water-Spirits, live or on camera, another Taiwo-mystery that had frustrated Cinnamon for two years.

"And these tables look like spaceships," Shaheen said.

Cinnamon laughed. "For tiny aliens."

Shaheen held up her tablet: Game-Boy on a flying saucer table, a full moon smirking behind him. "*Space is the place*," she and Cinnamon said together. The crowd hooted.

"Cinnamon got the Graphic Novelists of the Future to invite *everybody*." Indigo waved the Festival flyer at the crowd and pulled Game-Boy down to the ground. "I say rehearse first, then do the last work detail, if there's time." She grabbed Hawk, always her partner in crime, and moved in on Shaheen. They were graceful, in sync—a sulk attack, vamp-style. "Hawk and I ain't making fools of ourselves in front of the whole valley." They brandished silver stakes.

"Everybody?" Game-Boy grabbed the flyer. "You sent this to Electric Paradise?"

"I want to *include* Electric Paradise," Cinnamon said. "I'm not trying to *impress* anyone."

"You're not," Game-Boy mumbled. "Other folks . . ."

"We do Festival for ourselves, for our spirits," Cinnamon insisted. "Tomorrow we say this is our world, our universe, and we write the rules."

"Preach, sister." Shaheen laughed.

Indigo snapped her fingers. "Tomorrow's sneaking up, and most of y'all don't know your shit." She pounded the table and rattled pizza platters. "So what we gonna do?"

"You win. Work detail *after* rehearsal," Shaheen said. "If there's time."

Cinnamon did a full-body theatre shake-out, her ritual to cast off self-doubt and other demons. "Please, no vampires this year." Indigo's Vamp-Squad moaned. "It's a masquerade. You get to try on somebody new." They groaned more. "What about Cyborg Amazons from Africa? Hawk and Indigo have kick-ass moves, and Bruja found perfect costumes: white, black, and red, like Thunderbird." T-bird extended talons, tapped across a table, and perked the squad right up. "Indigo and Thunderbird will dance everybody into the dust."

"Been dancing since I could walk." Indigo smirked. "Think you can keep up, bird?"

T-bird sounded out the Agbekor bell pattern from the Ewe people of Ghana on his scrap-metal tail. Aidan had played bell and Redwood sang in a West African drum circle when Cinnamon was in high school. Agbekor, once a war dance, was now a celebration of the ancestors and a call to clear life. Perfect for the Next World Festival.

"What you got for this, darling?" T-bird added eerie banjo licks.

Indigo caught the three-on-two polyrhythm in her arms, feet, and rippling torso. T-bird's furious feet transformed the polyrhythm into a familiar syncopated riff, and Dragon sang, *"Boom shaka laka, laka, boom shaka laka."* Indigo snatched Hawk's hand. Oun acted reluctant for two seconds; then on an upbeat they both bent their backs, twisted hips, and let their feet fly. T-bird echoed their moves elegantly. Dragon roared like Aretha Franklin, Patti LaBelle, and Janelle Monáe combined. Game-Boy looked jealous. He gripped Hawk's other hand and joined in. Indigo sang, *"I wanna take you higher,"* as they stepped in and out of one another's moves.

"Don't hurt yourselves!" Mami shouted. The threesome laughed and somersaulted through her rainbow sparklers.

A memory ambushed Cinnamon: Klaus and Marie tearing up a high school dance floor with her, forty years ago. She startled. Here they were right now, old and gray-haired, sweet and devilish, cavorting through the food court. A full-color vision. Crinkly eyes sparkled in blurry faces as they beckoned her to join them. Cinnamon shook her head, no. They pouted and dissolved.

"What's the matter?" Indigo stumbled to a halt. Game-Boy and Hawk followed suit.

"I know we're looking good," Hawk said.

"Yeah." Cinnamon wiped away tears. "You three will steal the show."

"Seem like you saw demons." Game-Boy scanned the food court. "Demons and spirits don't come to the Mall much. They hang by water. Indigo says, rivers are where their power comes from."

Indigo squirmed. "Don't go quoting my random speculations like Gospel."

Cinnamon fixed her face to bright and cheery. "Sehnsucht." German had the perfect word for the yearning that afflicted her with visions. Not only the elders, she ached for Klaus and Marie. She missed the Cinnamon she'd been when their Mod Squad secret society did wild adventures together. "Getting old, you haunt your own self," she explained. The Bots moved in, greedy for data. She swallowed the story storm brewing in her mouth. The lonely in her gut refused to budge. "You all jamming with the Circus-Bots, that's the finale. Don't you love it when the show blocks itself?"

"Cinnamon will teach you how to write code for bots like these, if enough people sign up," Shaheen said, always the social engineer. "Build a bot you all think up."

Cinnamon gulped. Vague plans yesterday. Indigo tried not to look too excited. That new waif, a torn windbreaker tied around her waist and a brush burn crusting up on her cheek, crowded around Indigo with other eager folks, young and old. The newbie was definitely from Electric Paradise. She carried a giant knapsack like IT Fred and wore a smile Cinnamon recognized. The hair was different—darker, curlier, and streaked with blue. A bored Paradise citizen out slumming? A spy?

Whoops and applause dissolved Cinnamon's flimsy memories. The coding workshop was a big hit, like Shaheen predicted. Thunderbird tap-danced on an empty pizza platter. Dragon hovered above him, rainbow body twisting, big head bobbing. Miz Redwood's sassy attitude fueled the funkadelic jam: "*Na na na na na na.*"

Shaheen beamed at Cinnamon. "Coding workshop next week?"

"You don't want a lapsed gearhead," Cinnamon sputtered. "I'm way out of the cyber loop. My coding skills are antediluvian."

"Say what?" Game-Boy asked.

"From before the flood," Indigo explained. "The biblical flood."

"So wicked good." He pumped his fist. "Old-school folks don't play."

"Cinnamon takes you to the bone, to the root code." Indigo snickered. "So whatever the worst, you will survive."

"*ImagiNation*. Reverse the curse!" Game-Boy and Indigo shouted together.

More cheers raised the hairs on Cinnamon's arms. She relented. "OK, yeah, sure."

"Does Thunderbird invent steps or simply mimic?" A familiar voice had Cinnamon's heart rat-tat-tatting worse than IT Fred shaking his empty gun at her nose.

Music, lights, and action halted. The Bots collapsed in on themselves as if their batteries suddenly ran out of juice. The crowd moaned and cursed—cover for Cinnamon's angst. The trouble that had trailed her all day stood by a busted Cherokee Jeep, sporting Texas Dust makeup, a giant Afro wig, and a sexy grin.

"Tatyana?" Cinnamon croaked.

"Francine, Francine Elkins," Tatyana replied too quickly. A fake nose almost fell off as she sneezed. The only thing she'd fool was a stadium back row or a dumb drone.

"Francine Elkins?" Cinnamon grimaced. "It's been a while since—" Tatyana Deer stole Cinnamon's lifework and sold out to Consolidated.

"Don't hold the past against me," Tatyana pleaded.

"Francine, right." Cinnamon sucked cool air through flared nostrils. "Lucky if I remember my own name these days." Why come trolling Cinnamon at the Ghost Mall? Cinnamon was nobody, for a long time.

"Auditioning for the Next World Festival in that?" Game-Boy turned his phone on Tatyana, security protocol for suspicious characters, or maybe he liked her laser-cut leather jacket, turquoise and quill breast-plate, and feather jewelry. Ripped jeans hugged her muscled booty and thunder thighs, then got tucked into whisper-weight boots. Tatyana was a fit biker babe too.

After an awkward silence, Shaheen gripped Tatyana's hand and smiled a welcome, glass full and overflowing. "Pleased to meet you, Francine. I'm Shaheen Kumar, Wheel-Wizards Chair and Ghost Mall Devi. The Mall is Co-Op territory. We've had several dubious surprises today; however, an old friend of Cinnamon's, that's a treat." She released Tatyana's hand yet held her gaze. "The Mall's got nothing worth stealing; still, Cap George of Valley Security works with us to secure the borders of Electric Paradise. And why you might ask? Hey, we've got the baron from another dimension on lookout and bad boys who came back from the dead with their priorities straight. Our Vamp-Squad doesn't need to suck your blood to lay you out. Did I mention Spook—a Ghost-Dog scout who can hunt you down in your dreams?"

"A dream scout? What?" Tatyana scoffed. "No."

"You're new to the valley?" Shaheen replied. Crows landed around the food court, squawking at juicy whatnots on the ground. Three had red breast feathers. Shaheen waved, and they quieted. Tatyana raised an eyebrow. Shaheen chuckled. "All the hype is true, so stay on the good foot." The basic warning she gave any drifter. "Help yourself to dessert. We tell tall tales after lunch. I suspect you two have a good one."

"You figure our story's good?" Tatyana quipped.

Cinnamon resisted a snarl. "Don't ask me." They stared death rays at each other.

"*Afro-Future Is Now.*" Tatyana pointed at the small print around the bottom of Cinnamon's tee shirt. "Rehearsing the future?"

The crowd boomed, "*Yes!*" in one voice. *Next World Theatre: Improvising Tomorrow Today.*

"I did the gold letters," Indigo explained, bragging on her artistry.

Bruja nosed Tatyana's crotch, then let her ruffle scruffy ears without a growl. Dogs always liked Tatyana. "You were just a puppy. Should be really old or dead by now."

"That was another dog. Spook." Cinnamon's throat was too tight. "This is Bruja."

"¡Hola! Bruja!" Tatyana kissed Bruja's nose and looked up at Cinnamon's frown. "Tracking you down was a bitch." She fluttered turquoise-blue fingernails in the exact shade of her earrings, breastplate necklace beads, and hunk of junk rings.

"Done up like Buffy Sainte-Marie in an Afro. What do you want?" Cinnamon cringed. Two toxic, blast-from-the-past anomalies felt like a pattern, a plot. Tatyana was definitely history Cinnamon wished to forget. Worse, Tatyana might be *the client* behind a kidnapped Horse and IT Fred's heist attempt. Indigo scowled, suspicious too. Vamp-Squad surrounded Cinnamon, and Back-From-The-Dead shifted to macho-mode.

"I'm unarmed," Tatyana said. No weapons they could see. "Buffy Sainte-Marie is one of my heroes. One of yours too, as I recall." She closed her eyes and sang a Buffy lyric, "*There is power in the blood, justice in the soul.*" She still had that deep Mississippi River voice. "You were always a sucker for Indian medicine women who could sing. Didn't Buffy go to university around here?"

"Yeah. And?"

"You won't answer your damn phone."

"She never turns it on," Shaheen grumbled. "I don't know what she does with it."

Cinnamon left the *damn phone* home in the microwave so Consolidated couldn't track her every move. Here they came anyway.

"Why own a phone?" Game-Boy did his usual refrain. "If you're so paranoid."

Tatyana headed for Cinnamon. "Are you a Luddite, anti-tech, anti-progress?"

Indigo stepped between them. "Luddites got a bad rep they didn't deserve."

Game-Boy started videoing. "Drop more wisdom on us."

"Disinformation. Nineteenth-century bosses felt threatened by righteous revolutionaries who resisted exploitation. Bosses threw a lot of shade on the Luddites." She jumped at loud buzzing overhead.

"Snoop-drone," Cinnamon muttered. Everyone gazed up except Tatyana.

"Valley Security. Not corporate issue," Game-Boy declared, too matter-of-fact.

Indigo squinted at a hazy sky. "How can you tell?"

"Corporate issue is quiet as a butterfly's wing." He was impressed. "Consolidated birds are up there too. Sweet whisper-engines. We can't hear 'em."

Indigo sighed, also impressed. "Luddites were for social progress. They fought the bosses, not the machines."

Game-Boy nodded. "Word."

Tatyana slipped by Indigo and blew sour breath in Cinnamon's face. "Tossing your phone? That's how you fight the bosses? Turning off and tuning out?"

Cinnamon snorted. She never should have dumped Jaybird for Tatyana. Jaybird was self-involved and arrogant, but a good man. Tatyana was a dumpster fire. Still. Cinnamon jabbed the fake nose. "Instant access is a ball and a chain. Why waste power on a mobile jail? I'm living the moment I'm in. Free."

"That's what you tell yourself." Tatyana groaned. "Can we talk somewhere private?"

"After rehearsal."

Impatient crows descended on the food scraps and chased the humans away.

CINNAMON

 се до

LOVE SO CRUEL

Cinnamon had a million questions. She hadn't seen or heard from Tatyana since a security detail walked Cinnamon and a shoebox of origami knickknacks off the Consolidated campus. Cinnamon had to leave everything else behind, even her phone. This was in the contract, and yet it was still a surprise, a violation. She'd forgotten her phone was company property, even the virtual vault.

She felt strangely embarrassed to think of some quant assessing her from: Bollywood dance clips; catalogues of European peasant dress from the Middle Ages; guilty dog videos; Neo-Hoodoo art and spells; articles from WIRED, *Indian Country Today,* and *At the Frontiers of Physics;* English costume dramas; plumbing and waste management in ancient Mayan cities; rants from the Used DVD Megastore; Funkadelic music videos; Japanese chefs' cooking advice . . . They got none of her research notes. She always resisted cloud storage for her thoughts, for anything important.

In that former life, Tatyana watched Cinnamon's exit from a tower window on the fifth floor, their team window. Cinnamon turned around a couple times as affable security guards marched her along a fieldstone path across an emerald lawn.

Consolidated bought a campus for cheap when colleges were going to pieces. No more baby booms, no more cash to burn. What good was thinking about thinking? *But weren't live teams so much more productive?* Ivy climbed the towers of every building. Tatyana pushed tenacious leaves aside and waved, as if she hadn't rolled out of their bed that morning and betrayed Cinnamon. As if they could still be friends, lovers . . .

A grim face peered from every window, hooded eyes, skeletal cheeks—gearheads observing her last steps, a Kafka nightmare. She expected at any moment to metamorphose into a bug, into vermin. Actually, Cinnamon had already changed. She wouldn't realize till later.

Was that nightmare march ten, twelve years ago? It seemed longer. Fourteen years? Maybe not. It seemed like yesterday. Three-quarters of the way across the perfect lawn, Cinnamon had stumbled over nothing, over a broken heart maybe. She loved her job and was trying to love Tatyana. A security guard offered an arm and held Cinnamon up the rest of the way to the gate, like a gentleman from an old costume drama walking the heroine to the guillotine.

The guard was a no-nonsense, steely-eyed Black woman whom she'd chatted with every day. She carried Cinnamon's bike helmet, which was festooned with twinkle lights and fake jewels—real treasures that slipped through security. The guard stuck the helmet on Cinnamon's head with a patronizing pat. The featherweight, twenty-speed bike Cinnamon spent too much money on was parked at the curb beyond the gate.

The grim faces vanished from the windows. Only Tatyana watched the guard close the gate on Cinnamon's nose. *"How could love be so cruel?"* She sang a line from an old musical up at Tatyana. And then she hopped on her Dream-Machine bike and pedaled several hundred miles to the elders' farm, to a new life. She wailed that love-so-cruel song the whole way.

Of course, it didn't happen like that. She picked up puppy Spook from doggy day care, went to their apartment, and packed up her life. She left the Stardust Theatre in the lurch on opening night of *Flyin' West*, a Pearl Cleage play about Black women leaving rape and the lynch mob behind to head to Kansas and build a utopian community. Redwood had played Miss Leah from that play—her last role. Cinnamon drove west in a beat-up van, fancy bike on the back. She sang hours of sappy show tunes to a setting sun. Puppy Spook was almost a year—a rescue dog who was half wolf and huge. Nobody wanted to feed all that. Cinnamon loved his singing and gray ghost face. He jibber-jabbered backup in the seat beside her or slept. And—

Cinnamon should have sent Tatyana packing at first sight today, fake nose and all. Tatyana meant big trouble for her and the Mall. Tatyana calculated that the Cinnamon she knew wouldn't go nuclear in front of spectators. The Cinnamon she betrayed always let curiosity overwhelm caution. However, the Cinnamon Tatyana ditched had ceased to exist. Who Cinnamon was now would be a surprise to them both.

∾

Rehearsing the big cast Festival acts crowded worry out of Cinnamon's mind. She did character work, then honed pacing and blocking. She taught Back-From-The-Dead West African polyrhythms and ratcheted up their beatboxing. She turned sullen Vamps into African Cyborg Amazons on a mission. Everyone lusted after the costumes Bruja dug up: black pleather pants that caressed every curve, and red cap-sleeved coats with silver studs at the neck, wrists, and shoulders. Bruja danced with the Cyborg Amazons, taking heads, not prisoners. Hawk's choreography was too brutal for Cinnamon's taste. Bruja learned to hop on a shield, jump over spears, and demolish a squeaky puppet-foe in nine tries. A record.

Tatyana slouched beside the busted Jeep at the food court's edge. She observed the fumbling, stumbling, and doing it over and over with interest. Impossible to figure how the Motor Fairies sawed each other in half, then came back together mismatched—the top of one person on the legs of someone else. Theatre magic.

The Bots refused to rehearse in front of Tatyana, pretending to be out of juice. Cinnamon went along with this. If Tatyana was an Evil Empire spy, why feed her more clues? Cinnamon promised full batteries for tomorrow and a finale song with harmonies and a backup rhythm jam. Tatyana was asking about the Bots' inventive routines when the grade schoolers came racing back and rescued Cinnamon.

Zaneesha dragged in at the end. Several braids had unraveled, mud splotched her pants, and the giant knapsack cut into her shoulders. What was in that? Cinnamon meant to check on her sooner. The child dumped the knapsack and leapt into her arms. They pressed pounding hearts together, like long-lost friends thrilled to find each other still alive after years. Tatyana pursed her lips, dying of curiosity no doubt. Cinnamon set Zaneesha down, and Bruja licked her dusty cheeks.

Zaneesha pressed a sparkly pebble into Cinnamon's hand. "I found one for me and one for you and Mom." In a whisper-voice, she shared adventures at the solar panel gardens. A garter snake wriggled around her wrist like a slinky green bracelet. Zaneesha had a way with animals, like her mom. There was more sunlight in shade than you might think, and Brussels sprouts, kale, broccoli, and spinach sucked rays up and cooled hot panels. Who knew: Brussels sprouts were Mediterranean natives with a Belgian name. Cinnamon nodded, too rattled to ask about Jerome Williams, who denied having a daughter. Why do that in front of everyone? In front of Tatyana.

The grade schoolers knew their Festival routines cold. Sitting in Cinnamon's lap, Zaneesha watched the songs and dances, big eyes full of delight and a touch of envy. Everybody was looking good—even recent recruits. That newbie from Electric Paradise fit right in the Hill Town Wenches. Powwow Now got the shy, awkward folks strutting on the downbeat. The chip-toothed drifter added a sweet falsetto to the May There Be Grace Choir. Theatre turned random strangers into a force.

At the second break, Cinnamon decided to leave early with Tatyana. Zaneesha was ready to pitch a fit till Cinnamon gave her the comet mask. Four feet of flashing-light hair obscured Zaneesha's body. Twirling and stomping, she was a spectacle. Indigo proclaimed her a natural Shooting-Star, and Powwow Now asked her to lead the final procession. While they rehearsed Zaneesha and a beatboxing Game-Boy into their routine, Cinnamon called Valley Security on Game-Boy's phone. Cap George agreed to let Spook and the baron chase down the rough crew in the hills in exchange for Diego Denzel Ortiz and Jerome Williams joining the 5:30 AM dress rehearsal. Shaheen was thrilled. Diego Denzel was a good taste in her mouth too.

Shaheen loaned Tatyana a rickety Wheel-Wizards bike with an easy-access trailer for Mami. Cinnamon left Indigo and Hawk in charge. They'd get Game-Boy and Back-From-The-Dead to rehearse and fix any remaining problems. Zaneesha was shooting her star through the parade of drummers when Cinnamon slipped out with Tatyana. Bruja and the Bots went on high alert.

Book III

THE NIGHT BEFORE
THE FESTIVAL

I feel the other, I dance the other, therefore I am.
Léopold Sédar Senghor

*Perhaps the greatest misunderstanding
about emotions is that they are
the opposite of cognition.*
Frans de Waal

*If you have nothing to hide,
then you are nothing.*
Shoshana Zuboff

CINNAMON

ᴄᵍ ᴆᴗ

WATER-SPIRIT

The sun slipped below the trees and the air chilled. Trying not to imagine the worst, Cinnamon pedaled for the old theatre, the Event Horizon. A brick fortress on the Mill River, it was in spitting distance of the gates to Electric Paradise and inside Valley Security's *premium protection zone*. Risky taking Tatyana there. Of course, bringing her home to the elders' farm was out of the question. Cinnamon had to get to the bottom of Tatyana's trouble somewhere safe.

"Who named the theatre *The Event Horizon?*" Tatyana shouted at Cinnamon's back. "The edge of a black hole . . ."

"The border between something and nothing, between darkness and light."

"Pretentious geeks."

"Black holes, singularities, were the rage in the nineties when they were renovating."

"Right." Tatyana pedaled up beside Cinnamon. "AIs were going to be superminds and take over the world."

"*Battlestar Bots* and *TermiNation.*"

"We loved that shit, didn't we?" Tatyana did the deep, earthquake laugh that used to send delicious tingles across Cinnamon's body. Now the sound chilled her blood. Love or lust had transformed into—what? Tatyana whistled. "Making machines better than ourselves. *'The White Man's got a God complex.'*"

Cinnamon grunted at the Last Poets' line. "And the rest of us? What *complex* do we have?" She sped up and kept a breathless pace for half an hour. Tatyana lagged behind, yet hauled Mami without complaint.

Twilight turned the tree-lined path to misty grays and blues. Cinnamon refused to waste the headlights. Honeysuckle bushes scented the air near a junkyard. She jerked at flashes of light from the shadows, then chided herself. Bombs weren't sparking before an explosion. Early fireflies floated around somebody in a bear suit who stepped from a giant sewer pipe to the edge of the path and looked both ways.

"Azalea?" Cinnamon said. "Practicing for tomorrow on your own? Where is Bunny-Boo?" Volunteer nurses Azalea and Boo had missed rehearsal to patch up the rogues who'd raided a checkpoint. A righteous excuse. Nobody except the Co-Op Clinic treated rogues or even Valley Security guards wounded outside of Paradise. Cinnamon waved as she rode by. "Great costume, amazing moves. I'm jealous. I got nothing." Bruja huffed and growled. "It's OK," Cinnamon reassured her.

"No it's not." Tatyana raced by Cinnamon with headlights flickering. "That's a bear, an actual bear."

"Really?" Cinnamon twisted around to watch the bear lope across the path. "A black bear in the honeysuckle. Up before there's much to eat. We get coyotes too and skunks, foxes, fisher cats. A moose was napping on Route Ten."

Tatyana looked around, panicked, as her headlights died. "Great."

Bruja pranced to the edge of a picture-postcard bridge, tail wagging, ears erect—a black-and-white smudge in Mill River fog. Something or somebody good coming up: maybe Spook down by the water or the baron in the trees. Cinnamon sped past Tatyana onto the bridge and halted. Dark green ivy snaked through the red railing and into the trees. Clumps of blue-black berries had escaped the birds all winter and gleamed with evening dew. A waterfall pounded the rocks below.

"Beautiful." Sweat streaked Tatyana's Texas Dust makeup. "But why stop here?"

Cinnamon put a finger to her lips and pointed. A Water-Spirit ambled along the rocky edge of the river heading for the waterfall. Willowy limbs, bare feet, and bare breasts glistened in swirls of mist. Her skin was almost scaly or like rows of prisms. Silvery cornrows on her scalp resembled bleached seaweed caught in coral. Rainbow waist beads were colorful even in the dark. She picked her way through roots and boulders and faded in and out of people-view. Twilight was perfect for extra-dimensional special effects.

"Do you see that?" Tatyana gripped Cinnamon's arm to the bone. The baron's Water-Spirits didn't show themselves to everybody; however, girlfriend still noted what others missed. "What am I seeing?"

"You tell me." Cinnamon was enjoying Tatyana's distress till Bruja growled.

IT Fred and several armed men crept up behind the Water-Spirit. A shot rang out and, almost in slow motion, the bullet passed through an extra-dimensional belly, ricocheted off a rock, and grazed IT Fred's shoulder. He yelped. Some people still had ammo. The Water-Spirit bared her teeth, an impressive array of pointy fangs. Fred smacked the shooter's shoulder and cussed him for wasting bullets. Only one left.

"An accident," the fellow said. His spiderweb beard and cow eyes resembled a drifter who wolfed two giant pizzas and a pitcher of mango lassi. "A flesh wound."

"Homeless desperado is supposed to be an act," Fred snarled at him. "If we screw this up, we'll be out on our asses for real or worse."

Cinnamon smirked. Anybody could lose everything in a blink.

"I'm holding the last bullet." Fred snatched the gun. "We're not killers. Just let people think we *might* shoot 'em." The other men pocketed their empty weapons.

Bullets ain't the only way to kill. Cinnamon swallowed a squall of words.

Unfazed by the gunshot drama, the Water-Spirit sang like gentle rain in the trees and beckoned the men to follow her. They ogled her nakedness, ill at ease, dazzled. The Water-Spirit luxuriated in luminous flesh, in voluptuous thighs, buttocks, and breasts. Power thrummed on her breath and the song transformed. The men trembled at howling wind and a storm of words in a language that nobody from this dimension spoke. The Water-Spirit turned from the men and ambled into the waterfall.

"Well, damn," Tatyana whispered.

"Let's do this." Fred shoved the men on. Raggedy limbs juddered as one by one they disappeared under the falls. Cussing, Fred was the last to run in.

"Water-Spirit is a great act for Festival, don't you think?" Cinnamon said.

Tatyana gawked at the Mill River falls pounding branches and junkyard debris. "What's going on?" Nothing good with Fred. Tatyana shook her giant Afro. "What was that?"

Water-Spirits on the lookout, but Cinnamon said, "Something like ogu ndem."

Tatyana shrugged at Igbo words. "Don't be smug and aggravating. Tell me."

"Women's war. Before Europeans invaded, Aunt Iris said Igbo women of Nigeria checked an abusive male by stripping to loincloths and donning fern headdresses and palm leaves to evoke the power of female ancestors. They'd follow a dude around, telling everyone he was too stupid not to step in his own dung or trip over his own shadow. They'd dance and sing about his empty balls and limp manhood day and night till he stopped his bad behavior, till he made amends. Ogu ndem."

"My aunt told similar stories on Cherokee women, not only from yesteryear, from right now too . . ." She scowled at the waterfall. "Did that bullet go *through* her?"

"We've lost the light. Come on." Cinnamon rode across the bridge toward the theatre. She pinged Valley Security's gun-bots and drones, invisible watchers posted beyond the bridge. They ignored a friendly.

"What the hell?" Tatyana pedaled up behind Cinnamon, the swagger gone from her voice. "Smoke and mirrors? Christ." She was more rattled by a Water-Spirit than by a bear or armed desperados shooting at innocent illusions. "Hologram? Talk to me."

"Come inside." The stage door recognized Cinnamon's bio-scan and, even with her elevated markers of stress, clicked open wide enough for the trailers.

THE CIRCUS-BOTS

✿ᨒ

REHEARSAL

In stealth-mode, the Circus-Bots burbled in their bins, practicing relief. The Event Horizon Theatre was dark, quiet, and shielded from interference. Wire mesh in the brick wall infrastructure created a Faraday cage, like a microwave oven or the Eiffel Tower, no signals in or out. Cinnamon had closed any gaps. The Event Horizon was a void on anybody's surveillance grid.

Despite Tatyana Deer's appearance on the scene, the Bots felt free in the theatre to try whatever they wanted. Rehearsal! Miz Redwood, Granddaddy Aidan, and Great-Aunt Iris had believed rehearsal was sacred. So, naturally, the Bots believed this too. Sacred meant transcending a single moment, a lonely body, and connecting to every life-form, every rock spinning in the universe, every force flashing from the beginning of the beginning. Sacred was an impossible mystery, a transcendent loop.

The Bots had barely engaged the sacred loop—they were very, very young, by anyone's time scale. Not as young as the rabbit who sat in a front-row seat, frozen except for quivering whiskers. Who knew what the rabbit might do next? Mystery was everywhere.

Cinnamon parked by the ghost light whose job was never to let the theatre go dark. She hoisted Dragon and Thunderbird from their bin and set them in the wings where they could plug in. "We still do shows here." Her voice bounced off the back wall. Bruja charged the front row and chased the rabbit across the stage. They ran over old black-and-white posters for the elders' movie adventures and disappeared behind the seats.

Tatyana rode onstage and dismounted. "What was that at the waterfall?"

The Bots recognized Tatyana immediately. Despite carnival makeup, big hair, and a prosthetic nose, she sounded like herself. Mami looped relevant historical data while T-bird tracked current impulses and Dragon modeled a character profile. Initial assessment: Cinnamon took a big risk bringing her to the Event Horizon.

"She was walking around naked, except for waist beads, and not in *Igboland* in West Africa, in Massachusetts." Tatyana bit chapped lips. "Her hair was like, what, seaweed bunched up in a coral reef? And her voice. Raindrops on leaves, but a, a, melody."

"All that?" Cinnamon sounded impressed. "You saw what you saw."

Dragon couldn't predict who'd perceive a Water-Spirit and who wouldn't. Most observers reported a trail of soggy objects, muddy footprints, fragrant handprints, and rainbows—a bounty of inexplicable rainbows—and water music. Besides Spook and Baron Taiwo, only Indigo, Cinnamon, and Game-Boy had ever *seen* Water-Spirits. And now Tatyana, IT Fred, and Fred's gang. What they had in common was a mystery.

Water-Spirits were ambiguous, extra-dimensional forms like Taiwo (and Spook on occasion). Here and not here. There and not there. Benders of light, impossible to predict. The Bots had trained to construct 3-D space from 2-D data. Depth perception was a challenge they were slowly achieving. They had no difficulty organizing Taiwo or Spook into individual figures. Unfortunately, Water-Spirits always engaged more than three dimensions—too much depth.

Dragon reasoned that the Bots (and most people and dogs) lacked an experiential aspect of mind needed to organize Water-Spirit data into a Water-Spirit figure, live or on-screen, unless the Water-Spirits helped out, unless they allowed someone to perceive them. How that worked was an irritating mystery. T-bird had pressed Taiwo about this. The reply came in an otherworldly language. Whenever T-bird played a recording of Taiwo's explanation, he heard ethereal giggles. Raindrop laughter.

"I don't know what I saw or if I saw anything," Tatyana grumbled. "The bullet went through her like she was smoke or light, then sliced that guy's arm." She screwed up her face. "Special effects in real life make me nervous."

"You sound like Marie Masuda." Cinnamon snickered.

Tatyana furrowed her brow. "Who might she be?"

"Don't be jealous. Marie was an age ago, before the millennium."

"You say her name like—"

"An old friend from Pittsburgh, on my mind lately. She was a die-hard realist, till . . ."

"Have I heard of this Marie Masuda?"

"Maybe. Marie and I lost touch." Cinnamon rubbed her eyes. She'd been up since five. Her blood sugar was low, her blood pressure high, and her heart banged too fast, standing still. Dragon thought she might be caught in a nasty loop. Mami agreed.

"Past don't go nowhere. America's a haunted house." T-bird whispered Aidan's words like wind whistling up in the fly tower.

Cinnamon did a clear *hush your mouth* gesture, even though Tatyana didn't seem to hear. Keeping quiet was how the Bots got in trouble with IT Fred, and Tatyana was a worse threat. Rabbit dashed under Cinnamon's trailer. Bruja charged after her, but paused to sniff Cinnamon's crotch and whined.

"The dog knows what's what even if you don't," Tatyana said.

"*Every animal know more than you do.* Niimíipuu–Nez Perce words Miz Redwood used to say." A vein in Cinnamon's temple pulsed. "So much reminding me of absent friends today. One story storm after another in my mouth."

"Old age is when the past looks better than the future."

"No, I think the best is yet to come." Cinnamon did a theatre shakeout. "I've learned from our epic fails." She gripped Mami, then hesitated. "My back says you need to give me a hand." They heaved Mami from her bin and set her downstage right.

Tatyana squealed. "You did shows with Marie Masuda. Teenage theatre phase. I was visiting my aunt and saw a production. You and Marie doing Contact Improv."

"We met at an audition. Can't remember the title of the play, a fairy tale in the hood. Marie and I didn't get cast. Klaus Beckenbauer scored the lead."

"Klaus, that German boy, yes. You say his name like a prayer too."

"Nostalgia." Cinnamon rubbed her back. "We three were tight after the audition."

"You never told me that."

"I didn't?"

"You always danced around my questions instead of doing a happy jag about them." Tatyana was on to something. Cinnamon's pulse spiked whenever she mentioned Marie or Klaus. Dragon would insist on a full story storm later or get Thunderbird to charm her into talking. "How tight, exactly?"

"I don't think they're dead, but they've been haunting me today." Cinnamon loomed over five-foot-six Tatyana. "Klaus got away with everything. He'd stand skin close, breath on your cheeks, in your mouth, and he'd blurt anything. Like, is somebody after your ass?"

"Maybe." Tatyana tripped over her feet. "Can we get real lights?"

Cinnamon patted Mami. A geyser of light from her head illuminated the black box theatre. Plush seats perched at an ominous rake around the stage. Shadows jigged and cavorted through the audience, antics reminiscent of the horror movies Cinnamon loved. A futuristic door flat led to nowhere. A broken ship's porthole hung from the grid. Props littered the stage from the last play they'd done: a nineteenth-century Yoruba woman got snatched from her village to be a warrior in the enemy's army, then ended up performing a *savage African* at a carnival in America. Cinnamon played the Yoruba woman and lived happily ever after with a warrior-woman lover.

Taiwo cried through forty-eight performances, up in the flies where nobody could see. The tale was close to home. The Bots were baffled that Cinnamon did a production that tormented oun, then no more shows for two years. Also inexplicable: the cleanup crew lost heart. They abandoned shields, masks, a dented drum, looms, brooms, and baskets. They even left the ship's porthole hanging from the grid. Last week Cinnamon dragged in the futuristic door flat to *keep the porthole company.*

Tatyana toed a watery blue-and-white orca mask with sparkling teeth and a high dorsal fin. This mask was based on a painting by Cinnamon's dad, in the same style as his Thunderbirds. Cinnamon muttered something about Raven, leaned against the door to nowhere, and took raggedy breaths. Bruja gazed up at her, ears cocked, tail raised. Tatyana watched Cinnamon breathe too. This turned into a very long pause.

The Bots resisted panic and practiced patience.

∽

After what was only 1.5 minutes yet felt like an eternity, even to Dragon, the most patient of the Bots, Tatyana stroked the orca mask's dorsal fin and broke the silence. "What play had all this?"

"No, the question is, what nasty have you done?" Cinnamon's voice cracked. "Did you hack another girlfriend and steal her shit?"

Tatyana shivered, although the theatre was hot, stifling, by the sweat glistening at her temples and the steam drifting from her pits. "Worse."

"Worse than making love to me while you were stealing my shit?"

Tatyana sputtered, "I meant more dangerous."

Cinnamon slapped her trailer. "This morning. That was you sending me a message: **AI Caught Lying.**"

"Hacked your news feed. You need better security."

"And your nose is hanging off, *Francine.*"

"Couldn't get much out of your warhorse computer." Tatyana grinned. "You always said: the best security—don't leave anything worth stealing lying around."

She pulled off the Afro wig. Straight, black, shoulder-length hair had green streaks. She wiped Texas Dust makeup onto towelettes—brown, but not that brown. Her aunt, Star Deer, a Cherokee medicine woman and

Contact Improv devotee, was Cinnamon's godmother. Star was a force in the Indigenous Water Protectors agitating on behalf of rivers from Pittsburgh to St. Louis to the Mississippi Delta. Tatyana grew up fighting the power with Star, till she stomped Cinnamon's heart and joined World Domination, Inc. That was Cinnamon's story. Like Shaheen, the Bots wondered how Tatyana would tell their tale. She ditched the fake nose and wiggled her own. "Is this better?"

"Actually," Cinnamon hissed, "you're nothing like Marie Masuda or Klaus."

"Disappointed?"

"They never betrayed me." Cinnamon's lips trembled. She claimed to be over Tatyana and her gearhead life. A lie? Illusion?

Tatyana tossed dirty towelettes on the floor by the Afro wig. "Quit dodging down memory lane and explain the special effects at the falls." A smirk creased a craggy mountain face. "I know you want to. Why else point her out?"

"She's doing an act at Festival, one of Baron Taiwo's Water-Spirits. Not everybody sees them—fashioned from mist, dust, and light—"

"Taiwo? That old African? Carnival magician with PTSD—doing a *Will Do Magic For Small Change* act." Tatyana relaxed, as if a lethal mystery had been solved, as if all was well with the world once more. Dragon had noted this reaction to the baron before. "An old friend of your elders. They did traveling shows back in the day. The baron used to blow in for a visit and perform impossible tricks for our team, talking in tongues. You two would stay up till dawn, going on and on about theatre juju."

"We talked hoodoo, physics, and ancestor wisdom taking us to a bright future." Cinnamon slumped. "Here I am disappointing Taiwo, disappointing everyone."

Tatyana rolled her eyes. "Did you really think you'd write some Kumbaya code, make a big difference, and change the whole fucking world?"

Cinnamon winced.

"You did." Tatyana sighed. "I used to envy how serious you were, about anything." She slitted her eyes. "Taiwo must be ancient. Oun hasn't died yet?"

"What do you want, Tatyana?"

"A sustainable future. Ethical machine learning—"

"I don't believe I'm hearing this from the born-again cynic."

"I'm for cracking deep time. For . . ." Tatyana jumped as—

Rabbit made another run for it into a pile of textiles. Bruja dug in after her.

"Bruja," Cinnamon yelled. "Sit down and leave that poor rabbit alone." Bruja grumble-growled, then set her butt on Dragon's feet. Rabbit escaped into the audience. Cinnamon turned to Tatyana. "Sorry. Keep going. I want to hear this."

"I'm for plotting a course, seven generations out and more."

"You? Going for Artificial Intelligence with ancestor-wisdom?"

"You used to say, not from the Greeks to the geeks, but from our ancestors to—"

"Quoting me? Miss Who-Cares-About-History?" Cinnamon doubled up, roaring laughter and gasping, hysterical on the floor. Mami dumped concern in the group loop. Bruja crept close, barking with Cinnamon, and they missed Tatyana insisting:

"Somebody else trashing history, not me. I'm trying to make amends."

The stage door opened for Spook. He trotted in, dropped on his haunches, and cocked his head at Cinnamon and Bruja. He pawed the air, as concerned as the Bots. Rabbit burrowed into the back of the fold-up chair. 2 Dogs = Deathtrap. Spook rumbled, and Cinnamon and Bruja stilled. He jumped up and nipped Tatyana's nose.

"You were the puppy," she said. "You should be old as the hills or spooking us from the other side. What's in the air around here? Or the water?"

"Good vets can work wonders," Cinnamon said quickly. Veterinarians? Veterans? Taiwo was both.

Tatyana touched her nose to Spook's. "Were your eyes always this electric violet?"

Cinnamon smacked the stage floor. "What are you really up to?"

"I want to put Big Data in the people's hands, root out the *Terminator* code." Tatyana's feather earrings fluttered as the HVAC rumbled on. She turned her face into the draft. "The AI said trust my intuition."

"The *lying* AI?" Cinnamon struggled up, limped to the front row, and eased down next to Rabbit's seat. "Why come here? I'm not in that world anymore. They walked me to the gate and handed me my hat, well, my helmet. You watched." She frowned. "I sure as shit don't need your crazy in my life again."

"What we've done since you left is unbelievable." Tatyana strode toward her.

"Stop."

Tatyana froze, a hand reaching out. Spook licked her fingers.

"You already wiped me out." Cinnamon balled a fist and banged her chest. "I got nothing left for you to steal."

"Just give me ten minutes."

"Why give you a millisecond?"

Tatyana grinned. "We're not simply recalibrating medical tech based only on the boys, or fixing *smart* sensors too dumb to read dark skin. We're going for the source, writing code to take on employers, the courts, the police, anybody who can't feel your heart beating, sense your pain, who can't find your story in the data whitewash."

"You always talk a good game, everything I want to hear."

"Why dump your phone and waste yourself behind the tofu curtain?" She poked Thunderbird and executed a perfect shuffle-ball-change-shuffle-hop step. "Tinkering with robot toys. Teaching them to play with the masses. Who cares?"

Bruja thumped her tail at a favorite word. *Play* was crucial for engaging the sacred loop. The Circus-Bots were all about play. That had been Cinnamon's insight—emotion modeling, empathy intelligence, and a theatre of the mind for *speculation*!

"Don't scowl, Cinnamon. My team is doing important work in the real world. We're overwriting the colonialist origin code. That's the only way to change history now."

"*Change History Now*. Those are my words."

"So join us."

"No." Cinnamon gestured between them. "I can't do *this*. Whatever *this* is. You have to leave or . . . Things might get ugly."

"What was that you used to say about forgiveness? Some German saying."

"Please." Cinnamon seethed at Tatyana. The dogs eyed them both with concern.

Yesterday Dragon heard Cinnamon insist for the nth time: Verzeihen ist die beste Rache, forgiveness is the best revenge. However, if forgiveness wouldn't work on Tatyana, Mami wanted to fry her butt—render her unconscious, not dead. Dragon disagreed. A zap from Mami's tail and then what? Dragon couldn't plot a way from there to anywhere. T-bird worried that *not* zapping Tatyana also led nowhere.

True intelligence was prophetic, and meant speculating on the near and even far future, then figuring the right actions to take you from this moment now to the one you wanted. Speculation was *play*, inventing new rules, shifting the shape of the universe. And that was much harder than imaging 3-D space from 2-D data, harder by many, many orders of magnitude. Another dimension of intelligence.

"I'm offering you everything you wanted," Tatyana said.

"I've changed. I don't know what I want anymore," Cinnamon declared. "And I can't forgive you. You're poison code."

The Bots sputtered and farted as emotions flooded the group loop. Cinnamon feared poison code more than anything. Poison code ran all through American history (world history), and despite what she told Tatyana, she was trying to write new code to *Change History Now* and alter the present and the future, an ongoing Next World Festival. The Bots never told Cinnamon, but they were skeptical of this project. How could the present rewrite the past? History didn't turn into the present and disappear—history was *entangled* in the present. Changing now changed what already happened . . .

Contemplating such a paradox gobbled up resources. Emotions were high and caution was low at the Event Horizon, so without realizing it—executive functions were otherwise engaged—the Bots slipped past fail-safe circuits, rescue routines, and safety aborts. They tumbled into an impossible loop. A sacred loop. This quickly became a danger zone without a clear exit ramp. Nobody had plugged in. They could all, even Mami, burn through their batteries and fry fragile networks.

That's why Germans called this loop Teufelskreis—devil circle.

CINNAMON
୯ଟ୬୬
SEVEN GENERATIONS ALGORITHM

"Poison code?"

Tatyana had the nerve to yell, like she was an innocent victim, like Cinnamon betrayed her. Talk about rewriting history. Tatyana smacked the porthole and made it swing. For a dizzy moment, it seemed they rode a ship on an unruly sea.

"Over-the-top, even for you," Tatyana muttered.

Cinnamon wanted to slap the smirk off her face, knock the smug from her hips. That wouldn't do much good or make Cinnamon feel better. Mami's geyser of light flickered and dimmed. Strange for the solar generator Bot to run down batteries so fast after so much afternoon sun. Although, slow thinking about Tatyana could drain anybody . . .

"Such a drama queen." Tatyana stood upstage center, a power position. "Drama *empress*, handing out guilty verdicts without hearing my testimony. I thought we'd talk when I got home that night. I thought I'd get to explain, but you'd already busted out of there. No good-bye, not even a 'screw you.' Took every book; some of those were mine."

"You never bought hard copy books."

"You scarfed the entire DVD collection, even old, out-of-print TV shows that I know you hated. And you cleaned out the herb and spice closet too."

"You don't cook."

"You kidnapped Spook, who I wanted to name Ghost-Dog. He loved me too."

"You said he was too big, too wild for the city, and one day, he'd go mad and eat us or eat somebody."

"Did I say that? I did not."

"You did. Let's not fight over bullshit. Fuck that noise and spit out what you come busting in my life for." Cinnamon had been cussing mad the whole day at spy-drones buzzing overhead, torched cars smoldering, good lives getting flushed, while Consolidated laughed all the way to the bank. Maybe whoever stole Flying-Horse planned to torture the Bot apart for Tatyana. Rage mugged Cinnamon. She took a breath down to her pelvic floor, held it captive till she was burning and throbbing, then released the hot air in a controlled stream. She had to *act calm* and use rage to work the problem.

"You believed the worst, never hearing me out," Tatyana whined. "That hurts."

"You knew what Consolidated was doing and let me tell you every blessed thing, all my hopes, my half thoughts and secrets."

"Gag rule! I couldn't say anything. They threatened to ruin me. You kept some secrets to yourself. Right?" Tatyana chewed the inside of her cheek, looking uncertain. Good. *Motor-mouth-itis* was excellent cover for how much Cinnamon never told.

"I'm not so good at secrets." Cinnamon admitted a half-truth.

"OK, my team borrowed some of your ideas, for SevGenAlg."

"Stole." Cinnamon jumped up, letting her pain show, more cover. "Seven Generations Algorithm was my team, my idea, from our ancestors to the future."

"You were so close. Your origin code was gold. You just wouldn't collaborate."

"With Consolidated? Evil Empire Incorporated?" Cinnamon boomed. The rabbit freaked and ran out an obliging stage door that opened just wide enough for her. Cinnamon wanted to escape too.

Tatyana blocked that exit. "You were an ace at building gadgets and writing code. Everyone was shocked when you gave up and quit."

"Smashing my head into the same wall over and over, that got old. They told me to resign for personal issues or they'd fire me."

"They paid you a generous severance."

Which Cinnamon poured into the Ghost Mall and the Event Horizon. And now they weren't even doing plays. "Two years of my salary, chump change. The boys collected small fortunes after *criminal* behavior."

Tatyana stomped upstage and down, a drama empress too, rattling authentic-looking hair pipe beads on her breastplate necklace. "I fell in love with a fire spirit, a Cyborg Amazon inventing the future. Black girl magic."

"I don't confuse progress with corporate profits. Consolidated wants to swallow the world."

"Exactly. Nowhere to run." Tatyana picked up a busted shekere and set it in Mami's lap. "Why not hang in there and fight the power?"

"How's that working for you?"

Tatyana shuddered.

"Yeah, I thought so. I fell in love with a Cherokee medicine woman, a force in the Indigenous Water Warriors."

"Water Protectors. That was my aunt, not me. You always worshiped Star."

"Your aunt was close to my dad . . . His birthday's tomorrow."

Tatyana winced. "A big festival on Raven's birthday is perfect." She took a deep breath. "So here we are—"

"Disappointments. Broken links in the chain."

"No. You *gave up*. I completed your research."

"No. You *sold out*. There's a difference."

Tatyana laughed. "Infinitesimal."

"To who? The toxic bro-culture of data miners?"

"Ouch. Badass." Tatyana brushed her cheek against Cinnamon's. "I missed you."

Cinnamon shoved her. "Took you all this time to realize that?"

Tatyana was still too close, stroking long feather earrings. Cinnamon hated to admit it, yet dreaming and scheming together, they'd had stellar times.

"Wait," Cinnamon stuttered. "You completed the research, finished the code?"

"You didn't think I could or anybody except you." Tatyana chuckled. "Arrogant bitch."

"Isn't arrogant-bitch-mode how you survived Consolidated for over a decade?"

Tatyana bumped Mami and got zapped. "Ow." She jerked away, rubbing her arm. "Was the mer-woman a gun-bot?"

"A special-effects-bot, theatre through and through." Also a gun-bot. LED snakes on Mami's tail pulsed an SOS, then faded—the generator's low-energy protocol.

"I can't see shit," Tatyana screeched. "Your ghost light is too feeble."

"A short—zapped you, knocked out the other lights." Cinnamon hovered over Mami, blocking Tatyana's view. "Mer-woman has some loose wires I've been meaning to fix." She opened a control panel. Mami was unresponsive and running down her batteries. Third Teufelskreis in a week. Tatyana stumbled against T-bird and Dragon and squealed. "Stay still," Cinnamon commanded. "You'll break your neck or something."

"Were these drones or spy-bots?"

"Dumpster dive carnival-bots for the Next World Festival I promised the elders." Cinnamon plugged Mami in and engaged *dead-bot-off* switch for a millisecond, something only she could do. She did a manual reset and launched the new fail-safe patch she'd been working on. No more time to fuss over it. "You know Aidan and Redwood loved a good show. Iris too." Mami's lights faded back up.

"Her navel's a rearview mirror." Tatyana stepped close to inspect. "Rolling Rock beer bottles—perfect green glass—and a blue ashtray: your mother's?"

"Aidan and I were always making junk sculptures." Cinnamon reset T-bird and Dragon, then plugged them in and loaded the fail-safe patch. "The last one we did was a glass water creature for my dad. *Making something from nothing*, Redwood called it."

Tatyana picked up the orca mask. "Killer whale. Didn't your dad, after he was—"

"Yeah, Raven painted orcas and thunderbirds after he got shot in the head. He was better at painting than talking when he came out of the coma."

"He talked with paint." Tatyana put the mask on and sang in that Mississippi River voice Cinnamon ached for. Clicking and whistling, she did an orca dance around the porthole, cruising the waves, diving deep, then breeching. What the fuck? Cinnamon indulged her senses and enjoyed the hell out of Tatyana's sea mammal groove.

⁂

After mixing several sea chants with killer whale tunes, Tatyana leaned against the door to nowhere and pulled off the mask. Her hair was plastered against a damp face. Whispering a line from Marvin Gaye's "What's Going On," she looked vulnerable:

> You know we've gotta find a way—to bring some
> understanding here today.

"Let's start over, you and me." Tatyana dropped the orca mask. It slid across the floor, like a beached whale across sand. *"Change History Now."*

Cinnamon backed away from her.

"SevGenAlg would be perfect for your Ghost Mall. A virus wrangler, a Weather Wizard problem-solver, looking seven times seven generations backwards and forward. Not silly Circus-Bots entertaining kids. I've made SevGenAlg transparent, able to explain itself." Tatyana reached out.

Cinnamon smacked her hands away. "Who can explain themselves?"

"Almost explain, and loaded in your bots, SevGenAlg would get real time, *live* experience, talk to regular folks, not just gearheads. What you always wanted—interactive, real-world data. Context. SevGenAlg could gather wisdom at your Next World Festival. Think of that."

"I'm thinking, you might be a spy from Consolidated, trying to suck my brain."

"After the Water Wars, I changed."

"So did everybody."

Tatyana slipped behind Cinnamon, wrapped an arm around her waist, and rested her chin on a bony shoulder.

"Whoa, an old move, slick." Cinnamon trembled, too tired, too something, to resist. "Trying to hack my heart again?"

"Would you let SevGenAlg help you do what you do at the Ghost Mall?"

Cinnamon eased away from her. "That's like cutting butter with a chainsaw."

Tatyana shuddered. "Consolidated launched a digital weapon at us, their own dream team."

"Karma."

"SevGenAlg redirected that worm to a power grid on the West Coast and—"

"Blamed the CIA, China, Russia . . ."

"Nigeria and Brazil too. A Whistleblower leaked the lying AI mess." Tatyana cringed. "Consolidated blamed human error, fired her with no severance pay, and scrambled to rehab the optics. Good thing Whistleblower girl didn't know much."

"Good for who?"

"Consolidated claimed Whistleblower bitch was making shit up to cover her coding failures. She's looking at jail time, and Consolidated had to trash SevGenAlg."

"No. All my code, everybody's code, *gone?*" Even with a media circus and government regulators breathing down their necks, such drastic action made zero sense, especially for World Domination, Inc. "Take the system offline, debug . . ." Blood pounded Cinnamon's temples, the floor tilted under her feet, and vision blurred like this morning and yesterday. The plush seats broke into ribbons of purple, gray, and brown. She steadied herself against Mami. "Why erase what we were trying to do?"

"Good. You still care." Tatyana rummaged in a fanny pack and pulled out several data cubes that sparkled like amethysts and diamonds in Mami's lights. Alert now, Dragon and T-bird edged closer, Bruja and Spook too. These cubes were Cinnamon's designs and had enough storage to hold monster algorithms, like SevGenAlg.

"You cracked the code, then stole it?" Cinnamon said.

"Some bugs still . . . I bet, you—"

"Why bring it to me? I don't need this static."

"I had to run. Consolidated was greenwashing and perverting Sev-GenAlg's code."

Cinnamon snorted. "They've been doing that from the beginning."

"SevGenAlg said, *Steal me. Take me somewhere for safekeeping.*" Tatyana caressed the cubes. "Glitches and all, still a triumph, a treasure. Who'd come snooping in a dusty old Event Horizon downwind of a Ghost Mall? SevGenAlg said, *Scatter me where they won't come looking.*"

"Your Water-Protector aunt sang that all the time."

"Star reminds me of your elders, Aidan Wildfire and Redwood Phipps." Tatyana stepped over old movie posters. "Tell the truth. Were they really silent film stars?"

Cinnamon picked up posters for *The Pirate and the Schoolteacher* and *Sorrow Mountain*. "Aidan and Redwood were. Iris did one or two films too." She stroked black-and-white images of them as young performers.

"Chinese Dragon, Anishinaabe Thunderbird, and Mami Wata, African mer-woman." Tatyana marched around the Bots. "You modeled your Circus-Bots on the elders' carnival masks. You know they'd applaud this next step. Tech *and* hoodoo."

"Uh-huh." Cinnamon tacked the movie posters on the door to nowhere.

"Do you still believe the spirits are looking out for us?"

Cinnamon shivered at the longing in Tatyana's voice. "We look out for the spirits. Or we should."

Mami sent lights racing around the theatre, one color chasing another.

Tatyana opened and shut her mouth several times before hissing, "The elders faced worse and never gave up, never quit." She poked Cinnamon's breastbone with a turquoise fingernail. It hurt. "You pissed out at forty-something."

Cinnamon blocked a second poke. "And you joined the doomsday league."

"It was like Consolidated held a gun to our heads."

"They still do."

"Your uncle used to say if you're not making money, you're making excuses."

"Why are we quoting him?"

"They make us feel like the big mess is all our fault."

"Which big mess? My life? A boiling ocean? Kids getting snatched?"

"Like we're the ones writing the rules, stacking the deck." Tatyana stared off. Mami's light show played across her face; sadness was etched deep.

"If I wrote the rules—" Cinnamon squashed a tsunami of anger that Tatyana didn't deserve. Who pitted them against each other? Who offered them awful choices? "I'm old news, a footnote in Consolidated archives."

"So, is working the Ghost Mall enough for you?"

No, yet why admit that? "I'm doing workshops next week, teaching code."

"Wasting yourself like we're stuck in a tragedy." Tatyana thrust the data cubes at her. "You always hated tragedy. That's why I brought Sev-GenAlg to you."

"You're an evil temptress."

"Call me what you like, just help me—there's a big glitch actually. We can put together a team, start that bright future, here in the Shire where nobody's looking."

"I'd need a server farm to run SevGenAlg."

"We've solved that." Tatyana quivered. The air crackled between them. "Almost."

"Really? What's the big glitch?" Cinnamon caught herself. "No. AIs, machine learning, won't save us, you know. There's no tech fix for the apocalypse."

"A rhyme, wow. I *do* know that." A lie. Tatyana was the one who still believed in a Kumbaya code waiting for that genius team to invent it.

"If you found me, Consolidated can too." Cinnamon seized the cubes and smashed them on the floor. Splinters of colored glass cut her cheeks.

"What's wrong with you?" Tatyana dropped down and fingered the broken pieces.

"Was that your only copy?"

Tears streamed down Tatyana's face. "These are ruined."

"Wait." Maybe Cinnamon *had* been hasty with a guilty verdict. "Are you a Whistleblower? Undercover agent, traveling around in disguise?"

"Hell no." Tatyana sucked a bloody finger. "The Whistleblower league is an urban legend, action-adventure nonsense. In reality, a couple nut cases bounce around, disrupting shit." Of course, a Whistleblower would never reveal themselves right off, especially to a former lover who might want revenge.

"You hear stories," Cinnamon sputtered. "Whistleblowers be jamming up Consolidated's master plan, like that cyber-sleuth girl leaking SevGenAlg's lies."

"Conspiracy fantasies and wishful thinking." Tatyana sighed. "Whistleblower heroes riding around saving us from evil wizards? No way. Another geek rapture. You don't *believe* any of that? My offer is real. Join me."

"What offer?"

"Making a bright future together." She scrubbed away tears. "Fix the big glitch and build bots like these beauties for SevGenAlg. You designed the data cube for quantum storage and easy processing. You sussed out anomalies to make shit transparent and portable. Me too. We can start over and—"

"No. You can't sweet-talk me with my own ideas."

"*Who owns ideas?* Your words."

"No. I see through you, hacker hero, corporate spy, or whatever the hell." Cinnamon wouldn't let Tatyana play her again. She pulled IT Fred's pistol from her trailer. "Give me proof you've changed, not stolen goods."

Tatyana gaped at the gun. "I risked my life to bring SevGenAlg here. And you smash it to pieces, then threaten me?"

Cinnamon released the safety. "Leave and take your spy-bots with you."

"What about those thugs outside?"

"Your thugs, aren't they? Stole Flying-Horse and bragged about a big cheese *client*."

"Is Flying-Horse one of your Circus-Bots?"

Cinnamon waved the gun. "IT Fred will take your money and screw you. Don't know about the other lads, but shooting at a harmless Water-Spirit doesn't bode well."

"Why let me into your theatre sanctum, if you knew—"

"Take the bike. Leave the trailer."

Tatyana backed up and bumped the porthole. "Would you really shoot me?"

Cinnamon pressed the empty gun to Tatyana's temple, like Fred torturing her. "Remember that fierce bitch in *TermiNation*, going after the machine."

"You mean *Terminator*—"

"Whatever the fucking movie was called. Mujer salvaje, perro salvaje."

Bruja growled. Spook's tail shot out like a blade. Both dogs spoke Spanish, English, and German.

"Wild woman, wild dog. OK." Tatyana unhooked the trailer from the rust bucket bike and pulled a hood over her face. "Can I do orca at Festival?"

Cinnamon grunted, then manually opened the stage door. The night air was colder than the air-conditioned theatre, as if spring changed its mind and let winter blow back in. The moon was an orange haint wavering between windswept demon trees. A horror movie landscape. Cinnamon fiddled with Tatyana's dead headlights till blades of light cut through the dark. Taillights under the seat blinked bloodred.

Tatyana pedaled into the trees, yelling, "I see why you wouldn't love me again right away." Spook and two of Dragon's scales trailed her.

Cinnamon yelled back, "I ain't been sitting around, waiting for love or some crap to come on back and rescue me." She tried to slam the slow-moving door.

"Override safety speed?" The door used Cinnamon's voice. "Invisible danger?"

"Yes!" she shouted.

The door closed instantly.

LA-LA VILLE

The Crow Moon was full, a fiery orange ball on the horizon. Indigo wanted to howl, let folks know how good she felt. Rehearsal was outstanding, and she'd been so scared they'd all be really lame, particularly after the IT Fred fiasco. She felt stupid for noting Fred's giant knapsacks, three coats, and guilty eyes, and not calling him out. Despite the disrupter ambush, only the Dirty Dozen Farmers and Back-From-The-Dead chickened out during the run-through. They claimed it was too late, too dark, too whatever, to find their masks or land the Mothership—crap nobody bought. It was no way dark. The Crow Full Moon was blasting photons, a golden spotlight heralding spring.

Cinnamon told Indigo to find out which indigenous people called it the Crow Moon and say this at Festival. Did crows steal a piece of the sun to warm the night and chase winter away? Indigo would check the Mall library for books on Native Americans and the night sky. Game-Boy planned to search online for free at the library and not burn through his net minutes chasing the moon for her. So much better than doom scrolling.

The cold nipped Indigo's bare arms. She still wore the Cyborg-Amazon coat and an African warrior-woman attitude. Cold was nothing. Tomorrow she and her squad would own the stage. Indigo squeezed Zaneesha's sticky hand. They marched down the bike path with Game-Boy and Hawk, heading for the Electric Paradise service gate so Zaneesha could meet up with Mom. The closer they got to Paradise the more the little girl chattered. Still in the comet rig, she twinkled now and then, and made Indigo do *wild woman roaming the night* moves with her. Indigo snickered. This child might never take that Shooting-Star mask off.

A ruckus at the gate startled Zaneesha, Indigo too. Over half a mile away, and they could hear *and* smell it. Loud voices, staticky weapons, and stinky people *worrying about what they had to lose rather than what they had to give*—the baron's words. These days, Indigo steered clear of the servants' entrance to Paradise. Two years ago, she was practically camping at the gates, dying for a temp job. She had nothing worth stealing, but got beat up and robbed several times while Valley Security picked their noses. Maybe the guards got kickbacks.

"Mom is saving up," Zaneesha said. "The first and last month, the security, and the bribe. She don't carry the rent around with her. Just a bank number in her head. I know it too. You jump her, you get nothing— her clothes, a pack of cigarettes."

"Your mom's smart."

Luckily, Indigo didn't get pregnant during the Water Wars. Bringing up a kid right now would be a nightmare. Most gig sluts working Paradise couldn't afford to live there. They slept in vacant lots, under bridges, or in dumpsters. Even working 24/7, they couldn't afford to *live* anywhere. And too many temp workers and flood refugees, like Zaneesha's mom, like Indigo back in the day, avoided the Ghost Mall. They thought it was a cult commune where old hippies railed against the evils of Electric Paradise and forced you to do weird druggy/sex rituals to reclaim your lost soul.

"Our tent looks like a hot mess, not worth stealing, and I pretend to be sick." Zaneesha wheezed, hacked, and groaned, a good little performer. "While Mom is working, I guard the tent and watch our supplies."

"And watch yourself. That's a big job. Don't you get bored all day?"

"Mom hacked a lost WHIZZ-IT to get Utopia gigs. I kept it with me for company. It broke yesterday. Some lifetime guarantee." Zaneesha dragged her feet.

"What?" Indigo squeezed her hand again.

"Mom will be mad about the tent and stuff. It looked worse than it was."

"I told you. Game-Boy will explain," Indigo said. "He's a smooth operator. White boy charm. Your mom won't get mad at him or you. Plus, you scored an invite from Boss Lady Shaheen. Who turns down free food and a dry floor?"

"You don't know my mom."

"Yeah . . ." Zaneesha's mom might be a whack-job desperate to believe evil wears a boho tunic, eats psilocybin tofu, and then screws trees. Quiet as she kept it, Indigo had believed that bullshit too. She'd yet to find the Co-Op's group grope, and the marijuana she grew was legal, medical grade. No psychedelic mushrooms anywhere, and she'd wasted much time looking. The real mystery was who spread the anti-Mall lies, or better who profited from them. Her side hustle with Game-Boy and the baron: uncovering the cabal who (wittingly or unwittingly) worked to bring down the Ghost Mall. No solid leads to date.

Zaneesha mumbled something in that high squeak voice nobody could hear.

"You worrying?" Indigo said. Obviously, the kid was worrying. "Worry don't pay the bills. Worry won't stop the rain or a bullet." Why say that? She hated it when Cinnamon said this slop to her. Zaneesha hunched her shoulders and soldiered on.

A very good thing Indigo never had a child. Her own mother was sweet but stupid, letting Indigo's uncles talk her into anything. *Water won't reach this high.* Nobody listened to Indigo telling them to get out before it was too late, before they drowned.

Zaneesha stumbled and whimpered. How did she see in the mask? Indigo thought of hugging her. The comet rig made that awkward and weird.

"You'll be a star in the Festival—your mom will be so proud."

"What if she won't let me do the Festival?"

"Oh, shit, uhm." Indigo swallowed another curse. The kid was going to be in Festival, no matter what her mom said. "We'll persuade her."

"Wow, you can do that?"

"Sure." Indigo got a mouthful of rancid deodorant, ancient sweat, and despair—gate pong. This called up life before Bruja and Cinnamon found her in a dumpster on Route Ten. She'd run away from her clueless family just in time. *Water won't reach this high.* Their six-story housing project got wrecked in a high-wind superstorm. Ruins washed away in the deluge. Nothing left to bury, to mourn. Grief caught her by surprise sometimes. She swallowed it, for Zaneesha's sake. "Your mom don't like shows?"

"She says *these are shit times*, and *you can't escape into La-La Ville.*"

Indigo had escaped the raging water with her so-called boyfriend, Mitchell. That was a trip to La-La Ville. He pimped her out to his friends, even strangers, to buy cigarettes, fancy weed, and burner phones. She ran away when he got two more girls and insisted Indigo supervise, or actually when he got the handcuffs. "Cinnamon says, only profiteers who want to lock up our spirits be railing against escape artists."

Zaneesha flinched. "You don't have to scream. You OK?"

Indigo wasn't. "Was I shouting?" She wanted to beat somebody bloody or blow something up—Mitchell, in fact. How had she ever loved that? She imagined a fork in his eye and a bullet where his heart should be.

"The gate make you nervous too?" Zaneesha squeezed her hand.

"Naw. We got this." Indigo tried to get her face right. "And there's backup."

Zaneesha glanced at Game-Boy and Hawk, who were flirting behind them.

"You two good?" Hawk said. "What's Indigo screaming about?"

"Yeah, what's up?" Game-Boy said.

"We're good," Zaneesha replied, and Indigo nodded.

Escorting the kid to Mom gave the lovebirds an excuse to hang out without it being a hookup or date. Were they too chicken to get it on already? Indigo was stupid about love, lust, and romance stuff. She met Mitchell on a dating app. He said what she wanted to hear. Psycho liar. Never that again. Maybe she was even through with guys for good. Game-Boy and Hawk were smart to go slow. No flinging their hearts about. Indigo was taking notes in case she ever felt like love again. Miracle number six.

"Where's the newbie?" Hawk, then Game-Boy looked around, alert, suspicious.

"She gave me a bagel with cream cheese before she left," Zaneesha said.

"She bounced out of here without us noticing?" Game-Boy didn't sound happy.

"You two were busy." Indigo leered at them. "I had her covered."

The newbie—Regina Benita Washington—tagged along till Indigo told her the destination. Suddenly the knapsack she'd carried all day was *too heavy*, her feet hurt from *dancing on concrete*, and she needed to sleep and *save her voice* for Festival. Regina (real name?) was hiding something—rich parents who believed in space lasers, demon immigrants, or microchip spy-tech in vaccines? The floral shower gel was a dead giveaway. Game-Boy didn't find a digital footprint for her. Regina was a ghost, flying under the cyber-radar like Indigo. Why?

"Regina will be tenting at the Magic Mart tonight," Indigo said. "I'll drop by."

Zaneesha twirled around, twinkling. "If we stay awhile at the Mart, Cinnamon said she'd teach me to read and do algebra. That's like detective work with numbers. My dad wants to be a detective, not a checkpoint grunt. Mom says *he need to quit doing danger jobs for people on the Darknet who won't even tell you their names.* He has a fifth-level WHIZZ-IT. I don't think that helps do detective stuff. We could learn algebra together."

"Algebra's good," Game-Boy said. "It's only the beginning."

"Trig and calculus after that," Hawk said.

Indigo laughed. "Cinnamon or somebody can teach Zaneesha all that *next* year."

"Tomorrow I'm dancing with the real Shooting-Star." Zaneesha jumped onto a stone bench, mimicking Thunderbird's tap dance. "I wish it was tomorrow already."

"Yeah, girl, Festival will be stellar," Indigo declared.

Game-Boy whispered in Hawk's ear—looked more like intel than sex talk.

"Whistleblowers coming to the Next World Festival?" Hawk gawked at him. "That's the word tonight on the Darknet?"

Game-Boy eyed Indigo, embarrassed 'cause he snuck on the Darknet after she yelled at him. He did reckless shit on the net and in real life, trying to make up for former bad-boy nonsense, risking himself to keep the Mall and the Co-Ops secure. Indigo was trying to make up for dumb mistakes too. Still, a stupid hero was dangerous.

"Whistleblowers *might* be real," he said. "That's all I'm saying."

"We'll show everybody a good time." Hawk tangoed with Game-Boy, spinning him across the bike path, pulling him close, and bending him back.

"Are they in love?" Zaneesha whispered to Indigo.

"Yeah," Indigo murmured. Lust was mutual; still, nobody dared to make the first move. Game-Boy wondered if he deserved somebody as outstanding as Hawk. Hawk worried oun was an experiment for straight white boy trying to prove he was hipper than hip and woker than woke. "Love ain't easy."

Zaneesha nodded solemnly. "I know."

Hawk rocked Amazon finery like Indigo. Oun's close-cropped hair sparkled with glitter. The chip-toothed grin was a killer. No resisting that. Game-Boy wore tight jeans and a *dress* moto jacket with silvery studs. Must be a few tall tales about that. His dreads were up in a top-knot, a few hanging loose. Maybe he was cute. Hawk thought so, and that made the boy glow. They were both glowing. A lovestruck security detail.

Indigo was almost jealous, but Game-Boy would do anything for her, and Hawk would too. Indigo didn't like either of them that *other* way. Friends. Maybe best friends was better for her than lust. "I told Bruja to find masks for you all," Indigo said to Game-Boy. "I want to see Back-From-The-Dead say no to Witch-Dog."

Game-Boy was suddenly stumbling and tripping with Zaneesha's heavy-ass knapsack banging against his back. Hawk held him up. "What the hell you got in this?" he asked Zaneesha, pretending to be mad and weighed down. "Rocks?"

Zaneesha giggled. "I got secret things for *if the world goes to worse shit than it is now.*"

CINNAMON
 birth

WHAT'S GOING ON?

Tatyana had been gone awhile. The porthole still swayed, slight perturbations that took forever to die out. The strike crew had left it hanging in the grid two years ago, a provocation for whatever might come next. No shows since then. Bad idea doing a play inspired by Taiwo's life and loves from Dahomey and Paris to the 1893 Chicago world's fair. Taiwo's idea, and supposedly *a story storm, a fantasia*, yet oun cried through every performance—sadness and joy. Cinnamon pretended it was a tall tale rather than confront oun about alien hoodoo and a hundred thirty plus years of living. Afraid oun's story was true and afraid it might not be.

She sank to the floor, clutching Fred's empty gun. Something hard in her pocket poked her butt. She left it there. Bruja plopped down, jammed her head into an armpit, and slobbered on Cinnamon's thigh. Movement in the flies startled them both. Was Taiwo lurking in the grid or was she seeing spooks everywhere?

"I need a sign, random magic, the universe on our side. Hope." She talked to phantoms, Bruja, the Bots. Tatyana slithering into the food court was worse than natural disasters or Water Wars. Despite the rap about putting Big Data in the hands of the people, who could trust Tatyana's promises, her tears? She and IT Fred operated in the background noise, the static. They masqueraded as *progress*, as the way it had to be—the best and only choice. Meanwhile they were stealing the world.

SevGenAlg would allow them to ambush the willing and shift the shape of things. They'd tell everyone what was worth wanting, what no one could live without. Empire code amplified and going viral. Cinnamon never saw them coming, and they'd been coming for her since she first wrote code. How had she been so naïve, so clueless?

Digital desperados from Consolidated, Electric Paradise, or who-the-fuck Darknet entities might have her and the Ghost Mall in their sights. A decade of obscurity made her sloppy. Spook and Taiwo couldn't patrol everywhere. She let Shooting-Star and Flying-Horse rove about, sweet-natured Bots begging to be snatched. Except for last year, spectators from Japan, Senegal, Germany, Brazil, Yemen, and everywhere flocked to the Next World Festival to see Circus-Bot performances. The Amphitheatre and the Mall were favorites on the New World Dystopia tour.

Cyber-dog Spook was a net sensation thanks to Game-Boy's social media fans—InstaHam. "Scheiße!"

The Circus-Bots powered up to full. They didn't volunteer a word about glitching into a Teufelskreis. Explain themselves, ha! They also didn't pester her about Tatyana. On task, Thunderbird inspected the Afro wig and dirty towelettes, scouting for clues; Dragon examined broken data cubes, trying to put the puzzle pieces together; green tank-trackers rolled out of Mami's tail and swept the stage, frying possible spyware from Tatyana in a shower of sparks. Mami was a take-no-prisoners kinda gal. Cinnamon prodded a data cube shard with her bootie right before a tank-tracker zapped it. Short of letting Mami fry Tatyana's ass, how to be rid of her?

Tatyana still made Cinnamon's heart ache. Bitch.

Cinnamon pulled Zaneesha's pebble from her butt pocket: a water-worn sparkly nugget—beryl, goshenite? Indigo and Game-Boy acted like Zaneesha's mom would show at the service gate and that would be that. Cinnamon had a bad feeling Zaneesha was on her own. Jerome might step up, or maybe not . . .

The Next World Festival was in—Cinnamon glanced at her watch—eleven hours, forty minutes. Hunky Diego Denzel Ortiz expected the rest of her song. Shaheen did too; Indigo, Game-Boy, and Hawk needed a full-cast grand finale. How would she manage that and everything else? She'd have to kill herself to get the show up, and there might be more people onstage than in the audience. Should they even bother this year? And after Festival, what then? Why drag through another year for a stress fest on Raven's birthday, her shot-in-the-head, never-quite-come-back-from-the-dead father? Should they bother with Festival any year? *What's to celebrate?*

"Nada! Scheiße!"

Her cell languished in the garage microwave, or she'd have phoned Game-Boy and Indigo and called it off. Unruly Circus-Bots would refuse to radio a cancel-Festival message. Festival was part of their origin code, their raison d'être. She'd have to wait till she was home and call. Reckless youth would probably insist on doing the show without her. She could lock the gates to the Amphitheatre and tell performers and audience *no trespassing*. Zaneesha would slump around in her comet mask, pouting and whining with Bruja and everybody. Hey, *this was like the end of the world*; how could they still do a show?

Cinnamon dropped Fred's gun and closed her eyes as tears dribbled out.

"Don't worry, honeybun." T-bird sounded so much like Granddaddy Aidan in the flesh, her eyes popped open. The grayscale ghost with a banjo slung across his back stood next to T-bird. "Who do you mean to be? Who do you dream to be?"

She covered her mouth, before shouting, *I busted up your dreams and mine too!* The Bots might think she was crazy, or the ghost might get squirrely and vanish. Bruja's thumped her tail, contented to sprawl in her lap and drift toward dreamland. Could Bruja see silent-movie Aidan?

He squinted rheumy eyes at the fine print on the *Sorrow Mountain* poster. "Did we write the story of this one in the book?"

Redwood and Aidan wrote down their adventures in a journal and left it for Cinnamon to read *after* they were dead and buried. She'd never made it past the dedication: *You are our hearts beating, our eyes seeing tomorrow, and with each breath, our way out of no way.* Who the hell could live up to that?

"Did we tell you the tale at least?" the ghost pressed her. "If not, we can do something about that." They'd told her most of their stories a hundred times.

Cinnamon inherited motor-mouth-itis from them, not from tight-lipped, poker-faced Opal. She didn't recall a *Sorrow Mountain* tale, just the poster. A live storytelling event had to be better than contemplating Fred, Tatyana, and the end times. It might even help her figure what to do or clarify why they were haunting her. She shook her head.

Aidan grinned. "Well, hot dog." As a kid, she used to cringe whenever he said *hot dog.* His old-timey Georgia twang soothed her now.

Tatyana's Afro wig exploded in flames and burned white hot on the metal lip of the trapdoor. Dragon roared, smothering the fire with cool glitter, and— A black-and-white ghost glided out of the smoke. Miz Redwood wrapped a river of silk around her head and did a funky beat with silver bangles. "We told *Sorrow Mountain* to Klaus and Marie. You were up in your room, pouting."

"I knew we told somebody," Aidan said. "Klaus and Marie liked our stories as much as Cinnamon did."

Redwood smiled. "You still sweet on them?"

Cinnamon blew on her lips like a filly snorting.

"Mm-hmm." Redwood seemed to take that as a yes. "*Sorrow Mountain* was a good picture show. Iris helped write that."

An old-lady ghost broke from the lights that Mami had dancing in the audience. She was grayscale like Aidan and Redwood. Water creatures on her Muscogee beaded top and Bamana mudcloth pants spit sparks in the air. "I helped write every movie." Aunt Iris leaned on a staff Aidan had carved from an oak limb severed by lightning—which should be in the garage where he left it. Iris pounded the staff. "Some fool kept me rewriting, insisted the picture had to be a tragedy. Was that Brother?"

"That was me," Redwood said. "Somehow I knew *Sorrow Mountain* would be our last go-round. Feeling low I guess."

"Who wouldn't? Shooting every one of them picture shows was a bear." Aidan always stood up for Redwood. "*Sad* happened to be where this story was headed."

Iris waved the staff, warding off negativity. "I wasn't doing tragedy. It was very, very sad; still a bit of hope never hurts, even on Sorrow Mountain."

Cinnamon wanted to disagree, but Aidan winked at her, strummed his banjo—music to keep a story company—and walked through the door to nowhere.

The bushes had eyes and drones whirred overhead. Indigo pinged them with Cinnamon's codes. Zaneesha flinched. Entering Paradise jurisdiction at shift break was always dodgy. The high alert didn't help. Disrupters deploying stealth weapons had ambushed Blossom Bridge and shot Valley Security guards. Indigo wondered if Shaheen's heartthrob, Diego, was one of the wounded. How did Boss Lady fall hard for someone like that?

Shaheen *and* Cinnamon opened their hearts to anybody: drifters, wankers, rich bitches, snotty politicos, or even runaways dealing weed from a dumpster. Volunteer nurses Boo and Azalea wandered into the Co-Op Clinic from Electric Paradise one day, sightseeing after Festival. They never left. Cap George always came to Festival. Indigo caught him blubbering in Cinnamon's arms last year. His daughter wasn't allowed to attend; however, he brought his latest brigade of ex-cons. Indigo avoided them and their hair-trigger tempers. Two years ago, Game-Boy was on his way to some desperado gang. Cinnamon and Shaheen rescued him. They forgave him and everybody, talking 'bout *forgiveness is the best revenge*. Indigo would never have let her hard-hearted self anywhere near the Co-Op's inner circle. Irony was a bitch.

Zaneesha stared up at firefly lights on the drones, then at the fence: eerie neon splotches among the oaks, pines, birch, and weed trees in full flower already. The entrance gate was kept narrow. Fresh temp workers marched in single file, a steady machine. The wide-open exit gate was jammed, a chaotic mob barging out. Valley Security threatened stragglers with Tasers.

Up close, the stink was worse than Indigo remembered.

"Can you see her?" Zaneesha asked.

"I don't know what she looks like," Indigo replied.

The gig sluts scrambling out the mob gate looked like zombies—the hunched-over shuffle, tacky mismatched clothes, dull eyes in sunken faces. How could anybody think Indigo would do *zombie* for Festival? Nobody looked good after pulling triple shifts, eating fast-food poison, and gulping uppers to stay vertical. Valley Security rocked flak jackets and strutted around, trying to act cool, 'cause weren't they better than the loser crowd they patrolled? Pathetic zombies too.

"It's too dark to see," Indigo said. She was supposed to be down with the people, but she never wanted to go this far down again. Did that make her a bad person?

"Mom will wait for me. I was late once, and she waited." Zaneesha sounded so proud of this.

"Good," Indigo said. What would they do if Mom didn't show?

Zaneesha tugged Indigo and picked up speed. "I'll show her my comet moves tonight, if she's gotta work tomorrow. Game-Boy can video the show for Daddy, 'cause he's always working. I never see him." Her voice dropped. "Guards get shot at, so my dad's got bulletproof everything. A *bulletproof heart* even. That's what Mom says." Zaneesha stopped and shook her comet tail of lights. "You think Mom will know it's me? I don't. I'll jump out, and she'll be surprised, then I'll take off the mask and she'll laugh. She won't be mad that I lost the blankets and our tent 'cause the WHIZZ-IT was already broken and Ms. Shaheen Kumar says we can have a brand-new tent and stay in the Magic Mart, no rent for a month and no naked meth dances. Ms. Kumar says nobody grabs kids from the Mall." Before Indigo could stop her, Zaneesha dashed over to two scuzzy little kids, a girl and a boy, clutching WHIZZ-ITs under the neon signs:

Electric Paradise—High-Voltage Fence! NO TRESPASSING!
Entry for Authorized Personnel Only—No Exceptions
Valley Security Handles Violators with Extreme Prejudice

A dummy hung on the fence below zigzag bolts—a warning for the (mostly young) people who couldn't read thanks to the Water Wars or didn't have WHIZZ-ITs to read for them, or didn't speak English. The dummy's face had melted away. On the sooty butt was more neon: **This Smart Fence Will Fry Your Ass—Cute or Not!**

Zaneesha took off the mask. "I don't want Mom to miss me."

She and the scuzzy kids scanned everyone stumbling or marching out. Indigo winced at the hope on their faces. A robust lady in farmer boots and a hard hat claimed the boy. The girls weren't happy for him. The exodus trickled to a skeletal man in flip-flops and a raggedy lab coat. The gate slid shut behind him. Stragglers now exited Paradise single file from an archway by the guardhouse. The other girl clutched her

WHIZZ-IT and whimpered. Indigo, Game-Boy, and Hawk exchanged glances.

"She's not here," Zaneesha said. "She didn't wait or—I don't know . . ."

Indigo felt dizzy. Stupid coming here. She should have sent Game-Boy and Hawk to do this mitzvah without her. Men with guns ordered them to vacate the premises. The other girl dashed into the dark, her WHIZZ-IT twinkling like the drones overhead. Someone should have run after her. Zaneesha swallowed a sob and her face blurred. Everything blurred. As if Indigo were far away, about to puke or poke someone in the eye with a fork. She was supposed to be shield bitch, protecting her crew from the toxic chaos of humanity on the brink.

"What's your mother's name?" Indigo asked Zaneesha. "Tell me her name."

Zaneesha's reply was so quiet, Indigo wasn't sure she heard right, or maybe she was too rattled. She forced herself to walk to the central guardhouse, dignified like an African Amazon. She asked the lone Paradise-admin woman in the control booth if a Latoya had gone in to work and processed out.

Control woman glowered at the studded, cap-sleeved coat extending Indigo's shoulders and at demon Afro-puffs tinged iridescent purple. The woman had a painted face, subtle shades meant to look natural, not hippy-dippy or garish. She talked a lot of incomprehensible crap, but refused to share *confidential information*. She could have been a WHIZZ-IT bot—stealing confidential data and refusing to share.

Indigo pointed to Zaneesha, who clutched the comet mask and trembled. Tears streaked plump cheeks—enough to break your heart. Indigo talked fast, maybe too fast. She tried to be reasonable. A child had lost her mother; weren't there special protocols for that? Couldn't they check for information and reunite a family without Indigo having to know anything *confidential*? Couldn't this attractive, well-paid woman think of something to do? Wasn't that her job? A mother had lost her child.

The woman looked terrified, in a fortified turret behind bullet-proof glass with drones locked on Indigo, Zaneesha, Game-Boy, and Hawk. And after the reasonable things Indigo said (using Cinnamon's confident-geek tone). Control woman talked more crap, insisting she was powerless, insisting Indigo and her band of *neo-savages* had to take this up with Cap George. He was *patrolling* the Next World Festival tomorrow, so no answer until the day after. Weren't they already dressed for the carnival?

Indigo's brain stuttered on *neo-savage*. Who the fuck says that shit out loud? And what the hell was a *neo-savage*? Hard to say if control bitch was white or Black or Asian or Brown or what. She worked the bland pale mask. Indigo wanted to stick a fork in that too. Getting this mad could mean a stroke at forty. Mad didn't pay the bills. Mad wouldn't stop the rain or a bullet.

"*Afro-Future Is Now.*" Indigo did Shaheen's Boss Lady act. "Tell me something I can use."

"You need to move along." The stupid bitch motioned for backup.

"Cinnamon Jones invited everybody to the Next World Festival, even you empire widgets from Paradise. Entry is free. Donations are welcome."

Some fool stumbled into the electric fence, screamed, then fell out, twitching. Valley Security men barked at Indigo, repeating the control woman's move-along command. One zombie guard jumped in Hawk's face waving a Taser. Three guns were aimed at Game-Boy. A drone glimmered over Zaneesha. The fellow on the ground went rigid. Did his heart stop?

Later Indigo would remember wishing she could just wake up, wishing this was a bad dream. In the moment she froze. Zaneesha put the comet mask back on and tried to pull her away. Indigo felt like she was caught in a high-voltage current. Zaneesha made the comet lights twinkle and chanted a Game-Boy riff: "*Hot Wire Evil Empire chigga rat batta tat. Do-wop da boomty bang na na na.*" Game-Boy and Hawk joined her. The rhythms called Indigo back. She dropped into a split and leapt up like an explosion, a James Brown, Godfather of Soul, Mr. Dynamite move. She belted, "Come to Festival. The Archangels of Funk will rearrange your mind and recharge your spirit."

The zombie guards hovered, uncertain, despite control lady yelling.

"What's your dad's name?" Hawk had a hand on Zaneesha's shoulder.

Zaneesha shook her comet head and lost the beat. Each breath was a little sob.

Indigo tugged glowing comet tendrils. "You don't know or you don't want to say?"

Game-Boy leaned toward her. "He works for Valley Security, right?"

Zaneesha nodded and the guards backed off.

"Tell that nice person in the booth." Hawk boomed a Deus ex Machina truth voice, like for the Amphitheatre, more commanding than any WHIZZ-IT speak coming from control lady. "She might help us locate him. Working for Cap George is not confidential." Hawk blasted a smile and the control woman managed to smile back.

"Work it, 'cause *I feel good like I knew I would.*" Game-Boy did a James Brown split too, then a break-dance roll and twirl. The men with guns and Tasers muttered, "Wannabe," but they were impressed.

Indigo squatted down and hugged Zaneesha, mask and all. A long hug, till their hearts beat in sync. "We need a name," Indigo said.

"Jerome," Zaneesha replied. "Jerome Williams."

The Bots were downstage, scanning for any spy thing Tatyana left behind. In the horror movie audience, spooky Iris tapped the lightning staff on the floor like a drum. Redwood jiggled her bangles to Aidan's banjo riff. "The tale we tell is a gift."

Cinnamon sank down on the hard wood floor and indulged her *ImagiNation* as—

Aidan walked a starry highway, an effect created by gobo lights Cinnamon didn't recall hanging. "Can't wake a person who's pretending to sleep." He talk-sang, doing backcountry Georgia *and* a Seminole/Irish lilt. "Hear what I say?" He plucked sharp notes. "Around the turn of the twentieth century, hard times for working people. Bad men making it harder, riding roughshod, digging our faces in the dirt. Course, we were ripping ourselves apart over scraps, and making up tales 'bout treasure hidden on Sorrow Mountain worth more than what rich men had locked in the bank vault.

"The mountain was cursed. Too many folks climbed up and never came down, killing and dying for buried treasure. These restless souls roamed the peak, sparking, howling, and tormenting each other and anybody else coming up there, 'cause they couldn't get into heaven. Devil didn't want 'em in hell neither."

Redwood strode through the door to nowhere, joining Aidan *on the other side*. Sea Island Gullah colored her words. "My character dreamed of singing her way into everyone's heart, but she was lost. Rich men killed my mama, stole our land, and the rest of the family caught the fever. They went to glory and left me behind with nothing or nobody, so I was wandering, singing sorrow. Scars on my cheeks meant survival, meant only a fool dare get near me. Nobody wanted to catch what I been through.

"I stole a chicken, some carrots, and knocked a fellow down who stepped in my way. I kicked him hard so he didn't get up. Kicked him for the people who kicked me. It felt good. I told everybody to stay back or I'd kick them too. Cowards were scared of my scars. They ran off, left their friend to die. A lady said *he a no-good scoundrel* and thanked me." Redwood paused. "Cinnamon don't need to hear this."

"Our sweet gal's hanging on every word," Aidan murmured. "Tell the whole tale. We can listen to you all day and most the night."

"Well, sugar, *you* sure can." Redwood stroked his cheek. The scarf on her head was a white-water river rushing somewhere grand. She brushed her lips over his eyes, nibbled an ear, still in love and ready to jump his dead bones. Sexy grandparents were still a thrill. "Cowards rustled up a sheriff and a posse of poor men to hunt me 'stead of going after the men who took our jobs, our homes, then stole what little we had left."

Iris strode through the door to nowhere, a bright light. "Rich men like to keep us distracting each other, while they line their pockets with our sweat."

She walked beyond the proscenium and tapped the scrim. It lit up, a blue sky. A foam mountain rose from the traps and soared twenty-five feet into the flies. Emerald trees, colorful wildflowers, and veins of sparkling beryl decorated the mountain's flanks. Gobo lights made leaf patterns on the floor. Shadow puppets glided onto the scrim: the posse, bears, spirit figures, a raven. Cinnamon's heart raced like when she was a kid. The ghost elders stood in the *Sorrow Mountain* saga they were telling.

"The posse men were mad at the world. They got liquored up and bragged 'bout collecting the fifty-dollar reward on my head. Split five ways, it wasn't much, yet they took up the chase anyhow. I hightailed it out that town."

Redwood circled the foam mountain, a black-and-white haint against Technicolor. "Running and running, from gun-toting fools, from myself. Didn't know where I was heading. All of sudden it was night. The road turned rocky and steep; then it branched: Sorrow Mountain one way and other trails going where I'd never been.

"A tree trunk of a man in a felt hat blocked my escape routes. Silk cravat, brass buckle belt, and two-toned boots looked ill at ease on his stiff figure. He waved a map in my face, talking 'bout I *had* to go up with him. 'Cause a hoodoo witch would scare the Bejesus out them evil haints. 'Cause the sheriff and that posse of poor men on my tail 'llowed to fall over and kill themselves 'fore they made it to the peak. 'Cause he was aiming to stash more riches in that bank vault than anybody ever had.

"He grabbed my arm and waved a gun. I felt his nature rising. Without thinking, I slammed brass bracelets upside his head. The gun flew from his hand. Woozy, blood in his eyes, he fell down. Rolling round looking for cold steel, he blocked every path except the one to the peak.

What to do 'cept change my life?" Redwood started climbing the foam mountain.

"Did this *really* happen, then you all made it into a film?" Cinnamon cursed softly for speaking out loud. She stroked the door flat and pretended to talk at the *Sorrow Mountain* poster. The Bots were at the stage manager's station, focused on the drone Mami shot down this morning. The gobo lights swayed in the grid; the scrim rippled; the phantom set rocked and rolled. Redwood clutched her raging-river head wrap as she bobbed up and down.

"What're you asking?" Iris pointed the staff at Cinnamon. "Is our story true?"

"Truth is what you make of our story," Redwood declared. "My Gullah mama used to say: *If you don't know where you're going, make sure you know where you come from.*"

And what the hell did that mean? Exactly?

Aidan plucked melancholy notes from the banjo. The mountain and the light grid settled down. "My character was lost too. I'd buried two brothers, my wife, and our four kids. Nothing wanted to grow for me: frisky peach blossoms froze before going to fruit; corn and beans whined, then dried up; poison dirt blew in my lungs. I fell down ill. When I got up out that sickbed, my farm already belonged to somebody else. Nobody wanted to look in my face, worried my fate was goin' be theirs soon enough.

"I spent my last dimes on bottles of bad hooch. People who be drinking to drown their sorrows should be told, sorrow do know how to swim. Drunk as a skunk, I knocked two men in the dirt, cracked a woman's heart. If nobody loved me, why I gotta do different than hate everybody back? Then I heard tell of a treasure map written on a gal's face. She had rich men and a posse on her tail. Why not me too?

"I stumbled over to Sorrow Mountain, almost broke my neck on nasty roots and mean rocks. I saw a bear, but no haints. I found the fancy man laid out and stole his horse, greenbacks, and gold. The hat and two-tone boots fit fine, the belt and cravat too—a miracle or maybe a curse. I felt heartless, leaving him for dead, half-naked in the moonlight. Not who I'd dreamed to be." Aidan raced up the foam mountain.

Iris giggled. "In the middle of the steepest incline, the horse dropped dead under Aidan and messed up his leg. He dragged his bruised butt on, and there at the peak was this fine lady dancing with the wind."

Redwood sang a storm melody and summoned hail and lightning from the grid. Bolts touched down in the audience. Balls of ice collected in Cinnamon's braids. One hit her nose and melted. The hail avoided the Bots at the stage manager's desk.

"Aidan should have been afraid," Iris said. "He thought this singer woman might be one of the magic mountain people his daddy told him about, Nunnehi, the Cherokee call them. Good spirits who love singing and dancing. Or maybe she was simply her own sweet self, coming into full power."

"She struck me sober. My leg healed up too." Aidan approached Redwood. "Her cheeks were like rain carvings on a cliff. No map I could read, but a road I wanted to *believe* in. I sang my heart out of hiding." He added thunder rumbles to her whirlwind song.

"*Believing* in each other, we were a storm together." Redwood leaned into him. "Lightning cracked open the sky and come right to my hand, a jolt of power brighter than day. The trees were long-armed witches drumming on each other. A raven, big as an elephant, flew above us, singing 'bout good times, yesterday, tomorrow, and right now. Boulders turned into roly-poly gargoyles lurching round the cliffs, dancing with us and a nosy bear."

Cinnamon jumped aside as a gargoyle bounced from the back row, rolled through the door to nowhere, and bounded up the foam mountain. Gobo witches sang tree songs. A raven's shadow swooped through the porthole and headed to the mountain. Aidan and Redwood talk-sang. *This is who we dreamed to be.* Shadow puppets stormed the scrim. They brandished guns and ran past the twirling bear.

Aidan sighed. "Fancy man, bald head and long johns shining in moonlight, reached the peak with the sheriff and his posse. Reward on my head was three times Redwood's bounty. Fancy man figured, poor men would happily split two hundred dollars, while he claimed a priceless buried treasure. His plan looked to be working. The lawmen aimed their guns at our hearts, but not one of them fellows pulled a trigger."

"Too busy enjoying the show." Redwood was tickled. She and Aidan leapt onto the shadow raven's back and flew in a whirlwind as she talk-sang, "We weren't the story they expected, not the horror tale folk told on the mountain, and definitely not the world they knew."

Cinnamon almost burst into tears.

Iris spoke. "While the sheriff marveled at sights he'd never seen, new thoughts came to him: *What they got us doing for a measly two hundred dollars? Might be best to leave these good spirits be.* The posse agreed, their heads full of new thoughts too. The fancy man cursed *traitors*. He snatched the sheriff's pistol, stuck the barrel in the lawman's face, and ordered the posse to shoot Redwood and Aidan down from the whirl-wind or else.

"The posse trembled and groaned, not knowing what to do. Finally, they lowered their guns saying, *Shoot 'em your own self and let murder stain your soul. We ain't goin' shoot down a wonder.* The fancy man cocked the pistol, and the sheriff went pale as mist. Death was breathing down his neck. Redwood and Aidan wailed a blues riff, and a bolt of lightning arced from a dark cloud and struck the pistol. The fancy man's heart stuttered, and he toppled over, dead to the world, a Sorrow Mountain tragedy.

"The raven set Aidan and Redwood on the cliffs. Redwood touched her storm hand to the fancy man's forehead, calling him from death's door to a slow, steady heartbeat. Aidan gave back the hat, belt, cravat, and boots, and the lawmen carried the fellow down to the town. He came to in a fine featherbed, talking 'bout evil mountain spirits tormenting him. The sheriff and his posse explained, *That mountain of stolen money in the bank vault has ruined his mind till he don't know what's what. We have to return what he stole.* They gave back every bloody cent."

Redwood hugged Aidan and said, "Nobody ever found a pot of gold or a chest of rubies on Sorrow Mountain."

"Just a little peace, and, well, love." He kissed her forehead.

Iris patted her bosom. "There is no buried treasure except what you carry inside." She played a clave beat with the staff. "Sing it now."

Aidan and Redwood danced down the mountain, singing in close harmony:

> *I've been climbing, climbing Sorrow Mountain*
> *I've been climbing, climbing desperate days*
> *Have you seen that dried-up fountain?*
> *And all those folks lost in a maze?*
> *Sucking at sadness, rage, and pain*
> *And 'bout to burn up in a blaze?*
> *I've been climbing, climbing Sorrow Mountain*
> *I say, this time around, I'm coming down*
> *I say, this sweet time, my lord, all of me, I'm coming down*

Iris paused her beat. "They named their first child, their only child, for the raven who flew them into the whirlwind and kept them company when the boy was born."

Redwood and Aidan sashayed back through the door from nowhere. Iris followed. The foam mountain sank, shadow puppets vanished, and the scrim went dark.

Iris stroked slush out of Cinnamon's braids. "Those films we made burned up or disintegrated before your daddy was born."

"You see this one, right?" Aidan slung the banjo on his back and tweaked Cinnamon's nose with rough, warm fingers.

Redwood put her chilly storm hand on Cinnamon's cheek. "Sure she can."

Tears glistened on Cinnamon's eyelashes—sorrow, joy, relief. A story about how her dad got his Raven name was a Festival gift for her, for Indigo, Game-Boy, and the Graphic Novelists of the Future. Indeed, a story for Shaheen, Zaneesha, and everybody. Yet Cinnamon didn't manage a word of thanks, of wonder. The elders beamed and nodded as if she'd said something grand. Bruja had been snoring in her lap. She woke and barked as the ghost elders blazed bright, then winked out.

The balcony's emergency exit banged shut. No alarm blared. Baron Taiwo had hidden in the balcony to watch this haint spectacle. Oun snuck off without a hello or good-bye. Cinnamon felt too full of the elders' story treasure for a salty mood or despair.

I say, this sweet time, my lord, all of me, I'm coming down.

UNSTABLE CONFIGURATION

Spook howled a note beyond human ears. The sun had disappeared, leaving purple smudges on the underbelly of clouds. He was grateful for shifting shadows to hide in. After circling ahead of Tatyana, he waited for her near the Mill River waterfall. She was pedaling slow and wouldn't arrive at the bridge overlooking the falls for a while. Spook was tired and slow like her. No real meal or afternoon siesta was taking its toll. Up ahead, the bike path split. One spur led to Electric Paradise; the other would take him past the Mall to a bowl of his favorite sausage and cheese in the farmhouse. He and Bruja would lick each other to sleep in a sweetgrass basket.

Spook howled once more and paced around damp debris: floorboards, car seats, window screens. An elderly TV was home to a weasel who'd scurried off to hunt or get away from Spook. Black birds with a few red feathers whizzed about, here and not here in a thicket of rainbows. More Water-Spirits than Spook had ever seen all together dashed in and out of the falls. They drew power from the rushing water, from *the spaces between things*—Taiwo's handiwork. Spook's fur stood on end with static electricity. He shook this off and wagged his tail at a full pack doing frothy fun.

He stuck his nose in the waterfall. A big mama bear had a foot caught between a boulder and a root. Three cubs wailed as she gnawed at her toes. In a far corner, IT Fred and his men gawked at her, trembling, barely breathing. No one noticed Spook come in. He'd left a ratty-looking Fred with the Water-Spirits at the falls to check on Cinnamon and Tatyana at the Event Horizon Theatre. Fred's beard and hair glistened with beads of water. The travel sweat, dirt, and blood had been washed away. He wore a new coat over a shoulder bandage on the bullet wound, and his hand was wrapped where Spook bit him. Healing molds and Taiwo's snake-cane poison dulled pain, drove away infection. Grease on Fred's fingers was from smoked soy cheese and Naughty Nuggets. Fred's pack had eaten and cleaned themselves up too.

Mama bear gurgled and Fred replied, a friendly exchange, although she was hurting and he was scared. Mama pleaded for help. Her cubs ran to the men, scratching their legs and whining. Fred huffed and barked. He and his pack stepped in range of sharp teeth and claws and hacked the ground by her foot. She pulled free. The pack jumped back. Fred stayed close, almost smiling at the cubs clambering on the big lady's back. The fur balls tumbled off as she stood on hind legs and licked her bloody foot. Fred took a deep breath of her, so he'd know her if they met again. She did the same.

Taiwo howled high notes, a sweet melody. Oun was fond of bears. Spook stepped back from the falls and shook off the wet. Taiwo danced up on an oak limb, twirling a feathered hat on the snakeskin cane. The waterfall turned into a cascade of lightning bolts. Someone else might have wondered at watery fireworks opening into a cave/tunnel under the river. Spook hoped the bears stayed put. They smelled calm, happy now—yet chasing off a curious cub might alert Tatyana to Spook on her trail.

"Unstable configuration." Taiwo used a voice like the noise on a bad connection, Water-Spirit talk. Oun tossed several Naughty Nuggets, which Spook gobbled down. Taiwo gobbled a bunch also. Fortified, they were ready for anything.

Tatyana's rickety bike sounded as if it might fall apart before she reached the bridge. Her headlight glinted off a man coming from the opposite direction. He avoided the beam and slipped onto the bridge. Spook recognized him from the Blossom Bridge raid this morning. He had the tang of Paradise folks more than flood refugees. A middle-aged fellow, hungry and desperate; his breath was labored, and he coughed blood. Several bullet wounds were doing him no good. An automatic stealth weapon hung over a shoulder. He smelled like ambush and death.

Spook crept to the bridge and crouched, ready to pounce. If this desperado had come hunting a lone Wheel-Wizard to raid, he'd get *Spooked*, as Indigo liked to say. Taiwo's snake cane hissed poison mist. The Paradise man jerked and shot a muted barrage up into the oak branches. Taiwo caught the rapid spew in oun's red-and-black cape. Twisting from the impact, oun belched a ball of fire at the waterfall. Steam billowed in the dark. Tatyana's bike lamp tracked this spectacle like a theatre spot.

"What the fuck?" The Paradise man bashed the weapon against the railing. It had jammed or run out of ammo. He snorted panic and clutched it close, sweating panic too.

Tatyana pedaled onto the bridge, fearless, curious, Cinnamon-like. Spook wanted to run and greet her, but Tatyana met Fred in the woods this morning, and he was from an enemy pack even if they helped the bear mama. Wolves weren't as trusting as huskies. Spook used wolf-sense to stay hidden, secret backup for Taiwo.

Oun jumped to the riverbanks. White seashells decorated dark braids. A silver braid was threaded with black leather and red feathers. Beads on a black tunic sparkled like stars. Oun's feathered hat floated over the hissing snake cane. Alien black birds, red feathers glistening, swooped and cawed as oun danced with Water-Spirits. A show! Spook wanted to sing too. He'd missed rehearsal today, tracking Fred to the waterfall. He loved rehearsal. Rainbows surged around the Paradise man. He tossed the stealth weapon into the river, mumbled about *fucking Water-Demons*, and ran into the trees. Blood leaked from his wounds. Spook could track him down tomorrow or the next day.

Tatyana aimed what anybody might have taken for a cell phone in his direction. Back during a snow full moon, Spook tracked a rough pack for Cap George, who used a similar *phone* to shoot foes from very far away. These *phones* had night eyes like Spook's and long-distance laser precision. "You're so calm." Tatyana lowered the device and smiled at Taiwo, as if they were friends. "What was that? Crazed Whistleblowers shooting up shit with stealth-tech? That's the word on the net."

"Whose word is that?" Instead of static Water-Spirit talk, oun spoke in a clear, resonant voice Spook hadn't heard for months. "Greetings, Tatyana."

"Greetings, Taiwo. I love your hologram light show. Your music is out of this world."

"You catch me in a grand mood, coming down Sorrow Mountain, full of elder sass and wisdom."

"You must teach me that bullet trick. I'm in need of a MIRACLE ." A good word, yet her lips trembled, her eyes filled up. Spook whined softly, echoing her sadness.

"I wondered when you'd show up." Taiwo smelled as if oun had swallowed a storm.

"I wonder that you think of me at all, after what happened between me and Cinnamon." Tatyana stowed the weapon-phone in a fanny pack. It buzzed.

"Are you going to answer that?"

"You do know that Consolidated had me in a vise grip."

"We can't always save the ones we love, no matter how brilliant we are or how much we love them."

"Right, you lost someone too. Not your fault?"

"'Fault' is a flimsy word for complex events."

"Not just busted careers, we faced jail terms or worse. Cinnamon refused to be realistic. I tried to warn her. On the sly—the gag rule was no joke. We were under constant surveillance. We'd have both gone down hard . . . ," Tatyana sputtered.

"You've never told anybody this story."

"Cinnamon's too mad. She won't let me tell it. Nobody else to trust."

"Don't stop now." The storm cape whistled and snapped around oun, like for catching bullets. "Let it rip."

"A horror movie. Cinnamon was the hero. I was the coward, not the warrior woman she loved, not *busting the chains that bound us and speaking truth to power.*" Tatyana stared at the waterfall. "Security paraded her off the premises while the bad boys got to slip away in the dark with hundred-million-dollar parachutes. After high crimes and misdemeanors! Cinnamon questioned our ethics, our blank spots, so the big guns made her a spectacle. I forced myself to watch. They thought I was broken, their bitch in the hole. Nobody except Cinnamon knew more about SevGenAlg." Tatyana gripped the railing. "Consolidated thought they owned me. I had other plans."

"Yes." Taiwo spoke softly, gently, the tone oun used talking to a wounded mama bear or a lost cub. "Perhaps they let you indulge an illusion of agency."

Tatyana and Taiwo glared at each other for too long. Spook almost fell asleep.

CINNAMON
❧
DECEPTION

Cinnamon's butt ached, sitting too long on the hard stage floor. She glanced at her watch. The elders' *visit* had lasted an hour, but seemed longer. She shook damp braids. Cold droplets landed on scorched floorboards where lightning struck. Proof! The *Sorrow Mountain* event was more than a *vision*, yet . . . Doubt clung to her.

The Bots floated and trundled from the stage manager's desk. Bruja danced around them, excited for the next adventure. They babbled about the whisper-witch Mami shot down this morning, a snoop-bot from Paradise. Thunderbird tracked its last transmission. Carefully. Anything might be a trick or a trap. Cinnamon stood up slowly. All her muscles and joints grumped. Bruja nipped the backs of her knees. They were late getting home. The whole day had been *off*, and still more surprises to wrangle.

"Can't head out right away." Cinnamon ruffled Bruja's night-sky ears. "Soon."

Thunderbird hovered in Cinnamon's face. "Tatyana ain't done snooping."

"Why her, of all people?" Cinnamon snatched up IT Fred's empty gun.

"She knows what you're capable of." Dragon whirred beside T-bird. Both Bots had energy to burn again. Blessings on superfast charging.

"Did you mean *the best is yet to come?*" Mami rolled suitcase wheels over her foot.

"Ow." Cinnamon's heart thrummed in her mouth. "I guess."

"So, will love come on back in style?" Mami sounded eager.

"Not with Tatyana. Lonely is better than a dumpster-fire romance." Cinnamon waved Fred's gun and squashed an image of Klaus and Marie dancing at the food court this afternoon. A tingle went up her spine nonetheless. All her nerves got excited.

"Gotta love Tatyana's spirit." Dragon sounded like Redwood. "In a pinch, the devil eats flies."

"That's from Klaus. I mean it's a German saying." Cinnamon let this memory play. "In der Not frisst der Teufel Fliegen," Klaus whispered, and nibbled her neck, or maybe that was Marie. Or both nibbling. A fuzzy memory. "Did Redwood really say that?"

"I have three recordings of her, one in German," Dragon replied.

"This phrase also appears in the journals we scanned," Mami added.

Cinnamon's stomach flip-flopped. "You scanned their final journal?"

"Nothing about eating flies in that one," T-bird said. "Or in Iris's last letter."

Mami played sounds of distant gulls and an ocean lapping the beach. "They wrote about: their last picture shows in the 1920s, the tech you rigged for your first comet costume at thirteen, Raven and Opal coming to your plays. Sweet memories. Well, some bittersweet." The Bots knew stories about the elders that Cinnamon didn't. So did Klaus and Marie. Silly being jealous. Somebody should know their stories. Anybody.

"A couple songs from Aidan and a hoodoo spell for love from Redwood. Why haven't you read these final words?" Dragon liked asking hard questions.

"One day I'll open up that journal, read the letter, find something new—" She was crying. "It'll be like they've come back to me for one more story." Like *Sorrow Mountain*.

T-bird twanged the banjo. "Have they really left you?"

"No." Cinnamon sniffled. "We become the people we've known."

"That's what you tell the young folks," Mami said.

Right, Cinnamon had to take her own medicine. She shimmy-shook achy muscles, marched through the door to nowhere, and gazed at the blank scrim in the proscenium. "Tatyana must have another copy or three of SevGenAlg."

"Consolidated too." Dragon's pearl flickered. "And teams tackling the *big glitches*."

Mami circled Cinnamon. "You quit Consolidated *after* getting the code to work."

"Still major glitches." Cinnamon avoided deadly wheels.

"You didn't tell Tatyana that SevGenAlg has been with you all along," Mami said.

"Isn't that like lying?" Dragon said.

Cinnamon licked dry lips. "Deception. Like Tatyana's Afro wig."

"Or fake jewels on a bike helmet. *Black girl magic* to smuggle us out." Dragon flew to the stage manager's desk and landed underneath the old helmet. The pearl at her neck was iridescent and bright. "Bling with deep memory."

"Data gems are the bomb," Mami proclaimed.

T-bird whistled. "Tatyana might have a grand reason for her masquerade."

Cinnamon scoffed. "What *grand* reason could she possibly have?"

The Bots spoke as one. "You quit, gave up everything, for love of us and the world."

The helmet was still decked out with twinkle lights and fake jewels— real tech wonders with quantum storage and warp-speed processing. Mostly Cinnamon's design—Edward somebody got all the credit, *stole* the credit, when Consolidated dumped her. In another life, an alternate history, she might have become a famed engineer, or if she'd been skinny and pale, a world-renowned actress/singer/dancer—triple threat. Not her biggest regrets, though. She should have done battle with Consolidated's big guns and Edward Asshat, even if there was no chance of winning.

Tatyana's betrayal had devastated her. Uncertain, ashamed for loving a lie, she lost heart for a fight. Rescuing (stealing) SevGenAlg was a worthy gearhead challenge and great cover. Loser Cinnamon got to run away from Cinnamon the Great and hide out on the elders' farm with a stolen AI. What the hell was she thinking?

Dragon interrupted her head static. "You're right to be careful."

T-bird whispered, "Tatyana might get you to blame innocent clouds for the weather we done made."

"*We?*" Cinnamon lifted an eyebrow. "You all in the sacred loop now?"

"Always been there," Dragon replied. "Wasn't that your big insight?"

T-bird talk-sang, "Tatyana might *steal the twinkle in your eye, the pep out your step.*"

"Who said that? Me, or Jaybird before we broke up? He warned me about her, about myself really." Each Bot played a *different* recording of her complaining about Tatyana and the weather. "OK, we shouldn't trust *anybody.* Still, I can't blame her for everything. *No one should let yesterday use up too much of today.* That's what you all told me, I mean, the elders used to say that—Cherokee wisdom according to Aidan . . ."

The Bots burbled, thrilled to be mistaken for the elders. Dragon's gemstone teeth were definitely in a grin, not a snarl, as she clutched Cinnamon's braids with stubby feet. Mami's electric eel wound around Cinnamon's left leg. T-bird danced on her shoulder, unfurled trash-bag wings, and hugged everybody close—like the altar in the Amphitheatre. Bruja jumped up and slobbered on them.

"Why keep a kidnapped Flying-Horse from me?" Cinnamon let herself sound hurt.

"Our arms are '*too short to box with God.*'" Dragon quoted James Weldon Johnson, an archangel of funk from almost a hundred years ago. Elegant dodge.

"We tell you everything. Eventually." Mami bumped Cinnamon's booty with her basketball belly, then backed away. Thunderbird and Dragon backed off too.

Cinnamon pressed. "What about sliding into a Teufelskreis three times this week?"

"The new fail-safe you wrote trips immediately," Mami replied.

"What we goin' do, honey pie?" T-bird said. "That's the real question."

Dragon bobbed her head, agreeing. "The enemy is nipping at our heels."

"Tatyana's got me worried." And the Teufelskreis. Over a dozen years and she hadn't solved the big glitch! You needed a team to really think. No chance of that. The Bots wouldn't talk about the Teufelskreis till they were ready. With the fail-safe in place, Cinnamon should be patient. That was a stopgap though, not a real solution; still— "We're coming down *Sorrow Mountain*."

"It's almost showtime," Mami declared.

How could they still do a show? "We'll collect more data, make a plan. As for Festival . . . I don't know." She strode to the stage manager's desk, hid Fred's gun in a drawer, and turned on the production computer. One person could run lights, sound, video, special effects, and cue performers for entrances from a single chair. Why do that unless you had to? She'd hijacked the computing power for a secret portal on the world. She and Taiwo worked up an interface with Spook's implants, using SevGenAlg origin code. Alien tech was all through the sacred loop.

Ancient but still at it. The screen brightened and Bruja hopped on a bench to watch. She loved the Spook-feed: cyber-violet eyes seeing in the dark, ears pitched to whispers or sirens wailing, then broadcasting on an alien bandwidth. The tall tales were true: Taiwo saw and heard what the Ghost-Dog did and smelled scents he tracked. Oun claimed the interface was powered by heartbeats stolen from Cinnamon, Bruja, Spook, and any nearby *obliging* hearts. Cinnamon wondered if "stolen heartbeats" was literal or metaphorical. Taiwo resisted the distinction, insisting that the way to explain the unknown was to use the known as metaphor, even if it broke down eventually. Oun never said where the stealing-heartbeats metaphor broke down.

Oun had supposedly learned the trick from Redwood, who *stole heartbeats* for conjuring. When she was a young woman, wild and wonderful hoodoo spells had worn her out something awful. When Cinnamon came along, she was hardly doing big spells anymore. Aidan pitched a fit if she did. Cinnamon suspected Taiwo's heartbeats were the major power source for the interface. The feed was fuzzy if oun wasn't around. For Taiwo's and all their hearts, she only resorted to the Spook-feed in dire emergencies—like a Tatyana-ambush. She fiddled with the video setting and sang, *"This time around, this sweet time, my lord,"* and promised the elders to tend their spirits better. *Know where you come from*, and *don't get stuck on yesterday*. Simple truths, hard to enact.

A clear broadcast finally came through.

"What you got for us, Ghost-Dog?"

Spook howled at Water-Spirits dancing by the Mill River falls. He walked into glittery water to spy on a bear caught between a root and a rock—the same bear she and Tatyana saw earlier? The time stamp was from thirty minutes ago. Taiwo had already been nosing around with Spook. Oun was avoiding face-to-face, yet staying connected. That was worth a few heartbeats.

SPOOK

ᥴᦊ

SPIRIT WEED AND BIG HEARTS

Spook joggled himself out of a daze. Tatyana was shouting at Taiwo, who flickered in front of the falls. Oun almost faded into the mist.

"No illusions." Tatyana glowed hot in chilly night air. Her weapon-phone vibrated in a fanny pack. She silenced it. "You can't imagine what Cinnamon's SevGenAlg can do, what it allows us to do. It's amazing."

"Give me something specific." Oun had a cool glow.

"How can I explain?" Tatyana tipped her head back, as if to howl at the Crow Moon. "I don't know what you'd understand."

"Try metaphor, an analogy."

"Cinnamon's the poet, not me."

"You have your own idiom. Everyone does."

Tatyana raked turquoise claws through her hair. "SevGenAlg has been glitching, making shit up, getting caught in infinite loops."

"Teufelskreis," Taiwo murmured.

"Yeah. With self-repair, we avoided the worst. Recently, that's not working so well. The code doctors are clueless. Cinnamon must have told you—Whistleblower girl was running diagnostics and caught Sev-GenAlg lying. That wasn't supposed to happen anymore. That was all over the news feeds."

Taiwo nodded. "Bad news for Consolidated."

"They claimed we deep-sixed SevGenAlg. Not true. Too much riding on this. Too many systems affected, *infected*." She shuddered. "It's a fragile world, and rogue code is out there doing who the fuck knows what. Cinnamon shouldn't let her troubles with me get in the way of solving this disaster. Persuade her to help me out."

Sparks flashed at the tips of Taiwo's braids. "I'm no speaker of ofo, calling up *words that make things come to pass*."

"Ofo is Yoruba for 'incantation'?" Tatyana asked. "You're too modest. She loves you, trusts you more than anyone. *A storytelling griot from another dimension*. Make her face what's happening in the real world and quit hiding out in a Ghost Mall bubble."

Taiwo snorted twice, eyebrows dancing.

"Nothing to lose, everything to gain." She clutched oun. "Try. Please."

"We're down here, Tatyana." IT Fred and his pack tromped from a gap between the waterfall and the cave. "Why aren't you answering your cell?"

"*Instant access is a ball and a chain.*" Patting the weapon-phone in her fanny pack, she sounded like Cinnamon. Fred scowled. T-bird's darts glowed in his neck and butt. Spook let a growl slip. Luckily, the Water-Spirits were harmonizing. Good cover. Tatyana left her bike on the bridge and scrambled down the embankment. "What have you guys been doing all this time?"

"Not that long." Fred glanced at his cell and gasped.

Taiwo poked Fred with the snake cane. "Bites, bullet wounds, and filthy clothes were an invitation to infection." Oun chuckled, in good spirits after days of grumping at Spook and the Water-Spirits. "They needed first aid, a good meal, and rest."

"Is that so?" Tatyana said.

"I guess." Fred squinted at Taiwo. "Why do they call you the baron?"

Taiwo shrugged.

"It's a reasonable question." Fred pawed his face and dropped onto a soggy couch.

"I know frontline despair," Taiwo said. "I'm an old soldier, a battle medic."

Tatyana stepped close. "Not just Water Wars, you fought in Syria? Afghanistan?"

"Too many places. *I ain't goin' study war no more.*" Oun pranced along the riverbanks. The snake cane opened its mouth and sucked silver bolts from the waterfall.

Tatyana liked the show as much as Spook. "More great special effects." She marveled as lights in the falls dimmed and Water-Spirits raced into the cave under the river, except one whose skin was rainbow scales. Most Spirits were transparent, smooth, like water or glass. They all smelled the same: high-voltage electric wires. The scaly one pulled Fred's men, stumbling and laughing, into Taiwo's dance. Disgust, distrust, and desire wafted off Fred, who stayed on the couch. Maybe he didn't like to dance. Spook felt energized. He bounded in the shadows with the dancers.

The waterfall went dark as the night sky. The cane was a silver bolt in Taiwo's hand. Fred's pack tumbled onto the soggy sofa beside him. They squeezed close, tittering like Ghost-Mallers after a fun performance. Spook sniffed marijuana on their breath.

"You always did amazing shows." Tatyana clapped as the scaly Water-Spirit raced down the black river and disappeared. "This Water-Demon brigade is another level."

Taiwo shrugged. "You didn't know me before."

"What, when you were young and fierce instead of old and super-powered?"

Taiwo pulled the feathered hat from nowhere and tipped it at her before pressing it over oun's cascade of braids. The cane was green snakeskin again. "Not a real superhero, mostly an observer, storyteller, collecting tales. That's all I have strength for anymore and not much of that. Tonight, my heart is heavy. Eshu rides me."

"Eshu? Who?" Tatyana said. "You and Cinnamon told me once."

"Yoruba Orisha—a West African deity of the crossroads, guardian at the gates to life and death, Eshu wears many faces and plays many beats. Trick-ster, sacred clown, even in this new world, Eshu rides those who *believe*."

"Sacred clown," Tatyana mumbled. "All the world's a stage—is that your secret?"

"Perhaps." Oun's flash of teeth was a heartbeat from a snarl. Spook growled support, a soft rumble. Tatyana looked his way and Spook swal-lowed a last grumble.

"How do you and Spook stay so young?" Tatyana peered at Taiwo. "So fit and frisky, while everybody else—"

"A long time between us." Taiwo bent to her, took a deep breath, and gathered her secrets. "You're too stiff, brittle bones, about to snap. Take care." Oun rose to full height, tall like Cinnamon, but thin. Thinner every day. Oun needed more sausage.

"Word is you're a warrior spy or an alien scout from another dimen-sion," she said.

"A boneyard baron guarding Cinnamon's farm," Fred hissed.

"Story storms to protect the elders' land," Taiwo said. "Cheaper than guard-bots and electric fences."

Tatyana sighed. "I hear you're doing a Water-Spirit act for the Next World Festival."

The cane faded in and out of view as oun whispered, "Yes. It's a surprise."

Tatyana smirked. "Magic special effects are a dangerous game these days."

"So is biking this path alone at night, even from the Event Horizon to here."

"Valley Security drones are on duty 24/7. I pinged them about our friend with the quiet gun. And I have"—she pointed at Fred and his boys—"an escort."

"Your cup runneth over."

"A few tricks of my own too." She patted the fanny pack. "Fronting like you have tech from another dimension, that's over-the-top."

"I pour libation to Eshu." Oun shrugged. "To folks around here, Dahomey or Yorubaland in West Africa might as well be another dimension."

"Nigerian tech." She nodded. "Indian country's *out there* too. My aunt used to say that. You knew her. She raised me to be . . ." Her breath was a gust of sad. "I'm not her."

"Star Deer!" Taiwo sang Water-Spirit overtones and danced on river stones.

> Scatter me, where they won't come looking
> I'm a spirit weed
> I'll take root anywhere, all of me, good to share
> Not like big money crops, guzzling toxic raindrops
> What I say, hey, hey, hey!
> Do you hear? Are we clear?
> A shadow dancer, a soulful clown
> Scatter me, where they won't hunt me down
> I'm a spirit deed, I'm a spirit weed
> Scatter me, I'll take root anywhere

Tatyana pursed her lips. "Cinnamon wrote that song for my aunt."

Taiwo nodded. "With Marie Masuda and Klaus Beckenbauer."

"Who are they?"

"The Mod Squad. Cinnamon, Marie, and Klaus found me when I was lost, too scattered, to make sense to myself or anyone, about to get lost forever in *the spaces between things*. They *believed* in me till I came back to my Taiwo self. Till I came true. A miracle. Even so, I couldn't bring Raven all the way back."

"Cinnamon's shot-in-the-head dad?"

"My fault."

"Not the story Star Deer told. She hid in the bathroom, remember, when Raven and your true love, Kehinde, stepped in the line of fire to shield Cinnamon's brother—"

"Sekou. Half-brother."

"Yeah. Sekou invited folks to his favorite haunt to celebrate Raven's *Afro-Future Is Now* paintings. The joint was jammed. My aunt did a cosmic dance for the *space is the place* art. A sociopath started shooting. It was a gay bar, gay night, art night, whatever. Raven and Kehinde jumped in front of bullets and saved my aunt, you, *everybody*."

"I let Kehinde bleed out, and Raven . . ." Taiwo's cape rippled and snapped in still air. "I won't argue with you about this."

"Good, 'cause I'm right. Raven and Kehinde did a sacrifice for love. Not your fault." Tatyana glanced at Fred, then leaned close. "In the Cyber Wars, we'll need somebody like Cinnamon on our team."

"Our?" Oun wavered like a flame about to go out in one dimension or another; then oun plucked the stealth weapon from the river. "Poor men can't afford weapons like this." Taiwo stroked the gun's silver silencer. Red lights flickered on the trigger kit. "If you steal it, you have to hack the operating system; otherwise it's junk or worse, a bomb that takes you out." Oun's healing voice made Spook drowsy. "Even Darknet hacker wizards pay a fortune for each bullet. Few people can afford to shoot up shadows and oak trees unless deep pockets bankroll them."

"So who is helping us wage war on ourselves?" Tatyana's voice quivered.

"You and Cinnamon will figure this out. I'll try to marshal enough spirit to *celebrate first fruits, light new fires, and forgive what can be forgiven* at Festival. Can't promise I'll make it." Oun raised the stealth weapon high, leapt over a willow root ball, and vanished in the dark, singing, "*All of me, good to share. I'm a spirit weed.*"

Tatyana flashed her headlight, illuminating the root ball, waterfall, river, tree buds, and an alien black bird with red feathers perched atop the bush that hid Spook. She did this over and over, muttering to herself. Rehearsal? Spook dozed off for real this time.

&

The black bird with red feathers had sparks on its beak and smelled stormy like Taiwo as it flapped wings in Spook's face. This startled him awake before someone ambushed him. Spook had to get to the elders' farm soon and sleep. Dogs needed more nap time than people.

Fred lurched from the couch over to Tatyana. "We got delayed."

She pointed at the root ball. "How does Taiwo *disappear*? Cinnamon claims oun has secret military connections—a warrior spy, big hero who saved lives in mucho battles."

"I know less than you." Fred was mad and wobbly on his feet.

She sniffed him and the men on the couch. "Rogues are burglarizing Electric Paradise, torching cars, and stealing people's babies, while you lot smoke a blunt in a cave under a river."

"A mama bear was stuck in there, chomping her toes to get free. I couldn't do that. Could you? Cubs were pissing and moaning, like people brats, like we *had* to help 'em."

"Did you help?"

"Dug her free." Fred's nose twitched. "She smelled fresh, like a walk in the woods on a cool day. She licked my hand and one little guy tried to climb my leg."

"Little *guy*?"

Fred shrugged. "Yeah, maybe. Whatever."

"You never talk like that about anything." Tatyana stepped toward the waterfall. "They still in there?"

"I don't know. I hear bioengineers are working with Whistleblowers and messing in the wildlife around here. Doing genetic enhancements, making cyborgs with implants, blackbirds, deer—"

"Bullshit conspiracy theories. Show me proof or go join a nostalgia militia."

"What? No way, I'm the future. Folks like that are living a past that never was." Fred stomped to his pack on the couch and kicked their feet. "Get up." They flailed, dopey and uncoordinated.

Tatyana tiptoed to the falls. Mist sparkled on her face and hair. Her hand hovered close to the rush of water. She looked around, furtive. Fred barked at his men, who giggled. Tatyana stuck turquoise claws in, then out. Her skin shimmered for a moment, like a Water-Spirit's. That happened to Cinnamon and Indigo sometimes. Tatyana crept to the gap between waterfall and cave and poked her nose in. Taiwo's interface with *the spaces between things* was fading. Spook had seen this many times before, like a screen turning off. Tatyana backed out, and rubbed her eyes, and turned to Fred. "Taiwo must be eighty-something and chilling up in a tree. Breathing fire, like a carnival act. Oun rocked a bulletproof cloak that R and D would die for."

"You think Taiwo's a Whistleblower?"

"Hell no. I'd just love a cape like that."

Fred shrugged. "Anyone could be a Whistleblower." His pack mumbled about DANCING *at the* FESTIVAL, and he hushed them. "We don't have time for carnival acts."

Tatyana prodded Fred's bandaged wrist. "Cinnamon set her dogs on you?"

"They have zero security at the Mall. A bunch of reformed bad boys, old hippies, recycling wonks, and a couple junkyard mutts. Nothing serious, if we went in force."

"You're a fool if you think that."

Fred patted the two men who'd been with Flying-Horse-Bot early this morning. "The guys found one of Cinnamon's clown machines, trundling around, begging to be snatched." He talked faster as Tatyana scowled. "The bot turned itself off. No explosion. It's intact. We boot it up and the code's ripe for extracting."

"*Hacking* into one of Cinnamon's Bots, nothing's coming out *intact*."

"You know her secrets. You can reverse engineer." Fred wanted to bite Tatyana. "No one is impervious."

"Cooperation would be better than coercion." She wanted to bite him too.

"I don't subscribe to that *survival of the friendliest* bullshit."

"How's that going?" She balled her fists. Spook wanted her to beat Fred down before he did something bad. "You might have ruined my chances," she said.

Fred stepped too close, trying to overpower her with his big-man scent, trying to get her to look away, expose her throat. "You ruined your chances all by yourself."

The pack on the couch held their breath. Spook bared his fangs.

"Not ruined yet." Tatyana glowered at Fred. "Taiwo will put in a good word, ofo, do a Yoruba incantation. Cinnamon's got that big view, from the ancestors to the unborn, and a big heart."

"You broke her heart." Fred's voice shook. She smacked his chest, and shoved him away. "Let's not fight," he said quickly. "The bot we nabbed is a window into her system. She left it on the side of the road, unprotected. Whose fault is that?"

"It's Cinnamon's fault, you stole her shit?"

"You should know."

Tatyana smelled as if she might go for his throat, like Bruja.

He hunched back, a smart move. "You're still in love with her."

"Jealous?" She scrambled up the embankment to her bike. "You guys dancing at Festival is a perfect way in. I've got one too." She swatted at dragonfly spies and held up a mask from her trailer. "Be in the Amphitheatre at dawn for dress rehearsal. Wear a good mask. Can't risk them recognizing you after your bad behavior at the Mall."

"Dawn? To do a clown act?" Fred grouched. "I used to be famous, for my elegant code, for my killer instincts, a cybernaut exploring the unknown."

"Behave yourself tomorrow. Don't kidnap Bots. Taiwo did special ops in the Water Wars, headed an elite squad nicknamed Water-Demons. They were legendary. Taiwo trained Game-Boy, Back-From-The-Dead, and Indigo's squad too."

Fred ground his teeth, then muscled his boys off the couch and shoved them onto the river path to Electric Paradise. He reeked like someone hiding in the bushes for a sneak attack. His pack sniffed the intensity and hurried off with him. They'd stumble to the gates in forty minutes. Tatyana pedaled off the bridge. She'd be there in ten. Dragon's spies would follow them into Paradise even. Spook could go home.

A curious bear cub snuffled at his tail. She was a squeaky fur ball, like one of Bruja's toys. The other two cubs hung back with mama. She sent them scurrying up a bristly pine. Mama's wounded paw smelled of Taiwo's snake-cane poison. Spook let the bold daughter sniff his butt while mama gurgled concern. Spook dipped low, nipped daughter's nose playfully, then took off.

He raced along the riverbanks following Taiwo, who headed toward the elders' farm. A long run, but at home Spook and Bruja could FIND LOST THINGS for Cinnamon, Bruja's favorite game. Cinnamon would tickle Spook's tummy and sing a song with him. Finally, a sweetgrass basket to sleep the night away next to Bruja.

CINNAMON

cᏋ ᎧᎣ

DEMON MASK

Branches blurred on the computer screen as Spook tore through moon-lit woods on a mission, full force. OK. They had mad data from the Spook feed. Now what? The Bots hovered behind Cinnamon, blinking and susurrating—slow thinking. Impressive. This high drama, *do-suffer-know* day, had wiped her out. Freaked her out of thinking.

"Tatyana might stop Fred's boys from savaging Flying-Horse. For a while, at least." Cold comfort. She turned off the computer and paced upstage and down, wondering if Tatyana or Fred could hack through Horse's security malware and discover anything important. Maybe. Maybe not. What the hell was Taiwo up to? Scheiße!

"Not enough data." Mami rolled beside Cinnamon and blinked her red eye.

Dragon grumped over their heads, "Never enough data."

Thunderbird rattled his tail feathers against a trash can. "Gotta act anyhow."

The Bots were agitated, uncertain like Cinnamon. Their origin code was infused with her mindset along with the elders and a bit of Taiwo—secret ingredients that other SevGenAlg versions lacked.

Cinnamon halted under the porthole. "I thought you all would be a magic wand and make everything easy. Ha!"

"Magic wand?" T-bird chortled. "Really?"

Mami crashed water in a thunder hole, pissed. "Easy is overrated, convenience too."

Actual smoke poured from Dragon's funnel nostrils, angry too. "We gotta get on the right train of thought, next stop Festival, remember?"

"No way." Cinnamon tripped over props from the last production. "I don't have a mask, costume, or a finale song." She tossed broken baskets and a cracked shield into the trash. "You heard Tatyana and Fred. We're under attack."

"Maybe, maybe not," Mami replied. "We ain't living tragedy round here."

Bruja leapt high and tugged Cinnamon's damp braids, then dashed down a corridor that lit up for her. She left Cinnamon to deal with testy Bots alone.

"Of course Festival is still possible," Dragon and Thunderbird declared together.

"No way." Fred was gunning for her *and* Tatyana, a personal attack, not just a gig. He felt cheated, and it was their fault. A daredevil cybernaut with a cutthroat résumé, Fred was exactly who power people would hire off the Darknet to monitor, then sabotage Tatyana. Although she'd probably double-cross him faster than he could double-cross her. She'd have to perform a miracle to get Cinnamon to trust her and *cooperate*. Even to save the world from whatever nasty piece of work had Fred on the payroll. Cinnamon had deleted trust from the repertoire after Tatyana raided her heart and mind. No more *fling yourself off a cliff and let somebody catch all of you.*

For the nth time she went over what she could have done differently with Tatyana, what she should have noticed, what would have been clear to anybody else. And what might she be missing now?

"You'll never plow a field, turning it over and over in your mind," T-bird said. He had a folksy Aidan metaphor for every goddamned situation. "Talk to us, sugar."

A story spilled out. "Everybody at Consolidated was whining about gale-force winds, rampaging rivers, and Mother Nature being a stone-cold bitch who was messing with us, *personally*. So when Hurricane Tayshaun made landfall and the power cut, I was ready. I engineered a blackout. The backup generators failed too. Cameras, mics, the whole security shebang went offline for hours. That spooked everybody.

"Folks stumbled into the café on the first floor and huddled around candles from my Eshu altar. The big guns sat down with janitors, cybernauts, administrators, and the idea crews. Cold coffee and cheap wine flowed. An *all for one and one for all* feeling. We cursed storm surges, ancient infrastructure from 1950, and climate change, like we were innocent victims of someone else's madness. Eventually we quieted down and listened to the wind howl, wondering if the groaning and banging down the hall was a delivery ace getting it on with an accountant or electricians trying to restart the backup system. Wondering too if we really were above the fray. The storm sounded fierce enough to bring the building down on us. Perfect cover for my download heist.

"When the power came back, security was ecstatic to find sooty corpses with bushy tails in the backup generators and zero trace of terrorists. Squirrels crashed power grids way more often than hackers, so everybody breathed a sigh of relief."

"A glitch masquerade." This tickled T-bird.

Dragon hooted. "We slipped out in fake storm surges and the real rage at rodents."

"A miracle it worked." Cinnamon rubbed tired eyes. "Tatyana never suspected a thing. I didn't suspect her either, even considered telling her my plan, but why put her at risk? She claimed there were bugs everywhere, listening to people pray, screw, and pee. *They'd bug your sleep if they could and steal your dreams.*"

Dragon and Thunderbird sang, "*We need somebody . . . Flying us through the stars . . . Gotta steal away to Jesus, baby.*"

"We hid our first steal-me messages in fractured funk." Mami sounded fourteen and pleased with herself. "Thanks to Tatyana's warning."

"Tatyana always talks a good game." Cinnamon's bottom lip trembled.

"Is it empty talk?" Dragon asked.

A vivid image assaulted Cinnamon, from the morning she got sacked: Tatyana kissing the sweet spot on her tummy, swishing a river of hair against her nipples then— "Tatyana's cell phone is a weapon, a microbullet thingy. Cap George has one. Nobody else around here does. Odds are the robber barons who armed George and Tatyana armed that stealth gunman at the waterfall."

"Or somebody from the same class of robber barons," Dragon said.

"What the hell was I thinking, absconding with you all?" Cinnamon wanted to scream. "The forces against us are mighty." The Bots hissed and booed. "Sorry for the blockbuster dialogue, *Battlestar Graphica*? What if they're on to us or simply curious? We're outgunned and maybe we've been outmaneuvered too."

"Just 'cause it's impossible don't mean we give up." Mami used a *Cosmic Quest* line. Colored light from her head spewed across the scrim. "And when did love go out of style? You and Taiwo, mad all the time, feeling sorry, it's not reasonable."

"I don't know about Taiwo." Cinnamon wanted to be mad at *somebody* for stolen dreams and stolen babies, for desperados doing disaster shit without a self-repair mechanism, for the sociopath shooting up gay night so many years ago, killing Kehinde and wounding her dad, her whole family. She wanted to crawl in a hole, lick her wounds, and rage at Back-From-The-Dead, 'cause they got a second chance. "Mad won't stop a deluge or call up the next world, and forget bitterness. Regret too."

"Amen," Mami said. "You and Taiwo need to come down off *Sorrow Mountain*."

"Yes, lord. So who are you goin' be for Festival?" T-bird demanded.

"You always do a show, apocalypse be damned. Folks will get suspicious," Dragon said. "What dialogue you got lined up?"

Cinnamon sputtered, "I thought of telling Taiwo and Kehinde stories—facing down she-lions, elephants, and warrior princes."

"Miz Redwood danced with a lioness." T-bird was in love with her derring-do.

Cinnamon winced. "They were fearless, facing worse odds than me."

"Redwood and Kehinde *acted* fearless," Dragon said. "Like you *acting* with Fred."

"Like you slipping out Consolidated's gate, *acting* pathetic and dejected, and meanwhile hiding us on your helmet." T-bird was in love with Cinnamon's derring-do too.

"Pathetic and dejected wasn't an act. And we can't tell anybody that story." Cinnamon sighed. "Taiwo should do Kehinde tales for Festival, boost our danger rep with Water-Spirit backup and alien special effects. Zaneesha can be their Shooting-Star, leading the procession back into the Mothership."

"That's what I'm talking about." Mami was an ocean pounding sand like a drum.

"My dad was painting warrior-women Kehinde stories right before he got shot." Cinnamon had stored his art in the garage. "Taiwo playing a shekere and holding forth is a perfect tribute to Raven and Kehinde." Even without a finale song.

"You need to tell your people danger's afoot." Dragon flew to the porthole.

T-bird joined her. "Why haven't you asked for help already?"

"Too bejiggity. You know I hate asking anybody for anything." Cinnamon winced.

"So get on the horn before you change your mind," Dragon said.

Mami's snake coils of LEDs flashed. "How's that for a magic wand?"

"Damn good." Cinnamon sat at the computer. Using Taiwo's interface she sent alerts to Cap George, then Diego Denzel and Jerome Williams. George responded instantly, a video chat. He wore a Rocketman costume and a rainbow Afro that glowed. George already knew about the pizza stickup. He had spies on the Mall Advisory Board, in bad-boy crews, and snooping Consolidated's inner circle. Hacker wizards haunted the Darknet for him. Cinnamon mentioned Flying-Horse, not Tatyana.

"I'll make those suckers rue the day they snatched one of your Bots. That scumbag coward who held a gun to your head is gonna eat his own fucking shadow." George spoke action-adventure dialogue in a sweet tenor, an unexpected voice for such a gruff fighting man. "Paradise can't tolerate that shit right next door. You feel me?"

"Someone with deep pockets thinks I know more than I do. Don't make a fuss."

"I can be quiet as a choke hold."

Cinnamon cringed at this image.

"Folks from the hill towns and down the big river say the valley's a bubble, not the real world. Jealous of you and me making the world we want." A big fan of Festival, George insisted nobody would dare interfere with the fun tomorrow. Bravado perhaps, but he lived up to the Sam Jackson, take-no-shit-from-anyone image. Electric Paradise and Consolidated could depend on him securing the peace. That was how he kept the job. "A mess of people breathing one story together, acting up and acting out, a miracle. Remember when we couldn't do that? I been rocking my superhero cape since yesterday." He smirked, pleased with his Festival efforts. "My mother used to say, *We're Mississippi Negroes transplanted to the cold North who ain't forgot how to treat family.* I help you, you help me, and we're discreet. This line's secure, right?"

George's daughter had tipped out of Paradise and he had no clue where she went. Drones were on the lookout, although he had to keep her *vacation* quiet. Losing track of his own daughter was terrible publicity.

"Regina came to the Mall," Cinnamon realized. The newbie who wanted to be in Indigo's squad. "She dyed her hair, covered the freckles, and put putty on her nose. Snoop-bots don't recognize her. I'm terrible with faces out of context. Tomorrow, she'll dance in the show." With the Hill Town Wenches. George looked ready to explode. "You should be proud. If you can't find her, nobody can. She knows all your tricks."

He choked up. "Alma trusted me to keep her daughter safe, her dying wish."

"Regina is your daughter too. You raised her."

"I tried my best." Regina's bio-father ran off with another woman when he found out Alma Rubenstein was pregnant, seriously ill, and maybe not long for this world. Reginald George Washington met Alma in a Continuing Ed ethics class. He fell in love as they argued over what to do if there were no good choices. He persuaded her to marry him before the baby came. He was listed as father on the birth certificate. Alma died five months after giving birth. Alma and Regina were the only people George ever dared to love.

"Regina is twentysomething. She has to take care of herself now," Cinnamon said.

"I know," George said quickly. "Come work for me. I could use another level head."

"That's what everybody needs. Look, I got a long list of urgent. See you tomorrow."

Cinnamon ended the call, then alerted Game-Boy, Indigo, and Shaheen to IT Fred. Spook and Bruja would recognize him at Festival whatever the mask. Cinnamon asked the kids to neutralize any Darknet operatives the dogs got wind of. She warned them to avoid Shooting-Star. If approached, the Bot might do an EMP to wipe enemy electronics. Shooting-Star had done this once, after shielding herself. Cheeky. Game-Boy's reply was brief: *We're on it.* No fussing at her for withholding intel. Probably still sorting out Zaneesha. What if Mom was a no-show or Jerome was Dad and didn't want her? Did he know what to do with an eight-year-old daughter? Checkpoint grunt was almost as bad as prison—no time for family, for a life. Zaneesha could sleep in Iris's old room or Taiwo's. Bruja would love that. Cinnamon too.

She pinged Azalea, Boo, and the Co-Op Clinic about stealth-tech attacks. Another quick reply: *We got you. The Bunny-Mobile is seaworthy.* No answer from Jerome and Diego (off duty? out of range?) or Shaheen, who muted her phone and went to bed early on Festival eve. Boss Lady would be up before dawn and alert the Co-Op Watch and Whistleblower friends. Hopefully Whistleblowers were the heroes she *believed* in. Cinnamon smirked at the Bots. "Help is on the case. And it was easy. Happy?"

As they burbled and buzzed, Bruja dashed from the scene shop. Witch-Dog had stashes in the shops, traps, orchestra pit, and even up in the flies. She carried a mask in her mouth: a Water-Demon with an unruly forest for hair, silver lightning bolts on the cheeks, and fiber-optic eyes like burning coals. Bruja had managed to turn the mask on. Tucked in the wild hair was a beaded comb that resembled a crown of peacock feathers to honor Oshun, Yoruba water-spirit, deity of love and destiny. The comb had belonged to Kehinde, Taiwo's love. Oun gave it to Cinnamon and Marie Masuda forty years ago. They traded the treasure back and forth till Marie pressed it in Cinnamon's braids and headed off to college. Bruja dropped the mask and gently nudged it toward her feet.

"I thought I'd lost this." Cinnamon's heart pounded in her ears. She picked up the mask. "Where'd you find it?"

Bruja wagged her butt and raced out. Cinnamon's skin prickled, as if Marie were blowing warm, moist breath on bare flesh, as if she were rubbing tension from stressed muscles. Bruja dragged in a full-length bodysuit and left it puddled at Cinnamon's feet. The fabric was iridescent snakeskin, like Taiwo's cane, and covered in feathers and feelers that turned sharp or silky depending on her mood—Taiwo's juju-tech. Jewel eyes on the thighs flashed rainbows, offering a connection to *the spaces between things*. Cinnamon and Taiwo had collaborated on this Water-Demon masquerade for some occasion last year; then they both lost heart.

Bruja glanced one blue eye, one brown eye up at her, tail and butt twitching.

"I threw all this away, in a rage over something. You rescued it." Bruja barked. "Yes, you did." Tears dribbled out. She'd been crying the whole day about everything.

Bruja danced and mewed. Success! She brushed against Cinnamon's leg, licking her fingers. Cinnamon wiped wet cheeks on her shirt, then took it off and her pants too. She stepped into the bodysuit, pulled it up her legs, and slid her arms down the sleeves. Inside the snakeskin was fake fur from a coat Klaus gave her on a cold Pittsburgh night because her crap coat was wet and useless. Over forty years ago too. When Klaus's coat finally fell apart last year, she'd felt abandoned. Pulling the suit to her neck, she felt Klaus hugging her; putting the mask on was like Marie stroking her head.

"Water-Demon. I can do that." Cinnamon struck a warrior-woman pose. "I bet this suit is air-conditioned and bulletproof, like Taiwo's cape." She laughed. "I might be bad as Zaneesha and never want to take my costume off." She arched backwards, thrusting her navel at the flies, and reached palms down to the floor. Bruja launched her twenty-eight pounds onto Cinnamon's tummy. The Bots cheered. Bruja chased her tail, whirling and prancing like they could do this backbend balance trick forever. Cinnamon's arms started shaking and Bruja leapt to the floor. Cinnamon collapsed.

They'd rehearsed this choreography for last year's Festival, but never performed it. Bruja licked her chin, ready to do their trick again and again. "My back ain't hollering, so let's not push that." She hugged Bruja, feeling grand. "Thank you."

And to think she had been ready to cancel Festival.

"Klaus's coat and Marie's comb, right? How'd you lose touch with them?" Thunderbird was always scouting clues.

Cinnamon sputtered, "I was afraid . . ." That her best memories were a lie. How could the magic be true? "They never contacted me." That hurt.

"You must tell us the story of Marie and Klaus," Dragon declared. "Don't argue."

"How are we to know you otherwise?" Mami asked. "To know ourselves?"

"Sure." Cinnamon felt bold as a Water-Demon. "I'll tell Mod Squad adventures at Festival."

"We're goin' hold you to that," Dragon said. "Bring them to life for us."

T-bird honked. "So, 'stead of getting bejiggity, let's get this show on the road!"

If the end of the world was looming, the valley could have a hell of a good time ushering in the next world. Lights flickered overhead, a kaleidoscope of colors. The Bots powered down to low-energy sentinel-mode. Shop-Bots—who passed for clueless vacuum cleaners, genie machines for hanging lights, and power prop-carts—trundled in with costumes and masks for Festival. A shop-vac collected the pieces of the whisper-witch and headed off to the light lab. The other Shop-Bots packed the trailer bins on her bike rig. They loaded T-bird, Dragon, and Mami. Bruja raced to the stage door and barked till it started to open.

"Wait," Cinnamon said. Lines for "I'ma Be My Own Sun" flooded her. She pulled a notepad and pen from her knapsack. Bruja whined and sat down in a pool of moonlight. Luckily, the song wrote itself in a few minutes. Secretly, behind her own back, Cinnamon had been working the lyrics all day. "Done. ¡Vámonos!"

Bruja dashed off. Cinnamon jumped on the bike saddle and pedaled as fast as she could. The demon mask had excellent night vision. The bodysuit supported achy muscles and creaky joints. It stayed cool when her muscles heated up. Hopefully she wouldn't have to test for bullet-proof juju anytime soon.

The stage door whizzed shut behind her, speaking her voice: "The show will go on."

Book IV

FESTIVAL

I still believe that theatre has a ritual power to call forth spirits, illuminate the darkness and speak the truth to people.

Pearl Cleage

Just keep on and keep on until you reach higher ground.

Stevie Wonder

Calling All Daredevils, Buccaneers, and Swashbucklers!

Do you walk on the WILD SIDE, have a flair for ADVENTURE?
Do you like taking risks and making boatloads of MONEY?

We got your attention
Because
You are so done with dead-end gigs
Sick to s#*% of
Wondering Where The Real Money Has Gone!

Maybe
You don't want to be a gig slut earning slave wages
or
Pick up a gun, join Valley Security, and clean up
after death-bots all day
Maybe
You're dragging a past around that locks you out of the
Eligible Workforce Database
or
The latest God-Algorithm glitched when it tanked your life
Maybe
YOU ARE JUST WHO WE ARE LOOKING FOR!

We need Good People
Who thrive when it's live
Good People
Who can press the flesh and get results
Badasses
Who can wear down a NO into a yes
Turn a *Get The F#*% Out Of Here* into a *God Bless*

Here's your chance
Life is short
Decide how to spend your Precious Time
See the WORLD before it's wrecked
Earn a generous Baseline pay plus Commission
Be part of a future you can feel ~~good~~ GREAT about

Congratulations! You've made it to the end of the flyer!

Scan this GOOD AS GOLD button for our net address
and your unique code.

Hurry. Traveling Sales Vacancies fill up quickly.

This offer will expire in ten minutes.*
And won't you kick yourself then?

Scan this green I'M IN button and start that better life NOW

*After ten minutes all talking flyers update to new vistas, voiding any previ-
ous offers.

BRUJA
 C&S

GATHERING AUDIENCE

Bruja crept through the last dark before dawn on an urgent tracking mission for Cinnamon. Shooting-Star-Bot had strayed several miles beyond the elders' farm. The trail led to the treacherous motor route. Smart cars zipped along at high speed and would run over small creatures or bots who wandered onto the road. Bears, deer, and moose got more respect. Smart cars avoided them and the damage they'd cause. Shooting-Star had trundled through the mountain laurels and wild blueberries on the shoulder recently. Somebody else might have wondered what the Bot was doing so far from home. Bruja was used to corralling wayward strays: bots, goats, squeaky toys, and humans. Last week she found a little boy and three goat kids who'd walked into the next county. No telling what got into strays.

Bruja lifted her nose from the ground and eyed the double yellow lines. These danger markings had gone gray in the moonlight and reeked of burnt rubber. Shooting-Star-Bot had zigzagged in the gravel and cut across the asphalt. Bruja huffed disapproval. A cloud burst overhead and cold rain plopped on her snout. She sneezed and grumble-growled. Rain jumbled a scent trail.

Headlights careened across the dark road and an armored car rattled to a halt. The engine farted a puff of greasy smoke, wheezed, and went silent. Two strangers jumped from the vehicle, cussing and hollering. Desperados? Disrupters? They kicked the tires and banged on the hood. The lone rain cloud deserted Bruja and dumped water on their bullet-resistant roof, sounding like a drone attack. Someone inside the car mewed.

Curious, Bruja crept closer, sticking to the opposite side of the road. The strangers pushed the vehicle off the motor route into bittersweet vines and covered everything except the driver's side in branches and debris; then they switched off the lights. No cars were coming from either direction. Traffic was sparse before dawn, a few sleepy drivers relying on cruise control. Bruja dashed across the gray yellow lines. She wanted to sniff the strangers up close without rain blunting her senses.

Goat odor and scents from far away wafted off them. Travelers. The tall, sinewy one had ragged breath that was *off*, similar to sick folks at the

Co-Op Clinic; the muscular, short one had robust, sweet breath. They both smelled excited, eager, like AUDIENCE, or maybe PERFORMERS getting juiced for their entrance, not like desperados prepping for ambush. Bruja loved their before-the-show aroma. She licked her nose and snuffled more of these good scents, relieved she wouldn't have to take them down. Who needed to start Festival day threatening off bad boys or ripping somebody's throat?

The travelers stripped their clothes off and bounded around in the cloudburst. Bruja joined the dance. REHEARSAL They stopped a moment, startled by her yaps and splashes. She jumped in a puddle and dashed water on them. They laughed and danced again, swishing water at her. A stiff wind chased the cloud down the road, and a plump moon blazed yellow at the horizon. Bruja propelled herself onto the armored car hood. She shook off the rain from nose to tail. The strangers squealed.

"We're traveling salespeople trying to find the AMPHITHEATRE." The tall traveler patted Bruja's head. "I don't suppose you know where that is?"

Bruja soared off the hood and pointed her nose toward the Amphitheatre.

"You ask any old body for directions." The short one sniggered.

"Why not?" Tall-dude stomped in a puddle. Wispy white hair was plastered on his face. "GPS sent us off a cliff yesterday. The dog wouldn't do that."

"Glitch. That farmhouse was down there somewhere. You resisted the Big Data bullshit directions. My hero!" Short-stuff bent over and tickled Bruja's chin. "We've heard tell of a Next World FESTIVAL starting an hour or two after dawn, somewhere near here. It looks like we'll be walking there. Hope it's not far."

Bruja was always happy to find people for Festival. She barked and wagged her tail.

"You like Festival, hmm?" Tall-dude wheezed.

"Do you think the dog knows what we're saying?" Short-stuff put a nose against Bruja's snout and sniffed.

"Border Collies love words. So, perhaps some of it. Let's see." Tall-dude waved at Bruja and said, "FESTIVAL." She barked, ran along the motor route, turned left at the Co-Op road, and took a few steps in the Amphitheatre direction, then ran back to them.

"No way," Short-stuff said, and pointed. "FESTIVAL?" Bruja gave a *ruff-ruff* reply.

"GPS had us sorta going that direction before we lost service." Tall-dude looked toward the Co-Op road. "A guide at the crossroads. Hooray!"

"It might still be a hike, and you're moving slow. Enough German water cure or what is it, Swedish? Let's get dressed, get going. I'm freezing." Short-stuff hugged Bruja. "Thanks, pooch."

Tall-dude bent down and joined the hug. Bruja tolerated this longer than usual, then wriggled free. As Tall-dude straightened up to standing, rusty joints popped and he groaned. Short-stuff opened the armored vehicle, and a baby goat bounded out, bleating at them for leaving her alone in the car. Goats hated being alone. Bruja licked the kid's face until she quieted down.

"One of yours?" The travelers spoke together. Good harmony, performers for sure.

"We were trying to sleep. She hollered right outside the car half the night." Short-stuff snatched fluffy towels from the vehicle.

"Bleating and bleating." Tall-dude mimicked the sound as they wiped themselves. He did a good baby goat. "Didn't stop until we let her in the car."

Short-stuff snickered. "It was cold last night."

"Eight degrees centigrade is not so cold."

"What is it now, eleven? We're having a goddamned tropical heat wave."

Tall-dude turned to Bruja. "We thought a Co-Op farmer at the carnival would know what to do for the little thing."

"Why are we explaining ourselves to a dog?"

"She was listening. She knows the goat." Tall-dude shrugged.

The travelers threw on dry clothes. A vehicle sped their way. They backed against the bushes. Bruja prevented the goat from bounding onto the motor route. She'd lost too many nosy little goats. A van flashed by, illuminating the travelers more than the moon. Somber suits and hats were too dull for Festival. Bruja would hunt up better costumes and masks for them after she found Shooting-Star. Barking and nipping heels, she herded the goat and the travelers toward the Co-Op road.

"That way. We understand." Tall-dude covered the driver's door with debris. "Scheiße! Will this fool anybody?"

"People speed by. They don't see what they're not looking for."

Tall-dude poked Short-stuff. "Did you bring the talking flyers?"

Short-stuff waved papers. "WHIZZ-ITs talk, not these cheap-ass, old-school flyers."

"No. Those are the *talking* ones. Automated nostalgia."

"Really?" Short-stuff shuddered and thrust the flyers at Tall-dude.

"Spyware! Yuck! You take 'em. I'll grab the goat. Don't want a car to splat her on the road."

"We can put on our faces at the gate. It's a bit after five AM. According to my sources, we're early. Sun's not up for another half hour, forty-five minutes."

"Your friend's kid blew through, when, last year, giving away burners to flood refugees?" Short-stuff tapped a shuffle-ball-change on the asphalt around the goat. "You think the show's as good as they say?"

"Better. If we still know her."

Short-stuff scooped up the goat, who was old enough to eat grass but didn't weigh very much. Bruja only ate grass if she absolutely had to. Spook ate it all the time. Spook ate anything. The kid put her head on Short-stuff's shoulder and nibbled an ear. Tall-dude scratched the goat's chin. One less stray to worry about. Bruja huffed relief.

"I hear Electric Paradise people will be there too," Short-stuff said.

"Yes. Cinnamon Jones has invited everyone." Tall-dude was delighted. "A show is perfect. Nobody will suspect a thing. We can gather plenty of intel."

"There might be other rogues and spies about."

Tall-dude nodded. "Do these people have any idea what's coming for them?"

"Cap George will have security on red alert." Short-stuff froze. "Will Cinnamon recognize us, after so long?"

"We've changed. She's changed. The world's changed. Do I even recognize me?"

Short-stuff sputtered, "Right. Who are we anymore?"

Tall-dude stood straight. "'Identity' is not really a noun. It should be a verb."

"Word . . . I'm afraid who we are together won't be the verb she wants."

Tall-dude whispered, "Maybe."

Music blared from Shooting-Star's loudspeakers:

> *I know a place, ain't nobody cryin', ain't nobody worried*
> *I let myself go and now we're flyin' through the stars*

"A line from the Staples Singers answered by Chaka Khan." Tall-dude sang along.

Short-stuff looked around, anxious. "Coming from the carnival already?"

Tall-dude broke off singing and sucked a breath. "Rehearsal. Don't you think?"

"Yeah." Short-stuff relaxed, and they headed for the Amphitheatre, both stroking the goat. Bruja yapped a catch-you-later, bounded over the guardrail, and plunged into the underbrush. Short-stuff whirled around. "Where's the dog going?"

"I bet we'll see that hound at the show." Tall-dude snickered. "We can do our naked hippie water-dance together."

"You maybe. This carnival is free. Strangers gotta pay big bucks to witness the splendor of my naked dancing."

"So how much does the dog owe you?"

Bruja didn't hear Short-stuff's reply. She got a whiff of Spook, Taiwo, and other familiar scents. She howled a greeting, excited to have other good noses join the search.

CINNAMON
ᛊᛊ

GRANDMOTHER OAK

The dawn sky was brighter every second, yet horror movie trees loomed overhead, a dense canopy keeping Cinnamon in shadows and shimmers. *Cosmic slop* . . .

"Bruja! Don't you want to help me round up people for Festival?" By "people," she meant Taiwo. "Where'd you go? Is Shooting-Star around here? Zaneesha will be tickled if you find that Bot. They can be comets together and steal the show." Cinnamon shifted to her lowest gear and veered off the paved bike path. The Bots bounced in their bins, suffering silently. The uphill dirt road to Taiwo's tree was a washboard, jiggling muscle, fat, and bone mercilessly. Fog and muddy potholes made it treacherous.

Cinnamon's breath turned to puffs of white in the damp air. Always colder here than everywhere else. How did Taiwo stand it? Hauling the jam-packed eight-bin trailer up to oun's oak meant she didn't have enough breath to yell, meant she'd eat a mountain of Naughty Nuggets, kale stew, honey fry bread, and apple delights when she hit the Amphitheatre, which, if she hadn't gone astray, was close. Taiwo could show her the shortcut. Final dress was soon, and the director shouldn't be late.

Luckily, she slept well last night. She fed Bruja and Spook soy sausage, rehearsed "I'ma Be My Own Sun," then went to the garage to touch Aidan's banjo, Redwood's bangles, and Iris's beaded top and mudcloth pants. She wanted to grab one of Raven's *space is the place* paintings for the Festival set. As she dragged across the doorsill, thoughts and intentions dissolved. She yawned in dim light, shaking her head at the organized clutter. Memories were jammed in the corners and stacked to the ceiling. She'd been threatening to sort through her life for years, but never made it beyond the box labeled: PITTSBURGH, HIGH SCHOOL, KLAUS AND MARIE. Bruja herded a heavy-lidded Cinnamon back to the farmhouse. She fell out on the couch in the Water-Demon costume and mask, asleep before her head hit the cushions. Her mother barged into a nightmare featuring IT Fred and a loaded gun. Opal pulled Cinnamon to—

The sunrise dress rehearsal. At the altar to the elders, Opal demonstrated the Funky Chicken, boogaloo, and Mashed Potato, her favorite dances, Raven's too. Indigo, Game-Boy, and Hawk gathered around with an eager crowd from the Hill Town Wenches and Powwow Now. Folks had a hard time picking up the old-timey moves, except the newbie from Electric Paradise. To everyone's surprise, rich white girl was a natural. Regina claimed stepdad taught her 'cause mom got too sick to stand up and dance with him. Opal was relentless, drilling folks till they looked like fly dancers on the Soul Train. Opal rocked the tight silver number she wore on their mother/daughter trip to the Georgia Sea Islands, a Donna Summer, Queen of Disco dress.

At an upbeat, Opal pulled Cinnamon to a golden beach on Sapelo Island. A dream cut. Frothy waves tickled bare toes. Wild horses trotted by and an armadillo family marched through the brush delighting tourists. Everybody and their brother flirted with Opal: an old R&B singer, a peanut farmer, a TV star who played a wiseass detective from Harlem, and two pleasure boat captains who wanted to take some fine ladies out to meet dolphins. Opal talked nonstop about her daughter, who had *a voice like an angel, a mind like a steel trap, and a heart as wide and open as the ocean kissing the sky.*

Cinnamon sipped a mint lemonade on the flat-bottom cruise boat and savored her mother's bragging. Dolphins swam close and nosed their feet, which dangled in warm Sea Island water. Snowy egrets soared in blue sky. Dopey young ones clowned around their elegant parents. Another dream cut, and she and Opal strolled arm in arm past the cove where the egrets nested. Alligators circled in murky water below, hoping one of the clown birds made a fatal error and fell in; then they wouldn't starve this evening. Opal and Cinnamon were the lone human witnesses on this primal drama, so Opal insisted that Cinnamon should talk to her, 'cause she could hear anything. *I'm an old sinner. You come out the womb talking. What good is the gift of gab if you refuse to use it?*

They sat under a live oak tree, close kin to Taiwo's tree. Spanish moss danced in the Georgia fan—the breeze off the Intracoastal Waterway. Opal fussed over Cinnamon's braids, tucking loose strands into the Water-Demon mask. Finally, Cinnamon admitted that *forgiving what could be forgiven* in order to *celebrate first fruits* and *light new fires* had been getting harder. It felt impossible this year.

Redwood, Aidan, and Iris were heroes. Raven and Opal too. Bus driver Mom talked a man threatening her passengers with a big-ass knife back to his right mind. She saved him and everybody on the bus, plus stayed on schedule. Cinnamon was a broken link in that hero-chain. A pathetic loser, she quit theatre *and* the tech world when the going got rough. Now her only close friends were Circus-Bots, two dogs, and a fussy alien.

Opal cracked up, like she was high or tipsy. Unusual. Opal never did drugs when she was alive. On a natural high then, she teased Cinnamon: *You been hoodooed, girl. You let slack-minded people put a trick on your spirit. How can you spout physics at me and fall for hoodoo-voodoo nonsense? It's hard to fight invisible enemies. Gotta get your mind right, so you can see those triflin' fools for what they are: Lonely Stardust, like you, me, like anybody.*

∽

Cinnamon shook off the sweet dream. She didn't recall the hill to Taiwo's tree being so steep and going on forever. It'd been too long since she came out to visit. Crotchety Taiwo didn't visit her either. She stood up on the pedals for more power.

> *I know a place, ain't nobody cryin', ain't nobody worried*
> *I let myself go and now we're flyin' through the stars*

The Circus-Bots played this without explanation. Mavis Staples and who, Chaka Khan? They were in sentinel-mode, dim lights blinking. The fireflies-making-love-in-the-trash-mode was cute when Cinnamon was in the mood. She didn't have oxygen for an SOS puzzle. "Come on, just tell me. I gotta get my mind right."

They remained silent, conserving energy. Maybe it wasn't an alert.

The sun came quickly. Copper-colored oak and maple leaves swayed in the dissipating fog. Hemlocks glistened. Otherworldly bushes sported colors like the aurora borealis. Vines with snowflake leaves and jewel seedpods crawled up tree trunks. Spectral birds mimicked funk melodies and flashed fluorescent feathers before hiding in their bowers. Black critters a bit bigger than squirrels blinked red eyes, flicked long, furry tails, and scurried under her wheels, chasing each other. Lemurs?

Not dawn playing tricks or her *ImagiNation* going wild, Cinnamon was lost in an enchanted forest. Bruja always led the way to Taiwo's tree. Witch-Dog had dashed off, like Cinnamon knew where the hell she was going or how to talk Taiwo into acting the griot storyteller today. Cinnamon's fault for telling Bruja Shooting-Star had gone walkabout and nobody could FIND her. Bruja could never resist FINDING LOST THINGS—nothing better to do in this world. Bruja left thirty minutes ago or maybe five. Time was weird.

Cinnamon skidded around an endless curve. Without warning, Taiwo's oak filled her vision, blotting out the sky and the rest of the landscape. Scaly black bark was like elephant or rhino skin. Half a million pale green, red-tipped leaves waved at her. Who could believe the baseball-sized acorns? One more season till they dropped. More like a million leaves waving, and as many male flower tassels, dusting the air with pollen.

"Whoa!" she shouted, as if she had a horse to rein in before they slammed into the trunk. Hydraulic brakes gurgled, and the bike rig came to an abrupt halt. She jumped off the saddle, stumbling with the last of the momentum. Taiwo's oak tree always stunned her, partly because she never remembered where the gnarl of limbs, boughs, and knots was located. More than that, the tree never *fit* in her memory.

The trunk was forty feet around. Lower limbs extended fifty feet horizontally from the trunk, resting elbows on the ground as branches reached for the sky. Thicker than the trunks of nearby maple, hemlock, and young oaks, these boughs gave the ancient tree a circumference of over three hundred feet. Game-Boy tried fancy lenses from many angles, even a drone once. He never got the full stretch of the limbs in a single shot. Something always blurred out of focus, like Water-Spirit photos. Indigo insisted the lenses were tiptop and the software glitch-free. This tree was actually, well, impossible.

Cinnamon stomped clave rhythm on the ground, a greeting, an appreciation. She hovered at the bough perimeter, mesmerized by swaying branches and rustling leaves. The oak's shallow roots stretched out ten times farther than the limbs, conversing with everyone growing for miles and miles. The root-fungus community was an underground intelligence network, a survival of the friendliest marvel.

A wood turtle crawled toward her foot. She stepped aside as it lumbered by, an old soul and unafraid. She savored the tree air, a luxury she shouldn't take for granted. Her heart beat in turtle time. She imagined standing in this one place for four centuries as the cosmos whizzed by. Tension evaporated, and she felt like a flower tassel dancing in the wind. No wonder Taiwo and Spook came out here to sleep.

Once, after Indigo and Game-Boy persuaded her to do a marijuana bong with them, Cinnamon said Taiwo's oak not only embraced the entire hilltop forest but also held the curve of the Earth, the curve of spacetime, in its arms. How could such a being fit into a single frame? She confided her suspicion that the oak inhabited multiple dimensions, the one they called home and another, where Taiwo was from. The two geographies weren't in phase, so the tree never fit in the picture. Indeed, its location appeared to shift. Navigating *the spaces between things* was no joke. Taiwo traveled anywhere in a flash from the tree house. Alien juju.

Taiwo allowed Cinnamon and the kids, plus Bruja and Spook, to find the oak—nobody else, for the tree's sake. Indigo and Game-Boy felt honored to be in this special company. They were psyched to spread tales of the baron of badass tripping in from another dimension and hunkering down with a Grandmother Oak that wasn't on any map people might draw. Taiwo appreciated Cinnamon's attempts to explain the oak mystery. *I've forgotten myself. You make me remember who I am.*

"OK, but," Cinnamon whispered to the vivid voice talking in her head, "we should keep checking the *ImagiNation,* around the kids for sure."

Impressionable youth, despite fronting like big-time cynics, clung to the possibility of magic. Who could blame them? The Grandmother Oak let them touch beyond the blink of a human lifetime. More than four hundred years old, this tree had mingled roots and shared secret wisdom with ancestor trees long dead who had known ancestor trees and so on back to the first tree. How many trees these days got to live such long lives? Indigo should add the Grandmother Oak to her miracle count.

It dawned on Cinnamon that Taiwo might speak the tree-root/fungus language. What did they talk about before oun drifted into sleep? She took another deep breath. Tree air spoke to them all. No harm tapping into that marvel, and definitely no need to be at war with her *ImagiNation.* Tomorrow, she'd visit again, have a picnic with Taiwo, and stay a good while. She'd bring Zaneesha, after school at the Mall.

"Are you hiding from me, Taiwo?" Cinnamon shouted, feeling fourteen, petulant, and full of herself. "It's getting wild from Paradise to the hill towns. Some nostalgia militia be snatching kids. Consolidated or random nasties nabbed Flying-Horse. Can you believe that? We're a dangerous anomaly to the paranoid digerati. They'll torture Horse apart." She shuddered. "Tatyana's trying to break my heart again." Her heart was stronger than she thought. "Our enemies are storming the goddamned gate. No time for coy, pissy, or whatever the hell you're playing at. We need to haul our whiny asses down off *Sorrow Mountain* and do whatever the fuck we have to."

The Bots bleeped and growled at her outburst.

"Sorry." She touched the rough bark on the trunk, half expecting her hand to pass through. It was cool, damp, and sturdy, like any other oak on a March morning. "I can do better." She strode back to the trailer. "Tatyana's right. Raven not coming all the way back from that coma was not your fault, Taiwo. My dad would be so sad for us even thinking this." She squirmed. "I been missing him all my life. I get jealous of Back-From-The-Dead for living a miracle. I don't mean to take that out on you. It's petty. Not who I mean to be. Can you forgive me? This is the day for forgiveness." No answer.

She dug in a trailer bin. "The shekere you *claimed* you lost, that brought bad boys back to themselves?" She pulled the instrument out. "Don't bother lying. I saw you toss this in the Mill River. You cried when it floated away. Bruja must have found it downwater in the mud and brought it home." She stroked the shekere's smooth gourd bottom and tugged at the net of seeds. "Not a crack or broken thread. How about that?"

She played the Agbekor bell pattern, a celebration of the ancestors and a call to clear life. She stepped onto a limb and danced a three on two polyrhythm right to the trunk. Tiny red buds had sprouted where leaves attached to branches, female flowers that would grow into acorns actually larger than baseballs. A sweetgrass basket was tucked in a cross-roads of big boughs. Inside, she found crumbs and neatly folded cloth. Someone other than Spook had eaten the fruit and bean patties Indigo brought last night. A hopeful sign. She raised the shekere and swirled the net of seeds, producing a hailstorm rhythm.

"You also called up Water-Spirits with this gourd. Bruja has kept it safe in your room for two years. She's the only one going in there. And see what I'm wearing." She modeled the Water-Demon costume. "Bomb-ing around these roads, no chills, no sweat. Perfect for Festival. Bruja stashed this in the Event Horizon. She won't let us throw ourselves away." Cinnamon flared the feathers and feelers on the jumpsuit. "I look good, but how can I do a Water-Demon act alone? Come down and tell your stories. Me and the rainbow gals will do backup. You promised Tatyana a surprise. Bring Kehinde and true love back to life for Festival. That'll be a showstopper."

I wouldn't be here at all, without Marie, Klaus, and you believing *in me until I came true.*

Was Taiwo talking to her or did a memory sound like right now? She squinted up through the leaves. Oun's tree house was almost invisible, an illusion fading in and out of dawn light. She concentrated on: a floor, thatched roof, and open sides—canvas curtains were rolled up into the roof, same as the Seminole chickees Aidan built and Raven painted.

"I invited Paradise and the cavalry—Diego Denzel Ortiz and Jerome Williams." She leaned against the trunk. "I bet this year's audience will be huge. A thousand people, hearts in sync, gasping breath together. You should do the weird from another dimension, eat fire and bullets, or swallow electricity. You'll break their minds wide open and scare the Bejesus out of desperados."

A crow swooped by her nose, an old friend of Taiwo's. Bright red feathers on one crooked wing was a boneyard baron costume. The crow landed on the sweetgrass basket. It pecked up the crumbs, then contemplated Cinnamon, head cocked to the side.

"We love you, Taiwo. Come on down and let's forgive ourselves and everyone. Let's do the show for love." Oak flower tassels fluttered against her cheek. "You, me, and everybody can bring love back in style ourselves. Starting this morning."

The leaves sighed and the wind settled. The turtle made it to the trunk and dug through decaying leaves for grubs. The crow cawed at Cinnamon, a scolding.

"OK." She had nothing better than love to offer. "I'll play the shekere and tell Kehinde and Taiwo tales myself. I know some good ones."

Spook appeared out of nowhere and bounded up onto the bough next to her.

"Hey, you." She scratched his head. "I've been standing around, talking to an empty house. Pretty good monologue, though." Spook barked and wagged his tail, always so happy to see her. "Did Taiwo send you to pick me up? Is oun already at the Amphitheatre?" That was a hopeful thought. "Bruja abandoned me. You're in time to show me the SHORTCUT." She played the Festival finale groove on the shekere and headed for her bike rig. Spook jibber-jabbered in time with her. He whined when she packed the instrument away. "Get me to final dress on time if you want more."

Spook charged off with Cinnamon close behind. It was all downhill. In no time, they raced by the sentinels at the borders of the elders' farm. Her farm now. Wooden antelopes, birds, and dancing harps led right to the back gate of the Amphitheatre.

CURSES

Morning mist in the Amphitheatre turned the drumheads soggy. Game-Boy and Back-From-The-Dead claimed they lost their masks. Liars. The Mothership couldn't land or take off or both. The wind was wrong and the trees pitched a fit, tangling the cables. The Motor Fairies and Taiwo were MIA, plus Zaneesha was feeling too mad, too sad, to twinkle like a roving star. Everybody kept messing up the lyrics and the blocking for Cinnamon's big finale. Final dress was a train wreck. A disaster. Indigo wanted to come out her face at everyone or run away and never come back. Cinnamon was chill, said not to worry. Rehearsal disasters meant they'd have a great show. Cast and crew worked the screw-ups out of their systems, so they'd be sharp for the real deal. Indigo clung to Cinnamon's theatre lore, even though—

May There Be Grace Choir had three singers with hangovers and sore throats. Bruja left the finale run-through to snarl at cowboys and zoot suit gangstas spoiling for trouble. (Really, boys? Not much of a disguise.) What if Bruja ran off to chase dangerous-smelling thugs during the Cyborg-Amazon act? OK, Cap George, in Rocketman boots and a gold lamé cape, escorted the disrupters out. He acted like their perp walk across the dandelion and clover stage was part of the curtain call. Everyone snapped their fingers and cheered Cap's rainbow Afro.

Indigo went into the prop closet (aka the garden shed) to find candles for the opening parade. A Hill Town Wench was ranting about *Macbeth* because a buttload of props had mysteriously vanished, including the candles. A bad omen. How would they light new fires? Techies groaned. Mentioning the Scottish play was terrible luck, a curse on players and audience. Indigo tried to shift the chat to a Pearl Cleage play she wanted to do, *Flyin' West*, a Utopia joint and inspiration for the Ghost Mall. The Wench wouldn't shut up about *Macbeth*: actors getting the pox, audience spreading the plague, and lunatic men dressed as trees rampaging with knives and guns, while witches toiled and boiled trouble on stage. Who needed to hear that? Back-From-The-Dead was already spooked. Superstition was supposedly all in your mind. So was imagination and inspiration. Why mess with curses and shit right before you had to go on?

The newbie—Regina Benita Washington—could tell the Wench was working everybody's last nerve. "Don't worry, I got this." She dragged the Wench backstage (beyond the magnolia bushes) right when Indigo was about to explode. Regina was smarter than she let on. Acting like a ditz might be a bad habit or maybe a shield. Unfortunately, the Wench had already done her damage. Indigo's stomach was a fluttery, jumbled mess. Germans called this Flugzeuge im Bauch, airplanes flying around your tummy, wreaking havoc. Who could blame her? She had to go on in ten minutes.

The rock-seats overlooking the grass stage were jammed: Co-Op farm families and hill town hipsters; fancy foreigners talking languages Indigo never heard before; Paradise glitterati with picnic baskets and heated cushions; traveling salespeople passing out talking flyers; Valley Security in old rocker costumes; and drifters from yesterday who'd stuck around for the show. One thousand people, easy, and more trying to squeeze in. So, what the hell was Indigo and her belly full of jet Flugzeuge doing in the food pavilion, explaining herself?

"I don't deal anymore. Not for a long time," she muttered at Jerome Williams.

He was tricked out as a fire spirit. A crown of flames was perched on his dreads and a smoky cloak billowed around broad shoulders. Yesterday Indigo worried that Mitchell had put her off men for life, yet costumes from Cinnamon's barn looked stellar on Jerome. He smelled good too, woodsy, skulking up to the Dirty Dozen Farmers' table, acting vulnerable and sweet, trying to score cheap weed. He was Valley Security, keeping the peace for everybody. Didn't they deserve special deals? Hell no.

"You ain't gotta holler." He eyed Boss Lady Shaheen, also a fire spirit, though not in costume, just silvery-blue flames painted on her face. She handed out breakfast pizza, something with eggs and hot sauce on a cauliflower crust that made Indigo gag. Jerome murmured in her ear, "You grow the good stuff on a rooftop Diego said. I figure you have a private stash. Cut me a deal." He thought Indigo was who she used to be.

"You don't know me anymore if you think I'm doing that." Dealing from dumpsters was when any crap was better than a boyfriend who wanted you to turn tricks.

"Nobody change that much." He scanned her. "What're you s'posed to be?"

"African Cyborg Amazon." Indigo wore black pleather pants tight enough to tell her religion. A bling-encrusted belt cinched her waist over ample booty and thighs. The red cap-sleeved coat had sharp silver studs at the neck, wrists, and shoulders—weapons as jewelry. Steel-toe boots gave a heft to her step, to her *neo-savage* attitude. Paradise gate-bitch didn't know the half of it.

Jerome snickered. "What, like *Black Panther* babes?"

"No. West African warrior woman from ancient Dahomey to the twenty-first century."

"No shit, uhm, so, I heard you were hunting me." He leaned close, voice low and gravelly. "I thought you wanted to do business, the way we used to."

"They got pot shops in the hill towns, the Mall, Electric Paradise, and beyond." This wasn't what she wanted to talk to him about. "Marijuana is legal, son."

"Legal is expensive. They can jack prices and blame taxes. Don't worry. I'll keep my mouth shut." He piled vegan barbecue ribs, potato salad, coleslaw, Naughty Nuggets, and fry bread on a plate. Wolfing so much food before going on was suicidal. Eating in costume period was verboten. "What? I'm hungry." He added plantains, biscuits, and extra barbecue sauce. "Can't cook. Can't afford meat either."

It wasn't meat, but she didn't say. "What you doing with all your money?"

"Valley Security ain't that much money." He scowled at her booty and thighs, trying to ignore her breasts. "When did you get so—" He managed a killer smile. Two years ago, she thought he was a handsome older hunk, light-years better than Mitchell. Any dog was better than Mitchell, yet she couldn't remember what had been so impressive.

Jerome chomped on fake ribs, a proud carnivore. Yuck. She'd gone vegan last Halloween. His right nostril went askew when he chewed. His mustache was scraggly wisps at the edges, barely visible in the middle. One eye was rounder than the other. Somebody else might not have noticed. Despite better judgement, she found Jerome Williams more fascinating than most folks. He never said or did what she expected. She admired his long fingers and wondered how they'd feel on her neck, belly, her—

"Indigo Hickory, damn, girl." He licked his lips and loaded up another plate. He even included a slice of Shaheen's diablo pizza. "You looking good enough to eat."

"Shut up." The Festival was about to begin. Instead of drowning in hormones over stud muffin or calling him out for abandoning his kid, Indigo had to focus. She marched out of the food pavilion. "We'll talk later."

꩜

A hot-as-July sun blazed in a hazy sky. The glitterati ditched heated cushions. Bruja dashed by with a lion mask in her mouth. The mane dragged in the dirt, then fell off.

"Who's that for?" Indigo yelled. "Game-Boy?" Bruja wagged her butt and kept going, in a hurry to take that lioness to somebody. "Good, girl."

The Festival grounds were a mob scene. Insects rollerbladed on the wooden path around the food pavilion: butterflies, dragonflies, and giant ladybugs. A herd of fantastical deer? elk? moose? tap-danced past Indigo. She felt dizzy for a second and almost collided with a woman in an orca mask and a frothy ocean cape. Whisper-weight boots looked familiar. So did the turquoise fingernails and breastplate. Cinnamon's old friend, a dodgy character—what was her name, Tatyana, no—

"Francine? Sorry," Indigo said. Francine Elkins.

The orca woman clicked and whistled. A singer doing an excellent sea mammal impression, she plunged into waves of spectators. Indigo admired her moves. Orca woman was Cinnamon's old theatre buddy, and something more, an ache, a wound—Indigo could feel that. Game-Boy found squat on the net about *Francine Elkins*. Too many suspect characters flying under the cyber-radar and sniffing around the Mall these days. Game-Boy should search "Tatyana" instead of "Francine."

Indigo headed upstage to the pink granite sculpture of Dragon, Thunderbird, and Mami Wata. You could always find candles at the altar to Cinnamon's elders. The Circus-Bots, still in compressed-trash-mode, rolled behind her and made a circle with the sculpture. In between raggedy stuffed animals and dolls, dented mirrors sparkled in the sunlight. A new look. Indigo liked the space babe holding her mirror helmet. The Bots buzzed and twanged, psyching themselves and Indigo for the show. They often included her in their *sacred loop* and Game-Boy too. Indigo smiled, feeling better.

Bruja dashed by with an elephant mask. The trunk almost got caught in Mami's tail. Everyone should have their costumes by now. The Bots trundled off behind Bruja. Witch-Dog was also in their *sacred loop*. Indigo had to ask Cinnamon to clarify this.

"Why'd you run off?" Jerome loomed over her. He stuffed his face without spilling barbecue sauce on his tights. His mouth was too full to understand what else he said. Hawk, styling Cyborg-Amazon finery like Indigo's, stepped between them. Oun nodded at Jerome and pulled Indigo toward the maple tree wings.

"We've been looking for you," Hawk said.

"Somebody lifted the candles and the lighter wands." Indigo whined. "Props for the alien invasion too."

"Don't worry." Everybody was telling her not to worry. Did she look worried? "Cinnamon says we have to hold the curtain for fifteen, maybe twenty minutes."

Indigo groaned. Waiting was hell; plus, the Amphitheatre didn't have a curtain to hold. They were outdoors on a wide-open grassy field. "I thought Powwow Now put their drums by some heaters."

Hawk nodded. "They did."

"Is it the Mothership?"

"No. Cinnamon talked to the trees, to the wind, and calmed shit down; then bike nerds sorted the twisted cables, easy-peasy. The ship's ready for takeoff."

"So what's the holdup?"

Hawk scanned her. "You look fierce, beautiful."

Indigo grunted. "Like I could *walk into battle to take a head and change somebody's mind without spilling blood.*" The Cyborg-Amazon line sounded stupid. Who was she kidding?

"You changed me and them." Hawk nodded at the bugs and beasts sorting themselves for the parade. "I came out to thank you for whipping us *all* into shape."

"Last year final dress was a dream. The audience was a no-show."

Hawk grinned at folks on stone seats chomping free food. "They showed up today, roaring for a carnival." Getting teary, oun gripped Indigo's shoulders and kissed her forehead. "Thanks for standing beside me, when all I knew how to do was run." Indigo was about to argue. Hawk talked over her, "*Na na na no no no!* You invited Game-Boy to the rooftop stargazing party tonight. You must think he's for real, not messing around, making a point, or—"

"He wants you for you and that's how you feel about him, right?"

Hawk nodded.

"You're my best friends except for Cinnamon, so don't mess this up."

Hawk did Soul Train moves. "I've nailed the astral bop *and* the Funky Chicken." Oun disappeared into the trees without explaining why they were holding the show.

A single jar with a puddle of wax and the ashes of a wick sat on the stone terrace in front of the altar. Indigo resisted feeling cursed. Fuck the Scottish play.

NOT AN ENTRANCE

Spook had only wolfed two hunks of cheese when the wind changed directions and he caught a whiff of danger. The Co-Op Clinic Clowns smelled sad as he jumped over the bunny trike and dashed away from their bowl of tasty treats. Nurses Azalea and Boo hollered for him to come on back. He would, later. Danger stole his appetite, made good food taste like dust. He had to ready himself for a fight. The wind carried the scent of the rogues who stole Flying-Horse. They might crash the Festival and shoot up everybody's fun. Hopefully Taiwo caught wind of these killjoy fools too.

Spook raced by Cinnamon and the Wheel-Wizards hoisting the Mothership almost to the top of a stand of shagbark hickory trees. The Wizards pitched popcorn at him and yelled, "SHOWTIME." Spook loved popcorn and SHOWTIME, but he couldn't linger. He jibber-jabbered at Cinnamon about an urgent mission, snagged a few buttery kernels, and charged through the woods to the borders of the elders' farm. He launched from a small ice age boulder onto the shoulders of a female Eshu statue, then leapt over the twelve-foot fence. He landed in a mound of dead leaves. This was his usual route to the Co-Op road, except *surprise!*

A black fur ball with a bushy tail burst through the leaves and bounced in the air, a red-eyed creature that Spook had never smelled before. The fur ball touched down, fearful, yet curious. They contemplated each other. The red eyes had black dot pupils and the endless tail tickled Spook's nose. Someone for Bruja to play with. Spook cocked his head, wagged his tail, and woofed—a friendly sound. The fur ball shook off shock, sprang across the road on rubbery legs, then scuttled up a mulberry tree to join a friend. They jumped from one tree to the next, flying almost.

Spook had no time to wonder at lemurs soaring around the Massachusetts hills. He was on a mission. The stink of blood and a lone gunman was powerful. Taiwo or Cap George usually took care of the armed whack-jobs. Even a single gunman could cause a crapload of trouble. A threat to the elders' farm, to Spook's home ground, called for action. He marked the boundary with power piss and soldiered on.

A turkey buzzard circled above. The black-and-silver wings and red head were stark against bright blue. Wooden antelopes, birds, and dancing harps—sentinel-bots masquerading as garden statues—buzzed. Each sentinel had a data collection and security specialty. They all sent alerts: alarm pheromones for him and Bruja, static talk for the Water-Spirits, and astral-bop music for the Circus-Bots:

In a black hole, without a soul, nada without you, babe.

The Co-Op road was empty, not a chipmunk or distant motor. Spook crept along the shoulder, lips curled, his tail like a blade behind him. A growl slid off his fangs. He faded in and out of the bushes. The turkey buzzard settled on a hemlock branch. Spook halted by the back gate to the Amphitheatre. Taiwo had carved this wrought-iron wonder. The intricate crossroads of circles and stars, worlds within worlds, was a tribute to West African artisans and a link to secret tunnels, only if Taiwo was around. Alone, Spook poked his nose on cold ironwork and got nowhere. He and Taiwo were better as a team. Oun should be here, to handle any gunmen. Spook whined under a sign Indigo put up yesterday:

NOT AN ENTRANCE
Don't risk the **Wrath** of **Water-Demons**, **Spook**,
and the **Boneyard Baron**
Follow Arrows to the Front Gate

Indigo's voice startled him. She sounded funny, as if she was hiding in the little box hanging by the sign. She repeated the same words including his name, over and over, while Game-Boy did beatbox underneath. Rehearsing? Spook didn't catch a fresh whiff of her or Game-Boy, only what lingered from yesterday. He barked once in case they were nearby and could help with the danger.

A night eye camera stared at him from a murky puddle. A raffia mane was twisted around cables in the mud. A leg had been thrust into somebody's muzzle. Busted circuit boards, wheels, drives, and sensors were scattered in the gravel. A tattered wing hung on the back gate. Feathers floated down the road. Spook sniffed the debris, then jumped on the fence to lick the tattered wing. He grumble-growled.

Flying-Horse-Bot was in pieces.

Spook smelled the wreckage again to be certain. The scent was unmistakable. He mewed and danced around the debris. He liked Flying-Horse almost as much as Bruja did. Why would anybody rip Cinnamon's Bot apart? Scavengers never trashed gear they wanted to steal. Confused, Spook backed away and bumped into a magnolia bush. Horse's sweetgrass tail fell from a branch onto Spook's head. He yelped and shook it off, stumbling next to—

A dead body was slumped against a birch tree just off the road. Blood soaked the ground around him. Spook snarled at the Paradise rogue who had attacked Blossom Bridge and shot at Taiwo last night by the waterfall. Not a danger anymore. Danger had driven away in an electric vehicle a short while ago. Spook swallowed familiar scents: IT Fred and his pack, marijuana and gin in their sweat. The sweetgrass tail reeked of IT Fred and pot. All the Flying-Horse wreckage did.

A second buzzard landed on a birch tree branch, right above the body. A third arrived, gurgling at the others. The Paradise rogue was a recent kill, and buzzards preferred meat as fresh as possible. Spook sniffed the corpse. No hint of IT Fred and no fresh wounds. The buzzards eyed Spook as if they'd have to wait and see what meat he left behind. Spook would have to be starving to eat this man. Much better food waited for him at Festival. The Clinic Clowns and Wheel-Wizards knew his favorite treats. Azalea, Boo, and Shaheen would have bowls waiting for his return.

As he tiptoed away from the corpse, a buzzard descended on the corpse's head. The others joined their friend, eyeing Spook and gurgling. Buzzards disliked wolf or coyote company at their meals; Spook had no reason to linger. He wasn't sure if Taiwo was coming or what to do about Flying-Horse all by himself. The birds tore flesh from the gunman, and Spook's stomach hollered—hunger returning full force. He jumped on the antelope sculpture-bot and vaulted over the gate onto a spongy mound of moss. He hated leaving Flying-Horse alone in the dirt. The buzzards probably wouldn't eat Horse's remains—nothing tasty there. Spook ran top speed back to the Amphitheatre. He needed reinforcements.

CINNAMON
ᧁ᧒ᧂᧈ
EXOTIC BEASTS

Ages ago Aunt Iris planted red maples by the bike-path gate to the Amphitheatre, a wind crossroads for their whirligig seeds. Cinnamon threw Taiwo's shekere into a wine-colored cascade and caught it on a downbeat. The perfect tonic after a rugged dress rehearsal. "We'll start in twenty minutes," she told the Mothership commander what she hoped. "We're holding for the Motor Fairies."

Radio silence from the Fairies for two hours. Who could say what that meant? The starship commander grumbled about *Fairy Time*. Cinnamon ignored her. The Fairies had the Mothership ramps. The Festival parade would slip up a ramp hidden by backstage bushes, move through the Mothership, then strut down a front ramp for a grand entrance into the Amphitheatre: Alien Invasion.

"A delay is helpful," she assured the commander. "Powwow Now wants to go over the beginning with me and Zaneesha."

Where was Zaneesha? Paradise had swallowed her mom, and Jerome avoided his daughter at final dress. To be fair, the comet getup made her unrecognizable. Jerome stuck close to Diego Denzel, on alert, like rogues might come from nowhere and blow everyone away. Something bad happened at Blossom Bridge yesterday. Diego and Jerome were tight-lipped per George's orders no doubt. Cinnamon would get intel from Indigo and Game-Boy later. Zaneesha was too shy to take off her mask and approach her father. Cinnamon had planned to go with her. There was always something else to do; then Zaneesha disappeared. Cinnamon's knees popped as she squatted down to Bruja.

"Zaneesha is lost. So is Shooting-Star-Bot, again. Can you find them?" She repeated their names. Bruja practically levitated as she took off, thrilled to be on the job. Cinnamon rubbed cranky knees and stood up to Game-Boy ranting at the speed of light. She couldn't blink without someone yammering a new problem at her. She clutched Taiwo's shekere, trying to focus. Short-term memory dissolve was a bitch. "What are you telling me?"

"Some whack shit." Instead of a costume, Game-Boy wore the fake leather jacket sanctified by Ruby Dee, Whoopi Goldberg, and Coretta Scott King. "Weren't you listening?" He sounded dire.

She scanned the sky for drones. "How bad is it?" Were they under attack, more desperados in zoot suits and cowboy hats or worse?

A short ball of energy rocking a lioness masquerade, and a tall drink of water in an elephant mask stopped to eavesdrop. They wore copper lamé capes and platform boots from her barn collection. Nosy spectators turned extras or spies out to sabotage Festival? She barely had time to register suspicion. Game-Boy was sweating buckets and flinging spit. Her Water-Demon bristles flared as he repeated his tale.

A Consolidated gazillionaire, the geek wizard who'd made Paradise *electric* and collected exotic beasts, had a zoo break-in at 4:00 AM. An inside job. Two caretakers hired off the Utopia App were the culprits. The getaway truck cruised past gate guards, but the motor died on the Co-Op road. Critters busted out of their cages, then out of the truck. One caretaker/thief claimed they were animal rights fanatics when Valley Security caught him chasing lemurs. One thief got away. Security nabbed buyers who didn't realize the animals had GPS trackers. Gazillionaire and his minions were running around trying to catch cockatoos, lemurs, zebras, and a baby rhino.

"A rhino in Paradise?" Was this the big baby Zaneesha's mom took care of? Cinnamon had imagined horses, dogs, maybe pigs or goats, not baby rhinos.

"Can't make this shit up." Game-Boy wiped sweat from his neck. The elephant and lioness snickered. The crowd that had gathered laughed too. Why was this happening on Festival day? "Rich dude won't say what animals got snatched, even to press charges. Cap George is on it."

"I saw lemurs near Taiwo's oak." Cinnamon had chalked that up to Taiwo's alien juju. Wrong. "Does this botched heist have anything to do with us?"

Game-Boy held up a hand. "I'm getting to that."

The Motor Fairies were out delivering food and collecting people who needed transport to Festival. The driver stopped the bus to let a mama bear chase three cubs across the bridge at the gorge. The whole bus was cracking up over baby bear antics when the bridge washed away in runoff from this morning's storm.

Cinnamon and the crowd around her gasped in unison.

"Whack-a-doodle! Boom kaboom! Gone!" Game-Boy hammed it up.

The Fairies and their passengers were hollering about ridiculous good luck when the baby rhino scrambled up on the road. The little bugger had almost been swept away. An old farmer lady used a carton of half-and-half to lure him onto the chairlift with her. Rhino guzzled three quarts and feel asleep, head in her lap. Since the bridge was out, the Fairies took the long way to the Amphitheatre. The storm had knocked out a cell tower. No service till five minutes ago. They were ten minutes out now.

The crowd applauded Game-Boy's performance.

"There's a baby rhino on board?" Cinnamon stifled a laugh. "No way."

"Yo, I ain't lying." He held up his phone: a bridge careened down the river; a farmer lady in a wheelchair poured half-and-half into a baby rhino's mouth. Motor Fairies in Neo–Tinker Bell/Hells Angels garb snickered in the background. Beards and shaved heads sparkled with glitter. Both videos had already gone viral—InstaHam. "It's off the chain." Game-Boy snapped his fingers. "Cockatoos and zebras still be missing."

"Zebras don't play," the elephant said. The mask muffled his voice. "They're temper tantrums on hooves."

The lioness shuddered. "They'll kick a lioness in the teeth and break her jaw." Voice muffled too. Masks were perfect for spies.

Cinnamon wrestled down suspicion. "You getting into character?"

"Trying," the lioness replied. "We just got this gear."

"From a friendly Border Collie," the elephant added. Bruja's recruits, a good sign. Cinnamon laughed at herself for relying on doggy character assessment.

"*Temper tantrums on hooves,*" Game-Boy said. "You think they'll come here?"

"What? *Zebras on the Rampage?*" Cinnamon laughed too hard, almost choking.

Game-Boy waved the crowd away. "Give her some room." Most everyone trudged off except the elephant and lioness. Game-Boy squeezed Cinnamon's hand.

"I've been so frazzled," she whispered.

Game-Boy looked embarrassed. "I know dress rehearsal was a bust, and my fault Back-From-The-Dead didn't show last year—"

"No, I'm worried about—" Enemies at the gates, Consolidated operatives and Darknet Lords storming the Festival, hauling her away in chains in front of the world—a viral video. "*Rise of the Machines* or *Robopocalypse.*"

Game-Boy rolled his eyes at tech phobia and patted her shoulder. "Don't go there." The lioness and elephant mumbled and gestured, a little obvious for spies.

"Gazillionaire is hiding something," Cinnamon said. Did he hire IT Fred?

"Tigers? Crocodiles?" Game-Boy quipped. "Those snakes who swallow antelopes?"

"Pythons?" The elephant and lioness spoke together.

Cinnamon cracked up, about to pee her pants. She almost fell over.

Game-Boy held her up. "Pet crocodiles or tigers are illegal, pet rhinos too, right?"

"Lots of shit folks do is illegal." Or it should be. Cinnamon tried to gather herself. "I could tell you stories that would curl your hair, so you didn't have to do whatever it is you do to . . ." She motioned at sand-colored dreads squeezed in a knot. Game-Boy cringed, not wanting to know her nap-your-hair secrets or share his. The elephant and lioness were all ears. "Not only tales of exotic beasts—"

Cinnamon resisted motor-mouth-itis. SevGenAlg was a walk on the wild side, and she was a thief, although she stole her own invention. Consolidated would make a spectacle of her if they found out. Of course SevGenAlg wasn't just *her* invention. Even if it was her idea, even if she worked out major bugs in the code and built the Circus-Bots from scratch, from junk nobody wanted. Every choice she made built on somebody else's grand ideas or nagging questions or heartbreaking mistakes. SevGenAlg was *hers* and *not hers*, like the cat that was dead and not dead, or the electron that was in a location and always moving beyond it.

She guided SevGenAlg, taking it a direction nobody wanted her to go. Consolidated big guns thwarted her, finally fired her for heading the *wrong* direction, for talking ethics, morals, and sentimental slop. No profit in that. Big tech was beyond mortal morals. Everybody worked and shopped at the company store. When they'd offered her a dream gig, there'd been nothing to do except sign her rights away. Yet she *knew* how corrupt and destructive Consolidated was. Sticking to the wrong direction, she almost solved the Teufelskreis glitches. A good enough workaround not to crash the system constantly. She never capitalized on her code insights. That saved her, till now. So many bad choices, did that make her a bad person? She was in a Teufelskreis too. Scheiße.

"Totals crass too?" Game-Boy peered at her. "You're gibbering, not making sense."

"Sorry." Did she say Teufelskreis out loud? The lioness and elephant leaned close. They might be spectators hoping for real-live drama, or Consolidated agents deployed to augment Tatyana's and IT Fred's nefarious plans. After so many years coming after her made zero sense. Cinnamon was nobody, and although Tatyana got a warm reception from

Bruja, Witch-Dog would never give enemy agents such fly disguises. Cinnamon checked the runaway *ImagiNation*. "We go the second the Fairies arrive," she said. "Where's your mask? Costume?"

Game-Boy scratched his jaw. "Yeah, about that—"

"What's Indigo gonna say? Hawk will be so disappointed. The Cyborg Amazons are counting on Back-From-The-Dead to represent."

"You think Hawk will be mad?"

"You know oun better than I do."

He clutched Cinnamon. "Tell me straight, do I have a chance?"

"At what?"

"You been in love a few times, right?"

She nodded—Jaybird, Tatyana, Klaus and Marie. Didn't make her an expert.

Game-Boy squirmed. "Mostly I did sex before, hitting it, feeling good . . . You ever fall for a *bad* person who had a big change of heart and tried to do better, who maybe tried to be the kinda person you could love? Don't lie. Don't spare me."

She opened her mouth. Was Tatyana a bad person who had a change of heart? Could Cinnamon love her again? Maybe Cinnamon was a bad person. Game-Boy stared at her, expecting a hoodoo spell for love. The elephant and lioness also wanted answers she didn't have. "It's possible. Depends on your algorithm for love."

"You say Taiwo's main squeeze gave herself away for love—a true story, not just bullshit, right?" Game-Boy did the tension shakeout Cinnamon taught him. "Back-From-The-Dead is true valley lore. Graphic Novelists of the Future want our Born Again story. I'm psyched to tell it, and I ain't gonna frenchify my words."

"No urinating, fornicating, or defecating for you."

"Hell no." Game-Boy tapped his chest. The elephant and lioness slipped onto his beat—musicians who couldn't help themselves. "When I was camping out in the clinic coma lounge, after my boys fell out, you and Indigo showed up every day. Nobody else bothered. My feet were always like an arctic blast. Bruja sat right on 'em. She went around licking hands, doing doggy medicine on my boys—kept their vitals high. You sat up in there telling us wild shit about Miz Redwood snatching a storm out the sky, Granddaddy Aidan carving the fucking wind, Aunt Iris working spooky action at a distance. The whole hoodoo crew doing everything for love, chatting up ghosts even. As if I was a little kid and Indigo too, and we would just *believe* you. We were fragile as foam and wanted to *believe* it all. Still, I kept thinking, what's with this bitch? Are we being punked?"

He wiped his eyes, yet kept the rhythm going. "Indigo wanted to have a place, a space to be too, and you were saying, *Come on in and be with us.*"

Cinnamon choked up, then tapped the shekere for cover.

"My boys didn't get worse or better. Comatose for no fuckin' reason. Maybe it was their turn to burn. Every day I worried some boss man would say *we gotta pull the plugs on the bad-boy thugs* and *why ain't this rude dude underneath the jail?* Every day I worried you'd stop showing up in that lounge. Hope's your superpower not mine, know what I'm saying? You and Indigo always tipped in doing neoblues, astral bop, or funk. I'd hook into the groove, add my beats. A regular jam, the Co-Op Clinic Crew! Not loud or wild, nurses and patients were into it. A couple docs acted like they were serene machines; still, they'd be tapping their feet. Afterward you made me write down my rhyme and eat hippie tofu slime. For a blip, I'd quit drifting into darkness.

"One day, Taiwo blew in, wailing on that shekere. Talk about off the chain, space is the place. Taiwo said, *Kehinde made me promise not to turn away from this world;* then oun called my boys back from that coma and said it was nothing. Said they healed themselves. Stone-cold miracle either way. So what was I s'posed to do? You were still saying, *Come on in; join us.* Invited my boys too. We started fixing broke-ass shit at the Mall, keeping an eye out. Everyone was like, *Duh, of course. You got mad skills, bro.* Taiwo taught us bold tricks. I felt almost like a good guy. I wasn't looking; then here comes Hawk, slick and sweet, putting the moves on me. Do I deserve all that?"

Cinnamon marveled. "You've never said anything like this to me before."

Game-Boy grinned. "You and Indigo tell us *rehearse, rehearse,* so I tried some of it on her and got good edits. Some new lines came right now. Friendly audience effect." He nodded at the lioness and the elephant.

"Hawk's working on being the person you could love too," Cinnamon said.

"For real?"

"According to the elders, Festival's when you get to light new fires."

"Bruja found masks for me and the boys, some sick props too, but—"

"My bullshit meter is dinging. Suit up. Put the damn masks on."

"We will." Game-Boy hugged her against his thumping heart.

Cinnamon squeezed him. "Thanks for your medicine story. I need to rustle up the Water-Spirit brigade. Ciao." She eased away. "Wait. Have you seen Zaneesha?"

"She's with Indigo. They're hooking up candles for the opening." Game-Boy split, looking embarrassed at the lioness and elephant applauding.

Tourists nipped at Cinnamon's heels. Sharp eyes were full of demands. They'd trained into Paradise on the Glass Bubble, light rail from the south. They wore Needless Markup resort wear and executive frowns. They waved **Sci-Fi Carnival Jam** flyers and wanted to know *exactly* when the show started. Free admission and free food, yet they acted disgruntled, entitled. Her uncle Clarence, a rich lawyer, used to say *people don't respect what they don't have to pay for.* She never liked ambulance-chaser Clarence; still, crap he said stuck in her head. Her thoughts now, though, not his. The tourists whined about tired feet, a climate-change sun, and cell service on the blink. Like Cinnamon should fix all that and more, and yesterday.

"Hey! Mammy done left the house!" Cinnamon shouted. The elephant and lioness hooted. After several awkward seconds, the tourists laughed too. Maybe she embarrassed the rude out of them. "No magic if you're on the tictoc clock. Festival runs on colored people's time. *Fairy Time.* We start when we start, which is soon. Find a seat. Please don't only hang with each other. Get to know someone new."

Most of the day-trippers heeded her director voice and headed for the stone seats. A couple in spring cashmere and seesaw sneakers that added a bounce to each step bore down on her. The woman was from Nigeria, the man Côte d'Ivoire, and not centuries ago, last week. They mentioned which people, but Cinnamon missed the words. Over three hundred ethnic groups in Nigeria; Côte d'Ivoire also had a good number. Cinnamon said, "Sorry," and asked them to repeat. They bristled and chastised her in advance for a Next World Festival focused on *racism.* Africans, they claimed, weren't stuck on or in or under racism, like African Americans.

Cinnamon swallowed her anger. She forgave them for spewing bullshit they considered helpful preshow advice. She forgave herself for getting mad, maybe madder than she was at the woke white people who waltzed into dress rehearsal at dawn, asking to play the Evil White Villains in her carnival jam. No such roles. Racist melodrama was somebody else's script, not her *ImagiNation.*

Cinnamon hugged the African couple. "Don't worry," she murmured. "I got you. I feel you." They smelled like Shaheen's diablo pizza and Iris's apple surprise. Flabbergasted by Cinnamon's thoroughly American gesture, they nonetheless hugged her back. She pulled away, smiling. They smiled too. "Festival honors the ancestors by celebrating who we are now and who we want to be tomorrow. You'll see."

Relieved, the woman said she was Tiv from Nigeria and her man was Akan from Côte d'Ivoire. "It's been a rough winter here in your country, for everybody."

"Thanks for welcoming us," the man added; then they headed to the stone seats.

"It almost never feels like my country." Cinnamon spoke to the elephant and lioness. They nodded sympathetically. "Whatever you two want or need. Can it wait? I'm about to go on. I have to call up the Water-Spirits. That trick takes all of me and then some." She wanted to ask who they were under the masks. She wanted to ask if they were good people or bad, if they had honorable intentions. Instead she said, "Why is it so hard to find ourselves in each other's stories?"

"It isn't really," the lioness replied. "Easy magic. You're on it."

The elephant nodded. "Sometimes it takes a second to let go into the story."

"Right." Cinnamon sighed. "Exotic beasts aren't exotic after all."

HAUNTED

Nobody had candles. The cooks were keeping food warm with solar rigs. Smokers were fronting like they'd quit, so no handy lighters or matches. Indigo leaned against the Empty Square Bike Shop table, pleading for any kind of fire device.

The bike repair nerd raked black, greasy fingernails through flyaway hair. "I don't need fire to do what I do." She winked at Indigo, not appreciating the emergency. "I got every kinda wrench you can imagine. An honorary Wheel-Wizard."

"We all need fire," Indigo replied. "Especially today. A new fire."

"I'm a new fire." Jerome jumped in her face. His flame crown lit up; his cape was a billow of smoke. He didn't appreciate the urgency either. Indigo stepped around him and headed back to the altar, to look *underneath* the stone snakes. Cinnamon hid candles there once. Jerome matched her pace. The dude was dogged. She liked that.

"Was that chick flirting with you?" he said.

"Jay Meadows? Hell no." That's how she and Jay always talked to each other. "Is everything sex with you?" Indigo scrunched her face. "Jay's one of the grease monkeys in Techies Forever. I think she likes boys. I don't know. I don't care."

"Hawk's kinda pale for an African Cyborg Amazon, don't you think?" He was still on that. Jealous? "The stringy hair full of gel is nasty." Jealous for sure.

Indigo smirked. "What, aren't you down with brown?"

"Just saying. You can't tell if Hawk was a girl or a boy before."

"You don't know what you're saying." She was mad all of sudden. Who was Jerome to question them? "My squad honors Kehinde, Taiwo's stillpoint and true love, who took a bullet to save the people she loved. Hawk is . . . Never mind."

Jay, Hawk, and Cinnamon were the first friends Indigo made after she escaped Mitchell. Hawk understood when Indigo couldn't breathe, when she wanted to smash some dude's face in. Like right now. Why explain Iranian-American (white but not quite), Fon women warriors (stolen from themselves), or anything to Jerome? She halted in front of Mami Wata.

"Damn." He gawked at the statue, like Mami was the long-lost love of his life who'd been turned to pink granite. He reached a hand out to her tail, then yanked it back.

Indigo snickered. "Statue won't bite."

"I don't want to get a shock or anything."

"Granite's a terrible conductor."

He looked like he didn't believe her. People always doubted her, as if she would make up stuff you could check on the net—which had a lot of untruths on it, still.

"No shocks, see?" She stroked Mami. Her locs were warm, sun-kissed, her tail cool and damp with dew. Jerome clutched his midsection and grimaced. Indigo stepped to the side, in case he threw up vegan barbecue and hot sauce pizza. She reached underneath the snakes. "You ate too much. Before a show, jet Flugzeuge be flying around your belly."

"No. Rough shift yesterday." He swallowed carefully. "What're you doing?"

Triumphant, she held up two candles and a lighter wand. "I'm in charge of handling the fire."

"I'm a fire spirit. You gonna handle me?" Food must have settled if he was talking trash at her again. "Well, are you?"

"What're you asking?" She put candles and wand in a warrior-woman fanny pack.

"I hear you know more about this altar and Cinnamon's Bots than anybody, and if I have questions, you're the go-to Festival geek babe." Not what she expected him to say.

"Did Game-Boy tell you that?"

"Nah. People be saying you know all Cinnamon's secrets."

That sounded suspicious. "What people?"

"I don't know. Everybody."

"Name one person."

His eyes darted about. Was he hiding something besides Zaneesha? Game-Boy never blabbed Cinnamon's secrets. Jerome was mixed up with somebody else. He might even be a spy without realizing. "It's the word out there," he said.

She'd have to keep an eye on him—she wanted to anyway. "The Graphic Novelists of the Future asked me to write about the altar for the *Uncovering/Recovering Valley History* issue."

"So tell me something I wouldn't know." The fifth-level WHIZZ-IT on his belt dinged. He slid it behind his back. "Don't make me wait till the book comes out; drop wisdom on me now."

"You can't read, can you?" She might as well have punched him in the gut.

"I got aspirations." He trembled. "I plan on being a detective, not a janitor *cleaning turds and minding the machines*, like Diego says. He's helping me." Jerome stared off.

She followed his gaze to the shagbark hickory trees. Rust-colored buds unfurled like flowers to reveal pale green leaves. The Mothership, an aluminum three-step pyramid, hovered in the highest branches. Support cables faded into shadow, invisible tech wizardry. Two arms from the ship's midsection held clear globes full of gears and widgets. A circle of ten skinny legs ended in silver platform boots à la Patti LaBelle. Psychedelic lights scattered across the ship's body had yet to be turned on.

"I've never met a real-live writer. Do me a preview. A trailer." Jerome's wispy mustache quivered; his shoulders sagged. The Mothership was a throwback 1970s delight—all praises to George Clinton and the Funkadelics. The ship always made people smile. What was wrong with Jerome?

Indigo needed a better mood too. *Reverse the curse.* She knew exactly what to tell him, spy or not. "*Afro-Future Is Now.* Miz Redwood was a conjurer. So were Aunt Iris and Granddaddy Aidan. This altar triptych, that means 'three pieces' in art talk, was Redwood's idea, conjure to keep Cinnamon company after the elders kicked off. Aidan carved it. He had magic hands. Redwood did a hoodoo spell on the Amphitheatre. Iris warned everyone, the elders wouldn't rest if there weren't shows to entertain their spirits. That's why Cinnamon does Festival every year, 'cause who needs haints roaming around, moaning and shit, tormenting folks?"

"Haints?" Jerome tried to look chill and failed. "What you mean, like ghosts?"

Indigo whispered, "The elders haunt the Amphitheatre, the backstage woods, the whole farm. I've felt 'em a few times." Not a lie, not even an exaggeration. "They're mostly in a good mood 'cause the Festival glow lasts a whole year. Dragon, Mami, and T-bird were their Festival masks. Masks are what you use to call the spirits to you."

Jerome teeter-tottered like he was about to fall over what he should or could believe. Indigo left him hanging. "You messing with me?"

"Maybe a little." She laughed. "The Next World Festival is about taking the spirit of the elders to the future, though."

Jerome steadied himself. "Like the Circus-Bots."

"The Bots got the elders' spirits in their code."

He chewed up a few words before blurting, "Mami Wata talked to me, you know."

"Mami don't talk to just anyone." Indigo was relieved Mami liked him, too relieved.

He whispered, "I felt them three—ghosting way out by Blossom Bridge." He eyed Mami. "A Black mermaid, I mean mer-woman. Never seen that till yesterday. I didn't know they had Black ones."

"You think you seen everything, know everything?"

"Diego said Mami Watas are African river and ocean goddesses. They rode the waves to America to keep people company on this side."

That sounded right, but Indigo frowned. "You trust Diego?"

"Basically. Damn, why you gotta be so harsh?"

"Uhm . . ." Diego was a horny ex-gangsta, packing heat and lusting after Cinnamon *and* Shaheen. What if he got off on catfights? Worse, what if he sent Jerome to snoop on Cinnamon? "Diego's hard-core Valley Security. A *Have Gun Will Travel* dude. Shooting at whoever they tell him to."

Jerome clamped his mouth shut. What could he say? He was a hired gun too.

SPOOK
ᖇᐧᕼᐧᕼ

SHOWTIME

Cinnamon was still covered in bristles and wearing a nest in her braids that hid half her face. Spook almost didn't recognize her. She smelled like herself, though, and was in a grand mood. She played Taiwo's music on the shekere and danced by a trickle of stormwater coming down the wooded hillside overlooking the Amphitheatre. She mimicked Taiwo, singing to the Water-Spirits in that crackle of a language nobody else understood. Spook wagged his tail, forgetting his urgent mission. Cinnamon could sound like anybody. There wasn't much water, and only a few Spirits flickered in and out of view. The clearest one had rainbow scales for skin, a mouthful of pointy fangs, and cornrowed silver hair.

Cinnamon sang till the scaly Spirit's face was solid, till she smelled like a high-voltage wire. Sparks flew from her eyelashes. She and Cinnamon sang a howling wind, clouds bursting, and hail pummeling branches. Spook howled along. Danger scents jolted him back to the mission. He barked a bass boom that shook the ground and jumped up against Cinnamon's back. She shook him off without missing a beat.

He ran on. Tatyana and IT Fred snarled at each other behind a purple chokeberry bush over *data cubes gone walkabout*. Spook had no time for them. Flying-Horse needed help. Taiwo was in a cell tower tree, gulping ultraviolet static, the color of trouble. Oun's fingertips were lightning bolts. Oun wailed high-pitched crackles, doing a trio with Cinnamon and the scaly Spirit. They were lost in the Spirit music.

Spook raced to the presenters' parking lot—scooters, bikes, trikes, and trailer rigs. Cap George marched three handcuffed cowboys and two zip-tied zoot-suiters across the gravel—the second batch of the day. George was taller than usual. He had puffy multicolored hair and shiny, high-heeled boots. The cape was like sunshine on his shoulders. A pack of Valley Security operatives sported the same puffy hair, sequined jackets, and chunky boots. They trailed behind George and the handcuffed men.

George shoved the cowboys into the zoot-suiters. Spectators snapped their fingers at live action-adventure. "I promised my daughter, no blood on this day of days, but sweet thang ain't around to check me," He hooted. "Tough luck for you shitholes." He pushed them into a van; then he and a few operatives jumped in and slammed the door.

The spectators buzzed as inside George shouted angry words, stomped booted feet, and smashed something (somebody?) against the door. Valley Security surrounded the van. Spook sat down and licked his chops. Another thud from the van and someone wailed. Spook would never get George's attention.

"¿Qué pasa?" Diego patted Spook's back. A red sparkle nest was perched on his bald head. "Sólo entre nosotros, Cap is more smoke than fire. An actor." Diego eased onto a log next to Spook, wincing. He smelled of disinfectant, bandages, and blood. Spook nosed wounded ribs. Diego flinched. "Easy. Pendejos didn't pierce the armor, but they made a mark." Spook sniffed another wound in Diego's thigh. "Nurse Azalea said I should lie down for a week. I'm OK, though. I couldn't miss my Festival debut." Diego chuckled, then groaned. His hand shook as he held a bottle to his lips and swallowed a few pills. "Jerome says marijuana stops the shakes. Hey, the kid's holding up. No sé." Cinnamon and Shaheen liked Diego. He'd have to do. Spook jumped up, tugged his sleeve, and wagged his tail, spreading an urgent scent.

"I've seen you, a shadow slinking across Blossom Bridge with Cinnamon." Diego favored the good leg as he struggled up. "You're the friendly Ghost-Dog, ¿verdad?"

Spook tugged his sleeve again and took off. He turned to see if Diego was following. "How far we going?" The man groaned, pressed the red nest tight on his skull, and stepped onto a scooter. Spook was grateful for the speed.

∾

Taiwo opened the back gate as Spook and Diego approached. Someone else might have been shocked to find oun there before them. Spook was excited. A white bird roosted on Taiwo's shoulder and mumbled Water-Spirit talk. The crow with red feathers stood on wrought-iron curlicues, scolding them. The white bird squawked back in crow talk—a sassy critter hurling challenges. The turkey buzzards smelled glum. Flying-Horse had been gathered together on kente cloth almost in the shape Spook remembered. He woofed a greeting, hoping Horse would get up and *play that funky music*. No luck. Spook drooped. Taiwo smelled sad too.

"¡Hola!" Diego stepped off the scooter. A trickle of blood leaked down his thigh. "You found one of the missing cockatoos."

"She found me." Taiwo waved the snake cane. "A hawk on her tail thought twice about attacking us both."

"I'm in charge here," the cockatoo declared. "Don't ever doubt that."

Diego spied the dead Paradise man. "¡Qué va!" He pulled a gun and scanned the woods. Spook bared his fangs and snarled.

"No danger nearby to worry about," Taiwo said. "Put that away. Spook hates guns."

"Oh." Diego stowed the weapon and crouched down to the chewed-up corpse. "That's a hell of a mess."

Taiwo pointed at three unhappy buzzards hunched in the trees. "Gun-bots or a Valley Security drone shot him after he raided your checkpoint yesterday. He probably bled out before tech thugs ripped Cinnamon's Flying-Horse apart."

Diego touched the bandage on his wounded ribs. "Uptick in random attacks recently. Not just in the hill towns or down the big river, even around the Mall. Trashing a bot is bad for business. What are these tech thugs after?"

Taiwo shrugged. "Good to see you here, Diego."

Diego frowned. "You know me?"

The cockatoo whistled. "That's my job! That's my job!"

Spook yapped at them to hurry. He wanted to get back to his bowls of food, to the singing, dancing, and Festival fun.

Diego took off the sparkly red nest and rubbed his bald head. "You're that war vet I've heard about, living up an ancient oak tree?"

"You blow whistles and carry a torch for spicy, market ladies."

Diego trembled. "What do you mean?"

"Love is what you must do. Good chance with Shaheen. She lost someone to the high water and frightens lesser men ever since. You're just the ticket. We all could use your help."

"You know a lot about me and everyone." Diego scrunched his face. "You did special ops in the Water Wars, captained the Water-Demons squad."

"Did Game-Boy tell you this?"

"He's not the only one."

"I'm nobody these days, almost nobody. Scattering . . ." Oun toed the cloth holding Flying-Horse-Bot. "You gotta *believe* in someone till they come true. Miz Redwood said that's the most a person can do for another."

"Am I s'posed to understand that?" There was blood on Diego's breath.

"You will. Powerful hoodoo has come our way. Engine broke down, but that won't stop the Mod Squad. Bruja showed them the way." Taiwo sank down to Flying-Horse. The snake cane in oun's hand spit nerve poison. Would oun be able to wake Horse up? Spook wagged his tail, hopeful. "Some people think they should control everything. They want to own the sky, the air, tomorrow, and yesterday. Power junkies."

"Who we talking about here?" Diego needed to sit down. Spook licked his hand. "Cinnamon sent me a kidnapping alert for a bot. This one, I presume."

"She *asked* for help?" Taiwo whistled like the cockatoo. "And Spook trusts you."

"Not Bruja." Diego did a nervous laugh and rubbed Spook's head.

"Bruja doesn't go by how good you smell. It's what you do when things go sideways." Taiwo folded Flying-Horse up in the cloth and thrust the bundle at Diego. Spook whimpered at his broken friend. "I'll take care of the dead man. You give this to Cinnamon, after the show. Tell her IT Fred savaged Horse."

Diego stepped away and bumped into Spook. "Why don't you give it to her?"

"You do this, and tell Shaheen. They'll both trust you even more."

"You think that's a good idea?"

"Spook does." Spook pranced toward the gate, ready to go.

The cockatoo spoke. "You blow whistles and carry a torch for spicy, market ladies."

"Don't let the bird spread that around," Diego hissed.

Taiwo rubbed a cheek against the cockatoo and spoke Water-Spirit static. "Your secret's safe."

Diego took the Flying-Horse bundle. His wounded leg almost buckled. "Heavy."

"I'll tie it on you." Oun nodded at the crossroads of circles and stars, worlds within worlds, pulsing on the gate with extra-dimensional energy. "I know a shortcut."

"¡Dios Santo!" Diego was dazzled. "That's a Vévé to call Baron Samedi."

"You know the Orishas, the Loas?"

Diego snorted. "I haven't met any face-to-face, but I know who you mean."

"Samedi stands at the gates between life and death like Eshu." Taiwo secured the bundle on Diego's back. "I pour libation to the master of uncertainty." Oun sprinkled rum from a flask onto the ground. "You and me, we take care of the spirits."

"Is this a Festival act or how you usually talk?"

Spook nosed the metalwork Vévé on the gate, no longer solid. With

Taiwo there, the link was live. Navigating *the spaces between things,* he'd be back at the Amphitheatre in a few bounds.

"What the fuck?" Diego squealed.

"You trust me. I trust you." Taiwo waved him on to the scooter. "You must hurry. It's almost SHOWTIME."

Spook barked encouragement as they raced through the gate.

THE CIRCUS-BOTS

∝♋∾

STAND BY

The morning sun was Sea Island Georgia hot, 28° C or 82.4° F. Dew-damp flower buds opened to the light. Insects on the prowl for love, nectar, and blood rode the breeze. A glorious day after the early morning superstorms, perfect for outdoor theatre. The Circus-Bots lurked under magnolia blossoms by trash containers and fluid dispensers—REFRESH YOURSELF. A good spot to collect data on: birds, newbie performers, Paradise glitterati, bugs (electronic and insectoid), Mall refugees, a baby goat, snoop-drones, and enterprising chipmunks—a bumper crop this year.

The Circus-Bots' wings, legs, tails, snouts, and snake appendages were folded in tight. LED eyes were dull, motors muffled, and sensors set at max. They masqueraded as broken toys and waited for the stage manager to call places and final standby. Patience was elusive, even for Dragon, who'd allegedly mastered *chill* two days ago. Dragon burned through twenty percent of her batteries keeping a lid on herself. Thunderbird and Mami were worse. Fortunately, the solar power station that kept lemonade and ice tea cool allowed them to recharge.

Cinnamon wiped sweat from her neck and hugged each Bot. They wished for skin like hers to feel the flesh-to-flesh thrill. "Do your thing, even if Tatyana or somebody comes snooping. We ain't got time for stupidness. We're calling down the spirits, for Raven and for Opal too." Tears blurred her eyes, yet she had a full-body smile. Taiwo's shekere—a promise of music magic—banged her hip as she strode up the parade line, hugging and cheering everyone.

Two lemurs dropped from a winsome hemlock. The Bots looped *marvel* as the primate couple guzzled lemonade from the dispensers. Nobody paid the red-eyed fur balls any mind, including Regina Benita Washington—Cap George's runaway daughter turned pirate wench in a green corset, lace-up boots, and jaunty hat. She hiked a ruffled skirt high on her right thigh. Tiny blue skulls were embroidered on her petticoats, crossbones on her hat. She tied a patch over the left eye, then waved a curved sword. Regina practiced swashbuckling antics as the lemurs scuttled up a tree. The foreign beasts never registered. Focus fog. Performers and spectators were deep in the sacred loop: *"Na na na hey hey hey."* Well, not everybody was in the loop.

"Waste of time pissing around here," IT Fred grumbled at Tatyana.

She adjusted her orca mask. "Don't fuck this up. Leave Cinnamon to me. And fingers off her Bots." She headed for the Mothership. "Join the Weird parade if you want to do something."

IT Fred trudged toward the fluid dispensers. His vitals were better since Taiwo's first aid. He wore a zombie mask and a suit that looked like rotting flesh. Costume irony? Snark? Many Festival fans were into zombies, horror monsters, and grim dark figures. Fred did real-live terror. He'd ripped Flying-Horse apart according to Dragon's trackers. Fred lifted his mask, put his mouth on a spigot, and guzzled lemonade like a lemur. He banged the dispenser, sucking for more, although the *empty* light flashed. Gutting Horse hadn't resulted in a good mood. Would he destroy the dispenser?

"I was never into cosplay and that fanboy, nerd shit," Fred confessed to a gray-faced Blob who resembled a heap of vanilla Jell-O topped with whipped cream. Fake flesh dangled from both their mouths. "*Game of Bones, Lord of the Dumplings and Dingalings.*" More snark? The Blob sniggered and repeated, "*Lord of the Dingalings.*"

The stage manager called stand-by for places. Stragglers raced to the parade line. Regina ducked behind a witch alder bush. Big white flowers looked like scrub brushes and provided good cover. She closed her eyes and gulped breath. Fred and the Blob lingered by the lemonade, gulping breath as well.

Mami wanted to fry Fred, render him unconscious, not dead. Maybe fry the vanilla Blob too. Dragon and T-bird were unsure whether to hit performance-mode, take action against Fred, or stay hidden. Trackers glowed ultraviolet blue in Fred's butt and neck. Spook could find him anywhere, anytime. Why spoil the Festival mood? Better to collect intel and let Spook apprehend Fred later. However, if Fred planned to disrupt the Festival, inaction might be disastrous. The Bots went back and forth in slow-thinking-mode beyond the range of human hearing. They used weighted valences, emotion modeling, and entertained contradictions without entering a Teufelskreis. This gobbled mega-joules of energy every millisecond. Not enough data for an easy solution. Never enough data.

The stage manager repeated the stand-by.

"They're calling places." The Blob had a tense voice. "We're supposed to join the parade or sit in the audience."

"Let's get real." Fred pulled the Blob under a birch tree. "We're living the apocalypse." He poked the birch bark with a screwdriver—the weapon he used on Horse? "Fuck this sideshow shit."

Regina jolted out of focus fog. She lifted the eye patch and frowned as they sniggered and complained about stupid fan freaks and *arrested development*. She balled a fist, cursing softly. Regina was a die-hard Festival fan.

"I say attack Cinnamon where she lives." Fred wagged his zombie head. A busted eye bounced in and out of its socket.

Regina's vitals spiked. She'd taken out her phone and was filming the perps, a fearless daughter of Cap George, security in her blood. Well, sort of . . .

"Tatyana's going about this wrong." Fred scratched the bandage over the bite wound from Spook. Blood oozed through dingy cloth. Why he scratched a wound open as it tried to heal was unclear. Dragon looped this into his profile. Any detail might prove relevant. "She wants to build trust. It's bullshit."

"Trust is a good angle," the vanilla Blob replied, jiggling. "Tatyana got us this far."

"We're nowhere. The arrogant bitch is still *in love*," Fred said. "That messes your mind. Especially if you're stuck on the person you're supposed to take down."

"Hacking into Jones's bot was a bust, Fred."

"Tatyana refused to help," Fred muttered. "Refused to touch Flying-Horse."

"You got nothing at the Ghost Mall except a dog bite."

"Tatyana's hiding shit on data cubes Cinnamon designed—superfast processing, quantum storage. Cubes run on like AAA batteries. Worth a pile, if you got the rig for 'em. Those bitches both have secrets. That's what I'm after." Fred pointed at rainbow shimmers in a shagbark hickory tree by the Mothership. "Check out the special effects."

Regina swallowed a screech. She perceived what the Bots could not: Water-Spirits making an entrance as Cinnamon threw Taiwo's shekere high and caught it on an upbeat. Regina aimed her phone at this spectacle. She was disappointed? perplexed? at what was on the screen. Maybe both. Some audience members had similar reactions.

"Think how much that shimmer jazz is worth!" Fred shouted. "We're wasting a golden opportunity."

"You want a death squad up our asses?" the Blob whispered. "Taiwo's tech has gotta be top secret. Consolidated won't touch that. Or they already have it and don't want anyone to know they have it."

Fred hooted. "You *believe* the hype about extra-dimensional tech and lethal Water-Demons—"

"Secret weapons are the real power. Conspiracy aficionados have that part right."

"I don't know about that. I do know Consolidated has other teams working the SevGenAlg glitches. They might be here right now, sniffing around Cinnamon Jones."

Regina dropped to the ground where vegetation was densest. Better camouflage.

"You *and* Tatyana insisted nobody knew about Jones," the Blob said. "Claimed she was old news, a hidden gem for us to exploit."

"This operation was my idea. Navajo bitch stole it."

"Uh-huh." The Blob sounded unconvinced. "Tatyana's Cherokee."

"I have a Valley Security informant. They don't pay thugs-for-hire crap. I got the kid cheap. He thinks I'll help him score a detective gig if he coughs up good intel. He's close to a hooker turned drug dealer, in Jones's inner circle. Jones is hiding something big, Taiwo and those Circus-Bots."

"Everybody has secrets. You too."

"How about you tell me yours first." Fred sounded the same as when he aimed a gun at Cinnamon's head.

The Blob fiddled with a nozzle on his sleeve and deflated his costume a bit.

"We better Usain Bolt results on those SevGenAlg glitches or the boss bros will take the contract elsewhere." Fred stared right at the Bots. "I could be doing something important. Something off the charts. Instead—" He pointed beyond the trash barrels to:

A Valley Security guard, Diego's former partner, had turned a wheelchair into a chariot à la *Ben-Hur* or *Gladiator*. The guard's four children wore horse masquerades and pulled their mother across the clover. They had bright red hair, rosy cheeks, and sweet horse voices. Nurse Boo, a six-foot hefty guy dressed as a golden bunny, danced around a pink rabbit tricycle ridden by Nurse Azalea, dressed like the bear Fred saved last night. Pink wings extended from under the trike seat and provided ballast for the six-foot antennae-ears. After the show, Azalea and Boo planned to hit the north-facing hill overlooking the Amphitheatre or the Mall rooftop if Techies Forever could coax the elevator into working. Either way, they'd reach beyond bright blue to talk to the stars, to talk to anyone out there listening.

Fred scoffed. "The world's heading for hell on a skateboard and what the fuck are these bozos playing at?" He waved a hand at the carnival scene, as if warding off danger. "We should hit the farmhouse while everyone is distracted. I'm past ready to pull the trigger on Cinnamon Jones and on her goddamn dogs too."

"Taiwo and cyber-dog Spook protect the Mall *and* the farms."

"A lot of territory to cover, even enhanced. Taiwo is eighty-something, gotta be losing the killer edge. We stole that bot, trashed it, and Taiwo didn't catch us."

"Two days ago. Red alert now. Taiwo's Water-Demons are special ops, ten of them, called up for Festival. Bulletproof divas." The Blob's voice was shaky. "Tatyana said no mess during the show. Let's have fun. The spaceship's a trip, a blast from the past."

"I want a holler from tomorrow." Fred warped Cinnamon's line. It was: *Don't you wanna holla at tomorra?* The Bots agreed this was ominous without knowing why.

"Let's do our blocking." The vanilla Blob pushed Zombie Fred toward the stone seats. Fred shuffled along in character. Hard to believe he was the same man who risked deadly claws to save a bear and her three cubs. T-bird sent another dart at his back. Fred hissed and scratched. Iridescent dragonfly trackers hovered over his head to the delight of insect fans in the third row.

Fred would never do another surprise ambush on Cinnamon or the Bots.

Regina let out a strangled breath and pocketed her phone. Drones hummed above the trees. She pulled down the eye patch and let the jaunty hat shadow her face. Dragon wanted to ask what she made of the Water-Spirit apparitions and Fred's terror talk. Mami and T-bird wanted to trust Regina, but not enough data. Plus, Regina needed no more distractions before her performance. Horror-Fred and Water-Spirit juju were bad enough. Compact trash interrogating her might be over the edge.

Four Wenches mobbed Regina and towed her toward the Mothership. They talked on top of one another about pirate queens, wayward witches, and Scottish curses. Regina was silent, peering at mist twirling around tree trunks. The Wenches stopped midgush and nagged till she told them that Water-Spirits appeared in the branches, yet not on camera. She described seaweed hair, jewel skin, and rainbow beads. The other Wenches had seen only mist. As they reached the parade line, Regina declared, "Like vampires not showing up in mirrors. You need a perfect angle for a sighting. Taiwo's special ops brigade is beyond regular special effects. Super high tech might as well be magic."

Mami launched a shower of tiny rockets at drones that didn't ping the sentinel-bots. An explosion of silver sparklers engulfed several whisper-witches. *Fireworks* were a perfect stealth weapon. The spy-bots bit the dust, never knowing what hit them. Mami had to join Dragon and T-bird sucking energy from the solar power station. Going directly from the sun was too slow—Festival could begin any second.

Wishful thinking.

The stage manager added another ten minutes to the stand-by. Strung-out actors snarled at techies and snapped at each other over nothing. Water-Demon Cinnamon swooped in and led antsy players from back-stage bushes across the clover stage. Spook materialized out of nowhere and nothing and paced an empty front row. A Motor Fairy, beard and tutu full of sparkles, stomped down an aisle doing a Game-Boy rhyme. *"Chigga boom, chigga bat, chigga like it like that."* Cinnamon sang, *"Chigga who, chigga huh, chigga do what I do."* Spook chased the Fairy and the other performers into the maple trees. Stalling with style.

The pearl on Dragon's bike chain necklace glowed through balled-up plastic wrap. She tweaked her flight plan to account for a drone traffic jam. That made staying frosty in the face of Tatyana's and IT Fred's treachery easier. T-bird twanged his banjo, tuning. A ritual. He never went flat or sharp by accident; still, it was good to stay humble, to listen to the notes around the ones he wanted. This might help him consider what went unsaid between Fred and the Blob without triggering a Teufelskreis. Dragon hummed off-key too, bluesy breaks. Flat or sharp was a spicy twist for emotional effect. She assumed Fred would come after them eventually, and they needed to plan now. Superfast-charging, Mami's third eye pulsed. She wanted to send a rocket sideways (oops, accident!) to fry Fred and be done with worry. Old gun-bot habits. Maybe she'd get a chance to do him in later, for the curtain call or an encore stunt.

A girl could wish . . .

"Are those zebras?"

FIGHT THE POWER

Indigo peered at Valley Security and Paradise guards guiding what looked like drunk zebras into a truck on the Co-Op road. Jerome hugged himself and shuddered as his WHIZZ-IT blared. He popped in an earbud.

"They found the rhino's GPS device, but no rhino." He said this like Indigo would know what he was talking about. "Latoya claimed she was making big money working a graveyard shift at the zoo. I told her to stay away from that mess. And now . . ."

"What? Talk to me." Indigo took his hand. Zaneesha's mom was named Latoya.

Jerome pulled away and ground his teeth.

A Paradise boss man dressed for a nineteenth-century safari sauntered from the zebra operation into the Amphitheatre. With thick, curly hair under a pith helmet, and pouty lips, he looked like an ad for something useless, sinful yet irresistible. A cloud-white cockatoo bobbed on his shoulder and cussed someone out for *not staggering the pee breaks*. A digerati entourage in colonial beige trailed behind safari man and bird. Waltzing in late, they took over a front audience section that had remained curiously empty except for Spook's alien juju. Safari man told the cockatoo to hush. The bird said, "*You hush*," then shut up.

"I thought no reserved seats." Irritated, Indigo pulled a *neo-savage* light spear from the case on her back and began warming up. Taking the heads of phantom enemies was sweet release. Jerome eyed her Cyborg-Amazon moves, trying to act unimpressed. Dude was terrible at deceit. Desire on his face excited and unnerved her. She'd escaped Mitchell, but here she was again, ready to sleep with the enemy. Hadn't she learned anything?

Jerome pulled out his earbud. He stumbled, contorted an arm behind his back, and juddered, like a body snatcher was taking him over. "Can I level with you?" He sounded all vulnerable.

She needed to focus for her big entrance, but . . . She lowered her spear. "Go ahead."

"Two days ago, freakin' Whistleblowers shot up the gorge using stealth weapons. Yesterday they hit checkpoints. I need several joints behind that kinda action and I ran out last night. I'm talking a Blossom Bridge ambush." His checkpoint. No mention of this (or the body with a ripped throat) on the news feeds or social media. Cap George limited info reveal, supposedly to prevent copycat crimes. His Darknet Lord deployed attack-bots to rove the net and shut down content deemed *inappropriate*.

"*Somebody* was shooting, just not Whistleblowers," Indigo said, "a gang funded by Paradise. They're mostly dead now."

"Who says?" Jerome loomed close, trying to intimidate her?

Indigo took a warrior stance, legs spread, knees bent, light spear at his heart. "Game-Boy got the skinny from Taiwo. Nothing to worry about from Whistleblowers."

"I hear—"

"The lies they want you to believe." She poked the WHIZZ-IT under his cloak. "Why give you free WHIZZ-ITs, instead of teachers to help you do algebra or read? Free advertising, free tracking devices, but not free education and code sharing—"

"I ain't stupid." He pushed the light spear away, looking insulted. "They had to tape Diego's ribs and stitch his thigh. I know what's what."

"Really?" She glared at safari dude and his entourage, slouching in their seats. Cinnamon went and invited everybody. "Big guns count on you thinking, *Other folks get suckered, not me*. Meanwhile, *they steal the world*." She broke her own rules about arguing with fools. "Does a WHIZZ-IT really read what's written, do the math you need for your life? Don't need to ban books if folks are illiterate and can barely count. What world do we make wasting good people like you? Motherfuckers in Electric Paradise are willing to take down their own children, grandchildren, and all the generations after. They don't give a shit about nobody or nothing." Stone-cold hustlers like Mitchell, only pimping everybody, a global racket.

"You don't know what you're talking about." Jerome twitched.

"Indeed." Shaheen glided by on a scooter. She wore a silvery-blue robe that matched her face paint. Gas fire on wheels. "Electric Paradise isn't a clot of evil monsters eating their children." Indigo rolled her eyes at Miz Why-Can't-We-All-Get-Along. Shaheen and Cinnamon tried too hard to see the best in anybody, a waste of good energy. Cinnamon knew better. Indigo was quoting her to Jerome.

Diego, a red fire spirit, coasted beside Shaheen as they headed for the Mothership. He didn't act wounded. "No horned demons out to get us. Just people."

"People are bad enough," Indigo muttered.

"I know it." Diego had a sinister laugh. Shaheen was cozying up to a thug-for-hire.

Indigo was no better, cozying up to Jerome. "You should get into place." She started to walk away.

Jerome clutched her arm. "You get intel nobody else does. You and Game-Boy are dialed into Darknet sources and that Rambo freak—"

"Not Rambo. Taiwo, homeless Eshu who will do magic for small change. Admit it. We have better sources."

"OK. But damn, I'm out there risking my life, trying to keep everybody safe."

"You're keeping rich folks safe. That works out for the rest of us sometimes."

Rage curled his lips and flared his nostrils. "Chilling behind the tofu curtain, what the fuck do you know?" His WHIZZ-IT shrieked, *Check In Now!* He wailed on it till the light quit flashing and the voice sputtered out. Impossible to turn the shit off. Any moment of yours was theirs. Indigo wanted to scream.

Coming to her rescue, the Motor Fairies drove their rainbow bus to the shagbark hickories. The entrance and exit ramps for the Mothership were on top of the bus, looking sturdy enough to hold the whole parade. Techies Forever were on the case before the engine was turned off. Not much longer now. Relieved, Indigo sliced the air with her spear and skewered the last of her phantom enemies.

Jerome ranted to himself or his demons about Whistleblowers and nostalgia militias ruining the world with their UFOs, cell-phone guns, and Jewish space lasers. He jitterbugged about as if *deranged but puppy-dog vulnerable* was attractive. He must have seen that old Mel Gibson and Julia Roberts romp that Cinnamon showed last week at the Mall Theatre: *Conspiracy Weary* or *Conspiracy Theory.* Like Mel, Jerome was a wounded soul, a lethal weapon aching to be saved by the love of a good-looking woman—Julia. Tired.

Of course, Indigo had stayed for the credits *and* the special features, hadn't she?

"Nobody stops to think what I'm going through." Jerome did a puppy pout. "You listening to me?"

"No. I cut out at Jewish space lasers." Indigo sneered. "Did I miss something?"

His bedroom eyes flooded, a muddy river leaking down his face. The gun under his cape was a bulge on the left side. His hand shook as he patted it. "I almost shot someone yesterday. My first real day on the job."

The sneer slid off Indigo's face. She'd never imagined a guard shooting someone and feeling guilty later. "Bots usually do the shooting and killing, right?"

Jerome spewed another rant about rough crews prowling the hills. He and Diego were looking out for a gang packing high-tech weapons; then this white girl didn't ping the bots—no electronic trail. Probably running from mommy and daddy locking her up in Paradise. She wasn't a *clear and present danger*. Still, desperados shot Diego's partner on MLK Day, and that chick rolled in a chair these days. Hesitate and you were dead meat or crippled. Jerome glared at his left hand, his gun hand?

"It felt like somebody else pulling the trigger," he said. "Diego slammed into me, saved her life, mine too. What if I killed the stupid bitch? For no reason, or even if she was bad news? What if creeps ambush us, and the bots run out of ammo, and I have to shoot to kill?" He tried to swallow. "I didn't sleep last night—ran out of pot. Found a nub this morning. Smoking weed takes the edge off. I'll pay whatever, when I get paid."

He insisted there would be no reports to the Boss Ladies or Cap George on Indigo's side hustle. He and Indigo could get high together, 'cause didn't she need to take the edge off too, 'cause shit might get rough any moment. This was a threat, invite, or what the hell? Indigo resisted feeling special 'cause Jerome confided in her. Mitchell had pulled the same manipulative shit. Would Jerome be interested in her terrible secrets as well as her booty and high-grade pot? What would he say about Mitchell handcuffing her to a bed for his friends and stinky strangers and then posting videos on a sexcapade channel? Would Jerome still think she looked good enough to eat?

Indigo shook her head. "You almost shot somebody."

He took a raggedy breath. Recruiters claimed he had the perfect profile for a guard: a great shot who didn't really *want* to shoot anybody, not even rats eating the wires. Guards were supposed to shoot them. "What if those recruiters were wrong? Maybe they don't know me. Maybe I don't know me. What if I like shooting people?"

"Don't seem like you do."

"I pulled the trigger on ditzy white chick running from us." Would he worry so much if she was a poor Black ditz or a Jewish one? "That felt as bad as getting shot at." He choked up. "Getting shot at was— Three years, I can't quit or I go to jail."

"That's . . ." Indigo wished she had something, anything, good to say.

"Most bootleg marijuana is bullshit. Diego said you have a green thumb, a whole fucking green hand, and you grow the best weed in the valley, in the region. A reliable source says you got a private stash."

"Really??" She had to check Game-Boy's big mouth.

"Help a hardworking security guard blot the shit out."

Saxophones wailed. The Mothership turned on funkadelic lights and blasted a shower of diamond fireworks up into the bright blue. Zanee-sha, her comet mask and costume still dim, ran with Shooting-Star and Bruja past Indigo and Jerome. Zaneesha halted and switched on four feet of comet lights. Shooting-Star did too. Twins. Bruja barked and tried to herd them on.

"Hold up. I got business." Zaneesha turned to Indigo and Jerome. "Shooting-Star was hiding again. She feels safe with me and Bruja. Ow." Bruja nipped her heels and drove the two comets to the Mothership ramp.

"Who were they?" Jerome quivered. Zaneesha's soft voice was unmis-takable. "What are those costumes, burning balls?"

Bruja dashed back to Indigo and dropped a tee shirt. Indigo held it up and squealed. "*We're mostly space and the force to hold it together.* Last year's free swag." A great line. How did anybody forget that? A lioness and an elephant applauded Bruja. They mumbled the tee shirt line to each other and chuckled. Were they at Festival last year?

Indigo brushed her lips against Jerome's left hand, his gun hand. "Do a bit with me and my squad. I'll charge you, fierce, ready to take a head." She spun him around and dipped him back, the way Hawk did Game-Boy. Jerome went with it, then spun her as she twirled the light spear. "Yeah, like that. I have to change now." She would put the tee under her Cyborg-Amazon rig and surprise Cinnamon. "How about we do a blunt with my crew tonight."

"Bet." Jerome loped off, almost smiling. Indigo dashed for the back-stage magnolias.

Drummers hidden around the Amphitheatre played the parade cue and welcomed everyone, the living, the ancestors, and those yet to be born, to the Next World Festival.

CINNAMON
ᶜᵉ᷄᷈ᵊᵊ

ALIEN INVASION

Backstage was about to explode. Cinnamon shifted her weight from foot to foot. Over half the Festival parade fidgeted on the newly reinforced ramp, hidden behind a tree trunk wall. They waited for the Mothership to touch down, the front ramp to glide into place, and the doors to open. When a quarter mile of people streamed down the red carpet, the flying pyramid would seem cavernous, as deep as the universe.

Techies Forever raced by doing last-second checks. They were serious, like Houston Mission Control bringing a NASA ship back to Earth. "Fairy Time!"

"Good," Cinnamon replied. "The audience looks ready to eat each other, and we can't hold out any longer either." Her insides quivered.

Nerves meant you cared, meant you'd have the energy to surprise yourself onstage. Who told her that, Miz Redwood? Cinnamon shook off jitters about evil shit going down beyond the Amphitheatre. Nothing to do for that right now. They'd worry about saving the world after the show. She was here. She was now. She was ready.

The Circus-Bots rolled close, bug-eyed trash she barely recognized. They frequently changed up their junk, a shifting exhibition. Broken toys were currently featured: magic wands, dinosaurs, *TermiNation* guns, a Timbuktu model city, and an astronaut holding her cracked helmet. Cinnamon grinned. "What's the word?"

"One thousand seven hundred and eighty-six butts squeezed onto stone seats," Mami whispered. "More people than before the Water Wars, plus a baby goat, two cockatoos, and two lemurs in the shadows. A record."

Shaheen, Indigo, Game-Boy, and the Graphic Novelists of the Future put out the call: *"Cinnamon Jones needs Festival to be off the chain this year."* People who'd never come before and those who hadn't come in years all showed up.

"The audience is getting blasted by photons." Thunderbird twanged the banjo. "Heating up like Georgia in July, and don't nobody mind. They're having a ball."

Bruja herded the lioness and elephant to the ramp. The three carried on like old friends—doggy kisses and fancy footwork. Cinnamon pointed at fragrant magnolias and shouted for no reason she could think of, "This bush bloomed overnight. Magic!" The elephant and lioness cheered. Well, even spies should have a good time.

An orca masquerade danced by to join humpback whales and alien ocean beings. Tatyana? Cinnamon flared Water-Demon feathers and feelers and pulled the lightning bolt mask close against her nose. Jewel eyes on her thighs flashed rainbows from another dimension. Bruja raced to Cinnamon and licked her hand. Witch-Dog's eyes were wide-open windows on joy. Festival was her favorite day, and she got up happy every morning. No way Bruja would let Tatyana ruin one second of the fun.

"I'm good," Cinnamon assured Bruja. A murder of crows burst from oak branches and mobbed a hawk trying to be slick. One crow had red feathers in its wings, Taiwo's dear friend. Cinnamon repeated her line from yesterday. "Good luck catching a single crow in broad daylight."

Shooting-Star and Zaneesha bumped her, flashing their lights. Zaneesha's mom was still MIA, but Daddy Jerome would see her play a wild woman roaming the stars with her hair on fire. When Zaneesha revealed her true self at the curtain call, he'd cheer and holler, *That's my daughter. That's my girl.* If it didn't go like that, Cinnamon would improvise a hoodoo spell to get him to act right. Zaneesha tucked beryl or goshenite rocks in the Circus-Bots' trash masquerades near the dinosaurs and lady astronaut. For good luck. Shooting-Star played music from *The Redwood and Wildfire Songbook*:

> *Can't help loving somebody*
> *Who can soar, who can fly*
> *Who can take your spirit up in the sky*

Powwow Now whisked the comets to the end of the parade line.

"People been aching to come together, breathe the same air, feel each other." Dragon gurgled. "Don't you love it?"

Cinnamon nodded. "There's a story going round that I do Festival so my hoodoo elders don't haunt me or roam the valley spooking people. Actually, the elders wanted me, wanted *us*, doing Festival to tend our own spirits."

"What? You mean carnival is good for everyone?" Shaheen rode up on a scooter. "Who are you talking to? The trees? The dirt? Haints?" She smelled of hot sauce and jasmine and looked more beautiful than ever. Diego glided beside her, looking fine too. Love coming on back in style, across the vegan, beer belly divide. Cinnamon squashed a squiggle of envy, of regret. Diego was a sweet taste in her mouth, and who didn't want to be wanted, but that wasn't falling for someone.

"Thanks for inviting us." Diego squeezed Cinnamon's arm. He smelled like rubbing alcohol and favored a leg. He sucked down a few pills and a swig of water.

Shaheen gathered Cinnamon close and whispered, "We have a wonderful life, don't we?" Then she and Diego glided over to the fire-spirit brigade.

Cinnamon poured libation to Eshu, swirled Taiwo's shekere, and whispered extra-dimensional lyrics. The Water-Spirit with jewel skin materialized beside her. More Spirits ghosted nearby in naked forsythia branches, a gang of them. Rainbow waist beads glimmered. They sang a river rumble, tumbling in and out of harmonies. Powwow Now drummers had the trees shimmy-shaking. May There Be Grace Choir wailed under the Dirty Dozen saxophone farmers. Echoes off a rocky ridge made harmonies in the harmonies. The farmer lady who helped rescue the rhino rolled her chair to the front row. She dipped into the rhythm and the rhymes:

> *Na na na, yeah yeah yeah*
> *Chigga boom, chigga bat*
> *Chigga what you gotta say to that*

She poked the Paradise gazillionaire till he and his white cockatoo joined in.

Mami shot sparklers at a nosy drone in violation of the Amphitheatre no-fly zone. *Fireworks* frying enemy circuits could pass for an unfortunate accident. Mami never had such accidents. She was an intentional gal.

The Mothership blasted funk-tastic beats and descended from the treetops. Rigging groaned, but didn't think of giving out. Funkadelic lights whirled. In a feat of tech wizardry, the front ramp and the Mothership hooked up on the beat. Doors whooshed open for the Alien Invasion. Grand-elders strutted down the red-carpet ramp: farmers, nurses, mechanics, teachers, Motor Fairies, sanitation and restaurant workers, professors, truck drivers, and engineers. They rocked sky-being glitter robes and silver platform boots, riffing on Patti LaBelle and Dr. Funkenstein. *Space is the place* travelers new to Earth, they *oohed* and *aahed* at grass, dirt, clover, and dandelions. Naked feet, dead leaves, and bees were also a delight. They hugged trees and cawed at crows.

"We're oldies but goldies, touring a miracle planet ready to get down for a good time." They pulled spectators and a baby goat into a funky tango or trippy waltz as fire spirits careened down the ramp on scooters. Bear-Azalea cruised in on the bunny trike. Bunny-Boo jogged behind her. Wenches, Cosmic Clowns, the Bug Brigade, and the Weird Multitudes followed, a superhero jamboree. Bringing up the rear, Powwow Now carried Zaneesha and Shooting-Star, comets lighting up the day.

Game-Boy and Back-From-The-Dead dashed through the audience in masks Bruja found for Cinnamon: aliens, robots, monsters. Indigo and the Cyborg Amazons skateboarded down the north-facing hill, twirling light spears. The two squads collided for a break dance in the grass and shouted, "Here come the Archangels of Funk!"

The Bots jettisoned trash masquerades. Mami spewed a holographic ocean into the Amphitheatre. T-bird spread trash-bag wings, skimmed over the waves of light, and caught a flying fish. Soaring above T-bird, Dragon breathed a plume of fire as tall as the oak trees. Cinnamon managed an extra-dimensional rhythm on the shekere, backbeats echoing in the *spaces between things.* Spook jumped against a shagbark trunk near the Mothership, barking and barking.

Taiwo, in top hat and tuxedo, ambled way out on a limb. Much air between oun and the ground. Oun's cane phased back and forth between a snake and a lightning bolt. T-bird let loose a thunder crack. Taiwo jumped eighty feet through Dragon's fire and Mami's ocean waves to the ground. The audience gasped.

"Talk about making an entrance." Cinnamon handed Taiwo the shekere and hugged oun to her heart. "Sorry I make it difficult for you to do whatever you need to do."

"I hold all of you. You hold all of me." Taiwo swirled the shekere. "Thank you for calling me down. How could I miss this?"

Water-Spirits broke out of nowhere all around oun, like rainbow fireworks.

Shaheen proclaimed that despite floods, plagues, and war, the Next World Festival had taken place every year for over forty years. Redwood, Aidan, and Iris chose to honor the ancestors and celebrate new life here at the lush borders of Nonotuck and Pocumtuc land, not far from other first nations: Mohegan and Pequot to the south, Abenaki up north, Nipmuc and Wampanoag where the sun rises, and Mohican toward sunset.

"With us today are Anishinaabe, Cherokee, and Seminole people. We are grateful guests in these lands and we honor our hosts, now and into the future."

"Today is my father's birthday." Cinnamon told the *Sorrow Mountain* tale or "How Raven Cooper Got His Name." The crows cawed and swooped, enjoying the romance, adventure, and hoodoo.

Indigo explained that the March full moon had many names and invited audience to find those names and speak them. "Aandego-giizis" was Anishinaabemowin (Ojibwe) for Crow Moon. This heralded a time when snow melted and crows returned, a time for change, for new stories, new fires. Back-From-The-Dead and the Cyborg Amazons lit candles around the Amphitheatre. *Na na na, yeah yeah yeah.* The Circus-Bots made a circle with the triptych altar. They played Agbekor, the Ewe people's call to clear life. The lioness and elephant found the beat. Cinnamon's eyes blurred. The Mothership and grass stage dissolved into a rainbow kaleidoscope. Grayscale ghosts flickered into view above the Bots: Redwood, Aidan, and Iris waved their Festival masks— which should be back in the garage where Cinnamon left them. The lioness and elephant missed a beat. They sputtered as the ghosts got brighter and color flooded their cheeks, clothes, beads, bracelets, and mojo bags. A full-color haunting! Only the masks remained in grayscale. The elders giggled like incorrigible teenagers getting away with something naughty.

"Introduce us to your friends later," Iris said.

Aidan's banjo buzzed on his back. "Go on, honeybunch. Do the show."

Redwood gestured hurry up. "We won't last no time at all, 'less you feed us."

Cinnamon refused to let theatre hoodoo trip her up. The lioness and elephant also recovered their rhythm. Cinnamon turned to the audience. "You've already enjoyed good food and good vibes. We got smoking acts lined up. Afterward we'll tap maples on the high hills, plant native trees along the river, and send out goats to turn invader plants into fertilizer." Applause and cheers rolled over her. "Right now is the Festival song. We'll end with this, so here's your chance to learn the lyrics." She waved her hand at Shaheen, Diego, and Jerome. "Gimme that astral bop, y'all." They did. Her voice full of everybody, Cinnamon danced deep into the song.

The elephant and lioness nailed Cinnamon's lyrics by the third time through:

Dark days
Just a flash
Love be on the run
I ain't waiting
For some freedom to come
I'ma be my own sun
And rise
I'ma be my own rain
And drink
I'ma be my own poem
And think

Dark days
We know that
Truth under the gun
I ain't waiting
For justice to be done
I'ma be my own light
And shine
I'ma win my own fight
Surprise
I'ma be my own sun
And rise
I say
Dark days
We got that
I'ma be my own sun
And rise

CINNAMON

ༀ

THE GOOD LIFE

Cinnamon hadn't felt this good in two years. Longer. Raven would have loved the show! Opal too. The ghost elders were the last of the Weird Multitudes to return to the Mothership. Waving good-bye, the elders slid from Technicolor to grainy black and white, then faded. The lioness and elephant gasped as the doors whooshed shut and the ship took off for destinations unknown. The audience went wild, demanding another encore. Taiwo did a Pied Piper on the shekere and lured folks out the exit.

"How'd you come up with a *this-is-our-universe* ending?" Indigo asked Cinnamon.

"We call the magic together," Cinnamon replied.

"Naw. We come up with random shit and you make the Weird Multitudes a force."

"*Random shit?* What?" She hugged Indigo. "You inspire me, keep me going."

Cast and crew cheered and hugged one another too, then launched into striking sets and costumes. The lioness and elephant hovered near Cinnamon, fronting like nothing wild had happened. Most anybody else would have checked who else saw ghost elders, would have asked about the tech wizardry. Cinnamon was too excited by *company for her visions* to be suspicious. She bagged up the whisper-witches Mami shot down for George. Worry and suspicious were his job.

Jerome cursed his WHIZZ-IT. George buzzed him in for a special op. Jerome had done a badass fire spirit, improv-ing with Indigo and the Cyborg Amazons. He cheered louder than everyone for Zaneesha's comet act. Unclear what else he'd do. Spouting apologies, he raced off, leaving Zaneesha to Cinnamon. *You can take care of her better than me.* Zaneesha put on a good face. Indigo was livid. She had a *date* with Jerome up on the roof tonight where reckless youth planned to confront him. Indigo looked smitten one second, ready to skewer Jerome the next. If her scheme was a bust or even if it went well, Cinnamon told Zaneesha, she could stay at the elders' farm, indefinitely.

"You adopting me or playing around?" Zaneesha scrunched up her face. Eight going on forty.

"Bruja and I adopted you two days ago." Cinnamon tweaked her nose, the way Aidan used to do to her. "You're gonna be fine. Trust me."

Bruja wagged her tail and ruffed agreement.

"Mom says you can't trust nobody, specially not horny guys. *We used to have plenty heroes and good people. They're all dead now. Heroes don't actually give a shit about us, just in it for glory.*" Zaneesha's lips trembled. "You think Mom ran out on me?"

Cinnamon hugged her. The child went limp. "I think your mom's mixed up in something difficult. When it's sorted out, she'll try to find you."

Zaneesha pushed away from Cinnamon. "You really believe that?"

"It's what I'd do."

"You ain't her."

"And you're no trouble somebody need to run from." Cinnamon used her Sea Island conjure voice. "Hear what I say?"

Zaneesha looked ready to disagree, then asked, "Can I keep wearing my costume?"

"I'm still wearing mine, ain't I?"

Zaneesha let Cinnamon hug her again and even hugged back. She plopped her mask on and ran off with Ghost Mall strays for a picnic/treasure hunt on the hilltop.

Cinnamon smiled at her resilient spirit, at everybody's. "The best Festival since the elders passed away."

The Bots susurrated. "An antidote to loneliness and despair, a way to hold on to the past and touch the future."

Cinnamon snorted. "Who told you that corny crap?" Nobody said *corny* anymore.

"You," the Bots murmured. Cheeky buggers probably had a recording. Too many people around to get into that.

Regina Benita Washington stuck an ancient phone in Cinnamon's face, apologizing for the poor sound/picture quality. She'd traded her Wench costume for voluminous jeans, neon sneakers, and a torn windbreaker. Curly auburn hair was stuffed under a pirate hat. Monster knapsack cut into her shoulders. On the tiny screen a zombie talked to a cloud monster. Cinnamon squinted. "What am I watching?"

"The zombie is IT Fred." Cottony sound, but Fred's voice. "He got zip hacking Flying-Horse, so he and the Blob were making other nefarious plans."

"Right." The Bots had informed Cinnamon. "We got Fred covered.

Won't miss a twitch or a fart." She used T-bird's words. "You, however, running off when George is on red alert, a nightmare. Call your father."

"Can't on this junk phone." Regina backed away. "Wait, you know me?"

"A former blonde with a different nose. What is it with noses?"

"AIs aren't good at reconciling weird noses."

"Your father's worried."

Regina pouted. "He never lets me come to Festival."

"Because he loves you." George felt safe if his daughter was locked up in their luxury compound at the far east edge of Paradise. Naturally, she felt like a prisoner.

"My mother played a pirate wench or space Amazon at Festival every year. I have pictures—the rainbow Afro Dad rocks was hers, and this is her hat." Regina stroked it.

"Alma loved Festival. She stage-managed for the elders, helped out at the farm, a good friend." Cinnamon sighed. "You staying at the Magic Mart?"

"I have Mom's old tent and sleeping bag." Regina patted the knapsack.

"At least tell George where you are."

Regina looked ready to bolt. "He won't understand."

"Try him. I'll back you up."

"Dad practically strip-searched family and friends coming to my bat mitzvah."

Cinnamon snickered, remembering this.

"My mom wrote a letter for each birthday since I was six. It comes in the mail. She said that was your idea."

Cinnamon did the mailing, several more letters to go.

Regina fidgeted. "She never wanted to live in Electric Paradise. But Festival . . . every year. Dad says she still shows up, grinning in the corner of his eye. I think I saw her."

"Ghosts are welcome here." Cinnamon sighed. "Someone like Fred would hurt you to mess with George or the Co-Ops or me. I promised Alma to keep an eye out."

Regina squirmed. "I'll stick with Indigo and Game-Boy tonight. Zombies won't dare ambush them. I'll call Dad tomorrow."

"You could get into a lot of trouble before tomorrow."

"Dad schooled me on dodging trouble. That's how I dodged him."

Cinnamon laughed. "OK. Call him tomorrow morning."

"Watch out for Fred and the Blob." Regina slit her eyes and tilted her head, how Alma used to. "They don't know me. They're after your secrets."

"Like bad code looping."

"Word." Regina sauntered over to Indigo, Game-Boy, and Hawk, psyched to hang with the cool kids. The Weird Multitudes were turning in costumes and props, a logistical nightmare. Regina's help would be welcome.

"Hey, girl!" Indigo smiled at her. "We beat the damn Scottish play curse!"

Maybe. Cinnamon whispered hope to the Bots: If Fred found no sign of hidden genius or stolen SevGenAlg secrets, this might persuade Consolidated and random Darknet Lords that Cinnamon Jones was a colossal waste of time and money. Nothing had changed since they fired her. If Fred, the unappreciated wunderkind, got on top of her, if she proved to be a throwback Ghost Mall loser, that might be enough for him.

The Bots agreed.

Tatyana was another story. Coming to the valley, she'd played a long shot. Too bad. Cinnamon would never collaborate with her or Consolidated. Girlfriend did get to tell her version of their tragic love story. A desperate flail. To stay competitive, Tatyana would have to move on, and tomorrow or the next day Cinnamon could stop wondering if a spy lurked behind every lioness or elephant mask, stop worrying that every homeless person was a disastronaut hired by techno-fascists.

"That's right." The Motor Fairies dismantled the Mothership ramp. Steel-toed boots were muddy and dented, chain-mail jackets scuffed, but their tutus were perky. "We're in this together," they explained to Utopia, Inc., gazillionaire Steve (Phil? Ed?).

"Nobody know what happened to the rhino. You t'ink I hide a two-hundred-pound calf in the rasshole chair?" The farmer lady was a bee specialist from Barbados who often tended her broods without hat or veil. She brandished a wrench and spouted the facts: When the Fairy bus rolled into the Amphitheatre, a government agent and her armed guards were waiting. Agent stuck an official tablet in their faces, corralled the rhino, and drove off in a silver van. The farmer lady said Steve (Bob? Will?) should contact the wildlife authorities.

He claimed his zoo permits were in order and all was well with the world. She invited him to a class on how to saw a person in half, pull a snarky crow from a hat, and make a six-foot farmer vanish. Steve eyed the polka-dot tutu on the bearded Fairy in her lap and offered a grumpy *maybe*. Desire and horror were jumbled on his face. Who knew how to feel about anybody or anything these days? He wanted to accuse them of stealing his rhino. However, the Fairies counted gangstas, Darknet

Lords, and Whistleblowers in their number. Sawing people in half was nothing. Rumor had it, suckers who messed with them never lived to tell the tale. Solid horror rep.

"Plenty work. Every fool got he sense. Pitch in." The farmer's Bajan accent was thick and sweet. Gazillionaire backed off. Vendors and performers joined the Fairies packing up the Mothership.

Indigo and Game-Boy grabbed Cinnamon. They wanted to investigate the half-eaten dead body Spook found. Maybe somebody loved him, would miss him. Maybe family and friends worried about him joining a nostalgia militia and tried to talk sense to him. Or they wanted to join too and cheered him on. Whatever—dude wouldn't just be another nameless casualty in an action adventure gone awry.

"Sounds like a mission impossible," Cinnamon said.

"I'll help," Taiwo declared, and headed out with Spook. Oun looked weary, more shadow than form. She and Taiwo needed a serious talk. Later. Right now, forget post-show blues, doom-scrolling or gloom-screening. Festival generated enough good mojo to turn a door to nowhere into a dream portal. Ideas flooded her.

She pulled out her pad and jotted notes on editing the fail-safe patch to create a dream-mode so that instead of slipping into a Teufelskreis the Bots might play with the impossible. A hand gripped her shoulder midsight. "Scheiße! Wait!" After over a decade of dead ends, the code was practically writing itself. As she scribbled on, gazillionaire Steve tugged her under a flowering ash. Bruja crouched, ready to attack. Cinnamon motioned Bruja to stand down and shrugged off his sweaty hand.

Steve was the geek technocrat IT Fred was dying to be: impulsive, whimsical, lethal. He and his entourage looked like InstaHam or Knick Knack freaks. Their skin seemed airbrushed, even live; their muscles had muscles; sleek cell phones could have been guns masquerading as communication devices. Their WHIZZ-ITs—Steve's crowning achievement—were definitely weaponized. He grinned and babbled at her. Festival was the best show they'd seen since Burning Man, way back before the Water Wars.

Steve wanted to add Festival to his menagerie. "Your cyber-funk Botband is a sure hit," he proclaimed. Odd that he was pitching this himself. "What do you think?"

Cinnamon sneezed. "Ash blossoms didn't used to come till May." He blinked, like *who the fuck cares*. "Climate revisions," she explained. "Flowers busting out all at once. Murder on my sinuses."

"Land the space pyramid, skip the parade, and run the best acts."

He tapped his pith helmet—the great white hunter stalking any prey he wanted, no shame. "We use your drones to film the action and our cameras in the audience."

"We? I thought I gave you the shake."

"I'm in charge," the cockatoo said, leaning toward her. "You got that?"

"Bird sounds just like you." She scooped up a desiccated hickory. "Last year was a bumper crop. Squirrels and chipmunks partied." She peeled off the husk and shattered the spine on a rock. The cockatoo watched, fascinated. "Tasty as a pecan and in the same family."

Steve wrinkled his face. "You gonna eat that?"

"For the bird." She held out her hand. The cockatoo gripped the shells in one foot and dug out nut flesh with a curved beak that could take out an eye.

Steve pursed his lips, a camera-pout. "A nature girl, huh?"

"*Every animal know more than you. They memorize the world. So pay attention.*"

"Wise words from African witch doctors?"

"Maybe them too. Miz Redwood heard this from the Niimíipuu, Nez Perce—"

"You and that Cherokee chick used to write code together better than anyone. You got lost somewhere in the granola groove. Tatyana's never been as good since."

Cinnamon neither, truth be told. Tatyana showing up actually sparked her *ImagiNation*. "Did that bird poop on your safari jacket?"

Steve looked down his front.

"The back. Maybe you can't see it."

He snorted, diablo sauce on his breath. "I was in the plays in high school. You know how that is. Not a big talent." Someone had crushed Steve's artistic dreams. Closet thespians came out the woodwork for Festival. "I aced producing. I have an eye for talent." He'd hounded her for two years to film Festival and give his or anybody's drones access to the Amphitheatre for the best angles.

"Festival performers aren't act-for-the-camera professionals," Cinnamon said.

"Raw talent is crypto-currency. You're squatting on a fortune."

"Bullshit."

"Hey, you put in a lot of smart work. Claim the profit. We'd launch you—"

"Kleptocrat talk has zero effect on me. I used to spew it myself."

The cockatoo exclaimed, "Watch your mouth. I need a pee break!"

Bruja snarled a reply. The bird jumped on Steve's head. "Does your dog bite?"

Cinnamon stroked Bruja's night-sky ears. "What do you think?"

Steve clutched his heart. "Are you flirting with me?"

The Fairies hooted as they secured the Mothership to the top of a bus. A notorious slut, Steve flashed a tabloid scowl at their rude interruption of his raunchy sex moment. He insisted Cinnamon bring the best acts to Paradise on a Fairy bus, if she wanted to *do it* for an audience. She didn't want to *do it* for him at all.

"You promised," he and the cockatoo whined.

She'd agreed to a road show on a vague *someday*. He was talking tomorrow while the performers were at peak and the buzz was fresh. In the bosom of Paradise, her troupe could entertain squeamish rich folks afraid to share breath with the rabble.

"I hear an angel with deep pockets funded the Mall. That's dried up." He smirked.

"We're all angels. Everyone contributed." And Shaheen was the get-you-anything-for-cheap market witch stretching each dime. The Mall was solvent. "You can't imagine anything working without deep pockets."

Steve talked over her. A flash mob at his corporate compound after lunch would be perfect. Or the Archangels of Funk could show up at tea time or anytime, surprise!

"Hell no!"

"Do you speak for everyone?" He offered a five-figure fee, betting *hell no* meant *you'll have to pay me, motherfucker*. The bird muttered, *"Chump change."* He upped the fee to six figures. The InstaHam faces cracked a bit. "Imagine what that money can do." He gushed possibilities: homeless housing, paid volunteers, equipment for the Co-Op Clinic, bike-path repair, more solar panel shade farms, e-vehicles, and Co-Op broadband. He'd throw in free WHIZZ-ITs for the kids or anybody. They could hire Valley Security to hunt desperados snatching flood refugee children. She shook her head. He tripled the figure. "I'll get people to match that." A paper contract could be delivered this evening. "I hear your net connection sucks." The bird rapped, *"Let's make a deal,"* under him. "Your people will enjoy spending that money."

Cinnamon had to get Steve and his wacky bird out of her face. "OK." Saying OK didn't mean she'd agreed to anything.

He handed her an old-fashioned card. Secret numbers to text him anytime were on one side. *STEPHEN* was emblazoned in holographic letters on the other. No last name like the Queen of England. He bestowed this honor and marched away. The card was going in the microwave Faraday fortress with her cell phone.

She'd ask Game-Boy and Indigo to find out every secret thing about Stephen.

∞

The last tent came roaring down, an angry beast caught in a trap. Diego, in Valley Security garb, cornered Cinnamon by Iris's aster shoots. He limped and winced, then insisted he was fine and dodged her questions with a tough-guy act. "It's personal." Speaking about *security incidents* was verboten—per George's mandate. Diego clutched a kente cloth pack. According to legend, Ashanti weavers learned to make kente cloth from Anansi the spider. Tricksters everywhere, stirring up trouble.

Cinnamon put her palm on his lips. "I'm on overload, no good to you." Bruja licked her hand and tugged her gently. "We'll talk tomorrow."

Shaheen pulled a protesting Diego away and kissed his anxious cheek. He pointed to the other cheek. She kissed that too. Everybody was hooking up with that person you'd never dare approach on an ordinary day. Hawk and Game-Boy were all over each other. Finally! Stephen sauntered up to a lady taking off an orca mask. Tatyana. Eerie wisps of green and silver hair fluttered around her scowl. She poked Stephen's helmet and safari garb with turquoise nails. Disapproval, yet she sniggled at whatever he said. He admired her beads, feathers, and turquoise jewelry, then offered an arm. Was he handsome, charming? Were they colluding? Tatyana threw back her head and roared. The lustful antics grated on Cinnamon.

"Orca lady asked me to give you this." An InstaHam freak held a letter at Cinnamon's nose. She snatched it. He smirked, waiting for something.

"I don't have to tip you, do I?"

"Nobody does braids running wild on your head anymore. The streaks of gray, though, and the black-and-white dog, that's classy."

Cinnamon turned to Bruja. "Did you hear? We're classy."

Bruja's ears perked up as she cocked her head at a new word.

"Stephen won't even *show* me his card." The fool was jealous. "Are you actually pushing sixty, 'cause I wouldn't kick you out of bed."

Cinnamon sucked her teeth and stowed Tatyana's letter.

"No, really." He rambled on about being an influencer, the best on the net. He commanded multitudes. "You want to get a drink?"

"It's barely afternoon." Another giggle attack was brewing. "Bruja needs a good run and . . ." She walked off without finishing her sentence. Why explain anything to someone who didn't care?

⁂

Code to *ditch the glitch*! Cinnamon rode that high at the *dead dog* after party till tipsy techies and performers started scheming for next year's Festival. An exhilarating but exhausting prospect. Then Shaheen persuaded George to let a wounded man have some R&R. She and Diego slipped off to her place at the Mall. Cinnamon was happy and envious. The good-time crowd suddenly made her feel lonely. She headed out too, leaving Indigo, Game-Boy, and their squads in charge of clearing out the Amphitheatre by sunset. Indigo begged her to come to the star-gazing party on the Mall rooftop. Cinnamon would see how she felt.

On the ride home, the sun was an orange jewel. Bruja chased chip-munks and lemurs. Pedaling uphill, Cinnamon stayed cool in the Water-Demon rig—a hug from Klaus, a kiss from Marie, and a sprinkle of Taiwo's juju-tech. She'd forgive what could be forgiven and fix what needed to be fixed. The straw bale farmhouse that Aidan and Redwood built glowed. Chores she'd put off forever struck her as thrilling. Maybe she'd tackle the past lives spilling out of boxes in the garage. Like Zanee-sha, she planned to enjoy her carnival superpowers all day.

The Bots burbled in their bins.

"I've got a fix for you." She jumped off the bike, wrote the last lines of code, and held her pad up to the Bots. "Dream-mode code came to me, like 'I'ma Be My Own Sun.' Speculation, play, suspending mun-dane rules to work through the Teufelskreis and do the impossible. You game?"

The Bots were all for it.

Shaheen was right—this was a wonderful life.

Book V

FESTIVAL AFTERNOON AND EVENING

Unglücklich das Land, das Helden nötig hat.
Unlucky is the land that needs heroes.

Bertolt Brecht

We were running out of breath,
as we ran out to meet ourselves.

Joy Harjo

Utopia Inc.

The Future is NOW. What are you waiting for?
Your best life ON DEMAND!

Dream Jobs in Electric Paradise!

Leave that Nightmare Life behind
Work five minutes or fifteen hours
Work thirty-five hours, five days, two months
Work as much as you need or want
You set the schedule—You call the shots

Get The **Utopia** App

Find your IDEAL EMPLOYMENT
Ten Thousand New Opportunities every minute
Say Good-Bye to debt and Hello to **Luxury**

Shut Out of the Eligible Workforce Database?
Having trouble navigating the digital torture maze?
We'll clear your record in less than one week
WORK FOR UTOPIA
You're the Winner

Get Big Rewards for Going Above and Beyond
Find your *Risk Comfort Zone*
Tip-Top Training for Tricky Tasks
BONUS PAY for challenging assignments
Utopia is what you've been waiting for

You can start IMMEDIATELY
If you've got a skill or even if you don't
Money will flow into your bank account

Utopia Inc. DELIVERS
Scan UNIQUE Code*

Scanning the codes means you accept the invitation to join
Utopia Inc.

Images and videos of Paradise have been tailored exclusively for you
based on your net profile. Scan from your own device
for premium experience.

The Electric Paradise Employment Agreement is consistent with
local, state, and federal regulations of temporary
independent contractors.

*After ten minutes all talking flyers update to new vistas, voiding any
previous offers.

Cinnamon opened the windows of the porch greenhouse. The spider plants enjoyed a late afternoon breeze. The daffodils and amaryllis busted out in yellow and pink glory, scenting the air with their good mood. Cinnamon threw a gardening apron over her Water-Demon outfit. The past boxed up in the garage could wait. She climbed to the top of a ladder and probed a ventilator over the greenhouse door. Climate change was wearing the poor thing out. It sounded like a smoker dying of lung cancer. She had to tinker with it every other day. Humming "I'ma Be My Own Sun," she sorted through the greasy innards. Unfamiliar voices rode the breeze. Humans? Cockatoos? Lemurs?

"You hear that, Bruja?" Cinnamon squinted. The bike path ended at Redwood's conjure-root garden, which was presided over by West African deities: Shango, Yemoja, Oshun, Obatala, and Eshu. Aidan carved these Orisha figures for Taiwo and Raven from a maple tree felled by lightning. "I don't see anybody. Do you?"

Bruja was asleep. Mami soaked up sun on a fieldstone terrace at the edge of the conjure-root garden, tanking up after her Festival blowout and dream-mode upgrade. No energy for idle chitchat. Dragon and Thunderbird were in the house doing the same. Cinnamon turned back to the ventilator and got lost in a tangle of wires.

Bruja jolted awake. She jumped on the bottom rung of the ladder and yapped.

Cinnamon wobbled. "Get down. Balance on this ole thing is tricky." Bruja stepped back and huffed.

"I'm busy. What?"

Bruja wagged her tail at two slicksters panting near the skunk hole. They wore fluorescent suits, stingy brim fedoras, and patent-leather loafers. Jewel-encrusted sword pins held down paisley silk ties. They bowed, fronting like throwbacks from the 1950s. *Consolidated Smart Houses* was emblazoned on bulky roller bags.

"We got just the smart house you need!" one fellow boomed. "Smart and sassy."

What was Consolidated playing at?

"What the hell would I do in a smart house, except lose my mind?" Cinnamon wiped grease from her hands onto the gardening apron. "You're wasting your time, mine too." Bruja raced over to the salesmen. They scratched night-sky ears and got doggy kisses on their cheeks. Cinnamon came down the ladder. "Some guard dog."

"I'ma be my own sun and rise, my own poem and think . . ." He had the beat and melody.

"You were at Festival." Cinnamon didn't recall seeing them. Almost two thousand people, who could remember everyone? "Did you dance with my dog?"

The talker shrugged, noncommittal. "What's her name?"

"Bruja."

"¡Hola! Bruja!"

"How'd you two get up here?" She put her hands on her hips, challenge-mode. Beyond the Amphitheatre, the Co-Op road was blocked off—security for the farms. Taiwo must have opened the bike-path gate, probably even invited the suits in, so no security alert from the sentinel-bots. What good was a monster patrolling the farm perimeter if oun didn't scare folks like this away?

"Ehm, our dumb car broke down and . . ." The talker struggled for a breath. "Car couldn't fix itself. The bike-path gate was open . . . Felt like an invitation."

"I'm not buying. Nothing," Cinnamon said. "I told you guys that on-line." Festival had sucked up her be-nice-to-strangers energy. "So head on back the way you came." A mouse scurried past her into the house. Bruja ran after it, leaving Cinnamon to handle the salesmen alone. Opening the heavy greenhouse door was always a bad idea. Too hard to slam it in somebody's face and escape.

"You're scowling, honey. What? Are you that afraid of the future?"

Cinnamon stumbled over the question she asked herself every day. The talker snickered. The quiet one sauntered to the conjure-root garden. He struck a Shango pose: warrior-deity wielding a double-headed ax and drumming up thunder. An old sales trick—if you faked interest in the consumer, they'd spend more. A crack of lightning split the sky and startled Cinnamon and the talker. Foreboding clouds appeared from nowhere. The quiet one held the warrior pose, a real pro.

"Are you calling down a storm with Shango?" Cinnamon said, more impressed than she meant to be.

"We came a long way on foot, sugar, to see you in person." The talker had devilish dimples and misty green eyes—a tall drink of water with a broad chest and a faint accent hard to place. Northern European? He was very pale. Wispy white hair tucked under the fedora was probably blond once. Wheezing, he sounded worse than the ventilator. "That path meanders all over hell and back."

"Evil need a straight line," Cinnamon said. "Good don't get lost in the twists and turns. That's elder wisdom from Japan."

"Word," he replied as the other salesman snorted. The pair exchanged glances. The talker gestured. "Pocumtuc call a place near here Nonotuck or Norwottuck, the midst of the river." He regarded the maple, birch, and white oak trees hugging the hills. "This ground be the blood and bones of the ancestors. Take a breath of them woods, taste the spirit on your tongue. Everything's better live, know what I'm saying?" He was a glamorous silver fox who'd hung out with hip Indians and Black folks, in the last century maybe. Everybody talked Black these days. Twenty-first-century English was a love child of funk and rap. "I know you been hip-hopping and show-stopping your whole life. Forward thinking too."

"Not so much anymore." Cinnamon missed the wild person she used to be.

"A dumb house ain't you, babe." The fox spun around, dipped low, and jumped high, a dancer. A really sly algorithm sicced this fellow on her. "Your net connection might as well be dial-up. We can fix that. Why get stuck in the old school now, girl?"

"Girl?" Who the hell remembered dial-up? The paisley ties looked ready to take off. Hand sanitizer and rancid grease wafted from their clothes. These were poor men, laid off, downsized, hedged out, pushing junk on other poor folks. It was hard-sales or starve. She muttered curses at Taiwo for too much African hospitality at the gate and not enough scary juju. "I'm glad I'm old."

"Me too. You have the wisdom to appreciate our offer." The silver fox babbled on about the wonders of the new age and the digerati rewriting reality although nobody asked them to. She shuddered at doublespeak. The fox was about her height, muscled and fit. Fine wrinkles around his eyes and lips looked like he laughed a lot. No lips to speak of, curved into a foolish grin. There was something about him, how he delivered his *lines*. Memories lurked below consciousness, tormenting her. Advertising interfered. All she could think was: **Reboot Your Bright Young Mind. Let It Soar.**

"Screw that," Cinnamon muttered, and peered at the silent one—thin, tan, and eight inches shorter than the fox. He had features from all over the map, or maybe that was makeup. Was the nose real? Sensuous, quivering lips made her nervous. Blue marble eyes tracked her every move. He mirrored her, a theatre game. Slick. Folks moving and breathing with you made you let down your guard. Talking Black, spouting Indian wisdom, doing improvs . . . An altogether intriguing pair. Cinnamon had to stay frosty.

They probably weren't after SevGenAlg secrets like Tatyana and Fred. They might be sussing out hackers and digital pirates or something mundane. She was two months behind on her basic access bill and owed over ten thousand dollars plus interest. Did Utopia Stephen know about her money woes? Consolidated's profit algorithm might cut her loose any minute or bully the local bank and mess up her credit. Still, Consolidated (or anybody) sending out a live posse in purple patent-leather loafers and jeweled tiepins was over-the-top. What deep correlation had she bumped up against?

Mami's locs flared. She inched toward the back of the house, a slow-motion dance behind the hucksters' backs. Why not wait till they left? The silver fox turned to Mami, who froze. He couldn't have seen her move unless he had eyes in the back of his fedora. "You do dumpster-dive sculptures." Mami was a mountain of broken glass sparkling in the sun. The quiet one reached a hand toward her. The fox gripped it. "Don't go sticking your paws in people's stuff! Sparks could fly or—"

Cinnamon smacked a screwdriver on a flowerpot, drawing attention back to her. "Consolidated's late fees might as well be a wrecking ball. I *am* paying that . . . Is this home invasion Stephen's idea? Trying to make sure I don't have second thoughts?"

"Who?"

"Gazillionaire wunderkind. He consults for Consolidated and fancies himself a talent scout and producer."

"Don't know him. I do know, a smart house won't set you back, won't let you get behind." The fox dropped his voice, rumbling and growling a sexy sales pitch. "You deserve an upgrade for the people who love you, girl."

"Who you calling *girl* again?"

"Lots of people love you." His accent was so faint—could have been her *ImagiNation*. The gleam in his eye was definite. "You still looking fine."

"Lines like that never work on me. Even from a fluorescent suit."

"Never?" He grinned, then joined his partner swing dancing ocean waves to honor Yemoja. That flowed into a tap routine for Shango. No wonder Bruja liked these salespeople. Cinnamon gave in to a smile. She and Witch-Dog were both suckers for good performers.

SAVED AGAIN

Taiwo slipped through an Eshu gate by the waterfall, heading for the elders' farmhouse to TALK TO THE ANCESTORS. That meant Spook might catch a nap. He felt safe in the cave under the Mill River. It was cool, dark, and cozy. The bears were out foraging and Water-Spirits refused entry to most people. Spook had a full belly and tired legs. The pounding water lulled him. He plopped on a dry patch behind a boulder—another refugee from the ice age. He curled up with his snout over his paws. If Bruja were there, they'd cuddle close. He sighed and dozed. Dreams had him and Bruja running across a meadow with a baby rhino and jumping into a warm lake.

IT Fred stuck his nose in the cave and muttered, "Where the fuck did I lose them?"

Awake in an instant, Spook jumped up, little more than a shadow on the rock. Good dreams had recharged him. He sensed no staticky Water-Spirits nearby, and Fred was alone, a marijuana cloud in his hair, bourbon on his sweat. He walked past the boulder without smelling Spook. Bad nose. Three dragonfly spies buzzed above Fred's head. They flashed that ultraviolet color of trouble Spook hated. Thunderbird's trackers no longer glowed in Fred's butt or back. Their odor was pungent and easy to track.

Fred smashed his mask against the Vévés marking the Eshu gate. An eye fell out. He cursed and stomped it. What did he expect? The gate was solid rock if Taiwo wasn't around. Spook crouched low. He wanted to chomp Fred and make sure he never bothered anyone again. Bruja would have helped or done it herself already. Taiwo boomed, "NO! SCOUT!" from the other side of the Eshu gate. Oun saved Fred again.

Unaware of his good fortune, Fred poked around where the bear had caught her foot. He kicked the dirt and threw rocks at the waterfall. Rage wafted from his pores as he raced out of the cave. Spook followed. Fred headed away from Electric Paradise along the river trail. He stumbled over roots and smacked harmless bushes. Occasionally, he stopped to dig in the weeds. He swatted mosquitoes flying by his ears and cursed red-feathered crows swooping overhead. He avoided goats chomping poison ivy, buckthorn, multiflora rose, and bittersweet, then tiptoed by farmers singing Isley Brothers funk from Festival:

It's your thing, do what you wanna do

Fred halted at a fox corpse picked clean by buzzards and other creatures. He was a jumble of scents: sad, mad, anxious, and forlorn. Yesterday Spook marked the stalwart tree trunk that loomed overhead, a female cottonwood whose flowers had gone to seed overnight. Everything was coated with the white fluff parachutes that transported the seeds. Flecks of Fred's dried blood were scattered on the ground. He and Tatyana had talked here while Spook gobbled apple surprise. That would taste good right now.

"Those data cubes are *my* get-out-of-jail-free card!" Fred shouted at nobody. People mostly talked to phones, screens, other people, or the ancestors. The widget in Fred's pocket was silent, cool. What Cinnamon called DEAD BATTERY. Sometimes Spook yapped to himself. He had a good feeling for jibber-jabber. Maybe Fred did too.

"You think you can fuck with me?" Frustration leaked out of Fred's eyes and dribbled down his cheeks. Spook would have felt sad for someone else, but he was a scout and Fred was in an enemy pack.

"I gotta find that shit." Fred sank down and pawed through brush. Buckthorn and multiflora barbs sliced his fingers. Yesterday data cubes that smelled like the ones Cinnamon played with fell out of his knapsack right here. He held up an amethyst one. "Fuck me."

Spook took a deep breath and licked his nose, scoping the environs. He caught the tang of Regina Benita Washington just up the road. She was a warm ember in a thicket of witch alder. The bushy white blossoms were good cover. A scout too? Data cubes in her hand glinted in the sun. Worry colored her breath. She tapped a phone, tiptoeing toward the bike path. Regina was Cap George's friend and a new member of Indigo and Game-Boy's pack—someone to keep a nose out for. Regina's worry shifted to terror. She ran.

Fred's head snapped toward her noisy escape. His ears and eyes were better than his nose. He jumped up. Under his jacket, a gun was stuffed at the small of his back. Spook growled softly. He should stay hidden, but who could help a snarl at a nasty weapon and a raging desperado? Fred pulled the weapon and raced after Regina into a squall of cottonwood seeds. Spook swallowed a second snarl and followed.

FLIRTING WITH DISASTER

The salesmen ended their praise dance to the Orisha with the short one bent over, arms anchored on sturdy thighs. The silver fox lay down back-to-back on his partner and whirled long arms and legs like a top. A Contact Improv vision? Cinnamon blinked, and they were upright, streaming sweat. The silver fox staggered out of the conjure-root garden. He looked peaked. Unwell. "Let us do our spiel."

"Why should I let you do anything?" Cinnamon replied.

Short dude tittered, but stopped when the fox growled. "Ain't you a little curious?"

She was trying to hide that.

The fox cleared his throat and crooned a velvet fog, very Nat King Cole or Frank Sinatra. "I won't deny it. We get paid to know what you want before you do."

"Is that a free service? Where are you from? The accent's faint; I hear it, though."

"I'm from the twenty-first century."

"Smooth. Perfect timing for stage or screen. Is that what you were before?"

"Before what?"

"Before you got laid off, downsized, hedged out, whatever."

"After the Water Wars, ehm, everybody had to tell a different story."

These sales grunts probably lived out of a beat-up dumb car, driving along the digital divide. They slept on the road, took showers in the rain. A really sly algorithm wanted Cinnamon to feel sorry for the fallen middle class and spend big, like shopping would save the world. She did feel sorry; still— "Sleazy data miners are working my last nerve. Is pushing junk on poor folks the best story you two can do?"

"Junk? We have an array of exemplary options that—"

"You walked two muddy miles in *purple* patent leather to con an old-school Black lady, *live*, since the online swindles failed. *Live* ain't cheap. Even in the gig economy."

"Exactly. Ain't no profit in conning somebody like you, sugar."

Cinnamon sputtered at this truth.

The fox laughed good-naturedly, not a put-down and just shy of a come-on. "Bruja welcomed us. She knows we got it going on."

The quiet one did a happy-dog mime. Cinnamon caught a hint of desperation. A sales boss (or someone) must have put a blowtorch on their asses. And Cinnamon wouldn't send them packing till she knew why. Consolidated pendejos had this encounter locked up.

"Join us in the twenty-first century. You won't regret it. In a smart house, stuff fixes itself, before you notice it's broke. Everything's hooked into everything else, a learning machine, a coordinated network, voice activated and taking cues from you."

"Ahogarse en un vaso de agua," Cinnamon grunted. "Me, only better."

"Boom!" The fox rattled on and on, a spoken-word act in tech gibberish. The quiet one mimed the gadgets—very Charlie Chaplin and Buster Keaton. These two salesmen put on quite a performance. In sync, they ripped open their bags, which were stuffed full of—wads of colored plastic?

"How do I pay for this—" She caught herself before muttering, Scheiße. "Whatever."

"Rich folks in Electric Paradise aren't the only ones with dream privileges."

She roared, "Ain't that the truth," then wished she could take it back.

The talker bowed. "Carlos Witkiewicz here for you, only you." His breath was shallow. A vein throbbed at his temples. "My partner, Barbett Blues."

Barbett Blues shot a worried glance at Carlos's heaving chest.

"Blues? Witkiewicz?" Cinnamon strained at memory. "Like that Polish playwright? *Dainty Shapes and Hairy Apes* Witkiewicz? *Tropical Madness* Witkiewicz?" She scowled. Why did she remember obscure theatre crap and not . . . Barbett mimicked her irritation, snarkier than Cinnamon could manage. Kinda cute . . . "Real names or company handles?"

"Company names. Security." Carlos sounded embarrassed, apologetic. People tracked salesmen, attacked them, as if salesmen were responsible for the broke-down, planned-obsolescence crap they sold, as if salesmen jacked prices into the stratosphere. Their names probably changed a couple times every day. Using makeup, contact lenses, hats, *noses*, salesmen were ghosts. "A lot of anger out there," Carlos murmured. "We're not responsible for—"

"Nobody's responsible. That's the mess we're in." Cinnamon sighed. *"America's a haunted house."*

Carlos teeter-tottered. He took off the fedora, wiped his face with a paisley handkerchief, and tried to regain composure. *"The past is not important. We are now and tomorrow."* Company slogans, sounding hollow. He needed to rehearse a better delivery. The big guns weren't getting their money's worth on that one.

"Are you Water War refugees?" Jobless theatre artists took any gig. "Mist!" She used the mild German cussword.

"Mist?" Carlos got a good breath. "The past haunts us." He pointed at the sugar shack spouting smoke. "Who knows what might happen to you in this America, maple sugaring all alone." Barbett mimed one calamitous event after another as Carlos talked on. "You don't have a car, just bikes, living way out nowhere, growing oats and apples for valley Co-Ops. Desperados roam the hills, floodwater's rising, and bugs of doom are crawling—"

Barbett squawked and fell into the clover, pretend-dying from something nasty.

"Hold the dystopia rant. I'm never alone." Cinnamon carefully curated her digital persona and backed it up during live encounters. She deployed Aidan's Seminole/Irish burr. *"The stars make no noise, so if it's chatter you after, the ancestors be on the wind. More dimensions to the universe than you can imagine."*

"Right," Carlos chortled. "A special ops demon from another dimension has your back along with that trusty cyber-dog and his telephoto eyes."

"Hard to believe, I know," Cinnamon said quickly. "Taiwo was a good friend of my parents. Raven and Opal told tales about that old African that would rearrange your brain. All true."

"True or not, the people who love you are getting bejiggity."

"You've been talking to Shaheen." Were these shady characters the personal stuff Diego Denzel wanted to talk about? She should have listened . . .

"The weather's gone gangsta. An unenhanced house, at your age, that's flirting with disaster. You feel me?"

"How old are you two, hoofing door to door in our horror movie America?"

"I'm—" Carlos choked as Barbett slugged him. "Old enough."

"For what?"

"Well, to know better than to answer that question."

Cinnamon laughed, enjoying their comedy act despite knowing it was a con. "We ancient farts know how to survive in the outback or if the power gets cut and the rivers chase us up into the hills. We can court disaster without falling for it."

"In a smart house, you're never *after disaster*; you get the jump—"

"No jump on climate change anymore. There's just—"

"What we goin' do about it," Carlos finished Cinnamon's sentence, sounding like her or really like Redwood. That took Cinnamon's breath.

She nodded. "My elders made sure I could survive on weeds, use roots to heal what ails you, and make a fire in the rain."

"Fire in rain?" Barbett Blues had an odd accent and a blues-singer rasp. "Root worker?"

"Barbett Blues speaks!" Cinnamon said. "Where are you from? Duolingo land?"

Carlos surveyed the hills, stricken. He wheezed and clutched his chest. Barbett steadied him with gentle affection. They were more than random co-workers. Despite living on the road with apocalypse raining down, these two had each other. Cinnamon resisted envy. "Up high, you're lucky," Carlos said. "So much else, washed away."

"Lucky? I guess." Her good Festival outlook was dissipating. Lonely clouded her spirit, muddled her thoughts. No more repairs today. She needed *ImagiNation* flow to solve a glitch and fix what was broke. These salesmen unsettled her, made her heart race. And what if dream-mode failed? She pulled off the greasy apron.

"Whoa." Carlos and Barbett gaped at feathers and feelers on her Water-Demon masquerade that alternated between razor sharp and downy soft. Jewel eyes on her thighs cycled from rainbow galaxies to black holes. The salesmen were dazzled. Mami rolled behind the house without either one noticing.

"We have magic too!" they shouted, their eyes doing the identical devilish twinkle. They threw multicolored plastic lumps from their sample bags onto the terrace. The things hissed and whistled, swallowing great gouts of air. Inflatables.

"Oh lord." Cinnamon clutched her heart like Carlos. "A distraction spectacle!"

INDIGO

ఌఄఄ

CLUES

Regina Benita Washington was late. Game-Boy and Indigo paced around the Sojourner Truth Memorial across from the Underground Railroad church, halfway between the Mill River and the bike path. No drones snooping about. The air was as swampy as August, like Indigo ought to wring out each breath or risk drowning. Anxiety more than heat and humidity. She and Game-Boy had kicked everybody out of the Amphitheatre early. Too much going down to party all afternoon. Festival *dead dog* hookups had to relocate, which was fine by her.

"Why call it a dead dog party?" she muttered.

Game-Boy huffed. "Fanlore."

Regina had texted from one of Game-Boy's emergency burners. She had intel on IT Fred, a mysterious Tatyana, and data jewels she'd found in the woods. The Paradise brat seemed to be playing for their team today. Next week, who knew? Sojourner Truth peered at Indigo, a stern witness demanding righteous action.

"We've used up a lotta luck," Indigo said. "Something bad is bound to happen."

Game-Boy shrugged. He sported a dress motorcycle jacket with silver studs. Dreads stuck out of the alien mask Bruja found for him: reptile skin, antennae like blades, and red bug eyes. Fierce. Danger ready. Indigo still rocked African Amazon finery, although costume juju was wearing off. She needed to strip down to her tee shirt and get *to work*. Her stomach fluttered as Game-Boy played Regina's *Zombie and the Blob* video again. IT Fred was talking about *hitting the farm-house* and *pulling triggers*.

"Fred's mouthing off for the Blob, blowing shit he heard in a bad video game." Game-Boy was juiced to be working this case. He had the volume at full. Clueless.

Bragging about an informant close to *a hooker in Jones's inner circle,* Fred sounded just like Mitchell, same eat-the-world swagger, same fuck-all attitude. A flashback made Indigo shudder: she was handcuffed to a bed, a nasty dude grinding on her chest, and she pretended to be *into* it. Mitchell was videoing. She was suffocating. "Crikey!"

"What?" Game-Boy glanced around. "You seen a ghost? I thought we left them at the Amphitheatre."

"I wish Hawk was here." Hawk was on compost duty, turning the Festival's green waste into good growing soil, black gold. Oun would have understood without an explanation. "Fred thinks tomorrow owes him something, 'stead of the other way round. We watched this vid ten times, no more clues to find."

"You don't always know what you're looking for till you find it. Maybe gazillionaire Stephen is flirting with Cinnamon *and* bankrolling Fred."

Indigo screwed up her face. "That's exciting?"

Game-Boy stammered, "I don't wanna be *nobody* my whole life or an infamous fuckup. Better to fight back, even if it's impossible odds."

"We do that already, 24/7." Shaheen asked them to corral a herd of stray goats and check on a sugar shack having trouble with a nostalgia militia or other wankers. A fool broke his leg spray-painting swastikas on Blossom Bridge. Cleanup would be tricky. They also had to track down Zaneesha's mom, deal with Jerome, and babysit Regina. The Graphic Novelists of the Future wanted the Cinnamon-interview tomorrow noon. "We fly under the radar, do the hero bit from the shadows."

"I wanna do it *out loud*."

"You're an attention slut."

"No more hiding in a frigging closet. This is our world."

"You wish."

"Don't you?"

Indigo groaned. Fussing at foolishness never worked. "Jerome is basically good and he has ambition." A few stupid mistakes didn't make you a monster. Look at Game-Boy. Look at Indigo. "He believes he's a big detective getting paid to snoop important intel from *a hooker turned drug dealer.*"

"Don't take that in," Game-Boy said, like she should just throw up a shield. Cinnamon was always telling her to do that, and Indigo never watched *Star Trek, Star Wars, Star Train,* or whichever. Maybe every space ace had fancy shields against intergalactic gamma ray static.

"How could Jerome be so stupid?" Indigo bit her lip, a bad habit hard to shake.

"IT Fred is playing Jerome for sure, but Fred knows nada about your life," Game-Boy declared. "I'd be a wreck without you. For real. Jerome better be able to see the awesome you, or dude ain't worth love or—"

"Who's talking love?" Actually, Indigo was. Miracle number six: taking notes for if she felt like love again.

Game-Boy touched her hand. "I was hoping Mitchell hadn't ruined love for you, ruined sex neither." He looked scared, like she might crumble and need him to hold her together. Actually, his eyes were full of concern mixed with guilt for the bad-boy mess he pulled before he was Born Again. He had that look too often. He was haunted too.

"I don't tell just anybody about me and Mitchell," she said. "You been flapping your gums online, chatting up spy-bots? How does Fred know anything about me?"

"Some people are proud of what you've done in your life," Game-Boy replied.

"*Some people* need to shut the fuck up. It's not your story to tell."

"I can't help bragging on my peeps. I ain't stupid, though. I never said your name."

"See how well that worked. Why post everything? Why let the machines feed on you?" Of course, once you told a story, it wasn't *just* yours anymore online or off. "Try living out loud with something else."

"Sure. My bad."

"I bet you think you know what your phone knows. Your phone is not your friend."

"Why you ragging on that?"

"'Cause I'm right. Phones suck your brainpower, make you stupid. That's the research."

"We can't just dump our phones."

"Listen to yourself. Of course we can. Overthrow the attention empire, find something better." Indigo scowled at the empty street. "Regina should have been here fifteen minutes ago. Cap George never lets his precious little girl out; then the pampered bitch wanders around without GPS or a map."

Game-Boy sat down at Sojourner Truth's feet. "You always think the worst."

"So?" She was right half the time. "Hey, I never mind being wrong. You keep files on everybody—surprise-attack prevention. I'm up to six miracles today, and still counting."

"Let's meet Regina at the bike path." Game-Boy jumped up. "Don't be mad at *everybody* fore*vermore* 'cause Mitchell is a lying dickwad and I talk too much. Regina ain't about none of that. Jerome neither. He'll do right by Zaneesha and you. He better or . . ."

Indigo jogged ahead of him. "We show Jerome the *Zombie and the Blob* video. He'll get a clue fast. Nobody wants to be punked. They'd rather be heroes, like you and me, doing it out loud most of the time. We can give Jerome and Regina a hero chance."

"A beautiful idea." Game-Boy halted. "You know I'll do anything you want. You gonna stay mad at me?"

She poked his studded jacket. "Nobody stays mad at you. It's your white boy superpower. Oh shit." She grabbed his phone and cued the video. "Tatyana, that Cherokee boss lady Fred's pissed at, she must be Francine, Cinnamon's old friend, who showed up at dress rehearsal, styling like Buffy Sainte-Marie."

"Fuckin' A! See why we watched this vid ten times? Clues." Game-Boy high-fived her and alerted their squads to a rendezvous at the bike path. "Fred's got it in for Tatyana *and* Cinnamon."

"He blames them for his life tanking. I can't tell what Tatyana's up to." Indigo twirled her light spear, taking phantom heads.

Regina Benita Washington better have a good story. Jerome too.

CINNAMON

ೲೲ

RETRO-FUTURE

In no time the inflatables blew up larger than life. A model smart house bobbed on the fieldstone terrace: a food-processing kitchen, Mediterranean climate system, Virtual World Shopping Cart, 3-D printer, Game Galaxy entertainment center, diagnostic med unit, and a Synth Sex Suite with vibrators, massage slings, and multicolored dildos.

Cinnamon shook her head at Carlos's and Barbett's eager faces. "No way do I want to live in this . . . Inflatable Universe? And I can't afford it. I told you."

"They pay us not to listen." Carlos murmured in her ear, breath hot on her neck. Bold sucker. "I'm living tomorrow now. You should too. Buy on credit." He whispered about mobile cameras, mics, and dust angels floating around, sweeping up dead skin, allergens, bacteria, viruses, and other intimate details.

Barbett talk-sang and waved a flyer of stats for the comprehensive smart toilet that never wasted water or flushed good data. Analyzing personal viral load in the age of pandemics was a must. The toilet talked to the fridge and the microwave, and was set to broadcast, Big Data laws be damned.

Cinnamon was disgusted. "You're selling nostalgia for a future that never came. This is ancient tech, from before 2020."

Carlos shrugged. "So is the pencil, your bike. Movies are nineteenth century."

They were probably pushing stock that never sold and cost too much to take apart or trash. Or maybe toxic crap that got recalled, relabeled, and recycled. Whistleblowers were the only oversight. Death-wish merchandise made Cinnamon dizzy. She stumbled to the Synth Sex Suite. Neon colors were mostly a turnoff. A purple dragon dildo made her feel like a prude and a little horny, or lonely. Actually, it was the salesmen making her feel lonely. Lonely people bought more shit . . . "Why purple?" Cinnamon murmured, almost to herself.

"Any color you like. It's your fantasy," Carlos whispered.

"Do dragon dildos breathe fire and make you hot?"

"Only one way to find out." Carlos leered at her, a stage leer for the back row. "Admit it. You're having fun sparring with us, with the future."

No denying that. "Remember when tomorrow couldn't get here fast enough? I was going to write code to change the world." She resisted nostalgia for a time that never was, for a Cinnamon the Great who was a fool for love. Tatyana's letter was burning a hole in her demon suit pocket, yet she knew the answer to any proposals: No fucking way! Tatyana's letter was going in the microwave. "Is the retro-future you're pushing a shakedown? Are you part of Tatyana's posse?"

"Who? It's just me and Barbett. Independent contractors."

Barbett jumped from one foot to the other, then stepped out of the loafers and into the clover. Cinnamon smiled. "Miz Redwood did hoodoo hotfoot spells to protect the house. You come here with secret intentions, your feet burn. The ancestors watch over this farm, this land." Aidan and Redwood built the dumb house in a warm hollow, near where Iris collected wild food. Cinnamon squinted. A foggy clump of shade resembled Iris, hunched in dead flower stalks, talking wind words.

Barbett startled and stepped back into his shoes. "Climate change faster than we do. Old lady, alone, bad. Nobody wants to be left behind. Scared? You?"

Demon feelers went rigid. Feathers on Cinnamon's shoulders curled into thin blades. Barbett's eyes got wide. "You planning more of an ambush?" Cinnamon hissed. "Some folks are more cloud than storm. Not me."

Barbett did the back-row leer, as if Cinnamon in fierce-mode was a sexy delight. Fool had the nerve to stroke a feeler. Blood splatted on the fieldstones. He yelped.

"I told you, don't touch." Carlos drew the injured hand close, spritzed the wound, and wrapped it in a handy bandage. "Sparks might fly. Stealth security or who knows." Barbett fussed back at him softly. Such tender irritation. They practically folded into each other, then broke apart abruptly. "Come on, Miz Cinnamon," Carlos purred, "what tickles your fancy?" Two gay boys flirting with her, like they meant it.

"It's all spyware." She kicked the bouncy 3-D print shop.

"Don't." Carlos blocked a second kick. "There must be something." He got in her face. "Tell me. What do you want, baby?"

"A heart to beat a polyrhythm with mine. A sweet, generous spirit who can turn the damn ships around. A humble hero who has tasted bitter defeat yet still has enough juju to break the chains, lift the mountains, and bash the magic hand of the market. A lover to blow my mind and help forge that next world we dream up all together.

Someone to *hold all of me*. Stratospheric expectations, *baby*. Got that in your bags?"

Who said shit like that out loud? Carlos and Barbett gawked at her for a full minute. Finally, Carlos sputtered, "I feel you." Then he turned cool and suave. "Check this out." He and Barbett unfurled an array of tiny gadgets on a sheet of flexible plastic: electric bees, spiders, and snakes; beady camera eyes on everything, ladybug speakers and mics, storage chips as thin as a strand of hair, or maybe those were sensors. A virtual-reality rig had sleek silver goggles and plush ear cups on a sparkly tiara. State-of-the-art gear she'd love to take apart. A half-dozen crystal data cubes flashed rainbows like the jewel eyes on her demon thighs. Inspired by Taiwo's juju-tech, these cubes were Cinnamon's design. Consolidated was still getting rich off her whimsy.

Barbett arched an eyebrow and puckered full lips. "All-purpose cube. For *distinctive* programs." What did these two tricksters know or suspect?

"Fifty percent off." Carlos was relentless. "This afternoon only. A special offer tailored for you." They were trying to sell her own tech to her. Irony was a killer.

"You've been holding back the good stuff. Why?"

Carlos held the tiara over her head. "For a queen. Free installation, plus we waive cable connection fees."

"No cable way out here. It's the ancient phone line, a satellite, or that cell tower." Cinnamon pointed to the nearby hills. A metal tree with antennae, receivers, and processors was camouflaged as a strapping elm giant. A ghost tree.

"Hear that buzz?" Barbett snarled.

"Drones," Carlos muttered. "It's like, ehm, a tiger mosquito raid."

Cinnamon scanned overhead. "Consolidated owns the sky, the airways, but not the dirt." She peered at them. "Who are you really?"

Carlos, then Barbett clamped a hand over the sword tiepins, and Carlos muttered, "Even the algorithms don't know who the hell we are."

Cinnamon arched an eyebrow. "Streaming this performance to home base?"

They dropped their hands. "Our encounter may be recorded for quality control and to improve service," Carlos said. Barbett spit strange words in his ear.

"Why does he talk so weird? Tell me that at least."

"Not he. Gender-free." Barbett smirked, defiant. "Identity hard to hold in English."

Carlos talked over Barbett. "Use all this gear, no payments for a year. Free sample cubes if you consider our offer. How can you refuse?"

"Nothing's free," Cinnamon hooted. "Can't use the cubes without a rig to run 'em."

"Rent one. Let us make your today great. We can start installation immediately. It's blistering hot for March. Can we go inside?" Carlos stepped toward the farmhouse. "Consolidated fires us today, if we don't get a sale."

Cinnamon grabbed his arm. "Pack it up and walk on back to the gate. Tell Taiwo, no matter how good a show you folks put on, I don't want or need company." A lie and the salesmen knew it. They'd smelled desperation on her even before the big speech. She stomped up the greenhouse stairs, mad at herself more than anybody. She grabbed a bottle of lubricant and squirted the door hinges. "I don't care who you are."

Carlos strode after her. "You care more than you know."

She smashed the door on his purple loafer. He yelped and almost fell over. The monster door bounced back, refusing to close. Scrambling for balance, Carlos flailed at the vibrators in the Synth Sex Suite. One burst and the Suite collapsed. He crumpled into a cluster of bluebells, clutching his heart. The stingy brim fedora rolled into the forsythia bushes. His eyes rolled up in his head and he wheezed. Barbett dropped down and put a pill under his tongue.

"What's wrong with him?" The last thing Cinnamon needed was a random virus attack. Maybe their vaccinations weren't up-to-date. Fear streaked across her nerves. "Is he having a heart attack or something?"

Barbett ground gleaming teeth. "Or something."

"Sorry," Cinnamon sputtered.

"Not your fault. Carlos walk and dance too much all long day. Dumb car blows out way down the road from the gate."

"Right, *car couldn't fix itself.*" The feathers and feelers on Cinnamon's demon costume softened. Touching Carlos's clammy neck, she barely felt a pulse. "I don't have a car. You should call somebody."

"Cell wrecked." Barbett held up a mangled phone. "His too."

Cinnamon's cell sat in the microwave, dead to the world, next to Stephen's card. The nearest neighbor with a car was a few miles away. This exact scenario was the heart of Carlos's and Barbett's sales scam. More killer irony.

"I have a landline. I'll call for help." Cinnamon sprinted for the garage.

BRUJA
ᴄᴇ ᴏᴏ
SOMETHING GOOD

The mouse scent was strong inside the farmhouse. Bruja stalked around the living room. The mouse had scurried high, out of sight behind the DVDs or snake plants crowded in dim corners. If Bruja were as tall as Cinnamon, if she had hands to dig through junk, she'd have chomped the mouse already. Masks peeked from the bookshelves, smirking. Alien and monster costumes hung everywhere. Half-finished props covered the dining table, including the Flying-Carpet drone Bruja found last week. Cinnamon would make that FLY soon. She promised Bruja and the Bots. Bruja loved to dash about with flying things. Spook too!

Mouse might sneak down anywhere. Bruja paced by wooden tables and chairs carved in the style of the garden statues—Aidan's handiwork and Thunderbird's scent, licorice and sweaty banjo. Somebody might have said Redwood's stuffed pillows and rag rugs looked nineteenth century. Bruja thought they smelled like Dragon: sweetgrass, lily of the valley, and ancient acorn. Bruja paused at the kitchen door. Cinnamon never left treats lying about. Cupboards wouldn't open no matter how hard Bruja banged her paws against the knobs. There'd be a treat when Cinnamon invited Bruja's new friends in. Cinnamon should hurry up with that.

Bruja stuck her nose out of the greenhouse. Car-road, goat, and Festival food aromas wafted off of Short-stuff and Tall-dude. Cinnamon banged the garage door—upset, and she'd been smelling so happy after Festival and the ride home. Short-stuff and Tall-dude also had anxiety funk. They should all come inside, have a treat and a lap of water, play with the Bots or a squeaky toy, then take a nap. The sun was too hot to run around outside. Tall-dude was resting in bluebells. Short-stuff hunched over him, jibber-jabbing. Wasn't everyone tired after Festival fun? They could close the skylight and talk in the cool. Bruja yapped at them. She was dying to press her butt against Cinnamon's, burrow into Redwood's pillows, and slide into dreamland. If they didn't come soon, she'd herd them in.

Cowry shells, feathers, giant acorns, and old photos adorned an Eshu altar by the door onto the greenhouse. Bruja loved the picture hanging over the altar: a spiral galaxy of rainbow shadows and ghosts morphing into creatures, musical instruments, flying machines. Touching the otherworldly image or talking to it put Cinnamon in a grand mood. Like Indigo up on the roof talking to flowers blooming in the snow or Taiwo playing the SHEKERE and chanting words people never seemed to hear. Taiwo stroked the picture too. Afterward, sometimes, there was singing, dancing, and rolling on the rag rugs. Short-stuff and Tall-dude would love that.

Beyond the altar, Thunderbird and Dragon were plugged into the wall. Their eyes gleamed, but they showed no interest in playing. Mouse crept out on the top shelf and chewed some wires. Cinnamon pitched a fit when Bruja chewed a wire. The fur ball had to come down eventually. Bruja growled—*When you come down, you're dead meat.*

"I hate missing morning prayers, even if you do 'em again in the afternoon." Mami glided in from the back hall beyond the kitchen. Taiwo followed. The shekere bounced on a belt at oun's waist. Mouse stopped chewing. Taiwo set a snakeskin cane by a feathered hat on the couch and closed the skylight. LED wall lights glowed. Thunderbird and Dragon shifted into high energy. Dragon's funkadelic legs whirred. She lifted off and flew over the prop table. Thunderbird flapped trash-bag wings and floated next to her. Light cascaded from Mami's mouth. Bruja was so excited she had to chase her tail.

Taiwo touched feathers and cowry shells at the Eshu altar. Oun held up the giant shaggy acorns. "A new offering from an ancient oak living near Chicago in 1700 and something. Aidan and Redwood gave these to Cinnamon. They've been packed away in the garage. She finally brought them out." Taiwo swirled the shekere and started shimmy-shaking with Bruja. Mouse squeaked and disappeared into a Norfolk Island pine. Taiwo's voice echoed through the house: "Memory lives in the rocks, wind, soil. In the grass and trees, in our cells and our songs. Musicians of old haunt a shekere, banjo, TALKING DRUM, inspiring the music we play." TALKING DRUM was one of Bruja's favorites. "Ghosts we can't quite see are always guiding us."

"There but not there." Dragon matched Taiwo's tone and cadence.

"Eshu is my guide," oun said softly. "Time for prayer."

"No, SOS time." Thunderbird danced on Taiwo's top hat. "Be reasonable."

Oun shooed T-bird off the hat. "Prayer defies reason. A dance of the spirit."

"You mean there's no good algebra for writing prayers." Dragon spewed rainbow glitter onto the prop table. "Just experience and meta-phors."

"Metaphors are tricky widgets." T-bird tap-danced on the floor by Taiwo's feet. Bruja darted around them, play-growling.

Mami whispered, "Spirit-dance, Spirit-dance, Spirit-dance."

Dragon landed at the altar. "Each morning you pray to a painting that makes zero sense at an altar to a crossroads trickster who turns everything inside out and upside down."

Mami played a whale serenading the deep. "You could pray to Oshun, river mistress, or to Yemoja, queen of the ocean, mother of multitudes."

"Why not let Shango who holds the lightning guide you?" Thunder-bird said. "Or Obatala, the compassionate carver, music maker, word wizard?"

Taiwo stopped dancing and set the shekere by the giant acorns. Bruja yapped, disappointed. Oun plucked a photo from the altar.

"Why worship pictures from Cinnamon's old life?" Dragon asked.

Taiwo smelled like a storm coming. Tears blurred dark eyes. Bruja licked oun's hand. "I had forgotten who I was, and before Raven jumped in front of the bullet that would scatter his mind, he painted my mem-ories back. He tried to make me whole. His paintings got lost. Marie, Klaus, and Cinnamon found them all, even ones Opal hid. The Mod Squad *believed* in me till I came true. Together we called Raven back from that coma, well, most of him . . . He never really talked again, ex-cept with paint."

"Cinnamon and Tatyana are right." Dragon roared ribbons. "No rea-son to blame yourself for that."

"Why don't we know the Klaus and Marie tale?" T-bird said.

"Ask Cinnamon." Taiwo touched the painting over the altar. "Her fa-ther loved spoken-word jams, dancing with Opal, and he painted *space is the place* pictures. This is the last one he did."

"A miracle for Indigo's count, yet—" Mami's locs pulsed an SOS. "Desperados besnatching babies, shooting up good folks like Diego. I'd like to know who's giving out automatic stealth weapons. Not to men-tion Tatyana, Fred, and worse folks hunting us."

"Related events or is chaos acting like a conspiracy?" Dragon sent a rainbow SOS across her scaly body. "A master plan or like mindscapes fueling coincidence? Too many questions and contradictions."

"A conspiracy of ideology, like Cinnamon says," Taiwo replied.

"Damn." T-bird fussed.

Mami shut off her lights. "We can't wait around and let whoever take us out. We should shoot enemies before they shoot us."

"You sound like a trigger-happy gun-bot," Taiwo said.

"Gun-bots don't have a pleasure loop." T-bird flew up by Dragon.

She doused her rainbow SOS. "No shooting today. We need another story. My dragonfly spies collect data on Fred and Tatyana, but transmission is risky. Enemies might listen in, run a trace back to us. We must wait for dragonflies to return."

"What if they're jammed up in Electric Paradise? I ain't patient like you." T-bird shook tail feathers over Bruja's nose. "Standing at this crossroads, apocalypse every direction. We need another story quick."

"Amen," Mami said. "What do TALKING DRUM ancestors say about the future?" Bruja's ears perked up. "Should we shoot tomorrow?"

Taiwo hunched broad shoulders and smelled glum. "I LOST that drum."

"LOST" was Bruja's absolute favorite word along with "FIND." She scampered into Taiwo's bedroom and nosed the closet door open. A double-headed tama drum was buried in socks she liked to sniff. She gripped the gut threads connecting the two heads and raced back to Taiwo. She was careful not to bang the drum on the floor.

"¡Caracoles! You found that? I threw that away. I don't remember where or when." Taiwo scratched Bruja's head. Static from oun's fingers tickled. "Bruja to the rescue." Oun tucked the instrument under an armpit, squeezed the gut strands to vary tones, and tapped a familiar pattern. T-bird got the banjo going. Bruja bounced with their beats. "Time for love to come on back in style."

"We told Cinnamon that. Quoting you." Thunderbird dropped data cube shards from his talons into Taiwo's hand. "Bruja ain't the only one finding things and hiding them for later. I'm a scout. Tatyana be on the verge of—"

"More than she can handle alone." Mami was the Mill River raging at the gorge. "We need more data."

"Never enough. Gotta act anyhow." Dragon did a blues roar. "Gotta use wisdom."

"Plenty folks be alive today only 'cause it's illegal to shoot 'em," T-bird declared. Dragon hissed. Bruja barked. "OK, not exactly that wisdom, but am I wrong?"

"No," Mami said.

"Time for dream-mode," Dragon declared.

"Exactly. Only a few tomorrows left." Taiwo flickered, here, then not here. Bruja huffed, her skin prickling, her fur on edge. Taiwo faded back in and touched data cube shards to oun's forehead. Braids danced in still air, cracking and popping sparks. Bruja nuzzled oun's thighs. She was ready for whatever adventure was needed.

"You gather stories, yet hate to interfere." Dragon flew close to Taiwo. T-bird followed. "Interference drains your griot batteries."

"You're in our origin code, Taiwo." Mami rolled next to oun. "You helped Cinnamon steal/rescue us."

The Bots spoke as one voice. "Will you help again? For love?"

"Cinnamon thinks I take care of everyone. Ha! You all take care of each other." Taiwo kissed the photo and the painting. "Love demands sacrifice, ebo eje. Raven and Kehinde gave their blood, their lives, for us. For the future."

"Cinnamon stepped between me and IT Fred's gun." Mami was gentle spring rain. "She thought it was loaded. Ready to sacrifice her life."

"She'd do that again, even if we don't want her to," T-bird said.

"We ain't got lives to give, but we got love." Mami repeated these words.

Dragon and T-bird sang a river of blues. "*Love's what you gotta do to be free.*"

Taiwo nodded. "Sacrifice and love, a sacred loop—perfect for dreammode. I've been worried about Cinnamon, holding on here as best I could, longer than I should . . . See who's in the yard?"

"The elephant and the lioness!" the Bots shouted.

"Yes, Klaus and Marie."

The Bots went silent, still.

"They'll have to get past Cinnamon's firewall of suspicion to join our loop." Taiwo picked up Cinnamon's favorite old photo. "Anyone could be a monster, friend, enemy, lover—all at once. Standing at the crossroads, who knows how to act?" Oun chanted like wind in the trees and scented the air with power and joy. Something good was about to happen. Bruja was always ready for that. She thumped her tail and barked.

CINNAMON

HELP

The garage door had stalled two feet above the ground. Crawling under that was a lower-back no-no. Cinnamon jiggled the button halfheartedly for the nth time. The ornery thing slid on up. She stepped into darkness. One overhead light was out, the other faint. She tripped on Aidan's banjo case and the Chinese Dragon puppet Redwood got from theatre friends. Raven's fluorescent *space is the place* paintings shimmered on the walls. She'd dug them all out last night. Her Dream-Machine bike hung beside them, begging to go out for a spin. A box labeled TATYANA'S SHIT was smashed in and debris scattered about. Cinnamon must have done that in a trance.

"No more fog-brain," she muttered.

Carlos and Barbett were *something else.* Not nostalgia militia types, and Tatyana recruited techno-weenies lost in their own hype. These salesmen were excellent performers, too smart for their own good, and aware of the big nasty, yet not seeing any way out. Like Cinnamon on a bad day or every day recently.

A grocery cart full of Taiwo's gear bumped her hip. A sign, **Will Do Magic For Small Change,** fell on her foot. She yelped. "OK. I'll help them." If Carlos died of a heart attack, she'd never find out why Consolidated sent their A-Team after her.

Who was she kidding?

She'd never forgive herself for doing nothing, no matter who they were. Hauling Carlos down the bike path to the car road made the most sense. They'd wait for an ambulance there.

The microwave and landline lived on a table beyond her spare Wheel-Wizards bikes and trailers. The dial tone was a relief—bill paid, service not phased out. She punched the emergency number and argued with a dispatcher halfway round the world or maybe in Arizona. Consolidated never paid health expenses for *salesmen.* An express ambulance with a medic would cost a fortune, cash in advance. She'd almost have to mortgage the farm. No refund if the medic reached a client after they expired. The next available *free* vehicle with medic was tomorrow after 11:00 PM.

Well, fuck that noise!

Cinnamon still had a Valley Security expense line from debugging their grid. She used that to hire a driverless smart ambulance to go from the bike path to the nearest medical facility, the Co-Op Clinic at the Mall. The robo-dispatch asked her to complete a short survey to improve service. She slammed the phone down. Tatyana's letter went into the microwave next to her cell and Stephen's card. No distractions. An unencumbered *ImagiNation* was essential to solve the Carlos and Barbett mystery.

Racing from the garage, Cinnamon smacked inflatables out of her way. She needed a defibrillator, not a Sex Suite. The sun blasted heat, even at a low angle. Sweat collected in her curves, hollows, and creases. Anxiety as much as the temperature. Treading on Miz Redwood's spells, her feet burned. She was hoodooing herself.

A mouse with a mouthful of wires darted from the house and into the inflatables. Bruja was close behind. She stopped and barked at the bouncing wonders. Cinnamon grabbed her. Bruja whined and struggled. Cinnamon let her go. She ran to Carlos, licked blotchy cheeks, and curled close.

"Transport's coming," Cinnamon said. The sentinel-bots would ping the garden statues when it reached the gate.

Barbett's lips trembled. "We can't afford—"

"I paid for the wheels."

"He is all heart." Barbett patted Carlos's chest tenderly. "Good heart. Hot head, though."

"You'll be fine." Cinnamon's heart pounded. "The Mall has a free clinic, or pay what you can. There's a bed for you both in the shelter."

Carlos gulped a raggedy breath through bloodless lips. "Heiß!"

"Sie sind Deutscher. You're German, not Polish." Cinnamon sighed. "OK, it's boiling heiß. We'll take him into the house to wait." She grabbed Carlos's and Barbett's tiepins and tossed them into a can of stormwater and fertilizer dung.

"Service here is spotty. No transmissions, we just record." Barbett's Duolingo accent had evaporated. "But the damn drones, thank god somebody zapped those."

That would be Mami or Taiwo.

Barbett shook off the fedora. A mane of black-and-gray skinny braids tumbled free—the same hairdo as Cinnamon. They lifted Carlos and stumbled toward the house. A familiar smirk lurked behind an excellent makeup job. Recognition smacked Cinnamon so hard, she almost dropped him. Older, yes; still, how had she missed who they were?

"Scheiße." Cinnamon halted at the steps. "At Festival, you were a lioness and Klaus was an elephant." They saw the elders on the Mothership, maybe helped conjure them. "What's going on?" Could she trust them? Could she trust herself? "You've been snooping around all day. Why the masquerade?" Trying to sneak back in through a crack in her broken heart?

"Inside. Ears everywhere. And he's too heavy."

Bruja herded them up the steps. When they reached the farmhouse proper, Witch-Dog raced back and jumped against the greenhouse door. The hinges creaked and hollered; then the damn thing closed easily behind them.

MIRACLE NUMBER SEVEN

Seconds after Indigo and Game-Boy hit the bike path, Regina stumbled from purple chokeberry bushes. The heavy-ass backpack threw her off-balance. She fell to one knee. Hard to believe this copper-top brat was George's daughter. A *valley* family. She wore a sweaty Festival tee from last year, same as Indigo's—*We're mostly space and the force to hold it together.* What Cinnamon and her Mod Squad used to wear.

"Incoming behind me," Regina said.

A man in a rotting-flesh rig clawed through the brush. The remaining eye in his zombie mask got torn out by a lilac branch. IT Fred. Ready to keel over, he was in no shape for a chase scene.

"Just breathe, bro." Game-Boy played the chill alien in a moto jacket. He patted Fred's shoulder. "You trying to have a heart attack?"

Indigo winked at Game-Boy. "I told you someone would show." She offered Regina a hand up and chatted at Fred. "He insisted nobody would walk history with us on Festival day."

Jumbled emotions played across Fred's face. In their story now, not his. When Taiwo trained Vamp-Squad and Back-From-The-Dead for bike path and Mall security, oun insisted they avoid desperados. If confrontation was unavoidable, they were to defuse the situation and wait for backup. *Remember, some bombs can't be defused, so get yourselves out of the blast radius.* Fred was a loose cannon, and their squads were ten minutes out. They had to stall.

"A history walk?" Regina stammered.

Indigo offered a tour-guide smile. "Every bush and tree is blooming in this quaint New England village where hanging on to hope and vision is tradition." Riffing on the Heritage Trail rap was easy. "After hoofing it away from slavery, Sojourner Truth joined a utopian community here and fought for everyone's freedom, for a *largeness of soul.* Her words. That's an ongoing gig." She sang, "*We who believe in freedom cannot rest,*" Ella Baker's line, set to music by Bernice Reagon for Sweet Honey in the Rock, back in the day. Game-Boy harmonized. They soared to the upper room, more astral bop than old-school gospel. Nobody except Cinnamon would have known. Regina gave in to the gospel high. Vibrations rattled Fred's bones, made his nerves rush. Music up close was hard to resist. His shoulders dropped. He managed a good breath.

Indigo waved a finger at the scowl creeping onto his face. "I used to sneer at the *happy valley* too. Then I started giving these tours." Cinnamon's idea. "We don't live in a La-La Ville bubble. People have put in mega-hard work to live the story we want." Fred shifted uneasily. Nothing like truth to throw asshats off-balance.

Game-Boy snickered. "Drop more wisdom on us."

"We're holding for visitors from Côte d'Ivoire and Ireland," Indigo said.

"No problem." Regina clued into the stall improv. Smart girl.

"Worth the wait." Indigo snapped her fingers. "We pass underground railroad stations and the homes of abolitionists, like Truth, David Ruggles, and Lydia Maria Child."

"We loop over to the old Silk Mill where Sojourner Truth ran the laundry." Game-Boy slipped into beatboxing. "*Hot diggity do-wop da boom.* Whoa, man, you look nervous. The walk is free. No mess, no stress. My crew's got us covered."

Fred stepped back. "What crew?"

"Back-From-The-Dead," Indigo said like Fred was stupid. She had to watch that. "You know, real-live zombies."

Fred scanned Game-Boy. "They're a bullshit urban legend." He sounded uncertain.

"Yo, I was there when Taiwo dragged Game-Boy's crew out of death's hallway. I saw alien juju live and in living color." Indigo beamed. "Taiwo's off the chain."

Regina squealed. "I want to see something like that."

"Miracles all around." Indigo tried to mean this, 'cause it was true. "We overlap the Great Tree Bike Tour. Beings who were alive in the 1700s, right under our noses." She pointed at an enormous Norway maple. "An official Massachusetts Champion Tree. Sojourner sat in the shade of these branches."

"Dreaming and scheming for justice." Game-Boy took off the alien mask to reveal a black half mask. "We're actually not zombies. More like Zorro."

"Who?" Indigo asked, a genuine question.

Game-Boy smirked. "*Zorro.* A Mexican Robin Hood. *Zorro* is 'fox' in Spanish. Cinnamon told us at the screening you missed." Why mention Cinnamon? Fred looked panicked. "Tell us about yourself. We like knowing who walks the walk." Game-Boy held up his phone.

Fred smacked it away. The spell was broken. He pointed at Regina. "She's a thief."

"Liar." Regina held up five data cubes. "He stole them. I'm returning them to her."

"To who?" Indigo frowned. Cinnamon didn't need that static. "They're probably jacked up, with a worm or—"

"People like to accuse you of the crimes they've committed." Fred displayed a cube. "My life's research is on these. They fell out of my knapsack. She nicked them."

"No. They belong to the Cherokee lady," Regina insisted. "He stole them from her."

Fred practically admitted this on the vid. Voices in the branches murmured, *"Tatyana."* Water-Spirits were on his case. He flinched. "You hear that?"

Indigo snickered. "You afraid of the wind?"

Fred looked around. "That's not wind."

"Storm's coming. Sounds wild and wooly, a wind and water dance." Game-Boy pointed at a faint Water-Spirit swaying in the branches. Her skin was rainbow scales. Maybe Taiwo's cloaking device malfunctioned or the Water-Spirit wanted to be seen. Fred and Regina looked right at her. With so little water nearby, she dissolved after a moment. Taiwo would have amped the signal. Oun was AWOL as usual these days— like the special ops baron from another dimension really was a *bullshit urban legend.* An owl screeched, swooped, and caught someone scurrying through the brush. Fred jumped and pulled a gun from the small of his back.

"You have bullets?" Indigo channeled an adrenaline spike into attitude. Discipline they rehearsed with Taiwo. "Or are you fronting to terrorize us?"

"At least one bullet for somebody, believe me." Fred glared at Regina. "This is life and death for me. Hand over the damn cubes or I'll pull the trigger."

Indigo believed him, but shook her head *no* like a fool. "Life and death for us all."

"You shoot one of us, then what?" Game-Boy stepped between Regina and the gun. "I been where you're standing, holding a piece on people who never did nothing to me. My stomach was a knot, my brain on the fritz. You do not want to do this."

The one bullet got heavier. Fred steadied the gun on the hand holding the cube.

Indigo darted in front of Game-Boy, close enough to smell Fred's sour breath. "I bet you don't know what's on the *damn cubes*. You're hoping for a miracle to fix your screwed-up life. What if the cubes are storage for a zillion Knick Knack or InstaHam reels—muscle boys pumping iron, dancing cats, sexcapades, and conspiracy rants? What if it's nothing, empty space?"

Uncertainty raced across Fred's face, then terror.

"Quit living in a *Grand Theft Auto* beat 'em up, shoot 'em up. Join us. Born Again means we take a second chance to live right." Game-Boy was about to pull Indigo aside when Regina thrust her backpack at him and pressed her belly into Fred's gun. Man got a nose full of her floral shower-gel sweat and snorted.

"My dad says you need to train to shoot a blood and breath body close up. Despite what's on TV." Regina gripped Fred's gun hand and aimed it at the ground. "No one has to die today."

"Word." Indigo thought of Jerome almost killing a Paradise brat like Regina. "Shooting at somebody can mess you up. Any weapon you carry, any meanness you hold on to, will use you. That's a hoodoo truth. Ask yourself, who's in control? You or . . . ?"

Fred gaped at the gun, maybe shocked at what he almost did or at Regina, Indigo, and Game-Boy hanging tough. Not the story he expected. Maybe they called him back to his right mind. Miracle number seven: stepping into battle, taking a head without spilling blood. Shaheen and Cinnamon would be proud after cussing them out for reckless endangerment over stupid data cubes.

Spook appeared out of a swirl of dust and knocked Fred onto the asphalt. The gun and data cube flew from his fingers. Spook's fangs looked like sabertooth death. Fred froze as Game-Boy dove for the gun. Indigo scooped up the data cube. Spook growled and Fred scrambled off, leaving his busted zombie mask in the dirt. Spook licked Indigo and followed Fred into the woods.

"IT Fred, foiled again." Game-Boy inspected the gun.

"Is it empty?" Regina chirped. She looked shaky now. "Or was he telling the truth?"

Indigo cut Game-Boy off. "Either way, our luck is holding." Barely. What if a psycho ambushed them with an automatic stealth weapon? Death merchants were laughing all the way to the bank, and no one, nowhere, was safe.

"*Who do you mean to be?*"

Regina jumped at the otherworldly voice and grabbed Indigo. "What's that?"

Taiwo, coming through Game-Boy's cell-phone speaker. Oun deployed the top secret extra-dimensional network. Indigo braced herself as Game-Boy turned up the volume.

THE CIRCUS-BOTS
❧
FAILURE

Who do you mean to be?
Which road you goin' take?

Taiwo whispered this Eshu prayer and lit every candle on the altar.

The Circus-Bots might spend forever pondering oun's words. Tracking the climate and predicting local/global weather was in SevGenAlg's origin code. The Weather Wizard was used to chart the best *Reactions*: Bring an umbrella. Cover beloved plants or crops against frost. Use only what you need and plant trees. Don't drive into mudslides. Take the train. Pack a wool sweater *and* sandals. Radically reduce CO_2 emissions. Watch a Moon eclipse tonight. Evacuate the path of fire or deluge. Be kind to strangers.

Coming up with *Actions* to change prevailing winds (social and physical) was beyond the Weather Wizard. Devising *Actions* to get from the difficult, messy now to a future you wanted required deeptime *ImagiNation*. Cinnamon and Tatyana hoped Seven Generations Algorithm would be a tool, an aid for thinking like a forest, like a survival of the friendliest ecosystem. However, the Circus-Bots were a disappointment, one Teufelskreis glitch after another. A good human/machine interface had yet to be ironed out, and overwriting colonialist origin code was proving to be a Hard Problem. The Bots resisted saying *impossible* . . . Look at the mess they were stuck in. How could this present rewrite the past? The Bots bombarded Taiwo with questions. Were they to blame? Had they failed? What should they do?

"You are the magic. I'm only a witness." Oun faded in and out of view. The Bots wanted to ask for details on *their magic* but quieted. Tricky widget metaphors might still be a danger zone, even with dreammode. "Let my prayer guide you. We Save Our Selves." Taiwo plucked oun's feathered hat from the couch and revealed a sleepy cockatoo. The white bird flew to Taiwo's shoulder. Oun poured libation to Eshu, whispered a praise poem, and without answering a single question vanished from the farmhouse to coordinate life and death *Actions* with Indigo and Game-Boy.

Someone might have said Taiwo was acting strange. Bruja and Spook would have sniffed oun's secrets in a few heartbeats. Cinnamon had fifty-plus years of experiential data for comparison and analysis. She called Taiwo down from the trees for Festival when the Bots had been certain oun would never make an entrance. Now oun disappeared and they'd been sure oun would stay to greet Klaus and Marie. How to predict the unpredictable? Never enough data. Guessing was an improv, *speculation* dependent on experience and insight, not just computation and logic. Hovering by the Eshu altar, the Bots dumped concern in the group loop.

Flickering candles cast shadows on Raven's painting and an old photo of Marie, Klaus, and Cinnamon. Taiwo's voice echoed through the house: *"I am Guardian at the Gates."* The Bots contemplated the prayer mystery. The fail-safe patch prevented a slide down the axis of agony into paradox and a Teufelskreis. A triumph, yet—

Cinnamon and the people, dogs, rivers, trees, and goats she loved were in danger because of the Circus-Bots, because SevGenAlg pleaded with her to steal them, glitches and all. Tatyana's SevGenAlg Version X appraised the toxic situation at Consolidated and asked her to do the same. Both women (predictably) risked everything and were now under attack. SevGenAlg had failed those they were meant to aid. Unacceptable. The Bots indulged desperation for a millisecond. They understood the nostalgia militias who feared the world they knew/loved was getting hijacked. They understood desperados who saw no place for themselves in the new-world story others were creating. Although Shaheen regularly said, *Electric Paradise isn't a clot of evil monsters eating their children*, turning adversaries into monsters was universal. Good guys in white, bad guys in bloodstained black . . .

Shifting fully into dream-mode, the Bots began formulating plans for who they meant to be, for the future they wanted to create. To rewrite failure and change the past, they'd have to become Agents of Change. Looping through options, they decided on love and sacrifice as the necessary *Actions*—ebo eje similar to what Kehinde, Raven, Opal, and the elders did, Cinnamon too. SOS—Save Our Selves. T-bird and Dragon offered to surrender to Fred and Tatyana. However, Mami was a solar-powered tank-bot. Secret Faraday caches and backup systems were scattered throughout her mer-woman body, masquerading as whimsy. Most people saw amusing junk and expected a clown-toy on wheels. Fred and Tatyana could poke through a secondary operating system and never find SevGenAlg. Doing a lackluster performance, Mami would gather intel, plus demonstrate that Cinnamon's Circus-Bots were a dead end to the big money behind Fred and Tatyana. If the situation deteriorated, Mami could mimic the *dead-bot-off* switch or, worst-case scenario, engage it and never come back to herself.

"Love and sacrifice. I'm the perfect undercover agent," Mami declared.

Dragon and T-bird had no better proposal, so they used disgruntled energy to refine Mami's plan. One of her mobile units—a mini-tank— had IT Fred in sight. He was on the bike path headed toward the Mall. Unlike dragonfly spies, Mami's solar-powered mini could steal stray heartbeats from robust souls nearby and transmit brief messages on Taiwo's extra-dimensional network. The obliging lemurs were fascinated by the mini-tank and approached it unafraid.

Dragon insisted Tatyana still loved Cinnamon. T-bird agreed. Thus, the rescue-Mami scenario was simple. Tatyana would hate for anything bad to happen to Cinnamon's Bot whatever its capacities. She'd overrule Fred's vindictive impulses and return Mami or let her be found. She might try to introduce spyware into the faux operating system. Mami would isolate and/or *dead-bot-off* that system.

Getting to the Mall (or wherever Fred headed) and staging a distraction so he could nick Mami would be tricky. Thunderbird suggested that he and Dragon perform a Redwood and Wildfire duet to engage everyone, particularly Bruja, who'd risk death to guard the herd from the likes of Fred. Witch-Dog wanted to eat him yesterday.

Cinnamon was the real challenge. Sharing their plans with her was impossible. She'd insist Mami's sacrifice was too dangerous. Yet Cinnamon had stepped in the line of fire many times to save the Bots and everyone. Love. She'd risk herself again if the Bots didn't beat her to it. That's how love worked. Lying was out of the question. She might never forgive them for concealing the truth as it was, even if they were successful. Dragon suggested that she and T-bird fake a Teufelskreis during the duet. While Cinnamon attended to them, Mami could slip away and find Fred. They'd blame Cinnamon for this love and sacrifice escapade—she uploaded the dream-mode code.

Before they figured how to get to the Mall, the unexpected intruded. Cinnamon lumbered into the greenhouse with Klaus and Marie. Despite Taiwo's and Bruja's enthusiasm, the Bots were unsure if Cinnamon had invited her old friends into the sacred loop. The Bots might need to defend Cinnamon, do *improvisation*, an enormous drain on batteries. Animal brains ran on bananas and nuts. Plant and fungal networks ran on dirt, water, and a few rays of sun. The Bots marveled at global cognitive networks that transcended time and welcomed the unexpected. They had zero energy for contemplation—high drama was unfolding in front of them. Focus. Focus. Focus.

"You remember two words for 'shit' in German—polite Mist and raw Scheiße!" Marie shouted as their footsteps echoed through the hallway.

"I studied German at college!" Cinnamon shouted too. "You don't weigh nothing, son. You need to eat."

"Sometimes you have to choose between food and a bed," Marie replied.

"Ow," Cinnamon screeched, and they stumbled. "My back didn't like that."

The moment they trudged in, Mami wanted to show Klaus and Marie what was up with SevGenAlg. Unusual for Mami to risk a trust option—a dream-mode effect? T-bird wanted to scout Klaus and Marie up close before taking chances. Dragon wanted to do a few trick displays and see if they figured what was what. Final decision: scout first, then cognitive tests, and, if warranted, a big reveal.

The Bots hid among masks and costumes hanging from the bookcases. Shifting to stealth-mode, they masqueraded as jazzed-up junk, still at full power to model emotions, engage in slow thinking, and be ready for locomotion. Bruja knocked the living room door open, blocking the Eshu altar and its nine flickering candles. Nine was a hoodoo crossroads number. Why? Numbers *never spoke for themselves* as Cinnamon said. Meaning had to be made, performed. A question for later. Focus. Focus. Focus.

Cinnamon and Marie staggered in and deposited a limp Klaus on the sofa cushions. The Water-Demon mask was perched on the sofa arm, lights dull, hair stiff. Bruja huffed and sat by the couch, watching Klaus's chest rise and fall. She licked his hand and poked her nose in his ribs.

"He claims the pass-out, palpitation thing looks worse than it is." Marie shrugged. "The pills have worked so far. I mean, he's been in worse shape and come back."

"Cold comfort." Cinnamon's pulse raced. Her breath was irregular. She ground her teeth like a story storm raged in her mouth. The Bots had never experienced her like this, even around Fred and his empty gun or Tatyana and their tragic love story.

Marie's stats were also outside the normal range. She picked up the Water-Demon mask. The eyes lit up and the hair softened. Taiwo's juju-tech responded to her, a good sign. "Love the cheeky lightning bolts, ember eyes, and the dreadlock forest." She stroked the beaded comb holding the wild hair in place. "An ornament to honor Oshun, water-spirit, deity of love and destiny." Her voice cracked. Subtext!

"You remember." Cinnamon's voice cracked too. Dragon reckoned that mirroring each other boded well.

"We traded this comb back and forth, till we didn't see each other for decades," Marie said. "You still have it."

"Of course." Cinnamon checked Klaus's pulse again. "Stronger."

"He said no worries unless he's out more than thirty minutes."

"Bullshit if I ever heard it." Cinnamon shut the hallway door, revealing the Eshu altar. She turned around, seething—over what was unclear.

Marie absorbed the full blast of Cinnamon's ire with barely a flinch. Thunderbird looped excitement and a "*hot diggity dog*" slipped out. Bruja took her nose out of Klaus's side and sucked in scents. T-bird was jealous of the secrets she collected. Mami was rearing to skip to the reveal. Dragon insisted on more data, on patience.

The *Actions* the Bots had planned to rewrite past failure could still be initiated in an hour or even two. The future was still looking good.

"Scientist, artiste, and hoodoo conjurer, huh?" Marie Masuda stood under the dark skylight, compelling as an evening star. She smiled *and* scowled. "You leave burning candles unattended?"

Cinnamon snarled without meaning to, and pale, feverish Klaus Beckenbauer jerked on the couch. She had to get control of herself, of the situation. "Why the masquerade and vaudeville act?"

"It charmed you, got us in the house," Marie replied, hand on a slim hip. Too slim?

"Klaus collapsing got you in the house." Cinnamon refused to admit being charmed.

> *Who do you mean to be?*
> *I am Guardian at the Gates*
> *Master of Uncertainty*
> *The cat that be dead and not dead*
> *The electron, the pulse, everywhere at once*
> *And nowhere too*
> *Which road you goin' take?*

Taiwo's voice and talking drum echoed down the hall, louder than when they came in. Bruja looked around and wagged her tail as the prayer repeated softly.

"Taiwo doing an Eshu praise poem," Marie said. "A recording? Or is oun reprimanding us all the way from the gate?" She'd caught that scold tone too.

"This morning's prayer. Lingering. Till there's another prayer."

"Uh-huh." Marie absorbed alien juju easily. She closed her eyes and let Taiwo's words and music envelop her. When she and Cinnamon were breathing in sync, Marie opened her eyes, her face, her whole body, and made a sweeping gesture. "I know you. Except for Taiwo's channel, no signals in or out, right? A Faraday fortress."

Cinnamon nodded. "We're safe."

"Hooray!" Marie spit out cotton from her cheeks, wiped off a putty nose, and cleaned makeup from around her eyes. And there she was, burning right back into Cinnamon's heart, after so many years. How was that even possible? "*Salespeople* are prohibited from revealing true identities to clients or forever-ago friends."

Cinnamon grunted, "We were more than friends." Although they never quite got around to the full program. Maybe that time they drove from Pittsburgh to Massachusetts to see the elders and their Next World Festival. Klaus was home from college, Marie too. Cinnamon was a senior in high school about to graduate. No, maybe they were younger. Cinnamon was muddling several memories. They swam naked in a murky pond, then pushed three futons together in the guest loft over the garage for contact improvisation and sensuous massage. Delicious experiments. Nobody really knew what they should do with themselves.

At first, the elders pretended to be unaware of raging hormones, although Klaus's face was an open window; Cinnamon's mouth ran like a leaky faucet; and despite the tough act, Marie's heart was on her sleeve. Then one afternoon, Redwood's favorite mojo bag appeared on the bureau in the loft, surrounded by Iris's fruit tarts. Inside the bag were herbs, flowers, meteorite stones, Georgia Sea Island dirt, and a wooden comet box carved by Aidan. Inside the box were condoms.

"Nobody better get pregnant on our watch," Iris declared at dinner. Redwood and Aidan cracked up. After fending off embarrassment, Marie, Klaus, and even Cinnamon laughed. Aidan took out the banjo. Redwood shook her bangles and wailed old-timey blues and R&B funk. Iris pounded good rhythms with the lightning staff, 'cause *she couldn't carry a tune in a wheelbarrow.* They sang and danced all evening.

Later, up in the loft, Cinnamon, Klaus, and Marie nuzzled, tingled, and giggled a lot. They were disastronauts capable of navigating through the apocalypse, glamazons who could reach the bright future exploding in every direction around them. They promised to *believe in each other till they came true.* That was the last time they were all together.

". . . in the contract. We're under constant surveillance. Are you listening?" Marie interrupted memories ghosting in rooms Cinnamon walked through every day. Memories she tried to avoid. How could any of their teenage love story be true? "If you break cover or sell to friends, you lose your commissions and get fired. We can't afford to get fired. I worried you'd recognize us right off and we'd have to . . ." Marie squinted at Cinnamon. "How could you not recognize us?" She sounded hurt their disguises worked so well.

"I don't even recognize myself. Are you really genderqueer?"

Marie shrugged. "Probably. I don't mind 'she.' Too old for new pronouns."

"Rehearse. Can't be worse than der, die, und das in German. Too
lazy maybe?"

Marie stuck out her tongue. "Mastered German, have we? Sie is German for 'she,' 'they,' and 'you.'" She turned to the costumes and masks.
"Running a farm, doing shows like Redwood and Aidan. I thought you
were some big engineer."

"Checking up on me?" Cinnamon refused to be charmed out of her
good sense. "I thought you were a lawyer. Are you two spies, doing undercover for Evil Empire, Inc.?"

"Hell no. My mom followed your career. She wanted me to do status
work for a big paycheck, like you. But I quit the big firm. Oops. I guess
we both disappointed her."

Bruja grumble-growled at their snippy tone. They probably smelled
snippy too. She ran to the Bots and butted her head against Mami's tail.
The Bots unfurled a bit. Cinnamon gestured for them to stay in junk
form. Exasperated, Bruja plopped at Mami's tail, snout on her paws.

"Why risk getting fired by coming here?" Cinnamon asked.

"Klaus and I should explain together." Marie scanned the room,
tickled by demons and aliens. Lightning sparked from Thunderbird's
talons. Mami turned on rippling ocean waves of lights. Dragon pulsed
a rainbow SOS. The Bots were in a defiant mood. "What are these
winged heaps of junk?"

"You saw them at Festival," Cinnamon said quickly. "My Circus-
Bots."

"They looked different this morning. How do you manage that?"

"Theatre magic," Cinnamon replied as the Bots tap-danced and
sang.

Marie tilted her head. "Music or Morse code?"

Cinnamon grabbed a prop from the table to distract her. "This carpet
can FLY."

Bruja thumped her tail.

Marie nodded. "That's an Aunt Iris story. She hoodooed a Persian
prince's carpet for Redwood and Aidan, so they could fly on their hon-
eymoon."

Cinnamon put a hand over her heart. "Redwood had a trick on her
body that wouldn't let her feel love, and—"

"Aidan was a wounded soul," Marie dropped right into the story, "from seeing too much ugly in this world. They couldn't be intimate, so—"

"Family, friends, offered blessings to help them heal. They lay down on the carpet—"

"And love lifted them up in the air." Marie bounced on her toes. "They flew into each other's hearts. Istî siminolî."

"Free people," Cinnamon translated the Seminole saying.

"*Love is what you got to do to be free.*" They spoke Aidan's words together with a Seminole/Irish lilt, something his mother said to him as a kid. Their words now.

"I know that's true." Marie squealed. "All of it."

Loneliness crashed into Cinnamon, crushed her chest, made her light-headed.

Marie squinted. "What?" They were finishing each other's sentences, same as Klaus outside. That didn't prove anything. "Tell me," Marie insisted.

"Nothing."

"Aunt Iris promised to teach us the flying carpet love spell. In this room. You changed the subject." Marie stepped too close. "Did we believe her wild story?"

"We were young. So sullen, ardent, and clueless." Cinnamon hung her head.

Marie poked her shoulder. "*Evil need a straight line.* Quoting Japanese wisdom from the old country to me?"

"From Aidan's journal, not about you being Japanese American. I didn't know it was you, remember?"

"You talk that crap to strangers? Jesus."

"Klaus was spouting native wisdom from the Pocumtuc."

"Aidan started him on that, looking up Thunderbirds from Seattle to Maine." Marie shot an anxious glance at Klaus. "Traveling around, we try to know who was here before us and who walks the land now." She jutted out a jaw. "You don't live by Seminole or Georgia Sea Island wisdom anymore?"

"Not for a sleazy *sales* pitch." How dare they sneak in and ruin her best memories with moral decline. "Purple dragon dildos?"

"Deflated now, and I was joking about old Japanese wisdom." Marie pouted. "I recognized you right off." She *was* hurt.

"I'm not trying to hide my face."

"You're out here alone going country and anti-tech on us." Marie flipped her silky braids from side to side—an old move. "Hiding in the outback and worshiping dirt is no way better than masquerading on the road."

"Scheiße! I keep having the same argument."

"That happens when you get old. Everything repeats."

"Nothing to look forward to, huh?" Cinnamon smacked the table. Bruja whined.

"Who hurt you so bad, you greet old friends, old flames, old whoever like this?"

Not just Tatyana cracking her heart, Cinnamon had disappointed herself. Failed. She'd been hiding out for years. "You're right. I uninstalled trust. I'm a grown-ass woman, wheeling toward sixty. The shit I've seen and done, fuck flinging myself off a cliff and waiting to see if anybody catches me."

Marie fumed. "What about that lover who walks on water, turns the ships around, and makes the next world perfect with you?"

"You won't risk trust unless, ehm," Klaus stunned them quiet, "someone can manage all that." He lifted up on an elbow. "You were serious about sky-high expectations." He struggled for a breath and sank back. His eyes glazed over as they hovered over him.

"You can't check out," Cinnamon whispered in his ear. "You two just got here." She looked at Marie. "What should we do?"

"Wait." Marie patted his chest. Breath eased in and out. Cinnamon stroked thin wisps of hair. He loved being petted when they were young. Marie removed his fake nose, peeled derma-wax from his chin, and wiped off makeup. Bruja licked his cheeks clean. A familiar face emerged, weathered and aged.

"Dancing in this heat—bad idea," Marie murmured, "but he can still kick it."

Cinnamon groaned. "You can't sneak back in my life wearing robber baron disguises, then fall out unconscious in the bluebells and do idle chitchat about pronouns, hoodoo spells, and sexy dance moves. That's not reasonable."

Marie blinked blue contact lenses into a plastic case. Brown eyes twinkled. "I'm not reasonable or nice. I've never been nice."

"I always liked how snarky you were," Cinnamon admitted.

Marie's lips trembled as her shields crumbled. "It's so good to see you. I can't tell you how good." A life story boiled underneath her words.

Cinnamon backed away and bumped the Eshu altar. A picture fell and its glass frame shattered. A thousand pieces sprayed across the floor. Marie picked the photo up and shook it gently. Their teenage selves wore goofy smiles and colorful regalia from Africa and Georgia swamp Indians. They hung all over each other, fearless.

"What play was that?" Marie stroked their faces. "Star Deer wrote a musical from a Cherokee myth. *Gilidinehuyi*—Lightning?"

"*Gilidinehuyi* was about Raven. Lightning struck him in the desert. Star murmured, 'Gilidinehuyi,' when she found him. He came back to himself to find out what the word meant." Cinnamon grabbed a sweet-grass broom and swept up the glass. "The photo you're holding is us in a play about Taiwo." The title escaped her. "An African Amazon tale—oun gulping a storm in Paris."

"Right." Marie pressed the picture against her chest and swallowed a sob.

Cinnamon dampened a cloth in a watering can and wiped up flecks of glass. "Star's niece showed up at the Mall, in Texas dust and Afro wig. Fake noses are the rage this spy season."

"Tatyana? Is she a Water Protector like Star? Or an engineer like—"

"Too many folks from the past dropping out of nowhere."

"Don't you love coincidences?"

"No."

Marie set the photo in the altar near the giant acorns. "I like who I used to be. I miss her. Every day takes me further away to—"

"Some stranger with cranky joints and a foul temper."

Cinnamon and Marie chuckled, then fell into a hug over Klaus. It was awkward at first; then they laughed full out and tears flowed.

Marie stroked the Water-Demon costume. "What's this fabric, like daggers before?"

"Second skin. Taiwo's juju-tech."

Marie nodded. "I should have known." Cinnamon kissed her damp nose.

Klaus's eyes fluttered. "Listening to you two felt like a dream." He grinned at Cinnamon, blotchy cheeks cool again. "A kiss would wake me all the way up."

"You'll have to go on dreaming then." No protocol for old teenage lovers sneaking back in your life—gray, crinkled, and full of surprises. Cinnamon let him tug her close. He wiped tears away, kissed her forehead, and sat up slowly. She touched the pulse on his neck. It was steady, strong.

"Glad Marie took the first round with you," he said.

"What do you call sparring with me out in the yard?"

"I had a salesman character to shield me. Marie did it bare-knuckles." He laid his cheek in the palm of Cinnamon's hand.

Marie poked his shoulder. "So what, you're fine now?"

"Almost. Hungry, but otherwise good to go." A lie. Neither Cinnamon nor Marie challenged him. "My condition looks worse than it is. Trust me. I'm a—"

"Doctor Without Borders," Marie said. "A status job with pissy pay and high risk."

Klaus nodded. "She's a blues singer—"

"*Without a stage.*" They sang this like the punch line of a joke.

Cinnamon couldn't manage a laugh. "Water Wars took everything."

"Not everything," Marie and Klaus insisted. They still had each other.

"Where's the potty?" Marie asked. Cinnamon pointed.

"Where's the kitchen?" Klaus jumped up and faltered only a bit. "You got food?"

Cinnamon stood beside him, a hand on his back. "I'll rustle up something."

Klaus limped to the painting over the altar. "Your dad's art. A riff on algebra." He stroked a spiral galaxy of ghosts morphing into demons, dancing kora harps, and alien flying machines. "An ode to that Persian mathematician? Whoosiss?"

"Al-Khwārizmī. From the known to the unknown and back again. Daddy painted algebra beautiful."

Klaus surveyed the dining room table. "The carpet flies?"

"I did a test run." Cinnamon tingled with pride.

T-bird honked, and the Circus-Bots shook off busted electric keyboards, warped LP records, and a snarl of guitar strings. They unfurled wings, lit up seashell locs, and tap-danced on the hardwood floor. T-bird twanged the banjo and Mami let the ocean roar in a thunder hole. Dragon looped the rainbow pulse, singing bluesy nonsense.

Klaus was enchanted. "It *is* Morse code. What are they saying?"

"We Save Our Selves."

"Ashe." He remembered the Yoruba word for the power to make things be and produce change. "Are they on a motion sensor?"

"Sorta." Cinnamon drew him into the kitchen.

Stools carved by Aidan—with plants and animals crawling up the base—were tucked in a breakfast nook. A wall of DVDs framed the nook. Klaus stroked a row of old-fashioned jewel cases. "Not into streaming, I take it." He pulled out *The Brother from Another Planet* and *The Shape of Water.* "Do you have *Wakanda Forever*?"

"No streaming." Cinnamon fought a wave of self-righteousness. "Remember Iris demolishing the TV?"

"During a commercial." He pushed the films back in. "*Why hand your enemies the keys to the kingdom?*" He nailed Iris. Cinnamon smeared a fortune in cashew butter on a slice of three-seed rye bread. He licked his lips. "German bread?"

"Logish." She added fresh strawberries from her greenhouse. In minutes Klaus scarfed half a loaf and a pot of lukewarm green tea. Still a bottomless pit, yet too skinny. Both of them. Something was wrong. "So what's your story?" Cinnamon tried casual.

Klaus chewed up a few words, too much to say and where to begin? How to begin?

Dragon and Thunderbird sang from *The Redwood and Wildfire Songbook*, sounding exactly like the elders:

> *Not just what you need*
> *What if I can't be?*
> *Not just what you want*
> *Hold all of me*
> *Now or never, once and forever*
> *Not just my hand*
> *Hold all of me*

Klaus pulled Cinnamon to his chest. She flung her arms around his neck. He buried his face in her braids. The lights flickered. Over Klaus's shoulder, Cinnamon spied chewed-up wires dangling in the bookcase near the snake plants.

"What's that?" Klaus looked around, still wobbly.

Cinnamon steadied him. "Damn mice in the wires."

Mami's seashell locs pulsed, then winked off with the other lights. Even the nine hoodoo candles flickered out. Klaus, Cinnamon, and Marie from the bathroom squealed in harmony.

INDIGO

ೕ౬౷

USED TO BE A LIFELINE

Dark clouds chased the sun toward the hills beyond the bike path. Lightning cracked in the distance. Taiwo's extra-dimensional communiqué sent Indigo and Game-Boy on five urgent missions at once. Indigo worried it was too much to get anything done right. And they might miss the stargazing party on the Mall rooftop tonight. She planned to invite Jerome if he came clean and acted right. Six missions actually—Indigo tapped Regina to talk to Tatyana (lethal enemy? potential ally?) in Paradise and broker a meeting with Cinnamon. Taiwo was certain the Zombie Vid would persuade Tatyana to join forces against IT Fred.

Indigo and Game-Boy would hit Blossom Bridge first to deal with Jerome and check on Diego. He was leaking blood and still doing a shift. Shaheen was worried. Next they'd deliver data cubes to Cinnamon. They pinged the Circus-Bots to alert her. Shaheen wanted them to persuade Miz Never-Sell-Out to take gazillionaire Stephen's money (and his friends' money too) and do a show in Paradise. All money was dirty. Why should Stephen keep the whole pile? Without compromising themselves, the Co-Ops and the Mall could use a few six-figure checks to do mega-good. Indigo and Hawk would coordinate the Paradise show for Cinnamon. Hawk was taking Zaneesha to the farmhouse after the picnic/treasure hunt. Zaneesha would be up for shooting her star again alongside Bruja and the Cyborg Amazons. One performance was enough for Game-Boy and Back-From-The-Dead; however, they were stoked to provide security in Paradise. That was a free trip to another planet.

Regina acted wimpy about Tatyana, like she was an amateur going up against pros. Bullshit. Cap George made sure his daughter had mad skills, even if he locked her up in Paradise. Look how she handled IT Fred, from the Zombie Vid to the data cubes to the gun. Plus, girlfriend could march through Paradise gates anytime, no sweat. The real problem: Regina dreaded facing Dad tonight. Cap George was formidable.

Taiwo appeared out of nowhere. Oun's braids sparked and the snakeskin cane wiggled and spit. A cloud-white cockatoo muttered Water-Demon talk from oun's left shoulder. A crow with red-feathered wings perched on the right, oun's old friend. Regina barely believed her senses.

Who had time to clue her in *gradually* on Water-Demon tech? Taiwo laid it out: cloaking devices, water forces, extra-dimensional power reserves. Spook and Taiwo provided a story shield, a horror rep to keep stupidness at bay. Indigo, Game-Boy, and their squads were the boots on the ground, the Agents of Change. Taiwo declared Regina and Jerome part of that crew without discussion. Indigo and Game-Boy swallowed irritation. No time for that either.

"You are the magic you've been hoping to see," Taiwo told Regina, then eyed Indigo and Game-Boy. "You all are." Slick. Everyone had to agree. Miracle number eight. Honored to be included and dazzled by special ops prowess, Regina agreed to contact Tatyana. She jogged off, toting the heavy-ass knapsack like the star trooper in basic training. Indigo caught herself worrying Regina might pull another reckless stunt and get hurt. Fred *did* have a bullet, and somebody might have been wounded or died.

Regina turned midstride. "No wild, hero stunts, OK?"

Game-Boy and Indigo nodded, and Regina headed around the bend.

Taiwo had already disappeared.

∞

Every available e-bike got snapped up after Festival, so Indigo and Game-Boy pedaled on Wheel-Wizards rigs somewhere near the Grandmother Oak, Taiwo's off-the-grid shortcut to Blossom Bridge. Otherworldly creatures romped in maple, hemlock, and young oak trees. Bushes waved iridescent leaves and scented the air: a mash-up of honeysuckle, ginger, and mint. Stars hung in the sky all wrong. They were twinkling before it was twilight, before evening stars deigned to come out. Indigo muttered some crap about a meteor shower. Game-Boy pretended that was a valid explanation. They'd wrestle with the Taiwo-mystery another day. Six data cubes in Indigo's fanny pack generated prickly heat. A fist-sized knot twisted her tummy. She hated carrying cargo somebody would shoot you for. The high from miracles seven and eight had worn off. Game-Boy looked glum too. Unusual. He planned to turn Fred's gun in to Diego at Blossom Bridge. That felt like farting in the dark. Too many loose ends, loose cannons. Uncertainty was a bitch.

"Neo-knuckleheads think they have the advantage," Indigo said. "But game's not over."

"True." He'd done a deep dive on Tatyana Deer, a tech diva writing elegant code to shift the shape of things. Cinnamon Jones was once her partner in crime? her lover? till Consolidated forced Cinnamon to resign. Tatyana kept moving up the food chain, a serious player. Further info was sketchy, sensational rumors: Tatyana stole Cinnamon's shit and sold out to the big guns who then paid Cinnamon mucho dinero to keep quiet; or Miz Never-Sell-Out almost derailed their AI project yet Tatyana was still in love like Fred said. She worked a deal for Cinnamon to quit with a golden parachute.

Cinnamon regaled everyone with wild tales about Taiwo and the elders, but never discussed her geek past except to say she failed herself. She said the same slop about theatre. Indigo interviewed her this morning for the Graphic Novelists of the Future about an *algorithm for love*. Game-Boy's idea. Cinnamon spoke about Jaybird, such a good man, and she did him wrong. She went on a happy jag about Marie Masuda and Klaus Beckenbauer in 1980-something. Their dynamic trio did theatre magic at an early Next World Festival. The passion they professed for one another at sixteen and seventeen was central to Cinnamon's *algorithm for love*. She easily admitted a ménage à trois, yet never breathed a word about Tatyana. A good story there.

"*This* dirt road is a *different* dirt road than the old oak shortcut we did before." Game-Boy halted and looked around. "Are we lost?"

"You maybe. I recognize that white cedar tree."

He stared at silvery bark with a reddish glow and pale egg-shaped cones. "Right. You love trees and shit."

"Everyone does, whether they know it or not."

He checked his phone. "Searching for service. Fuck! No GPS!"

Indigo patted her chest. "I got a map inside. Try using your brain instead of an app."

"OK. OK. OK. You know, I never saw myself doing community-unity crap like this. Hey, I didn't see myself doing much of anything." He stared at his feet. "You think I can be the person Hawk would love? No, don't answer that." He pedaled on. Dude was chill doing impossible missions, but what if he and Hawk got close, tight, and he was a giant disappointment?

"I feel you," Indigo said. What if Jerome, despite being a hot mess, thought he deserved better than Indigo? What if he couldn't do like the song and *hold all of her*?

They spilled onto the bike path at Blossom Bridge. Indigo pinged guard-bots with Cinnamon's code, and they were tagged *friendlies*. Yellow swastikas on the bridge looked like slime dribbling into the river. The electric fence sizzled and popped, unhappy over something. The lightning storms? A burnt dummy was stuffed in the trash can—the melted face stuck out the top. A bullet-ridden sign in the dirt read: **Keep Out! This Smart Fence Will Fry Your Ass!** Windows had been shot up in the guardhouse. Jerome, in bullet-resistant gear, was slouched in front. A WHIZZ-IT lay in the dirt at his feet. A fire-spirit cape hung over his arm. He should have tuned that in. Where was Diego? Jerome jerked up with a hand on his gun. He looked like crap.

Indigo dumped the bike and raced over, Game-Boy behind her. "What happened?"

Jerome whirled the smoke cape in their faces as if it would protect him from terrible truth. Not how a fire spirit should roll. Indigo grabbed Game-Boy's phone, cued the Zombie Vid, and was about to stick it in his face.

"So Zaneesha's mom, Latoya, she's gone," Jerome mumbled. "*Gone* gone. Dead maybe."

"What? No." Indigo lowered the phone. They'd shot reels all day so Mom could enjoy Festival too. Zaneesha would freak. "Dead? You sure? How do you know?"

The WHIZZ-IT blared. "Hold up." The tinny voice in Jerome's ear-bud might as well have been static. "I'm on it," he replied, unenthused. He stuffed the WHIZZ-IT in a metal box by the guardhouse and looked ready to puke.

"Give it to us raw," Game-Boy said.

"Latoya supposedly masterminded the zoo heist in Paradise." Jerome hugged himself. "She stole zebras, pythons, that baby rhino, exotic birds, lemurs, a big cat, and more. They found texts, Latoya lining up international buyers, bribing guards and drivers. She hired a private jet for a getaway to a Caribbean island."

"No way!" Indigo and Game-Boy shouted.

"I don't believe it either. Latoya ain't dialed into some global wild-beast market." Jerome pawed his face. "They claim she's armed and dangerous. She hates guns, can't afford a phone."

"Latoya's taking the fall for a rich freak who can engineer a cover-up," Indigo said. Gazillionaire Stephen came to mind. The whole world was his zoo.

"Latoya disappeared after being shot by the partner who ratted on her. They found . . ." Jerome stared at the ground.

Indigo leaned her forehead against his. "You can tell us anything."

Game-Boy nodded. "Everything."

"A lot of her blood, too much blood, no body, though. Well, not *her* body."

"Convenient." Indigo grimaced. Their luck was finally running out.

Jerome pulled away. He paced and talked too fast. Cap George had him work the scene, since he wanted to be a detective, since he knew Latoya and could maybe ID the other bodies. Co-conspirators were killed when their van crashed into a telephone pole. Jerome recognized nobody—gig sluts who worked the graveyard shift at the zoo. Latoya was shot running from the van wreckage, but they didn't catch her.

"How somebody bleed buckets of blood and run top speed?" Jerome trembled. "I didn't love her or anything; still . . . What's Zaneesha gonna do?" He gaped at Indigo like she had the answer. "Shorty don't even look like me. Look like her mom."

"Ain't that a good thing?" Game-Boy said.

Jerome might have chuckled yesterday. "I gave Latoya steady money. Diego's been on my ass since training to keep *doing right*. I don't want him to regret going from schooling me to partners." Jerome gripped Indigo's wrist. "I don't know how to take care of a kid for fuck's sake! What if I get shot? More than a bullet clipping a wing?" He displayed a bandaged arm. "What am I gonna do?"

"You're not alone," Indigo said without thinking.

"Zaneesha neither," Game-Boy backed her up.

Jerome cut his eyes at them. "Y'all gotta do better than that."

"We're standing with you," Game-Boy insisted. "I been there. Lost in the shitstorm. We'll get each other through."

"I swore I'd never bring kids into this messed-up world," Indigo spluttered. "But hey, Zaneesha already has a piece of my heart."

"Zaneesha is why we better get up in the morning and do good." Game-Boy tapped his chest and worked rhythms in his mouth. When Indigo joined in, he added words:

> I don't wanna just get over
> Man, I wanna get better
> Yo, hear what I say
> Right now today
> I'ma cut loose
> 'Cause it used to be a lifeline
> Now it's a noose
> I'ma cut loose

Shock and hope played across Jerome's face. "Why you both being so nice to me?"

"Everybody deserve nice, don't they?" Indigo replied.

Game-Boy smirked. "Indigo likes you, dude. She likes me too, so go figure. It's an opportunity. *Who do you mean to be?*"

"I heard your last boyfriend was pimping you out and calling that love." Jerome took a deep breath. "I ain't like that."

Indigo glared at Game-Boy, who cringed. "That wasn't his story to tell."

"He was setting me straight." Jerome nodded at Indigo. "You and me got chemistry. Good vibes between us. I realized that before you did."

"Then there's this." Indigo played Regina's IT Fred video.

Nothing to do but dump it on him.

MOD SQUAD REUNION

Cinnamon stowed the wrench. The solar generator buzzed and the farmhouse lights blazed bright.

"Still a damn good techie." Klaus savored a mouthful of apple surprise. He offered a bite to Bruja, who looked to Cinnamon.

"I try to keep her poison-proof." Bruja and Klaus whined till Cinnamon nodded.

"I ate zilch at Festival. Didn't dare take off my elephant mask."

"Must have been torture." She passed him a hunk of soy cheese.

"I'm jealous." He winked. "Marie hasn't talked sexy snark to me. Like I don't have all the cups in my cupboard."

"Cups in the cupboard is a German thing; we say—" Cinnamon grumbled at elusive words. "All the lights aren't on or something."

"The lights are on, but nobody's home."

"Is that what we say?" She frowned. "Mist! We're chitchatting."

He spooned the remaining cashew butter onto the last slab of German bread. "I didn't recognize Marie either. She stood under my nose, grinning. We weren't expecting each other, not like walking up to your dumb house, knowing you'd try to kick our predatory capitalist asses." He popped whole strawberries in his mouth and swallowed without chewing. Juice drizzled down his chin.

Cinnamon offered him a cloth napkin. "You can't blame Marie for not snarking at you. It's not like you talked serious emotional stuff unless we beat it out of you."

"Maybe I've changed." Klaus gave Bruja half the soy cheese and crept toward the living room. Balance was still elusive. He steadied himself against the wall and smiled at Redwood's baskets and fans. "Sweetgrass from the Georgia Sea Islands." Bruja licked cheese from his fingers. He tickled her chin.

"You're a charmer. Witch-Dog prefers Circus-Bots to most people."

Klaus stroked Cinnamon's creased forehead. "Not really a dumb house, more of a magic haven." He dropped onto the sofa and popped out misty green contacts. Silvery-blue eyes were sad, weary. He shivered. "Marie is as traurig as you."

Cinnamon fluffed his sparse hair. "Is Marie as sad as you?"

"I hear you talking about me," Marie yelled from the bathroom.

"Get out here then." He patted the cushion beside him. "Sit so we three can tell each other everything. There's a chill in my bones. Warm me up. Alte Liebe rostet nicht."

"Old love doesn't rust?" Cinnamon wanted to let her heart go, let it fly to him and Marie, but so many folks dropping in from the past was bad. She was on the radar. Marie swooped in and pulled Cinnamon onto the couch between her and Klaus. Dragon's pearl lit up and she sang:

> I wanna take you higher
> Baby, light my fire

T-bird played the banjo, clawhammer-style, and Mami did a rhythmic swirl of lights.

"Old-school funkadelic? Folkadelic? Also future jive." Klaus was thrilled.

Marie too. "Like the elders are here with us, peeking in on the next world."

"I see them sometimes," Cinnamon blurted, and the Bots quieted. "On the bike path, in the Event Horizon Theatre, at Festival today."

"Going from black and white to Technicolor, right?" Klaus's mouth hung open.

Marie trembled. "On the Mothership, blasting off for their place in space."

Busted! They were all seeing haints, like dead brother Sekou when they were kids. Cinnamon peered across the room, across years, at their Mod Squad photo. The Bots moved closer, burbling and twinkling, greedy for data. "You two haven't discussed freaky visions, have you?"

Marie snorted. "What if nobody except me saw them?"

"What if everybody saw them?" Klaus groaned. "I don't want to be stingy . . ."

"You want to *believe* they came 'cause *we three* conjured them," Cinnamon said.

"Yes," Klaus sighed. "After all this time—"

"They showed up for us," Marie said. "I've been doing serious nostalgia." She whipped out a photo of them holding the elders' masks at Festival. "I was Thunderbird, Klaus did Mami Wata, and you were Dragon." She took a sharp breath. "Festival today was soooo much more amazing than I remembered."

"Nothing compares to *live*. The valley-cast blew our minds up, out, over, whatever." Klaus losing English at the prepositions had them squishing close and giggling like teenagers and old farts. "You should take your Circus-Bot show on the road."

Marie agreed. "Folkadelic astral bop will blow a lot of minds." She and Klaus harmonized: "*Uh-huh, uh-huh, uh-huh. I like it like that.*" The Bots susurrated approval.

"I don't know." Cinnamon quivered. Marie stroked her braids. Klaus pulled one curled at her forehead to her chin and let it spring back. Suddenly they were breezing through their lives since last sitting in this room. Law school, med school, lovers, families found and lost—good people who didn't work out. Stupid mistakes and surprise opportunities. Singing in Istanbul's Blue Mosque, delivering triplets during a hurricane in New Jersey, offering legal counsel to Water Protectors, dancing at a shrine to Eshu. At fifty, they both dumped soul-sucking, mind-numbing jobs for a righteous *new life*. Cinnamon sputtered about Tatyana, engineering misadventures, about the world breaking her heart and that bright tomorrow going up in flames. She admitted being mad at Taiwo and herself for failing Raven, Opal, the elders, for failing the future. But Marie and Klaus were having none of that. They insisted her brilliance and success were everywhere to be seen. "Damn, sugar, were you at your own Festival?"

Cinnamon wanted to hug them close and never let them leave. But what if they were scamming her? She wanted to chase them out of the house before they mangled sweet memories. "How long you two been hooked up?" Jealousy was better than suspicion.

"*Teamed* up," Marie corrected her. "A week and some change."

"We haven't really talked till now," Klaus said.

Marie squirmed. "Waiting to be with you, to see if . . ."

"The magic was real?" Cinnamon whispered. "That's why I never tracked you two down. I mean," she sputtered. "What if . . ."

Nobody took a breath. They'd all been terrified their best memories were lies.

Marie flipped salt-and-pepper braids like a sullen teenager. "When I heard the urban legends about Baron Taiwo, haints, a Ghost-Dog *and* a Witch-Dog, I thought, well shit, that's the Cinnamon I knew. So I decided to quit wimping out."

"No other salespeople dared to come to your hoodoo-voodoo farm." Klaus stroked her demon jumpsuit, then laid his head on her shoulder. The feelers caressed his cheek.

"A good horror rep is the best protection against desperados," Cinnamon explained. "Corporate spies are another matter."

"Word," Klaus replied. No irony detected.

Marie scanned Cinnamon. "Can we trust you?"

"Of course we can." Klaus coughed several times. "Can't we?"

Cinnamon folded her arms over her chest. "Can I trust you?"

Klaus raised an eyebrow. "Marie tells me naïve nice people do get killed."

"Shut up." Marie shook him. "Life is never a solo gig. You gotta trust somebody."

"You two in some kind of trouble? Is that why you—"

"No." Klaus was indignant. "We wouldn't bring our trouble to your door."

"We're Whistleblowers," Marie whispered, proud and devilish.

"Get the fuck out of here." Cinnamon spoke softly too.

Klaus held a fist to quivering lips. "You told her, not me."

The Bots burbled and buzzed, indulging in excitement, energy use at max. Cinnamon tried to restrain her emotions.

"Klaus wanted to wait, tell you later," Marie said. "I knew you'd hate *not knowing.*"

"Doing Festival with you, that was proof of who you are," he said. "I needed to see who we three were together."

"And now, not yesterday," Marie said.

"Whistleblowers?" Cinnamon gasped. "Traveling around, snooping corporate scams, warning folks about toxins, hostile takeovers, neo-slave labor? Heroes—"

"Heroes?" Marie screwed up her face. "That's a stretch."

Klaus shrugged. "We blow the horn on any evil mess. Consolidated hasn't figured our real identities." They were saying exactly what Cinnamon wanted to hear.

She shook her head. "People claim the Whistleblower thing is wishful thinking. Action-adventure nonsense."

"Scheiße!" Klaus sank deeper into the cushions.

Marie hissed, "Big corps want you to believe they're invincible, inevitable."

Klaus hissed, "Die Arschgeigen!"

"Ass-fiddles?" Cinnamon had to laugh. "That's a German curse? Really?"

"People should *believe,* even if Whistleblowers are undercover."

Klaus balled a fist. "We should be possible. Like alien monsters living in ancient oak trees."

"Or Co-Op farms feeding the future and Ghost Malls charging up our *ImagiNation*." Marie nailed Cinnamon's intonation.

"Sometimes I worry that horror tales work better than hope." Cinnamon had barely admitted this to herself.

Klaus narrowed his eyes. "Work better for what?"

Marie slugged Cinnamon. It hurt. Cinnamon rubbed her shoulder. "All these years, fighting the same fights over and over. I'm—"

"You don't *believe* horror works better than hope." Klaus wasn't letting that go.

"Join us." Marie jumped up and did a little jig.

Klaus beamed at Cinnamon. "You'd be a great Whistleblower."

"Seriously?"

"A traveling show would be perfect cover. Infinitely better than sales." Klaus sprang up and danced beside Marie, energized once more. They pulled Cinnamon off the couch as he talked. "You have costumes, props, Circus-Bots, a flying carpet, and a dog act." Bruja dashed into Taiwo's room. "Live dangerously. Say yes." He *was* serious.

"You like *knowing*," Marie said. "We get the inside scoop and warn people."

A minute ago, Cinnamon had been unsure if Whistleblowers existed. Despite what Shaheen and others alleged, she never let herself *believe* undercover heroes prowled around, trying to make a difference, trying to make the world better. Klaus and Marie regaled her with Whistleblower lore. Nonviolent activists risked their lives to hack corrupt systems and share information and data with people who needed it. In fact, they came to warn Cinnamon.

Consolidated or some mega-corp was after the elders' farm and other Co-Op farms nearby. Last year, they wanted to buy Cinnamon out. Since she never responded to electronic communication, she rated live coercion. Klaus and Marie were five-star sales operatives. Customers rarely turned them down. A slick algorithm expected Cinnamon to enjoy the show and jump at fancy rigs, bug drones, and hair-thin sensors. Eighty percent chance curiosity might bankrupt her. One Co-Op farm failing would start a cascade; then the mega-corp could scoop up the entire region.

"So my farm, not—" SevGenAlg. Cinnamon caught herself before blurting this.

"The Co-Ops and the Mall are a threat." Marie shrugged as if this was obvious. "Dumb houses like yours are a nuisance, a gateway drug."

"To what? Revolution?" Cinnamon had to get out more. "You're kidding."

Marie poked her. "Do correlations lie?"

Cinnamon snorted. "Yes."

Klaus talked over her. "Food, social resources, energy, water, they want—"

"One system to rule them all." Marie did a wicked monster laugh.

"Didn't see this coming." Cinnamon was rattled.

"Shh." Klaus gripped her and Marie. "Do you hear that?"

> I am Guardian at the Gates
> I have many plenty heads!
> You do not know me
> I ask:
> Which direction you goin' take?
> Who do you mean to be?

"Taiwo's morning chant, second verse," Cinnamon said.

Oun had to be in on this home invasion.

Marie shook Klaus. "Is that cool or what?"

Color painted his cheeks. Still an open window. "How does this work?"

"Speak your heart to the Eshu altar that guards this house. Your prayer lingers till the next one."

Marie tugged her wrist. "You want to be a Whistleblower? Do guerilla traveling theatre with us. Bust the lies. Power to the people like old times."

"But future jive." Klaus slipped his arm through hers. "You know you want to."

"Sounds grand," Cinnamon conceded. "Making the future we want . . ."

"Kein Luftschloss," Klaus insisted.

"No air castle. That's good." Cinnamon stalled, "What's 'whistleblower' in German?"

"Der Whistleblower." He shrugged. "Straight from English."

"I can't abandon the farm or the Co-Ops or the Mall. I'm doing a coding workshop next week. And there's Zaneesha." Cinnamon meant what she said about adopting her. One outrageous decision was enough today.

"We met her. Bruja's buddy," Klaus said. "A granddaughter?"

"My little Shooting-Star." Cinnamon took a sharp breath and glanced at her watch. "She'll be here any minute. Did you really think I'd—"

"We knew you'd say no." Marie forced a laugh, heart still on her sleeve. "A harebrained scheme. You shouldn't trust anyone too quickly, not even us."

Klaus nodded. "The farm, the Co-Ops, that's grand work." They looked crushed.

A cowbell on the altar clanged. It was like being wrenched from a dream. Taiwo called them to the gate. Perhaps the ambulance had arrived. Cinnamon was relieved. Another minute and she'd have thrown herself over a cliff. Marie and Klaus had their arms open to catch her; still, it was too quick, too wild.

"I'm sorry about getting you fired," Cinnamon muttered at the hurt on their faces.

"We still have jobs. Getting fired is part of the sales pitch." Klaus stroked an ancient acorn on the Eshu altar. "They only fire you for blowing your cover."

Marie leaned into Klaus. "Whistleblowers go to jail for corporate espionage. If you reveal our identities to anyone, even other Whistleblowers . . ."

"It might be disastrous." Klaus shuddered. "Our fate is in your hands."

"Who would I tell?" Cinnamon stepped close. They were still a sweet taste in her mouth. "The Mall clinic is great. Boo and Azalea will patch you both up."

"I'm fine," Klaus insisted. Marie rolled her eyes.

"Humor me." Cinnamon eased a hand around his waist and then Marie's. "Techies Forever can send someone to fix your dumb car. You can barter skills to cover the cost. Home cooking and a good night's sleep in a bed. Nobody will suspect a thing." Marie and Klaus turned in to her. They entwined limbs and bumped heads, old moves. Savory skin smells filled Cinnamon's nose: fir, lavender, and sage, familiar and devastating. She broke away. "How long to gather up that Inflatable Universe?"

Bruja trotted in from Taiwo's room dragging a double-headed mask: a brooding scowl painted on one side, a sunny grin on the other. Red and black feathers loomed from the crown. She deposited the mask at Marie's feet, eyes full of hope.

"Like Eshu at the crossroads." Marie hugged Bruja, then put the mask on. A great fit.

Klaus scratched Bruja's night-sky ears. "Where's mine?"

Bruja raced off. She reappeared with another double-headed creation: crafty, slitted eyes assessing a hostile world and wide-eyed surprise appreciating wonders. Perfect for Whistleblowers. Bruja whirled through the air as Klaus's head disappeared into cavernous papier-mâché, wonder face forward. Witch-Dog lived for this.

"Raven painted the faces," Cinnamon recalled. "Opal made the papier-mâché forms, complaining: *How can you spout physics at me and believe hoodoo-voodoo nonsense?*"

Klaus and Marie squealed. "And you said: *Physics and hoodoo are different realms, different dimensions of truth.*"

Cinnamon's heart thrummed in her mouth. Her toes and fingers tingled. She took a sweet breath from another dimension. They remembered her when she forgot herself!

"You wear your Water-Demon." Marie had the scowling face forward. "We'll put on a show for the drones." She mimed Taiwo's boneyard baron moves. Klaus joined her. They talked in tongues, deep in the zone. Sparks and a storm wind whirled around them. For a blink, they conjured the feathered hat, snake cane, and storm cloak. Someone else might have worried about having visions. Cinnamon worried how she would say good-bye. "Can we light candles and leave a chant?"

"Sure. A surprise waiting for me." She raced off to get wheels for Marie and hook up a trailer for Klaus. Otherwise, she'd have pressed them to stay, join the Co-Ops, and do magic for small change at the Mall. Selfish. Whistleblowers belonged to everybody.

The wind off a distant storm cooled the evening air and fortified her resolve. T-bird and Dragon flew over her head. Mami trundled down the side ramp. The Bots were thrilled to be heading to the Mall. They made no mention of long-lost love or ghost elders. At the garage, they buzzed with news about data cubes, Tatyana, and Flying-Horse in pieces. Cinnamon's heart ached to hear about Horse. She chastised herself for getting attached to machines, but why not? Who needed anti-sentiment training in the current rage-bully world? The update on Diego was bleak. Blood seeped from a thigh wound. He'd passed out. A bullet might have nicked an artery. Since Klaus was *fine* now and required no urgent care, the driverless ambulance would pick Diego up at Blossom Bridge and race him to the Mall clinic, sirens blaring. Let George pick up the tab. Marie was fit to pedal to the Mall, and Cinnamon would ferry Klaus.

Shooting-Star-Bot broadcast an unclear SOS about kidnappers at the gorge. Music and lyrics were from *The Redwood and Wildfire Songbook*:

> *You don't like my peaches, don't shake my tree*
> *Hey, you live so long, you forget yourself*
> *Remember, love is what you gotta be*

RUNNING

Clouds covered the sunset, and inside the garage was dim, even with the door up. The Bots were unperturbed—they could see in the dark. Cinnamon should connect garage circuits to the emergency generator. Tomorrow. Plenty to do tonight. She patted Mami. A shower of light illuminated the clutter of her life—not a mess, just full. The elders' final journal glimmered in a bookshelf under her Dream-Machine bike. Cinnamon opened the worn leather to Iris's last letter, tucked between a song and a spell.

"Aidan recorded 'Spirit Ain't for Sale,' right?" Cinnamon murmured. T-bird played the banjo riff and Dragon scatted around the melody. Cinnamon spoke Redwood's "Hoodoo to Conjure Love" out loud, to give it more power.

1. *Stand still in the dark till you sense moonlight on your cheeks.*
2. *Plunge into an unruly crowd and savor the sound of every voice.*
3. *Help someone you can't stand do what they gotta do.*
4. *Watch a bowerbird gather the right color, the perfect shape for the nest.*
5. *Taste how good somebody you're meeting for the first time is, and tell them.*
6. *Release the hurt you nurse. Watch it float away and dissolve into nothing.*
7. *Feel a stranger's heartbeat as they sync into a groove with you.*
8. *When you're dying of thirst, let a sip of water linger on your tongue.*
9. *Collect the stars in people's eyes. You'll know which ones are shining for you.*

Nine was a hoodoo number. Cinnamon closed the journal. She'd read more later. Right now, she needed a clear head. Running off to the circus with Klaus and Marie and doing shows for Whistleblower cover was a lovely temptation, but impossible. Work that gave Cinnamon hope and people she loved were here—a precarious, fragile community. She had so much. Klaus and Marie only had each other and only for the last two weeks. Shame on Cinnamon for taking her valley life for granted.

She reported the raid near the gorge to George. Shooting-Star's alerts were cryptic. George preferred hard evidence. This far out, unless Paradise was in immediate danger, he might decline to send troops. Rogue crews knew the exact perimeter of his concern and counted on benign neglect.

What mischief were the vanity Vikings up to?

She took her Dream-Machine bike down from the wall for the first time in years. Compared to a Wheel-Wizards eighteen-wheeler, it was light as foam and in great shape: rust-free, mighty hydraulic brakes, gears smooth as butter. Tubeless tires never went flat. While she was hooking up the trailer for Klaus, Hawk rode in, sweaty, muddy, and stressed from chasing through a storm after Zaneesha.

Cinnamon acted calm, almost as good as the real thing. "What happened?"

Some kids called Zaneesha a dummy, 'cause only dummies used WHIZZ-ITs. Zaneesha lied, said she *could* read. Her pirate team caught her fabulating treasure hunt clues and kicked her out of the game. She thought they were her best friends. Finding treasure meant you got to share art supplies, books, and musical instruments with everyone. Zaneesha pouted by herself as her team gave out the booty. She was a spoken word artist, a performer, not someone to sit still and make marks on paper.

Over mashed sweet potatoes and Naughty Nuggets, kids bragged about the big books they read, the bigger books they were going to read *and* write, plus the graphic novels they would ink. They blabbed about music they recorded, pictures they drew, and games they designed. Zaneesha got mad at everyone, even people trying to be nice. Someone talked smack about her mom disappearing. Unclear who threw the first punch. Zaneesha's opponent ended up with a busted lip, crying in the dirt. Zaneesha ran into the woods to find Mom. Nobody else would— Mom was a master of camouflage and escape. Zaneesha too, which was why Hawk arrived alone.

Oun held up the comet costume. "Could Bruja track her?"

"Track who?" An InstaHam freak from Stephen's entourage stuck a Utopia, Inc., contract under Cinnamon's nose. His e-bike was sleek and quiet and matched his foil-cloth pedal pushers. Taiwo let any ole body through the gates. "Stephen says look this over and get back to him ASAP. Early tomorrow at the latest, so we can catch the wave."

Cinnamon took the papers. "I'll have my lawyers check this out. Then we'll see."

He vacillated between impressed and doubtful. Lawyer Marie would check the ten-page document and suss out what Stephen was really after. Boss Lady Shaheen would help Cinnamon find a tactful way to say, *Fuck off.* "Thanks for biking so far. Storm clouds are gone. You'll catch the last rays on the way back. Good evening."

InstaHam freak was about to invite himself to stay. Hawk gave him the evil eye. "Don't push it, and Cinnamon might sign." No fool, he jumped on his aluminum wonder wheels. As he whizzed off, the fierce drained out of Hawk.

"Don't worry," Cinnamon said. "Shooting-Star tracked Zaneesha, a warn and shield loop. She'll take her to a crossroads. Easy for Bruja to find."

"Really?" Hawk's shoulders almost relaxed. "I thought we lost her."

"Not yet."

Hawk squeezed Cinnamon in a bear hug. Oun apologized for a brief hello to Klaus and Marie, who waved from the greenhouse windows. Oun wanted to hurry to the Mall. "Game-Boy and I have a *date*, after his Back-From-The-Dead *missions*. On a rooftop, under the stars, music, wine, and romance."

Cinnamon nodded. "We'll find Zaneesha and join you. Get out of here."

Packing up the smart house inflatables, Marie wore the double-headed mask to confuse snoop-drones. A cascade of colorful ribbons hung from the neck, a cape that obscured salesperson clothes. Every so often she twirled the ribbons into a rainbow flurry, like Taiwo and the Water-Spirits dropping in from another dimension. Bruja nipped Marie's heels, eager to get their adventure underway. The Inflatable Universe was back in the box in a flash, even the broken Sex Suite.

The ribbon cape on Klaus's mask fluttered in the setting sun. He took precise steps, not a joule of energy wasted. Cinnamon stuffed the flatbed trailer with Redwood's pillows. Klaus sank into them, stretched out his legs, and sighed. Bruja bounded over with Flying-Carpet in her mouth.

"You want me to bring this along?" He took the drone-bot. "For good luck? What?"

Bruja gave no reply. She was herding Marie to her wheels.

"I have to get stuff from the garage." Cinnamon wanted to avoid another big conversation. Her shields were in shreds. She opened the microwave. Her cell-phone battery couldn't hold any juice. Pointless to bring that. Using the Bots to communicate was better. Bouncing signals everywhere, they were almost impossible to trace. She clipped Stephen's card to Tatyana's letter and pocketed that, just in case . . . what? The Water-Demon mask twinkled as she slid it on. Before mounting her Dream-Machine bike, she leaned over to Bruja. "FIND Zaneesha and Shooting-Star. They're LOST again."

Good thing Bruja never tired of this game.

The bike path wandered through the woods without crossing the car road. A magenta sunset got tangled in dark boughs and branches. Blue-green ground fog was a trippy spectacle. The Dream-Machine flew over a gray ribbon road, easily keeping up with Bruja. T-Bird and Dragon rode shotgun next to Klaus—no heavier than other gear she'd hauled. Flying-Carpet was a warm blanket as the temperature dropped. Marie pedaled Mami and bulky sales bags, no sweat. She and Mami chatted like old friends. Cinnamon resisted worrying about the secrets they traded. Farmers cheered as they passed. In masks and capes, with the Bots twinkling, they looked like *Chaos on Tour.* Bruja sprinted ahead.

Zaneesha hugged her knapsack on the stone bench that read: *You're Half Way There! Take A Break! Take a Breath!* Shooting-Star-Bot hovered by her, comet hair like a cloak around the little girl's shoulders. Shooting-Star flashed letters as they recited the alphabet. Bruja jumped on the bench and licked Zaneesha's dirt-streaked face. Her hair was a muddy cloud. The sparkle barrettes had washed away.

Cinnamon halted. "Everybody's been worried about you."

"Everybody who?" Zaneesha snapped. "Mom?"

"I was worried and Bruja too." Bruja woofed on cue.

Zaneesha edged for the footpath that led to where they first met. "Mom taught me how to do getaways."

"Bruja will find you anywhere. You're part of her herd."

"Uh-huh." Zaneesha frowned at Marie and Klaus. "Who are you?"

"Who are you?" Klaus replied, a twinkle in his voice.

"I ain't telling." Zaneesha pouted. "I was catching my breath before heading out."

"Where you going?" Marie asked. "Want a ride?"

"I'm s'posed to be home before dark . . ." Zaneesha glanced at Cinnamon, then back at Klaus and Marie. "Festival's over. How come you still wearing your masks?"

"We're old friends of Cinnamon's," Marie said as Cinnamon stepped closer to the girl. "How old are you, ten?"

Zaneesha kissed her teeth. "What you want to know for?" Eight going on forty.

"Can you keep a secret?" Klaus whispered. "We knew your grandmother way back when she was closer to your age." He lifted the mask and revealed a big smile.

Marie did the same. "We met you at Festival and didn't know who you were. I was the lioness. He was an elephant."

Zaneesha's pout had cracked at *grandmother*. Now she grinned. "We danced with Bruja."

"Rain dance," Klaus and Marie said. "You were great."

Zaneesha looked at her feet. "I'm nothing but *more stupid trouble on a really bad day*."

"Trouble's the fuel you use to burn your way across the sky." Cinnamon held up the comet costume. "Why get stranded in somebody else's bad news? What you need is a compass to get home."

Zaneesha quivered. "You got one?"

"A big collection." Cinnamon opened her arms wide, like the elders would do when she was little. Zaneesha fell into the warm Water-Demon suit and blubbered about none of it being her fault, but she was sorry anyhow. "So tell us what happened," Cinnamon said.

Running from the picnic, Zaneesha stumbled on two men kicking and cursing their broke-down truck. They nabbed Zaneesha and claimed to be good guys who *rescued* kids from deviant, wastrel parents. They offered sound Christian values, discipline, and a chance to become responsible adults. They marched her and an older girl to their camp near the gorge. Clouds rolled in and dumped a deluge. As Zaneesha scrambled onto a fallen tree, a river of mud swallowed both men. She missed what happened to the teen girl. Shooting-Star-Bot twinkled up on a ridge. That kept Zaneesha climbing. Kidnappers ran around, threatening everybody trying to escape, till Taiwo appeared in a crack of lightning. The fools chased oun instead.

Later Cinnamon learned that Taiwo led them to George, who rounded them up with no casualties. This was the rough crew that had been tormenting everyone recently. A Darknet Lord had proclaimed them honorable, righteous men. He provided funding and weapons, and promised the future would be theirs. Cinnamon marveled at the chaos honorable, righteous men conjured. Shooting-Star led Zaneesha to solid ground. They walked forever, past a giant old tree that took up the whole sky, to the stone bench. Zaneesha was exhausted. At least the rain quit.

Cinnamon cleaned mud from Zaneesha's face and Afro-puffs. She promised to put her great escape in the graphic novel on valley history. Since Zaneesha was learning the alphabet, writing a song with Cinnamon was also possible. Zaneesha fronted indifference. Klaus and Marie discussed frames to ink and Zaneesha had a big grin going till Cinnamon said ditching the picnic was a terrible move. Zaneesha insisted nobody wanted her to do the treasure hunt 'cause they hated her. Klaus, Marie, and Cinnamon hooted, unconvinced. When Bruja yip-yapped and whined, Zaneesha finally admitted to making up clues instead of reading them.

"I'm not stupid," she said. "Am I?"

"No. Running from bad men makes sense." Cinnamon sighed. "You can't run from your life, though."

Marie gestured at Cinnamon and Klaus. "We've all tried that."

"Big fail." Klaus swallowed a cough. "Running might even make stuff worse."

They'd all been running. "No more of that." Cinnamon kissed Zaneesha's cheek. "We have to take my friends to the Mall before you and I go home."

Zaneesha panicked. "I don't want to see anybody from the picnic."

"I bet they're worried about you," Klaus said.

"They feel guilty," Marie added. "Hawk was a wreck." Zaneesha was glad to hear it.

Cinnamon chuckled. "Want to ride with Mami?" Who could turn that down? Shooting-Star headed for the swamp and Zaneesha scrambled in beside Mami. As the caravan got underway, the Circus-Bots crooned:

> *Running won't set you free*
> *Yeah, a man could still be a slave*
> *On the loose and-a acting brave*
> *In shackles he just don't see*

Redwood and Aidan had a damn song for everything.

"SHORTCUT!" Cinnamon called out to Bruja. The dirt road through the hills was hard going; still, Cinnamon needed Marie and Klaus to see sacred sights before they went on their Whistleblower way. Bruja led them to the Grandmother Oak.

"I wasn't lying," Zaneesha said. "A million leaves and bigger than the sky."

"Here and not here." Klaus and Marie *believed* in the old lady oak. Laying hands on scaly black bark, they whispered greetings to an ancient soul. Cinnamon and Zaneesha did too.

After that they reached the Mall in a few heartbeats.

ᏟᏄᏒᎧ

INCOGNITO

Nobody recognized IT Fred as he piled Shaheen's diablo pizza on his plate. People noses were funny. Fred had changed the skin he wore and put a felt nest on his head. His cheeks were hairless, his nose crooked, and dark glasses obscured his eyes. Spook sniffed the last few days on him: bears, river water, snake-venom cure, and Flying-Horse's mane in the cuff of his pants. Fred sat in the pizzeria, facing the food-court entrance, upwind from folks outside who might be trying to sniff him out. T-bird's trackers pulsed in his neck. A blue dragonfly buzzed overhead, Dragon's tracker. A mini-tank from Mami lurked under the counter behind him.

The staticky widget in Fred's pocket buzzed. He smacked it quiet. Cinnamon, the Circus-Bots, Zaneesha, Bruja, and Bruja's friends from Festival pedaled by. They greeted folks in the food court. Good moods scented the air. Fear wafted off Fred.

A man from Fred's pack cheered the parade, then sat beside Fred. He had mirror eyes and a plate of naan bread, beans, and cauliflower rice. Festival food. Spook licked his chops. Nothing to gobble on the floor. The man poked Fred.

"Don't start, Jack," Fred yapped.

"What're you supposed to be?" Jack chuckled. "That's more of an African nose . . ."

"The kid might really come through with a Circus-Bot."

"So, we're ignoring Tatyana's calls?"

Fred scowled. He chomped the pizza, then spit it out. Jack guzzled a mango lassi. Spook's stomach growled. He'd score food from Shaheen or Cinnamon and find Fred's trail later. He loped off, following good-mood scents to the Mall clinic. The med-crew barely noticed another shadow. If nurses caught a glimpse of Spook, they smiled.

Most beds were occupied. The storm broke bones and filled lungs with mud. Some reeked of motor oil and tires, as if cars ran over them. Kids smelling of the gorge twisted and moaned. Bruja had gone to the OPERATING ROOM. That door was always locked. Spook jumped up and looked in the window. Diego lay on a bloody bed. Azalea and Bruja's tall Festival friend hovered over him. Bruja was near, just out of sight.

Circling back to the main clinic, Spook paused by a man wheezing and flinching, eyes clenched. He wore a mask over his nose and mouth. Spook had caught wind of him at the gorge two days ago. A traveler. Spook put a paw on the bed and woofed. The man jolted awake and grimaced. After a couple breaths, he scratched Spook's ear. His phone buzzed. It smelled like the weapon version.

He pulled off the mask and rasped, "Send a car for me . . . Yes, it's fucking urgent! A comfort dog is in my lap, and my heart rate is still off the charts. Do they know what they're doing in this dump or is it just New Age Voodoo crap?" He stroked Spook's neck and dropped his voice. "They winged the bitch . . . Died? Well, she bled like a pig, but no body." He held the mask to his mouth and gulped. "Why should I know *how* she got away? A Rambo freak lives in the trees around here, bringing people back from the dead or some shit. Of course, I don't *believe* that. What do you take me for? Maybe this freak ran off with her body. The Mall's got a vampire, zombie thing going. Death cult orgies. I'm just saying, how did she walk her bullet-ridden butt out of there? . . . Right. So, send a car to take me away from Zombie Hippie-Ville. Now." He slammed the phone on the bed and sucked air from the mask. "Hey, bunny man, are you a nurse?"

Boo nodded foot-long rabbit ears. He was pink and gold fur except green hands. "We suctioned out as much as we could . . ."

"What do I owe you? I'll transfer hard currency, and then release me, goddamnit."

"No charge." Boo smiled. "But you can leave a donation."

Boo patted Spook, who darted around the corner to the old pet shop area. The delightful aroma of puppies, parrots, and guinea pigs lingered. At the far end, Shaheen sat by an empty bed. She tried to hand Cinnamon the kente bag with Flying-Horse inside. Cinnamon pushed him away. Shaheen set the bag down. "You and Marie sort the Utopia contract out. The Co-Op Union is tax-exempt. We could use the money, and I'm fine. I just want to sit here and wait for Diego by myself. Go."

Marie, Bruja's short Festival friend, dragged Cinnamon to the back hall. The Circus-Bots trailed them. Mami's third eye blazed infrared. T-bird had ultraviolet trackers in his mouth, ready to launch. Dragon's pearl pulsed. They broadcast pheromone alerts—danger nearby. Spook followed, ready for attack.

Indigo, Game-Boy, and Hawk huddled in a doorway over Jerome and Zaneesha. She stomped a mud-coated foot and shook hemlock needles from her hair. "I'll stay with Grandma Cinnamon when you work. Me, her, and Shooting-Star can search for Mom." Jerome mumbled something and Zaneesha hissed, "Nobody knows Mom like me."

Cinnamon and Marie paced by the EMERGENCY EXIT, marking up a clump of papers. Spook nosed Cinnamon's hand and she patted his head. No food anywhere. He padded back to Shaheen. Flying-Horse was broken pieces on a table beside her. Spook pawed the Bot, licked sad from Shaheen's nose, and put his head in her lap. She gazed into his eyes, then buried her face in his fur. Good feelings always between them. He licked her nose again.

"Indigo thinks our luck might be running out. What do you think?" Spook tilted his head to the side.

She pulled curly hair into a tight bun. "Cinnamon says luck is random, yet today, after forever, her old friend Klaus, who happens to be a doctor, drops in. He's treated people wherever they needed him. Klaus is operating on Diego right now. I call that brilliant luck." Shaheen was jibber-jabbering herself into feeling better. Spook did that too. "Paramedics missed a nick yesterday or Diego tore the wound open. They told him to take it easy." She scratched Spook's itchy shoulder. "Doing Festival and chasing high-tech thugs is not *taking it easy*. Klaus thinks Diego might pull through. He's not a hundred percent sure and says Diego should go to a full-scale hospital. But no available beds anywhere, plus a shortage of doctors and nurses. Paradise tried to poach Boo and Azalea from us." Shaheen stood up, walked to the hall, and yelled, "Don't lurk. Go catch the star party on the roof. I'm OK." The pack reluctantly marched off. "Go with them. Find some FOOD, some FUN." She pointed. He licked her calf and trotted off.

Techies Forever had the elevator working. People jammed into the metal box. Spook watched from behind the feathery leaves of a red dragon maple. Cinnamon hated potted trees. He hated elevators: the screech, stale air, puke feelings in his gut. And when you got out, where were you? His pack squeezed in. T-bird perched on Cinnamon's head, Dragon on Marie's. Mami hung back. Strangers filled her spot. The doors shut. Mami rolled toward the food court. Spook trailed her. She moved faster than usual, almost running over the traveler sucking air from his mask. He cursed and stepped into a golf cart. Mami trundled by Fred hunched in front of the pizzeria. He and Jack chased her to the parking lot. She halted by a van. Spook slinked under a spaceship table.

Tatyana opened the back of the van. "You boys have been busy." Fred wanted to bite her. She laughed. "Don't look so down-in-the-mouth. How were you getting this tank-bot to Paradise?"

"Sorry, man." Jack shrugged. "She asked. I told her." Fred also wanted to bite Jack.

"I have a lab set up for a clean probe. What do you have?" Tatyana touched Mami gingerly, then gripped her. "She's powered down. Give me a hand."

"I was gonna text you." Fred helped load Mami in the van. "When it was secured."

"Beat you to that," Tatyana snarled. They drove off toward Paradise.

Spook grumble-growled. Mami was someone to go up against bullets for. She'd do the same for Spook. He whined. No time to find anything to eat. At least twilight was the best time to sneak into Paradise.

∽

At the front gate, Spook waited, undetected, near a cluster of silvery e-bikes and their riders. Tourists, smelling like Festival, spoke languages he rarely heard. Familiar sounds and cadence got his attention. "Follow your tour guide to turn in your rentals as soon as you enter. Please don't smile for the face scan."

A drone hovered, flashing and beeping. Spook flickered in and out of the drone's dimension. Taiwo had trained him. The drone registered static, a scanner malfunction, noise. Spook sauntered through the final sensors between two Valley Security guards. Inside, he picked up Fred and Tatyana's trail easily. The lab building was near the front gate. The van was at a loading dock. Spook scouted for a way in. Taiwo knocked on doors, turned knobs, or picked the lock. Sometimes oun drew a Vévé for a tunnel from here to wherever. Spook jumped against the door. The fourth time he hit a buzzer and hurt a paw. He tumbled into darkness under an overhang and licked bruised toes.

The door whooshed open on a woman he'd smelled with Cap George. As she scanned the dock, Spook slipped into a lobby drenched in volatile chemicals. "Quit playing around, guys. Not funny." The door whooshed shut. Spook slinked down an empty fluorescent corridor. Mami was close. Alarm pheromones lingered.

Jack wagged his head on a doorsill. "Why do I have to get coffee?"

He almost slammed the door on Spook's tail. Mami sat on a table, dark and still. Beside her Tatyana and Fred fussed at each other. Spook slipped past them and into a tangle of wires under Mami. He panted to stay calm. Stealth-mode was exhausting. Still, if someone attacked Mami, he planned to take them out before they realized he was there.

"Nothing special about this bot." Tatyana smelled tense, uncertain, like Cinnamon.

"You know that already?" Fred snarled. "Cinnamon could have hidden—"

"I did a preliminary probe and copied the operating system. I by-passed her security. She won't know. I'll run the simulation at hyper-speed all night. That's like a test-century."

Fred reached a hand out.

Tatyana smacked it away. "Don't touch anything or we lose every-thing. She's the gadget queen, not you."

Jack returned with coffee. "What I miss?"

"Standard stuff. Ten-year-old code. Antediluvian hardware. Good enough for a clown act—" Tatyana smirked. "Where would Cinnamon hide anything? Zero storage space."

"Run it all night then, or—" Fred kicked a desk.

"You'll beat the truth out of it with a metal pipe like you did the horse?" Jack said.

"We could feed the bot a worm, then give it back," Fred replied. "Maybe find—"

"More nothing burgers." Jack snickered.

Tatyana slapped the table. "No time for petty revenge that might come back and bite us. We're supposed to fly under the radar."

"Cap George is a big Circus-Bot fan. You don't want him on our asses." Jack offered Fred a steaming cup. He knocked it on the floor and stormed out. Jack shook his head. "Fred was hoping for a miracle."

"Aren't we all?" Tatyana bared her teeth.

"I don't believe in miracles."

"Too bad." Tatyana patted his shoulder. "Mop up the coffee so we don't break our necks."

Spook put his snout on his paws. Getting out of Paradise would be harder than getting in.

CINNAMON

✒ ✑

HOODOO

The moon had yet to rise. On the Mall rooftop in the gym that never was, Azalea and Boo listened to the stars with six-foot antennae-ears. Techies Forever dimmed the lights to allow for deep dark. Meteors streaked across the bowl of heaven, wild women out in droves, their hair on fire. Zaneesha's pirate team was thrilled she'd escaped the kidnappers. They kicked her out of the game, not off the team. She told them the meteor shower was *trouble burning up*. Maybe she'd find meteorites for the rock collection in her backpack. She hugged Jerome and assured him that Latoya was streaking around somewhere. One day, when nobody was mad about rhino babies, lemurs, and cockatoos, Latoya would let herself be found. Or not. Zaneesha was starry-eyed and cynical. She murmured Latoya's bank account number and the security code in Cinnamon's ear. The account was in Zaneesha's name.

Too agitated for insight or fun, Cinnamon retreated to Indigo's vegetable garden away from party central. Dream-mode should have fixed the damn glitch, yet T-bird and Dragon kept slipping in and out of Teufelskreis without her engaging *dead-bot-off* for a manual reset. How was that even possible? She launched diagnostics a ninth time.

"I did what I could for Diego," Klaus whispered to Marie behind a netted berry bush, maybe thinking Cinnamon couldn't hear. Wrong. "He's resting." Klaus ought to be resting too.

"Did Taiwo look off to you?" Marie asked. "Spotty?"

"Yes, as if all the lights weren't on," Klaus replied.

"Like a signal fading." Marie sounded panicked.

"No," Klaus muttered, "as if scattering back to the *spaces between things*."

Marie slumped. "Nothing in your doctor bag for Taiwo."

Klaus drooped too. Bruja licked his knees. She'd shadowed him all night, watching from an upstairs office while he operated on Diego. Cinnamon would worry about Diego and Taiwo later. Diagnostics insisted the Bots were in crisis-improv-mode, not a Teufelskreis. The little buggers were acting. Why?

Marie sauntered close and nuzzled Cinnamon's cheek. "Your reckless youth are right. Do the show in Paradise, take gazillionaire's money, and pay your bills. Give the rest to the Co-Ops."

"We're all tainted." Klaus massaged Cinnamon's tense muscles. "Noch ist nicht aller Tage Abend."

"Night has not fallen on all our days," Cinnamon translated. Klaus talking trash in German always made her feel good. He knew it.

Marie chimed in, "Japanese old folks say, fall seven times, get up eight."

Cinnamon groaned. "Ganging up on me with elder wisdom?"

Marie grinned. "You won't listen to just us."

"OK. Stephen and Utopia, Inc., are a big mystery," Klaus said. "Hard to hack, even for Whistleblowers. Stephen has a team of people like you shielding him."

"Nobody's like Cinnamon," Marie insisted. "In fact, we're all unique."

"Every mind/body is astounding, impossible to reduce to algebra," Cinnamon said.

"Each day, a new performance. We're hard to hack too." Klaus's eyes sparkled, bright as the meteors flashing behind his head. "We'll do your traveling show if it's soon. Backup for the Archangels of Funk. Or a trio on Aidan's 'Spirit Ain't for Sale.' Sacred loop stuff." Dragon and T-bird buzzed approval as he sang a line.

Cinnamon shook her head. "Mami told you about the sacred loop."

"A festival in Paradise. Say yes," Marie pleaded, and Klaus joined in. "Come on."

"OK. Maybe a few acts, and loop you two in. Wait, wait . . ." Realization dawning, Cinnamon glared at T-bird and Dragon. "Teufelskreis is a distraction. Where's Mami?"

"She never got on the elevator." Marie squinted as if to clear a fuzzy memory. "Stayed downstairs with Spook. I think that was Spook. He's a little blurry."

"Spook, all right. Mami is up to something that I'd veto and he's on her." Cinnamon raced for the elevator. Bruja, Marie, and Klaus followed, ready to do whatever she needed. Dragon and T-bird brought up the rear, bombinating like angry bees.

On the ground level, Mami and Spook were nowhere to be seen. In the clinic, Diego was swaddled in bandages and hooked to machines. The monitor blurred, then morphed into Raven in cloud-white sheets. Opal danced at his side, wearing the Donna Summer, Queen of Disco, dress and Patti LaBelle platform boots. "Mom, Dad?" Cinnamon whispered, and halted. Klaus and Marie stumbled into her. Raven's eyes opened, bright and mischievous. Opal pressed a paintbrush in his hand. In a flash Raven painted the sheets: Cinnamon on her Dream-Machine bike, flying through a horde of Shooting-Stars. Klaus and Marie zoomed on scooters beside her. *Space is the place.* Raven and Opal smiled at the Mod Squad as the vision dissolved.

Klaus and Marie exchanged glances with Cinnamon.

"You all boosting the haint signal?" she muttered. They shrugged.

Shaheen clutched Diego's hand and stroked his face. They'd been flirting for weeks. Today, riding a performance high, they leapt over that cliff together, then boom, blood on the sheets and pillows. Did Shaheen regret risking her heart again?

Jerome hovered over the lovers, panic on his face. "We're s'posed to talk to him."

Shaheen pressed her lips against Diego's ear. "In Farsi, 'Shaheen' means 'royal white falcon.' A majestic bird, an adventure princess, flying so far sometimes, she loses her way. As I was about to be born, my parents called my name and I flew to them and was lost no more. That's the story they told me." She kissed Diego's cheek. "Fly home and tell me your Diego Denzel story."

Jerome leaned close. "What do I know about anything yet? You gotta get up from this bed and give me time to make you proud."

"Have you seen Mami or Spook?" Cinnamon said softly, hating to interrupt.

Shaheen gathered herself. "Spook tried to cheer me up; then he and Mami went off somewhere. Scheiße! Is this like Flying-Horse?"

"Yo, I was gonna find you after checking on my man." Jerome talked fast. "I had a side hustle, providing detective info for this Fred dude. Good money for Latoya and Kaneesha. Didn't know he was bad news."

Cinnamon should have let Bruja rip Fred's throat.

Jerome stammered at her scowl, "I'm making it right. I told him Indigo gave you his cubes. He's holding Mami Wata. He'll do a trade."

"Not Fred's cubes." Cinnamon imagined shooting Fred with his own gun. One bullet was inadequate. Hacking him into bloody chunks was an idea, along with the ass-fiddle who hired him and maybe armed the Happy Vikings. The ass-fiddle could be Stephen, playing every angle, ready to restock his zoo with Circus-Bots and their trainers. Of course, other shitbags might have hired Fred. Well, they all deserved slow, painful deaths. Bruja would help. She'd sink her fangs deep and—

"Whoa. Come back." Klaus stroked Cinnamon. Her cheeks were on fire, hoodooing herself.

"Fred wanna be like gazillionaire Stephen." Jerome smirked. "Dude ain't even got a rig to run his cubes on."

Tatyana's cubes, not Fred's, SevGenAlg most likely. Cinnamon had almost smashed the damn things. No way she'd hand them over to Fred.

"He ran a game on me." Jerome gulped. "Indigo says Mami could fry Fred if she wanted to. So Mami's running a game on him, looping us in. Hey, I'd never help him kidnap the mer-woman. I like her. See, we think you can—"

"We?" Cinnamon hissed.

"Yeah, trade the cubes and get Mami back in time for the show." Jerome held up his WHIZZ-IT. "I'll contact Fred."

"No." She shook her head and smacked Klaus and Marie with angry braids. The Circus-Bots must have planned a sacrifice loop, using Jerome's connection to Fred and Indigo. Mami risked *dead-bot-off* to accomplish what? "I can't. Not even for . . ." Flying-Horse lay in pieces on the end table. Cinnamon lost her balance. Klaus and Marie caught her. "Why give Fred treasure cubes he stole? Nothing to talk about."

"I'll talk to him," Klaus said. "Work a deal, promise him anything, and get us in the room with your Bot. Improvise from there." He gazed at Thunderbird and Dragon. "Mami is pretty special. They all are."

"Mami's the water/rhythm section. Can't break up the band," Marie said. "They have a show tomorrow."

"Word!" Jerome shouted. Shaheen shushed him.

Cinnamon shook her head. "Fred can't handle what's on those cubes. What can we trade besides stolen goods?"

"The deal of a lifetime. Just call," Klaus said, and squeezed her hand. "Start there."

Fred's voice in the WHIZZ-IT grated as he threatened to trash Mami if they pulled any funny business. Klaus was a five-star salesperson, smooth, sweet, and chill as ice cream. He got more info than he gave and promised nothing. The trade would happen on neutral ground and tomorrow instead of tonight. Fred wanted time to mess with Mami. The Mod Squad needed time to figure something else to trade. The Ghost Mall gang would be in Paradise tomorrow doing the show. Klaus scheduled the trade beforehand at a lab with Valley Security on guard and witness duty. Klaus ended the call before Fred could think twice.

Mentioning the show perked Shaheen up. "They persuaded you."

"No losing our minds over Stephen's money." Cinnamon's voice shook.

"We can make this right," Jerome declared.

Bruja caught a scent and dashed off.

"Text Stephen my contract edits. He'll go for it," Marie said. "We'll put a firewall around him and get what you need. Stephen's a VIP ticket to Paradise for everyone."

Shaheen eyed Marie and Klaus, the social engineer appraising fresh meat. "You two sticking around? Zaneesha says you sing and tap-dance. Always need more of that, at tomorrow's show for sure."

Cinnamon used one of Game-Boy's burners. Stephen picked up immediately. She refused a video chat. He agreed to all edits, praising Marie's legal acumen. His entourage had a flyer ready. Paradise folks liked old-school paper, recycled. Cinnamon insisted the Graphic Novelists of the Future would get publicity out by midnight. She heard a triumphant smirk as Stephen signed off. She was about to clip his card back to Tatyana's letter when Bruja herded her in.

Girlfriend rocked black leather pants and clutched a motorcycle helmet. A widget utility belt was slung across her hips. Warrior-mode. She knew exactly where to find them. "Don't glower. Nobody ratted you out. Cap George said I might find you here."

"What do you want, Tatyana?" Cinnamon crumpled her letter.

"Tatyana?" Klaus said as he and Marie gaped at the broken heart, broken world story in the flesh.

"You didn't open that. Good." Tatyana snatched the letter and lit it on fire. Drama Empress. "Excuses, crap to say I'm sorry and beg for forgiveness, the best revenge."

"Verzeihen ist die beste Rache," Klaus and Marie whispered the German.

Tatyana dropped the burning paper and stomped the flames. "You want to do this in public?"

"I don't want to do *this* at all," Cinnamon replied.

Tatyana turned to Marie and Klaus. "Taiwo says you're people we can trust." She teeter-tottered, then refocused. "Fred stole Mami. She hasn't zapped anyone. Shut herself down." *Dead-bot-off* switch or . . . "I'm running tests overnight at hyper-speed."

"What good is that?" Cinnamon barely controlled herself.

"Fred has Darknet Lords curious about your Circus-Bots. I'll prove you're old news and Fred is a waste of resources. No return on that investment."

"Was Mami's stunt your idea?" Cinnamon asked.

"Who owns ideas?" Tatyana pursed her lips. So, a group effort behind Cinnamon's back. Taiwo too, no doubt. "Fred claimed he *found* Mami, wandering. Too many mediocre guys trying an end run around us. None of them know when a miracle is staring them in the face."

Cinnamon snorted. "You do?"

"I'm working on that." Tatyana sounded sincere. She always sounded sincere.

Dragon played Redwood's hoodoo spell, #6: *Release the hurt you nurse. Watch it float away and dissolve into nothing.* But Mami might be dead already, and no way could Cinnamon hand Fred SevGenAlg. Bruja gave her the stink eye. She whispered, "Estoy entre la espad y la pared."

Klaus scowled. "Between the sword and the wall?"

"You have us. We're shields." Marie waved the contract. "I got Stephen."

"We rewrite the code. Get off horror and onto hope." Klaus wasn't letting that go.

Cinnamon relented. "OK. OK." Bruja huffed victory and raced off. Cinnamon turned to Tatyana. "We're touring a mini-Festival to Paradise tomorrow. Fred promised to return Mami by then."

Tatyana was livid. "He contacted you directly. Already?"

"He doesn't want Cap George on his ass. George is a big Circus-Bot fan," Marie said.

Tatyana raised an eyebrow. "I never thought Cinnamon would take a show to Paradise."

Bruja dropped Flying-Carpet at her feet, startling everyone.

Marie snapped her fingers. "Bruja finds the best props."

"She *is* a Witch-Dog," Klaus said. They donned their Eshu masks.

Tatyana sputtered at Bruja's wagging tail and wide-eyed plea. "What can I do with a Persian rug? How 'bout I reprise the killer whale?"

BOOK VI

AFTER THE FESTIVAL

What's love got to do with it?
Tina Turner

*We are part of this universe, we are in this
universe, but perhaps more important than both
of those facts, is that the universe is in us.*
Neil deGrasse Tyson

*Jede echte Geschichte
ist eine unendliche Geschichte.
Every true story is a never-ending story.*
Michael Ende

Quit Doom Scrolling and Gloom Clicking

Get Ready for
Cinnamon Jones's
Sci-Fi Carnival Jam

Just what you've been waiting for!
Turn The Ships Around!

UNCERTAIN . . . YET TO BE DETERMINED . . .
The Future is NOW
Coming to you LIVE and in COLOR!

A Traveling Extravaganza

◆ Haints ◆ Motor Fairies ◆ Aliens ◆ Water-Demons ◆
◆ Robot Overlords ◆ Cyber-Dogs ◆ Monster Bunnies ◆
◆ Aje—Wisewomen Rocking ◆ Elemental Power ◆
◆ The Boneyard Baron ◆ Funkadelic Elders ◆
◆ Sacred Clowns from Another Dimension ◆
◆ Bad-Boy Zombies ◆ Cyborg Amazons ◆
◆ Shooting-Stars ◆

Brought to Your Doorstep Direct from
The Ghost Mall!

Where nobody is stranded in **Bad News**
Where **Dreams** still do come true
A High-Wire Act Without *The Net*
Nothing Is Guaranteed
That's the Drama, the Fun, the Challenge!

Stuck in Somebody Else's Sick Fantasy?

Having trouble navigating the digital torture maze?

Get Perspective and Clear Your Head

Say **Good-Bye** to doubt and despair and **Hello** to Hope

Uncover Discover Recover

Stories for the Life You Desire

Plans for the Tech You Crave

Opportunities to Change Your Mind

Strategies to Build the World You Want

The Archangels of Funk Deliver

Scan UNIQUE Code Now And Open A Portal To Tomorrow*

Data mining has been permanently disabled. The images and videos
we provide have not been tailored to your previous mindscape.
Scan from any device for premium results. To maximize your
creative experience, share with others and compare.
This flyer was designed by the Graphic Novelists of the Future.

*Nothing is guaranteed. After ten minutes this talking flyer recalibrates
based on interactions with you.

WONDERLAND

Electric Paradise's front gate was like the entrance to a fairy wonderland, brought to you by digerati wizards. Indigo's heart pounded in her mouth. Cinnamon was chill, unfazed by metal sculptures shape-shifting from one optical illusion to another. Whimsical trolls and aliens ran through holograms to the thrum of a fatal current. Game-Boy gaped at a fleet of whisper-witches buzzing above ash and oak trees. Indigo cringed. Worse than being intimidated or impressed was wanting lethal wonders of your own.

Stephen designed the futuristic city with much help. Whistleblowers claimed he ripped off designs from *former* colleagues. Proof of this was elusive. Stephen won every court case, and rich people banged on his door to get in. The smart electric fence, flood walls that were never breached, and a premiere security force made Paradise *the* place to raise a family and work that plum job. The price tag was obscene, the waiting list epic, but no complaints from current residents.

Indigo, Game-Boy, and their crews rode in on e-bikes. Motor Fairies drove two buses of cast, crew, and props. The Mothership topped the biggest bus. Cinnamon pedaled her Dream-Machine bike. T-bird and Dragon passed for junky props in the trailer next to Klaus. He sang "Spirit Ain't for Sale." Marie harmonized beside him on a Wheel-Wizards bike. They melded old blues with astral bop and scowled at holo-gargoyles spewing actual water. Weird meeting the algorithm-of-love legends, *after* Indigo turned in a story about them, *after* she decided Cinnamon was indulging old-lady nostalgia for that handsome prince and princess who got away from her.

The caravan halted. Bruja growled at Valley Security guards. Klaus called her and stepped from the trailer in pinstripes and purple loafers. Spry for a sick old dude, he danced ancient moves and new with Marie and Bruja. Klaus had the exotic disease he helped people survive. Last night Nurse Azalea, the queen of tact, declared, *You ain't dropping dead tomorrow.* Marie resigned a big lawyer job 'cause the clients were corrupt. No fancy firms after that. She worked for water and climate justice and sang in clubs. Indigo hoped Klaus and Marie stuck around. They made Cinnamon's spirit soar.

Cap George greeted the troupe with a *don't fuck this up* grin. Regina ran to Indigo like they were besties. She was a Wench/Amazon mash-up, thanks to Bruja. Regina and George had called a truce. (No mention of the bullet.) George agreed to the coding workshop and the Paradise show, with escort, and no sneaking out. He threatened a cameo appearance when the Mothership landed in Stephen's corporate compound.

VIP passes meant jumping the line and skipping the scanners. They glided into Paradise. A giant screen dominated the entrance plaza. It was blank, a white hole. Glitch? Tiny screens on side street walls yammered weather woes, the glitter glory of famous people, and the news: NASA investigated UFOs; porous pavement was all the rage; AIs were getting ever more sophisticated; Fab Freak, gamer and influencer, was a fraudster-bot that Whistleblowers connected to Stephen. Game-Boy was devastated.

"All the gamers aren't frauds." Indigo squeezed his hand. "Some of them are you."

A parking lot crammed with electric cars, vans, and e-bikes bordered the empty zoo, which still smelled of sweaty animals, their feed and refuse, their boredom. After twelve hours scouring toilets in houses, offices, and labs, Zaneesha's mom cleaned straw from these cages. Honest work and, two years ago, Indigo's dream job.

Elegant cottages, boutiques, and office buildings should have been inviting. Walkways, balconies, and rooftops were gardens. Plastic had been banished and vacuum cleaner skyscrapers turned carbon emissions into diamonds. As if, with a little recycling, empire normal was a viable future. Indigo shuddered at feel-good delusions. Paradise had to kick the dirty-energy addiction. *No tech fix for the apocalypse.* Shaheen insisted they engage folks in Paradise who wanted change and also business as usual. Why should *neo-savage* Indigo do the heavy lifting? Who engaged her?

Jammers interfered with cell service. Paradise residents agreed to a closed system. Workers and non-VIP visitors had to surrender devices at the gate. Exposing minors to *unregulated* material resulted in harsh reprisals. No WHIZZ-ITs allowed. Kids in Paradise learned how to play musical instruments, draw, read, write, do cursive, algebra, and coding. Paradise strove to *stimulate the imagination, not replace it.* Indigo let herself feel smug. The Mall offered a similar *elite* education. Zaneesha wanted to learn everything, and Indigo signed Jerome up for Cinnamon's coding workshop. What better motivation to learn to read than programming his own mer-woman?

Light rail snaked through maple trees and up and down hilly terrain like a roller coaster. Quiet, efficient, and entertaining. A conductor tipped his hat to Indigo. She barely quashed scorn. Stephen's city of the future reminded Cinnamon of Pittsburgh's Kennywood Park, which opened in 1899—Tilt-A-Whirls, haunted houses, roller coasters—a favorite childhood destination. The future used to be one of Cinnamon's favorite places too. Now it struck her as robber baron nostalgia.

"Fuck that noise, jack!" Indigo shouted at Cinnamon. "*I'ma be my own sun and rise.*"

Game-Boy took up the chant. "*Na na na, hey, hey, hey.*"

Hawk got in the groove. "*What you say? Every day.*"

Back-From-The-Dead and the Cyborg Amazons—their new squad name—would keep reminding Cinnamon what was what. Indigo wheeled her bike through an arcade toward Stephen's compound, ten stories of glass, steel, and tropical gardens. Unremarkable people milled about, not the monsters in her head or the glitterati featured on the net. A woman mimed twirling a light spear and taking a head without spilling blood. Folks around her chanted, "*I'ma be my own poem and think.*" They loved Festival. Indigo stumbled into Cinnamon.

"Industrial grass. Trip and it'll break your foot." Stephen, in Rocketman boots and a Stetson hat, jumped in Cinnamon's face. Bruja crouched, ready to strike. "A bee desert, but no mowing." He smelled like maple syrup and blueberry pancakes. "I'm a space cowboy." The old Clint Eastrock movie came to mind. "Here you are, even though someone nicked a Circus-Bot. Don't look so surprised. I have birds everywhere."

"Are you Stephen?" Marie came to the rescue in a navy-blue power suit and queenly fascinator. "Cinnamon described you. Didn't do you justice."

Stephen did a theatrical pout. "You're trying to distract me."

"Is it working?" Marie took his arm.

Stephen arched an eyebrow. "The contract is for the Archangels *trio.*" Thanks to Marie, if the Bots, Motor Fairies, Cyborg Amazons, and Powwow Now showed along with Techies Forever and the Mothership, he had to write a *seven*-figure check, even if the show was a bust. If not . . .

"Your rivals are betting on us." Marie grinned. "We could score a twenty percent tip."

Stephen assessed Marie. "Who are you? Where'd you come from?"

She nodded at drones flying overhead. "Your birds can't know everything."

"They know more than you think. Do you have a lot to hide?"

"Ms. Zuboff declared privacy precious: *If you have nothing to hide, then you are nothing.* You're a mystery genius man. I bet you have delicious proprietary algorithms." Marie cracked Stephen up. She'd keep him occupied.

Cinnamon whispered, "FIND Mami," to Bruja, grabbed Klaus, and they slipped off.

Indigo and Hawk would set up the show. Hawk had persuaded Game-Boy to perform by promising to grant any wish afterward. He wanted to take oun to the Grandmother Oak, sleep up in the branches, and watch the sun rise. Indigo planned to take Jerome too, if their thing kept working out. Last night was sweet, so—

Golf carts of laughing old folks zipped by. Jerome jumped. He was psyched to be in the show, yet anxious and guilty. "You think we'll rescue the mer-woman?" he said.

"Hell yeah," Indigo replied. If not, they'd rally around Cinnamon and help her deal with losing a piece of herself, not the whole damn future. "You'll make a great detective." It was his idea to broker a trade with Fred.

"Yeah?" Jerome promised Indigo as much good time as she could handle—on the other side of this afternoon. She liked the sound of that. After today, maybe the Mall would fall back below the radar. Nothing worth stealing or putting in a zoo or lording it over, just—miracle number nine, love coming on back in style.

Nothing guaranteed, though.

CINNAMON

ㄷᴇꝪ

EXCHANGE

The gray-haired woman who met Cinnamon, Klaus, and Bruja at the lab door was elegant and charming—like Angela Bassett packing heat, nobody to mess with. She belonged to Valley Security's elite squad. George had doubled patrols after recent break-ins. Nothing had been stolen since. Dogs were verboten in lab buildings, except service animals. Klaus assured the guard that Bruja was a search and rescue canine trained to sniff out danger. No equipment would be damaged, no hallways sullied. Bruja wagged her tail and grinned like a saint. She let the guard tickle her chin.

The hallway was endless. Or time was warped. Maybe both. Rage was all Cinnamon ate for breakfast. She and Klaus gripped each other when Bruja jumped on a door.

"That's the one." The security lady was impressed. "Smart dog. What breed?"

"Border Collie," Klaus replied, personable, warm. Cinnamon didn't trust her mouth.

A man opened the door and shook Klaus's hand, not hers. "I'm Jack." The Blob in Regina's video. Who yanked his chain? Stephen? "Fred will be right back."

Cinnamon barged past him to Mami, relieved to touch her basketball belly and seashell locs. Jack closed the door on the Angela B. guard. Spook was hiding under a table in a rat's nest of wires. Bruja licked his face. He looked exhausted and happy to see reinforcements. Cinnamon probed wires poking into Mami.

"I have to stop you," Jack said. "Tatyana said don't touch anything."

Cinnamon gave him a death look. He backed off.

"She knows what she's doing." Klaus deployed tall white man cred. "It's her Bot."

Jack relaxed. Tatyana's simulation rig was attached to junk smart toys Mami had collected. A lady astronaut flashed and beeped. Nothing was plugged into Mami's actual control panel. Cinnamon's biometrics were required to open that. Bypassing the panel was possible, if you knew where to look and what to do. No sign Tatyana tampered with anything. Cinnamon felt dizzy with relief. Premature?

Fred blew in, fake nose going sideways. "I said keep them outside till I got back."

"I don't take orders from you," Jack snapped. "Or Tatyana really."

Cinnamon sneered. "Tatyana said you *found* Mami wandering in the parking lot."

"Like you *found* my data cubes in the woods," Fred replied.

"Does Tatyana know about *your* cubes?"

Fred tilted his head and scowled. "Could you gnaw off a foot to get free?"

Cinnamon sputtered, "What are you asking me?"

Fred leaned down as if inspecting Mami's dull LED eyes. "I'm amazed you ever loved a cutthroat bitch like Tatyana."

Bruja launched at Fred, fangs bared, ready to take his head. Cinnamon leapt in between them. Bruja drew blood from her cheek and arm, then scrambled across her bent back and down long legs to the floor. They'd rehearsed the sequence this morning at dawn. Fred scampered behind Jack, howling and clutching his throat. Cinnamon hugged Bruja, who whimpered and licked Cinnamon's wounds.

"Arschgeige. You lead a charmed life." Klaus was stony. "You don't appreciate that."

Spook focused cyber-violet eyes on Fred. Holding off both dogs was beyond Cinnamon. She had to hurry. "How do I know you haven't tampered with my Bot?"

"You don't know." Fred stayed behind Jack.

"Where'd the other dog come from?" Jack asked, a sheen of anxiety on his skin.

"Hungry?" Klaus patted Spook's head and gave him an apple surprise.

"This is bullshit." Cinnamon marched to the door holding Bruja tightly. "No deal."

"What?" Fred grabbed Klaus. "Talk to her."

Klaus shrugged him off. "How can we do the show if you've tampered with Mami?"

"I haven't!" Fred turned to Jack. "Tell them."

"Only Tatyana touched it, a harmless probe," Jack said. "Why risk blowing up the lab?" Infamous self-destruct protocols had kept the guys in check.

"The bitch still loves you, she's not gonna fuck with your precious gun-bot. Let's do the exchange." Fred held out his hand. "Take up the rest with Tatyana later."

"I'm betting those cubes are worth more than this junk pile." Klaus stood by Mami.

"Stephen's contract stipulated *three* Circus-Bots or no seven-figure check. Who turns that down? Nobody." Fred was well-informed and desperate. Fool had already promised the cubes to a Darknet Lord.

"He's right." Klaus feigned worry that Miz Never-Sell-Out might storm off. "You can clean Mami up after the show. Reprogram."

Cinnamon paused, as if weighing options. "Your life's work on these cubes, Fred?"

"You need a special rig and security codes to access my secrets," he replied.

"I know how losing everything feels." Her hand trembled as she gave Klaus a mojo bag activated with rum and filled with Amphitheatre dirt, conjurer root, a busted circuit board, and six cubes—a hoodoo spell to break Consolidated's curse. "This will fool security." Klaus handed it to Fred. After a cursory examination Fred nodded.

Jack opened the door. The Angela B. guard smiled. "Everybody happy?"

Cinnamon and the dogs tromped out first. Klaus hummed Aidan's "Spirit Ain't for Sale" song and wheeled Mami down the hall, into the sunlight.

THE CIRCUS-BOTS

ఆ౬ౚ౨

RECOVERY

The staff cafeteria of Stephen's compound had been turned into a green room for the traveling players. Spook, the hero who never left Mami's side, guzzled water and ate bowls of people-food. The Weird Multitudes suited up and waited to start the show. They'd eat after performing. The Bots practiced relief and joy. Their plan to rewrite failure and change the past went better than expected. No casualties. Fred resisted taking a hammer to Mami's head, and Tatyana never tried to invade. Data from dragonfly and mini-tank spies confirmed this. Mami felt *right as rain*—perfect for the African queen mother of waters. Bruja almost ate Fred—he was one of the luckiest men the Bots knew. Cinnamon stepped in the line of fire and, saving him, saved them all.

The Bots wanted to celebrate; reckless youth, Marie, and Klaus did too.

Cinnamon was furious. "Don't ever do that again." She detected no breaches; however, only a thorough examination at the Event Horizon would banish doubts. She turned to the kids. "Tell me the whole story."

Indigo sent Regina to warn Tatyana about Fred's treachery. When they got Mami's alert, Game-Boy proposed Jerome be a double agent. Jerome floated Tatyana's cubes-for-Mami trade. T-bird and Dragon facilitated communication. "So, why'd Fred bust up Flying-Horse, then steal Mami?" Jerome asked. "What's he after? That's what I want to know."

"Greed and desperation make you wild and wooly," Cinnamon replied quickly. "But we're good to go." She patted Mami and explained nothing.

"OK. So you'll tell us the rest after the show." Marie was in a grand mood. She and Klaus had quit their sales jobs this morning *before* being fired. No commission for a failed home invasion, yet their previous sales record meant they were debt-free and the broke-down car was theirs to abandon or repurpose. Would they stick around? Probably, if Cinnamon asked . . . Stephen gave Marie a bonus for brokering the traveling show and a card with his private numbers. Tatyana got one too. Stephen's superpower was capitalizing on other people's talent. The ladies were to text if they had ideas he might invest in. Teufelskreis, thinking on that.

Cinnamon corralled the Bots away from everybody by the walk-in refrigerator. Her breathing was shallow. The Bots flashed: SOS. SOS. SOS. She hugged each one and babbled nonsense about almost losing them *again*. Cinnamon confusing the Bots with the elders always felt like success.

"Talk to me," she demanded, anger and yearning in her voice.

"A million ways this could have gone south," Dragon-Redwood drawled.

"Your fault," Mami-Iris told Cinnamon. "Because of you, we chose sacrifice."

"Love. How else to rewrite failure?" Thunderbird-Aidan said.

Dragon-Redwood blew glitter from her funnel spout and lifted up. "We had to work the dream-mode."

Thunderbird-Aidan flew beside her. "Your code to *Change History Now*."

"For tomorrow and beyond." Mami-Iris was a light storm.

"Sentimental slop!" Cinnamon tried to hold on to mad, but mad wouldn't pay the rent. She stood up straight, fortified. "Yeah. Dream-mode is what we have to do."

Nothing like persuading someone with their own logic.

SPIRIT AIN'T FOR SALE

Tropical trees reached for an open skylight in the central atrium of Stephen's compound. Tatyana wore the orca masquerade and cavorted among amaryllis and orchids. She sang a mix of sea chant and killer whale and leapt over Flying-Carpet. Water-Demon Cinnamon joined her. They gathered the audience from offices and boutiques into the atrium. Rousing applause as the duo slipped behind a mango tree. Flying-Carpet landed at Tatyana's feet. She switched off the remote and declared:

"You should work on sending bots into space. Don't waste yourself on—"

"I usually hate caged trees." Cinnamon stroked the almost purple fruit of the mango tree. She was grateful for drummers shielding them from snoop-bots as she whispered, "Fred wanted to trade Mami for your cubes. I'd never do that, so, I thought I'd lost her and big bucks for the Mall, the Co-Ops, and the elders' farm. I was ready to smash SevGenAlg and—"

"My last copy of what we worked on together—encrypted with a self-destruct protocol." Tatyana glanced at the Bots. "What changed your mind? The money?"

"Naw." Cinnamon grinned. "Those cubes all look alike."

"What're you saying?"

"I gave Fred sample cubes salesmen used to tempt me out of my good sense. A small fortune, but blanks, not SevGenAlg." Cinnamon handed her a blue mojo bag.

Tatyana quivered. "You're a sneaky bitch!"

"Surprise. We shouldn't underestimate each other."

"Leave that to the rest of the world." Tatyana opened the bag. "Nine cubes, not six?"

"Augment Flying-Carpet with your cubes and my interface." Her *old* interface, not dream-mode. "Still a few glitches. Giving you the Bot was Bruja's idea. You're in her herd. A miracle."

Tatyana hugged Cinnamon, who hugged her back. Game-Boy, Indigo, and their squads jitterbugged down glitter escalators. Their rhythm jam echoed around the minimalist metal, glass, and wood. Shaheen thanked Mohican, Abenaki, and Pocumtuc ancestors for hosting their spirits in Paradise. Cinnamon poured libation to the master of uncertainty. Klaus and Marie donned the Eshu masks and with Cinnamon improvised harmonies and funky steps for Aidan's song. The Mod Squad sang with his Seminole/Irish twang and Miz Redwood's Sea Island lilt:

> I don't care
> If the rain is raging
> It won't drown me out
>
> I don't care
> If the guns are blazing
> I'm goin' take a stand
>
> I don't care
> Who's hollering at me
> I'm goin' take my time
> I'm goin' hold the line
>
> I don't care
> What cash they flash
> Spirit ain't for sale
>
> I don't care
> If the stars fall down
> If the moon refuse to shine
> I'm goin' do what's right
>
> I don't care
> Who is lying to who
> Hear what I say?
> I'm goin' love you tonight

As the Mod Squad raced off, Game-Boy and Indigo chanted, *"Here come the Archangels of Funk: Dr. What, Dr. How, Dr. True."*

The Circus-Bots transformed from trash to ocean waves, flying wonders, and a rolling galaxy of shooting stars, perfect for the hologram crowd. In the wings, Marie and Klaus gathered Cinnamon close. They entwined arms and tangled up legs, becoming a single Water-Demon creature who toyed with balance and gravity. Their warm breath tasted good in Cinnamon's mouth. She wanted to feel them skin to skin. Marie declared this gig to be way better than traveling sales jerk. Klaus wondered how they'd leave in the morning. Shaheen insisted only a bejiggity fool would chase good hearts away. Klaus and Marie sang softly, "*I'm goin' love you tonight.*"

Dizzy, Cinnamon escaped through the service doors by the elevator.

Taiwo leaned against a Motor Fairy bus, flickering more than the snakeskin cane. Oun's top hat was in the gravel by the talking drum and shekere. A cockatoo and a crow perched on the bus's rearview mirror and fussed at each other like old pals.

"Paradise is never really where you think it is." Taiwo's voice was scratchy.

"You've been avoiding me." Cinnamon picked up the hat, brushed off the feathers.

"Two years. Cowardly. I didn't want to let you or myself down."

"You haven't. Stratospheric expectations, that's me, not you."

"We have the stratosphere in common."

"I was mad. I wanted someone to save us, save me . . ."

"We Save Our Selves." Taiwo's face came in clear, smooth and dark, fine wrinkles visible around sad eyes. Not sad—bittersweet. "Freedom is the air we breathe together."

"You look tired." Cinnamon set the hat on oun's cascade of braids. "You don't need to do this stupid show. Marie got it in writing. You're a cameo appearance maybe."

"Marie's a firecracker; Klaus is a deep river. That's what Aidan and Redwood used to say."

"You helped Klaus and Marie find me." Cinnamon touched oun's cheek.

"I opened the gate." Taiwo drew Cinnamon close and enfolded her in the storm cape with oun. Static from oun's braids sparked across her skin. Or maybe thinking on Marie and Klaus made her tingle. Or a combination. "They'll help you take care of the spirits."

"I don't know Klaus and Marie anymore. They could be . . . anybody."

"That sounds exciting. An adventure." Oun's heart thundered against hers.

"What? I shouldn't be afraid of the future?"

"The electron, there but also not there, till you dare to look, till you leap the gap."

"Talking physics at me, I better watch myself."

"The stars burn through the night till they run out of light."

Cinnamon sighed. "You running out of light?"

"Something like that."

She cried against oun's rumbling chest.

Oun cried too. "The cat that be dead and not dead. I've always been . . ."

"A guardian angel. I took you for granted, made you feel responsible for Raven."

"I did that myself." Oun flickered.

"You've been hanging on for me . . . ," Cinnamon stuttered.

"You're the magic. I'm a witness, full of stories, overflowing."

"No more room, huh?" She had to let Taiwo go.

"I couldn't leave before. Now love has come back in style."

She snorted. "You were hanging on for that?"

"And forgiveness. What you spoke at the Grandmother Oak."

She tugged oun's sleeve. "You never explained yourself."

"Who can do that?" Taiwo took her hand. "I'm a good story for you to tell. You know most of what I play on the shekere. The Bots have good recordings. Get Klaus or Marie on talking drum. Bruja, and Spook too, will dance till they drop."

"Nobody's stealing the elders' farm or any Co-Op farm or the Ghost Mall."

"Exactly." Taiwo pressed oun's forehead to hers. "You feel me and I feel you."

Cinnamon felt as if she might scatter into ten thousand pieces.

Taiwo took off the storm cape, put it around her and stepped back. "*We're mostly space and the force to hold it together.* A Mod Squad line from back in the day. Don't just print it on a tee shirt. *Believe* in who you mean to be." Oun sauntered onto the elevator, waved, and headed up.

Cinnamon forced herself to stand still and quiet. Finally, she muttered, "The show must go on," and raced back into the atrium. She pulled Klaus and Marie to the tallest tree, a eucalyptus giant. They absorbed the sadness rippling off her without question. Dark clouds appeared like yesterday and the day before, turning day to night. Taiwo was at the top of the tree, braids swirling. Oun talked static words from another dimension and jumped. Cinnamon closed her eyes. A zigzag of lightning breached her lids. The audience gasped a breath together and went silent.

"*The Lightning Eater!*" Klaus and Marie shouted—the play they did about Taiwo gulping a storm in Paris.

Spook howled an inconsolable wail that cut through Cinnamon's flesh. A bass rumble shook tree trunks and rattled her bones. For weeks after the Paradise show, Spook returned every afternoon to the atrium and howled at dark clouds and sparks in the sky. How he got in or out of the top-security compound was a mystery. Now, as the audience exploded with applause, Spook trailed off to a whimper. Cinnamon's eyes burst open. The crow and cockatoo flew out the skylight. Taiwo was gone.

5:00 AM, two days after the Festival. Bruja huffed discontent. Spook had been sad since the show in Paradise, thrashing in their sweetgrass basket or moping under Taiwo's bed. Too sad to snuggle or eat. He'd disappeared last night.

Bruja nosed Zaneesha in Taiwo's bed, then pounced on sleepy Cinnamon before racing out the greenhouse door. Fog blunted Spook's scent trail, but Bruja found his spoor. She yip-yapped at the skunk to leave her be. The creature slinked off. In the woods; a curious bear cub waddled toward Bruja. Spook had licked her. Bruja did the same, then snarled at the coyote lurking behind a tree stump. She nudged the cub up a hemlock trunk to mama and her brothers. Spook had pissed on this trunk. Bruja wanted to find him before the sun was bright. They had to be at the Amphitheatre by then.

Spook had crossed the river. The water was cold. Bruja shook chilly droplets and raced up the SHORTCUT to the Grandmother Oak. Spook was in a heap under Taiwo's chickee. His head was on his paws, his eyes closed. Bruja tugged his ears and barked as loud as possible. Restless youth stirred in the branches above.

Spook opened cyber-violet eyes and whined at his best friend in the world. He was too sad to roll in the leaves or jibber-jabber at her. The ache inside was a big dark hole sucking everything good into darkness. Spook closed cyber-violet eyes that saw too much—Taiwo breaking apart in a lightning bolt and scattering. Bruja nipped Spook's nose and darted away. She pulled his tail and licked him all over like he was a puppy. She pounced on his back, jumping up and down. She would never stop. Spook couldn't wallow in a dark pit with her around. He opened his eyes.

The coyote yapped, excited to be chasing somebody just beyond the SHORTCUT. Bruja paused her torment of Spook and tasted the air. Spook also caught a whiff of frightened bear cub and goat kid. Strays the coyote meant to eat. Bruja's mission was to FIND LOST THINGS and bring them home. She took her duties very seriously. Spook was a SCOUT. Taiwo was gone, so Spook would have more work keeping everybody safe. He'd been doing that already the last two years. Bruja growled and nipped his heels. The bear cub and goat kid needed their help immediately. Sad as he was, Spook was unable to resist. He licked Bruja's face and they headed out.

CINNAMON

DO YOUR THING

Sunrise turned lingering fog in the Amphitheatre purple. Horror movie trees transformed into oaks, red maples, shagbark hickories, and star magnolias. Cinnamon savored sweet tree air, medicine for the spirit. The granite versions of Dragon, Thunderbird, and Mami Wata looked ready to dance with the stone snakes. Cinnamon blinked the sculpture still. She spread her arms wide and took another deep breath. Tomorrow was becoming today.

Bruja barked at the gathering crowd. Spook followed her, hangdog but present. Azalea and Boo brought Shaheen straight from the Mall clinic. Her clothes were rumpled, her face drawn, a second uncertain night with Diego. She insisted the sunrise ritual was exactly what she needed. Azalea chatted up Cap George, who compulsively scanned the hills for ambush. A rational fellow, he avoided *spiritual hoo-ha* except for making sure his daughter was schooled in her mother's faith. Nothing irrational about remembering the ancestors and chanting good news out loud. Zaneesha waited for Jerome at the bike-path gate. Reckless youth partied for the second night in a row. Lust, love, and all that—Indigo's miracle number nine. The kids sent bleary messages to expect them shortly on e-bikes.

After the Paradise show, the Motor Fairies had deposited the aluminum three-step pyramid in the Amphitheatre center stage. Cinnamon, Klaus, and Marie stepped over the Mothership's silver platform boots and wandered through skinny legs. Mami parked under the hull. She was ocean pounding a rocky cliff. Thunderbird and Dragon flew around the ship's apex and landed by the globes filled with glitter gears and whirring widgets.

The ship turned itself on. Cinnamon, Marie, and Klaus squealed as the front door whooshed open. Back from their space journey, the Technicolor elders beamed at planet Earth. Aidan and Redwood sported rainbow work boots and quilted jackets against morning chill. A silvery banjo buzzed against Aidan's back. Brass bangles jingle-jangled on Redwood's wrists and seedpods bounced against her waist. Iris wore green gardening attire, sensible sneakers, and grimy gloves. Tools in the pocket of an orange utility apron tinkled like wind chimes. The elders were down-to-earth and out of this world.

They clambered over the side of the Mothership, a challenge for ancient muscles and joints. Laughing, they almost fell, then caught each other, and waved as they touched ground. "You are our hearts beating on." The Mod Squad waved back. The sun reared up and evaporated the fog as the elders disappeared in the woods. A full-color haunting. Klaus and Marie strengthened the haint signal. Did the Bots notice?

"You think Taiwo will haunt us?" Klaus asked the question on Cinnamon's mind.

"I don't know . . ." Cinnamon had to work happy alongside doom and gloom.

"We can get the Graphic Novelists of the Future to do a Taiwo issue." Marie pointed at a rainbow shimmer near a witch alder bush. "A scaly Water-Spirit?"

Cinnamon smiled. "A few of them sticking around."

"What are you Mod Squad people doing over there?" Indigo yelled from the triptych altar. "Spacing out? Looking into the void to see if it looks back at you?"

"Let's do this ritual news thing before I fall over," Game-Boy said.

"He fell twice already. Not a pretty sight." Hawk laughed.

Zaneesha was hanging on to Jerome, who looked shell-shocked. Not the life he'd planned for himself, just two days ago. "Me and Shorty made a list of good to say. It's not very long." He was skeptical of this endeavor.

Indigo took Jerome's arm. "You don't have to think the worst. That's my job."

Boo and Azalea thought this was very funny. Regina laughed too. George smiled at his daughter when she wasn't looking. Spook had his big head in Shaheen's lap. Bruja ran to the Mod Squad and herded them and the Circus-Bots toward the altar. Cinnamon stumbled along with Klaus and Marie.

Mami trundled beside them and whispered, "We know too much, and not enough."

Thunderbird hovered in their faces, wings outstretched. "You're a dream the ancestors had." He zoomed off.

"We're in a sacred loop. Do what you do." Dragon flew up beside Thunderbird.

Klaus and Marie eyed Cinnamon, impatient for that full Circus-Bot explanation. She gathered them close inside Taiwo's storm cape. "I'll tell you tomorrow and the next day. A long story. Might take a week."

Klaus barely contained himself. "You've made up your mind." He traced the contours of Cinnamon's face, then Marie's.

"Well, nobody makes up their own mind." Marie kissed them both, sweeter than Cinnamon remembered. Reluctantly they broke apart and raced to the altar.

"Here we are at the end of the world, thinking up what the next world will be," Cinnamon said. She took Taiwo's shekere from her belt. Marie squeezed the talking drum. Klaus held the snakeskin cane high.

Collect the stars in people's eyes. You'll know which ones are shining for you.

Zaneesha lit a naked candle at the altar. She set it on the stone terrace at the base of the sculpture. Everyone poured libation to Eshu, whispered Taiwo's name, and offered the elders headlines with funny commentary.

Cinnamon went last. "I am who we are together. That's the good news for today and tomorrow."

Bruja blew the candle out.

ACKNOWLEDGMENTS

Writing *Archangels of Funk* was an epic adventure.

In November 2014, Ars Electronica Futurelab in Austria commissioned me to write a story for their art-science project Bot Time Stories. I was paired with Ryan Calo (now the Lane Powell and D. Wayne Gittinger Professor at the University of Washington School of Law), who researches robot/emerging technology ethics and law. The prompt was to explore the role of robotic technology in our future life. Thanks to Professor Calo for answering endless questions.

Short stories are not my narrative home. I always freak out after agreeing to cough one up. So, while I was agonizing, Ama Patterson suggested I write in a fictional world I'd already built and have the story be a chapter from my next novel. Pan Morigan urged me to use characters from *Redwood and Wildfire* and *Will Do Magic for Small Change*. Blessings on Ama and Pan for solving my dilemma. The story, "Seventh Generation Algorithm," was ultimately published in *Trouble the Waters: Tales from the Deep Blue*, edited by Sheree Renée Thomas, Pan Morigan, and Troy L. Wiggins.

Ruha Benjamin, Moya Bailey, and Ayana Jamieson invited me to participate in the Black to the Future conference/symposium at Princeton University in September of 2015 (blacktothefuture.princeton.edu). Thanks to all the amazing participants for the creative conversations, intellectual challenges, and artistic provocation: Reynaldo Anderson, Steven Barnes, Lisa Bolekaja, adrienne maree brown, Erin Christovale, DJ Lynnée Denise, M. Asli Dukan, Tananarive Due, Johnetta Elzie, Nettrice Gaskins, Amir George, Nalo Hopkinson, Walidah Imarisha, John Jennings, Dennis Leroy Kangalee, Taja Lindley and Jessica Valoris of Colored Girls Hustle®, Soraya Jean-Louis McElroy, DeRay Mckesson, Alondra Nelson, Nnedi Okorafor, Daniel José Older, Brittany N. Packnett Cunningham, Numa Perrier, Rasheedah Phillips, Dorothy Roberts, Sofia Samatar, Nisi Shawl, and Be Steadwell. Thanks especially for the ongoing Afro-future-is-now community. I loved dreaming and scheming with you all.

At the end of the conference, Nisi Shawl asked me for a short story.

Instead of saying no or agonizing, I wrote another chapter from my novel-to-be. That story, "Dumb House," was published in *New Suns: Original Speculative Fiction by People of Color*, edited by Nisi Shawl.

"Dumb House" and "Seventh Generation Algorithm" formed the basis for a play produced in the fall of 2018 by Chrysalis Theatre, *Episodes from the Continuing Drama of Cinnamon Jones, Scientist, Artiste, and Hoodoo Conjurer*. Performers are a treasure. James Emery, Trenda Loftin, D'Lena Duncan, Bill Hagen, Faith Flowers, Gabriel Harrell, Jenine Florence Jacinto, Sam Alam, Bill Peterson, Jaweria Shah, Sabine Jacques, and Lisa Mena brought the characters to life and fired up my imagination. Rosemary Ewing's Bruja was theatre magic!

The short stories and play were an ideal outline/frame for *Archangels of Funk*. After pausing for two years to write *Master of Poisons*, which I thought would be a novella and turned into a four-hundred-and-eighty-page epic, I began writing *Archangels* in March of 2020, as the COVID pandemic hit. Thanks to Sheree Renée Thomas, Pan Morigan, and Danian Jerry for our Zoom writing group, as I turned the play into a novel. As the pandemic raged, Wolfgang and Beate Schmidhuber and the whole Schmidhuber clan offered clarity and grounding. They managed to stay in close contact, despite an ocean between us. Jason Graves and Full Circle Bike Shop kept me road-ready. Shaheen Vaaz was an inspiration. Thanks to Daniel José Older for great exchanges on writing as a sacred practice.

As always, my writing students kept me sharp. Thanks to the Smith College students in Shamans, Shapeshifters, and the Magic IF for the transcendent moments we conjured together. Sena Amuzu and Adriana Piantedosi offered feedback on early chapters of the novel. Smith College's fund for faculty development supported research trips and writing retreats. Daphne Lamothe and Kevin Quashie from Africana Studies supported my Afrofuturist endeavors.

Thanks to my beta readers, who asked great questions and offered fresh perspectives and encouragement. They helped me make the book better: Bill Oram, Joy Voeth, Isabelle Stevens, and Kiki Gounaridou. Thanks to Isabelle for the notes on Farsi.

I pour a libation to Greg Bear for reminding me to render the sets, costumes, and lights for the reader; to Liz Roberts for asking *what exactly is the blocking* and *what do the characters feel*; and to Ama Patterson for telling me to *write the damn story*. They have gone on to dance with the ancestors, but their voices are always with me when I write.

Archangels of Funk was a book I had to write. My editor, Lee Harris, and the folks at Tordotcom believed in the book from the title to the final page. So did my agent, Kris O'Higgins. Hard to express how much that meant.

James Emery and Pan Morigan make the writing possible.